THEY RULED THE WORLD BEFORE MANKIND— and dinosaurs still live in our modern-day consciousness, capturing countless new admirers in every generation. And even as fossil finds fuel the ongoing controversy about what really happened to the dinosaurs, twenty-three of today's top explorers of time, space, and the imagination offer their own highly creative field trips to meet dinosaurs on their own territory, in our time, and in many possible futures:

"Romeo Falling"—She was stranded on a world humans had long ago abandoned, and not even her ship's computer could prepare her for the creations they'd left behind. . . .

"Down on the Farm"—She'd bought her first oviraptor as a pet. But then her hobby became a good way to make a living—at le_____ an end to her dinosaur

"Flight"—T_____ather. But now his fa_____-and their secret—were _____

"The Test of Time"—The time machine had saved him from being murdered in his own time, but how long could he survive in the Age of Dinosaurs . . . ?

RETURN OF THE DINOSAURS

RETURN
OF THE
DINOSAURS

edited by Mike Resnick
and Martin H. Greenberg

DAW BOOKS, INC.
DONALD A. WOLLHEIM, FOUNDER
375 Hudson Street, New York, NY 10014

ELIZABETH R. WOLLHEIM
SHEILA E. GILBERT
PUBLISHERS

First Printing, May 1997
1 2 3 4 5 6 7 8 9

DAW TRADEMARK REGISTERED
U.S. PAT. OFF. AND FOREIGN COUNTRIES
—MARCA REGISTRADA
HECHO EN U.S.A.

PRINTED IN THE U.S.A.

ACKNOWLEDGMENTS

To Carol, as always

And to Jean-Louis Rubin:

Bon vivant,
Hollywood mogul,
Gourmet chef,
All-around Nice Guy,

CONTENTS

INTRODUCTION

Dinosaurs just won't die.

Oh, sure, a meteor (or whatever) killed them off about sixty-five million years ago, except for those that had the good luck or foresight to evolve into birds.

Edgar Rice Burroughs killed them off in Africa, Caspak, and Pellucidar. Sir Arthur Conan Doyle killed them off. Ray Bradbury and L. Sprague de Camp killed them off. Claude Raines and Caesar Romero killed them off. Stephen Spielberg killed them off.

And yet they keep coming back. It seems that everyone loves them.

A few years ago I edited an anthology for DAW Books entitled *Dinosaur Fantastic*. It had some pretty good stories in it. One of them even won an award. Many of them were reprinted all over the world.

I thought that was the end of it. (Spielberg probably felt the same way when he yelled "That's a wrap!" on the set of *Jurassic Park*.)

But the public is never wrong, and the public is even more enamored of dinosaurs today than when this book's predecessor saw print. Between the books, the movies, the models, the CD-ROMs, the museums, the figurines, and the endless TV documentaries, dinosaurs have become a billion-dollar-a-year business. The public just can't get enough of them. One would almost guess that the word "dinosaur" has evolved from "terrible lizard" to "cash cow."

And since the customer is never wrong, DAW Books has decided to publish a second collection of original science fiction and fantasy stories about dinosaurs.

I had some trepidations when they asked me to edit it. I mean, after all, how many science fiction stories can you tell about dinosaurs before you start repeating yourself?

Well, I needn't have worried. In romance, you tell the same story over and over again, with different names. In mysteries, you tell the same story over and over again, with different plot details. But in science fiction, with all of time and space to play with, the practitioners would sooner die than constantly retell the same old story.

This book's ample proof of it. In the following pages, you'll discover a number of different theories—some serious, some hilarious—about why the dinosaurs became extinct. You'll read a story about a Pope who tries to convert the dinosaurs to Catholicism. You'll hear a dinosaur pour out his troubles to a sympathetic vampire in a neighborhood bar. You'll learn why there were no dinosaurs on Noah's Ark. You'll even learn why one science fiction writer tossed another into the La Brea Tar Pits during the most recent World Science Fiction Convention.

Most of all, you'll be entertained, because that's the business of storytelling, and no one does it better than the wildly imaginative men and women who ask *What if?* for a living.

—Mike Resnick

WHAT REALLY KILLED THE DINOSAURS

by Esther Friesner

Esther Friesner is famed for her humorous fantasy novels. In 1996 she added a Nebula for Best Short Story to her trophy shelf.

The hunting had been good that day. Yrg strode back to his lair with his hunger sated, a huge gobbet of raw meat clenched in his mighty jaws. If his mate had been only half as successful at the hunt as he, their newest clutch of young ones would feast and thrive. They would grow quickly, soon come to their full powers, and then take their rightful places as lords of the great world—fearsome carnivorous eating machines before whose coming all lesser beings would tremble and submit.

Maybe *then* they'd move out of the house. The thought of finally seeing the backs of the loathsome little ankle-biters sent pleasurable shivers of pride all up and down the titanic meat-eater's spine. Mind you, he had nothing against the young ones *per se,* it was just that every so often he was seized by the less-than-fatherly urge to rip their throats out. It was not a constant urge, but one which spiked every so often, most notably when the brats insisted on showing off all the clever things they could do with that peculiar-looking fifth digit they'd developed. They insisted

that it was fascinating: the way they could fold it all
the way across the inner surface of their forepaws and
use it to manipulate even the tiniest objects with
remarkable dexterity. Fine, Yrg could understand
kids and their manias of the moment, but why did
they have to insist that he be fascinated by it too? If
you'd seen one digit, you'd seen them all, to Yrg's
way of thinking. Seen and—most likely—tasted.

And then, those *sounds* the hatchlings made! First
one of them would chirp and chitter a series of noises,
then another would respond in kind. Why? Not for
any reason Yrg could fathom, unless they really
meant to drive him into a rage. These were not the
sort of sounds younglings had made in *his* day, no sir!
These vocalizations were too complicated, for one
thing, and there were so blasted *many* of them. As far
as he was concerned, there were a fixed number of
noises any respectable dinosaur of his kind needed to
make: the hunger noise, the pain noise, the warning
noise, the distress noise, and the show-me-where-
you-got-them-eggs-waiting-for-me-hot-mama noise.

As with the fifth digit, this noise-fixation of his
latest brood would be tolerable, except, here too, the
scaly boogers insisted that he learn some of the
noises. From what his poor, befogged brain had been
able to absorb, the noises *meant* things to the young:
things about as complicated as the noises themselves.
He'd gotten the hang of it, in time, and the younglings
were pleased with him, though he'd have been just as
happy to have been left in peace with his original
repertoire of eat/hurt/mate/run away cries.

"Now we can understand each other!" his first-
hatched male offspring had declared proudly.

"For . . . what?" Yrg inquired awkwardly.

"Well, so we can communicate more effectively, of
course," the youngling told him, accompanying this
information with *that* look: the one that as good as
said—without benefit of any noises whatsoever—that
he thought the old male was so stupid that if he fell

into a tar pit he'd need someone there to give him sinking lessons.

Yrg gave a grunt of comprehension, then repeated, "For what?"

The hatchling took in a deep breath and let it out slowly, accompanying it with expressive rollings of his eyes. This was a mannerism as new as it was annoying—to Yrg, anyhow. "Never mind, Pops, you wouldn't understand. What's to eat?"

Eating was something Yrg understood. In fact, there were only two things stopping him from eating this noisy, eye-rolling, extra-digit-fixated clutch of hideous hatchlings: the fact that it would break his mate's heart if he devoured their young, and the fact that his mate would then break his spine and devour *him.*

It was a female thing. Females were something he understood even less than the hijinks of his offspring, but at least it was an old, familiar mystery. Take the latest scheme the Fairly Large Sex had come up with: cooperative care of the young! The females had laid the bizarre proposition before the Great Council when they should have been home laying eggs. They described in loving detail how it would work: males and females both waiting around, minding the nest until the eggs hatched, then looking after the hatchlings after they were out of the shell. No more hasty matings and hastier farewells for the males, no more eggs laid and left to chance and the elements. No.

If we take better care of our eggs and our young, we won't have to lay so damn many of them in the first place. (So the leader of the females gave the assembled males to know.) *Squeezing out a dozen of those things at a sitting* hurts, *in case you didn't know!* Mutual parental care. . . . Where had the egg-bearers ever gotten such a wild idea?

From the plant-eaters, eh? Yrg could still see the Oldest One's heavy head slowly swaying from side to side in disbelief. Could anything good ever come

from the plant-eaters? Well, cutlets, yes. But apart
from cutlets, nothing. To think otherwise was either
purest ignorance or willful stupidity; the Oldest One
had made that perfectly clear.

After the females tore the Oldest One into several
fairly equal portions of warm, sticky refreshment for
the Great Council attendees to enjoy, the New Oldest
One allowed that it wouldn't hurt to give the plan a
try. After all, nothing ventured, no one devoured.

And what a surprise: It worked! In the time since
the New Oldest One had given his approval of the
females' scheme, Yrg and the other males noticed a
distinct improvement in not only the quality and
quantity of younglings added to the population, but
also in the females' tempers. Freed from the uncomfortable spectre of constant egg-laying, they no
longer viewed the males as unnecessary evils, to be
slashed open from guts to gizzard when there was
nothing better to eat and no howling hormones to be
satisfied into silence. This was all to the good, and
then some.

As many males knew (and as the Former Oldest
One had lived—and died—to learn) females were
often cranky when crossed, and sometimes they
didn't even wait to be crossed to be cranky. The
slightest thing might set them off, and there was
absolutely no reasoning with them, especially when it
came to the young. For the life of him, Yrg didn't see
why. Oh yes, granted that the actual physical act of
egg-laying was no picnic, but it was soon over and
done with. A couple of grunts, a squeeze here, a strain
there, and *POP!*: motherhood. Then you kicked a
little sand over the new arrivals and let time and sunshine do the rest. That's how a male would work it,
anyhow. No muss, no fuss, and if you felt compelled
to stop by a little later on and check on the eggs'
progress, you mighty even get an unexpected treat.
Sometimes one of the eggs was a dud. It wouldn't

serve to perpetuate the species, but it did make a mighty fine midmorning snack.

The word *snack* touched off something inside Yrg's skull, the part he used to keep his brain in. Now what was it . . . ? Ah yes! That hunk of meat still dangling from his jaws. He was supposed to be bringing it back to the nest to feed to his kids. He knew he'd put it there for a reason.

As the great meat-eater strode through the dense vegetation, he let nothing slow him, much less stop him. From time to time he felt something warm and fuzzy squish between his taloned toes. Probably one of the those pesky newfangled creatures—the furry nuisances seemed to be everywhere these days. How he hated tromping on them! Parts of them always got stuck under his claws, and they tickled terribly until he scraped them off. There was good eating on the bigger ones, but not much. By and large the hairy things were more trouble than they were worth, and the noises some of them made set his nerves on edge. Just thinking about the low, persistent, rumbling sounds he'd once heard from a pair of them during their mating season made his fangs curl.

At last he broke free of the forest and spied his home in the not-too-distant distance. His mate, Grkh, had chosen the site: a lovely little niche in the lee of the towering red cliffs. A spacious yet easily defensible spot which the sun warmed for most of the daylight hours and whose high stone walls kept off the worst of the night's inclemency. Most of the other mated pairs from their herd had made their homes in the same general area. As long as they all spread out to do their hunting, it didn't matter whether they nested close together. You needed surprisingly little elbow room when you had no elbows worth mentioning.

As he drew closer, he saw Grkh coming forward to greet him. The sight of the female bearing down on him at great speed froze Yrg in his tracks. This

wasn't like Grkh at all. Usually, when she spied him
approaching the lair, she went into a defensive posture: jaws gaping, muscles tensed to spring. It was
pure instinct, a leftover from the days before mutual
childcare when any male who approached a female
was either hoping for a quick mating or, in times of
poor hunting, a quicker meal. Of course any male
who wanted to use a female of the species for lunch
rather than loving had to be pretty desperate, or
maybe suicidal: Females were bigger and badder; and
they fought dirty.

Not any more, though, Yrg reminded himself. *That
was then, this is now. And now is full of new things,
more and more of them every day.* What was it that
Grkh called it? Oh yes: *progress.* As he recalled,
she'd even tried to turn the idea into a sound, the way
their kids did.

She was certainly making a lot of sounds now.
"Yrg! Yrg! No anger! Nooooo anger!" she cried as
she drew nigh. Her beady eyes were almost warm
with concern.

No anger? That was an odd request, coming from a
female. Normally it was the male's role to beg for
clemency from his mate over any one of a number of
offenses, real or imaginary. (Especially imaginary.
Most of the pain-cries Yrg had overheard in his long
life usually came when a male had done nothing
wrong but a female was in the mood to bite something. Thus he had come to learn, through the sudden,
violent deaths of others, that the worst thing a male
could do wrong was to do *nothing* wrong and admit
it.) Yrg was immediately on his guard. He dropped
the meat from his jaws and kicked it toward her as a
distraction.

She ignored the meat, still repeating, "No anger!
No anger!" Vaulting the brisket, she slowed her
pace and bowed her great head before him in a submissive posture he had only seen in other males. If

Yrg had had lips, he would have pursed them in consternation.

Before he could question his mate's bizarre behavior, the mouth of the lair exploded with an outpouring of young. A dozen tiny replicas of himself came streaming across the earth, uttering wild cries that set his scales on end.

"Pops!"

"Dad!"

"Father!"

"Papa!"

"Big, ugly, male oppressor, useful only for breeding purposes!" (That was one of the cleverer of the female fry, and one for whom he privately predicted a short life but a messy one.)

"Daddy!"

There was no dodging them, and no way he could get his bulky body up to enough speed for an effective getaway. Sickened to his very guts, Yrg allowed himself to be overwhelmed by a veritable avalanche of posterity. He bowed his head in defeat. Some of the females immediately took advantage of this to shove their snouts against his and make sucking, smacking sounds. He had no idea whether this was another one of the kids' newly invented ploys to rile him red-eyed, or simply their way of tasting him, for future reference. He hoped it was the latter.

"Hey, Pops, wait'll you see it! It is *so* great! You're gonna love it! C'mon!" The first-hatched male scythed his clutchmates out of the way with an elegant sweep of his tail. It did Yrg proud to see him in action. A maneuver like that would win the sprat any number of mating fights, thus ensuring that something of Yrg's blood would be passed on to future generations. For some reason he could not quite put a claw on, this struck Yrg as a vital thing. Yes, the master of such an elegant tailsweep could even be forgiven for digit-folding and noise-making in the first degree.

"See what?" Yrg asked in his most benevolent tone.

"You'll see," the little male said, and dashed back towards the lair, his co-hatchlings racing after.

Before following suit, Yrg turned a questioning glance toward his mate. She only rolled her eyes in just the way he'd seen some of the plant-eaters do in the instant before his fangs permanently rearranged their vertebrae. Come to think of it, it was the self-same facial quirk she'd used just before she'd permitted him to mate with her.

Surrender? Yrg thought, perplexed. *That means defeat. Defeat or hormones.* He sniffed his mate. No, there was no trace of the exquisitely rank scent of a female no longer in control of her own destiny, slave to the demands of her heart (and her ovipositor). So, defeat. But . . . defeat by what agency? Surely not by her own young! They were so small, so delicate, so tasty! Every inborn survival trait demanded that they defer to their elders in all things—and look adorable while doing so—or be gobbled up for insubordination.

"No anger," Grkh repeated, a pitiful, plaintive note coming into the words. "We just get this clutch hatched, growed. No want lay more eggs so soon! *Hurts.*" The massive female stamped one paw for emphasis. "Let be, let young do. No anger." And then, a sound entirely foreign to Yrg's ear-holes: "Pleeeeease."

He was not sure what this new *pleeeeease* noise meant, but he got the unmistakable impression that it was not a sound that the female made easily or willingly. Completely at a loss, Yrg made a gesture of acquiescence. *Let young be? Let young do? Do what?* He had the sinking sensation that this was not truly a plea for his permission. The thing was already done, and whatever it was, it was more than likely to be something truly terrible. While his mate picked up the until-now-spurned hunk of meat, Yrg went on ahead into the lair, his guts tied in a Turk's head knot.

"Hey, Pops!" The firstling male waved to him from the back of the niche that Yrg's family called home. "C'mon in, come closer, you've gotta see this. All the other families got one too, but I think ours is the best."

Yrg stepped gingerly forward, his huge head lowered, his nostrils flaring with suspicion. There was an alien smell polluting his lair: a pungent, warm aroma hideously different from the good, honest reek of reptilian life. What horror was it that his brood had brought into his most intimate domain? The nearer he got, the more aspects of the invading presence arose to make his flesh creep and turn his bones to stone. There was a cloud of—of—What were those wisps floating in the sunbeams? A pinch of them landed on his snout and sent him off into a fit of sneezing. And what spoor was that underfoot? Not his, not his children's, certainly not the droppings of any breed of dinosaur that *he* knew. It was not only the wrong scent, but far too small. A great dread overcame him, and in that icy moment, one of his disused synapses sparked to send a revelation to his brain. Now he *did* know what and whence those wisps. He had had to dislodge whole clumps of them from between his toes more than once. Even though he had not yet come near enough to actually see the thing around which his younglings crowded, he knew what it was.

"No anger?" Ha!

A cliff-shaking roar burst from his chest. *"Mammal!"* he bellowed. "You got *mammal* here!"

The young ones looked up, wide-eyed. "Well, yes, of course it's a mammal," said the too-bright-for-her-own-good female. "And we *do* know we're not supposed to play with our food, you *don't* have to explain it to us again, we're *not* stupid. However, in your absence on yet another futile mission to assert the superiority of the male through the overly simplistic ritual of hunting (which is rendered meaningless by the fact that most females of our species are

patently better at it than their mates) this creature
happened to wander into our lair and we have made a
communal decision to keep it."

Yrg stared at his daughter. "Hanh?" It was the first
new noise he'd ever made, and it worked like a charm
when it came to conveying absolute bewilderment.

One of the less-bright females took a stab at
explaining things to the dominant male of the household: "It followed us home. Can we keep it? It's
soooo cute. We'll take good care of it, I swear, you
won't even know it's here. It can have my food, it
doesn't eat much, I don't care if I starve right to
death, honest. Can we keep it, Daddy? Huh? Can we?
Huh? *Pleeeeease?*"

There it was again, that whiny noise his mate had
made at him. Coming from a large female it had been
merely disquieting. Coming from a small one, it
seemed to promise that if Yrg did not comply with the
utterer's request, that would not be the end of it. Further whiny noises would ensue, rising in pitch and
volume until his eyeballs would shatter under the
assault.

Yrg looked down at the subject of his offspring's
petition. The young had stepped aside to let him get a
glimmer at it. It didn't look like much. It was a
mammal, all right: hairy as a Kiwi fruit and with only
half the charm. He thought he recognized the breed. It
was curled up, sleeping peacefully, making that peculiar rumbling sound he'd heard come from others of
its ilk. As if by a miracle, a fresh tuft of the critter's
fur dislodged itself and floated up to alight on Yrg's
snout. His sneeze rattled loose a bushel of gravel
from the cliffside but did not disturb the mammal in
the least.

What was it the first-hatched male had said? Something about all the other families in the nesting
enclave having one of these? Yrg was not as smart as
his hatchlings, having been raised without the nurturing benefits of mutual parental childcare, but there

was something in the knowlege that *all* of his neighbors harbored one of these creatures that struck him as ... well ... What *was* the cognitive term he wanted—?

Oh, yes: *sinister.*

He had the *what,* though *why* he should react so negatively to such a seemingly innocuous bit of fur and flesh remained a mystery. It was a mystery destined to go unsolved, mostly because Yrg's personal world had gotten along pretty well up to now without wasting time on foolish things like puzzles, conundrums or unanswerable riddles. Deep within his brain, one of the most primitive yet tried-and-true circuits kicked in. It was this very mechanism that had given the dinosaurs dominion over the earth for uncounted centuries. It wasn't as fancy as opposable digits or sound-making, but it was sufficient unto the epoch: *When something smaller than you makes you feel afraid, don't waste time asking a lot of stupid questions; kill it.*

Yrg raised his foot and uttered his best killing roar, then brought the gigantic paw down. There was a very satisfying crunch, and the familiar feeling of gooshy stuff welling up between Yrg's toes.

A *lot* of gooshy stuff. Too much gooshy stuff for one little furball. Yrg glanced down and saw what was left of his whiniest female hatchling. Yuck.

"*Now* you've done it." The too-bright female confronted him. The nimble-footed mammal, unscathed, was perched on top of her head, its fur bushed out, its eyes flashing. It almost looked as if the creature was challenging Yrg! The very idea would have been ludicrous if not for the fact that the great meat-eater had just done something really, really stupid. Yrg didn't like being made to feel stupid. It made him overreact and do something even stupider to make up for it.

"Well, what *could* we expect from a male?" the too-bright little female was going on for the benefit of her broodmates. "It's not just the carnivores, you know; the male herbivores are just as likely to presume that a display of brute force is a fit substitute for reasoned dialogue between equals. It just does not enter their miniscule brains that the only way to go is a frank and open discussion between empowered—"

At this point the mammal had the gall to spit at Yrg. Yrg roared and stomped down a second time. This time there was much more gooshy stuff: He had taken out the too-bright female and two of her male siblings who were agreeing with her. The mammal escaped.

Now Yrg was mad. This was not a good thing in the best of cases. Not one of the most keen-eyed reptiles, a hunter by scent rather than sight, Yrg became the living illustration of the term *blind rage* when something really got under his skin. The killing fury possessed him. A dinosaur's home was his—his— Well, it was something pretty darn special, that's what it was, and he'd see himself at the bottom of the food chain before he allowed some wussy little warmblood to take over. He didn't care *what* the kids said!

Obviously he also didn't seem to care where the kids said it, for as soon as they realized that their precious mammal was in peril, the living hatchlings swarmed forward to beg their angry sire to spare its life. *Forward* was not a wise direction to take. *Away at all speed* would have been better, but younglings who have been raised in the sheltered environment of a two-parent nest and who have not had to fight for every mouthful of meat from Day One *ab ovo* have not had the chance to learn that you never try to reason with an adult on a rampage.

Afterward, it didn't take long for the dust to settle; not with all that blood to wet it down. Yrg stood in the midst of the desolation that had once been his home, looked down at the mush that once been his hatchlings, then up into the contorted face of a mate who had just realized how soon her reproductive hormones were going to kick in again now that the children were gone.

Yrg knew doom when he saw it. Grkh launched herself at him with a resounding, maniacal, carnivoricidal scream that made all of Yrg's previous bellowings sound like the peep of an asthmatic tree frog. Yrg's jaws gaped in terror, and by a quirk such a Fate has always delighted in dispensing in bulk to her abused children, those same jaws accidentally snapped closed on Grkh's throat just as the big female disemboweled him with a single stroke of her hind foot. Locked in death, the two dinosaurs keeled over with a crash, just missing the mammal as it hightailed it to safety.

Outside the now-silent lair, the little creature paused, heart thumping wildly. He was still panting for breath when one of his own breed came sauntering out of the underbrush, tail held high. They touched noses in the ritual greeting of their kind, then rubbed heads. The stench of death clinging to both their bodies communicated the fact that their master plan for sowing ultimately fatal discord among the giant reptiles was well underway. Already they could hear the distant sounds of other, previously stable dinosaur lairs all along the cliff face dissolving into hellholes of bloodshed and chaos. The mammals rumbled their satisfaction.

As they exchanged information in this manner, a third creature broke through a stand of ferns to join them and make his report. His eloquent whiskers touched theirs and as good as said, *Soon they will all be gone. Then the world belongs to us!*

Not so fast, the first creature communicated via a flick of his pointed ears. *The dinosaurs are not the only ones we must eliminate. What about all those damn lemurs? You can't walk under a tree these days without going deaf from their idiot chattering. It makes my fur stand on end. I say we wipe them out, too.*

How? the thirdcomer inquired. *Our tactics only work on* intelligent *beings, and they're nowhere near as smart as the dinosaurs.*

Why bother? the second creature soothed. *It's not like they'll ever amount to any kind of threat. Not to us, at least.*

I don't know. . . . Sometimes you'd almost think they were—

Forget it. You're just tired. Now come on, we've got bigger fish to gut. Who's the baddest mammals on earth? Who's gonna ditch the dinos? Who's gonna rule this world, huh? Huh? Huh?

And from three fuzzy throats at once there went up a sound more terrifying, more dominating, more awe-inspiring than any roar that had ever broken from the jaws of the outflanked, outclassed, and soon-to-be-extinct tribe of thunder lizards:

"Meow!"

ROMEO FALLING
by *Karen E. Taylor*

Karen E. Taylor is the author of three horror novels, and has been on the preliminary Stoker Awards ballot two years running in both the novel length and the short fiction categories.

"Goddamned piece of space junk!" I stopped my foot an easy inch away from delivering a sharp kick to the control panel. Yeah, the stupid ship was already down, but it was probably fixable; damaging it further wouldn't do me any good, despite how wonderful it would have felt.

"Good plan, girlfriend. Knock out all your controls while you're at it." The tones of the computer's speech module were sarcastic and comfortingly familiar, as they were designed to be, since they were my own voice patterns repeated back to me. I'd tried all the available voices and they'd all annoyed me. What I'd finally ended up with was very similar to carrying on a prolonged conversation with myself. But space was a big lonely place and I was all I had.

"No harm done. I stopped."

"Just barely. Now, don't you want to know what your options are?"

"Yeah, let me have it."

As things turned out, I wasn't in too much trouble. I'd managed to land with minimal damage when the warnings had gone off. I'd also managed to land on an oxygen-based planet, with acceptable food and water rations, should I be down for longer than my meager supplies lasted. That, however, was the extent of the good news. The planet was listed as non-humanoid/nonintelligent/nonpopulated, and the necessary parts for repair to my ship would take at least one or two months to arrive via auto-shuttle. In addition, I'd definitely miss my cosmetics drop off at Megalon IV. By the time I finally arrived, the tints would be all wrong, passé, last week's news. And undoubtedly the other company's ships would have already been there and gone. Damned pink monstrosities. Just the look of them made me nauseous; they should, in my opinion, be banned from space.

And none of this took into account the fact that this run was supposed to give me the down payment on a new ship. Now the missed drop and the repairs would set me back even further. I often wondered why I did this. There were times when I just wanted to give up on the whole thing, settle down somewhere, and make a life. Any life would be better than the one I had.

"Shit."

"Oh, and by the way, that reminds me," the computer voice droned on, smugly. Damn, I could be an insufferable bitch at times. "Your little emergency landing was a bit difficult on the sanitary facilities. I've ordered an extra pump and a valve or two along with the other necessities, but for now, you'd better go *alfresco*."

"Great. Just great." And now that we'd mentioned it, I realized that nature was indeed calling. "So," I said, getting up from my chair and slinging a holstered stunner over my shoulder, "Anything special I should be careful of out there?"

"No. Nothing much out of the ordinary."

"Good."

"Unless, of course, you count the dinosaurs."

My legs gave way underneath me and I thumped back into the seat. "The what?"

"Di-no-sau-ers," it said in my best derogatory fashion, "Prehistoric Earth creatures, dating back some 150 million years. The term itself comes from two ancient Greek words . . ."

"Yeah, yeah, I know what dinosaurs are." I sighed, seriously considering reconfiguring the voice module, convenient though it was for singing self-harmony. "But what the hell are they doing *here?*"

"This place is coded as a nonoperational recreational planet."

"Any information about why it's now nonoperational?"

There was a slight pause. "Overall incompatibility of the genetically designed lifeforms with the visiting lifeforms. Been closed down for about a hundred years. Supposedly nondangerous, though, so you should be perfectly safe."

I nodded slowly. "Thank you. Supposedly. Should be. I feel so much better." Standing up, I took a deep breath and headed for the exit. " 'Join the Merchant's League,' " I mimicked the vid-ad, " 'Grow rich beyond your wildest dreams and see the wonders of the universe.' " The computer gave a noise that could have been a snort. I agreed. Well, I thought, as I switched open the door, maybe the wonders part will be accurate.

The planet, or at least the part on which we'd landed, was breathtakingly beautiful. It had a sparse, almost Earth "Old West" appearance: sandy, rocky and flat with what looked like a small mountain range on the horizon. I knew that appearances were deceiving in this kind of terrain; those mountains could be immensely high. The air had a clear crystal scent and feel. Scrub brush grew in a scattered fashion, but a splash of not-too-distant green promised a watering hole.

Deciding to save that trip for a little later, and with

my hand firmly fixed on my stunner, I glanced around uneasily, but saw nothing more than a few small, purple, six-legged lizards, obviously indigenous creatures, possibly a food source for the purported dinosaurs. "Well," I said, "First things first." My voice sounded muffled, swallowed up in the vastness of the area, but was still loud enough to cause the lizards to skitter away for shelter. I spotted an appropriate clump of small bushes, squatted down among them and relieved myself, then laughed as I fastened up my suit. Why on Earth was I seeking privacy? There was no one here to watch.

Pardon me, I couldn't help but notice that you just thought about Earth. The voice was masculine, deep, drawling and seemed to originate directly inside my mind.

I spun around. "Jesus!" Lounging rather indolently against the side of my ship stood a six-foot-tall, bright red, leather-winged, lizard-headed bird.

Romeo, actually. And you won't need that.

"What?" My hand had been edging slowly toward my stunner.

My name. You obviously have mistaken me for someone else. My name is Romeo. I sense your fear, but assure you that you don't need your weapon. And since I mean you no harm, I will trouble you no longer.

With a sweep of his wings he was gone, diminishing first to a small v-shape, then to a speck in the sky, and then to nothing at all. My knees were shaking. I was thankful, as I quickly entered the ship and switched the exit closed and locked, that I'd relieved myself before the confrontation.

"Nicely handled," the computer commented on my return.

"Shut up. It scared me, is all. I was hardly expecting something like that, waiting for me. And it spoke, telepathically or something. Weird."

"I did warn you."

"Well, yeah, you did. Just barely. Get out all the files you can find about this planet and let's have a look at exactly what kind of Godforsaken place we're stranded on, shall we?"

I spent the next two days reviewing all that was known about this planet. There wasn't much. And what was there was old news. I watched some of the early vid-ads importuning rich space travelers to "Come and Partake of the Wonders of Prehistory." Not much of a slogan, I thought scornfully, but then the whole planet was a project that had been left entirely in the hands of the scientists who'd thought it up. Always a bad marketing idea. When things didn't quite work out the way they'd planned, they just closed it down. Idiots. They must've lost millions.

And their dinosaurs weren't really dinosaurs. They were genetic constructs of what these particular scientists thought dinosaurs should be. All of the creatures were artificially created with the data from original DNA samples collected and consulted, but not always used. The occupants of this planet were mongrels: put together from a piece of this and a piece of that, not pure and not simple, with incredibly long lifespans. Each species was encoded with a special, often stereotypical personality, to make them more amenable to the artificial situation. And in some cases, this personality type was ominously slanted to prevent certain types of instinctual behavior. Mostly, the system was designed to prevent wanton and possibly destructive overprocreation. The tyrannosaurs and some of the other carnivores, for example, were almost exclusively homosexual in orientation. The larger plant-eaters were reclusive loners and the smaller ones were equipped with a Messianic complex. Which, of course, explained Romeo's recognition of the name I had invoked.

In fact, all of these artificial personalities made sense to me from that perspective. It would take two members of the species to act out of type to enable a successful mating, thus maintaining the ecological balance desired.

"Except the personality for the winged dinosaurs," I concluded in discussing the situation with the computer, "they are listed as the hopelessly romantic type. How on Earth does that prevent procreation? I'd think it would mean they'd breed like rabbits."

"The files don't contain that information."

"Yeah, I noticed." I got up from the console and sighed. "Well, whatever these creatures may be, there's absolutely no indication that they present a threat to humankind. In fact, they seem to have been purposely designed to be totally benevolent to two-legged types."

"All available data would indicate that, yes. I concur."

I stretched my arms up over my head, sniffed, then groaned. "As for me, I think I'm way overdue for a bit of a bath. I've gotten a little ripe, cooped up in this tin can with no use of sanitary facilities except for a few bushes. And since my winged Romeo seems to have disappeared, I think I'll hit the watering hole."

"Take the stunner."

I shrugged. "Why? If anything on this planet wanted me, they'd have come for me already. They've had opportunities in my many potty trips. I can't hide inside forever, cowering in fear. So I'll just take a couple of towels and a bar of soap, if you don't mind."

"Suit yourself. But if something else happens, don't say I didn't warn you adequately."

I stuck my tongue out at the console on the way to the supplies cabinet. Did I usually sound that much of a know-it-all? As I walked out the door, towels slung over my shoulder, a cake of soap and a water-testing kit stashed in my pocket, I made a mental note to have the entire computer system reworked when I finally got off this planet.

Outside it was another beautiful day: sunny and hot, but not terribly oppressive thanks to the slight breeze blowing in from the mountains. Stiff and sore from two solid days of sitting at the ship's controls, I decided to jog over to where I'd spotted the waterhole. Yes, there it was, and more like a small, but deep lake. The water was clear, I could see all the way to the bottom, and nothing swam in this lake but more of the six-legged lizards I'd encountered before. I scanned the area for the skeletons of dead animals or any other indication that the water might be poisonous. To my relief, nothing at all indicated a problem. But, to be safe, I put a small drop of water into the testing-kit tube and sat it and me on a nearby flat rock, to wait for the results.

The sun was hot and a blinding glare came off the water. I unzipped my suit and stepped out of it, took off my undergarments and tossed them all into the water for a nice long soak. Then I stretched out on the sun-warmed rock, wiggled my toes, and closed my eyes, humming a song to myself.

I must've fallen asleep almost immediately, a combination of the heat and the peacefulness of the pond. I dreamed: a long, winding dream involving the high cliffs of the faraway mountain range and the sensation of soaring and gliding over the desert floor far beneath me. A voice sang to me in my dream, a beautiful song, a beautiful voice. Masculine, deep and slow-pitched, it warmed my soul much like the sun warmed my body, wrapping me in love and leather wings.

Excuse me, the voice sang, *I do not wish to disturb your rest, but I saw you here and knew that we must speak.*

No, I thought as I struggled to open my eyes, that was not a dream. I remembered that voice.

"Romeo?"

You remembered me. How wonderful.

I squinted up at him where he loomed over me, still confused with the heat and the dream.

You are not afraid of me now. That is good.

I realized when I sat up that he was right. I wasn't afraid of him, although I knew that I should be. This was a ferocious prehistoric creature, capable of shredding me to pieces with vicious claws. It didn't matter that I knew his kind had been created artificially, to be benevolent toward humanoids. It had been a hundred years since anything but dinosaurs had walked this planet; they could have developed some nasty instincts since then.

You should have brought the stunner, my mind said, or you should turn and run for the ship. But I wasn't afraid. I felt secure and totally relaxed as I sat naked on the rock and smiled up at this creature. He even seemed to smile back, though I knew that wasn't possible.

You merely sense my happiness at meeting you again. I do not actually have the facial muscles necessary to smile. You, on the other hand, have a beautiful smile. Such nice, white, even teeth. And your skin is such a glorious shade of red.

"Red?" I looked down at my naked body. He was right. My skin was almost the same shade of red as his. "Damn, I must've slept longer than I'd thought. This isn't my skin's natural color, you know, it's a sunburn."

It is still a beautiful color, don't you think?

I stared at him, then laughed, delighted and somehow not at all surprised that the masculine ego knew no barrier of species. "Yeah, I suppose it is."

He reached a wing over and covered my arm. *We are a perfect match.*

I shivered slightly at his touch and his words. The feeling of love from the dream washed back over me and I blushed an even deeper red. What did this creature want from me? Why was I even talking to him? I didn't need friends, didn't have time for them; didn't stay long enough in one place to keep them. And I liked my solitude.

But something deep within my mind denied that statement: the same thing that had warmed to his presence and his touch, that held no fear of his alienness. Personal contact was something I hadn't had in a very long time and I liked it. Maybe too much.

"Well, it's been nice talking to you," I said, avoiding his intent eyes, "but I came out here for a much-needed bath. So if you'll excuse me . . ." I stood up, verified the safety of the water in the tube and dove into the pool.

Cold. Damn, the water was incredibly cold. I came up to the surface sputtering and he still stood on the rock. I could hear him laugh inside my head.

I could have warned you about that, you know. But you didn't ask. There are warmer pools around. I will show you.

"No," I insisted through clenched teeth, "this is just fine. Now if you don't mind, I'd like a little privacy."

He stared at me for a while, then nodded. *Of course, I understand. You wish to bathe alone.*

"Yeah, thanks." I paddled over to where my suit still floated and fumbled around inside the wet material to find my bar of soap. I began to work up a lather in my hands, glanced back up at him, and said with a note of finality, "It was nice to see you again."

Romeo flexed his incredible wings then cocked his reptilian head at me. *Perhaps it is presumptuous of me, but I would like to know your name.*

"Oh, yeah, my name. I'm sorry. I'm Miranda."

Miranda? Do not be sorry, Miranda. It is a beautiful name for a beautiful woman. Until later, then, and he bowed slightly. Perhaps he was just preparing for flight, I couldn't tell. *I bid you farewell.*

"Yeah, see you later."

After he had disappeared from sight, I gently soaped my burned skin, washed my clothes and went back to the ship, singing softly to myself the song from the dream.

"Have a nice bath?" The computer's tone was snide as usual, but I was in too good a mood to rise to the bait.

"Very nice," I said pleasantly. "Do we have any sunburn cream in storage?"

There was a pause as it checked the records. "No. Nothing at all like that."

"Oh, well . . ."

Excuse me. I do not wish to interrupt. Romeo stood hesitantly at the door of the ship, clutching a bouquet of blood-red flowers in his right wing claw. *These are for you, Miranda.*

"Flowers?" I blushed again and the computer snorted.

"Thanks."

Crush them and rub the juice on you. I believe they will help soothe your skin where it has been burned by the sun. I would offer to do it for you, but I'm afraid my limbs are not designed for that purpose.

I smiled and took the flowers from him. "Thanks," I said again, "it's very thoughtful of you."

You are most welcome. He gave a gesture that could have been a shrug and flew away.

"Flowers? From an admirer?"

"From a friend. For medicinal purposes."

"Uh-huh. I felt the tension between the two of you. You have an admirer."

I shook my head and gave a nervous laugh. "Give me a break, will you? We're different species."

"Different species, maybe, but we have scientific proof that the creature is a hopeless romantic. I would advise no further contact with him, nor with any of the other species on this planet."

That did it. I could put up with the snide comments, the sarcastic tones, but I didn't need a stupid machine making decisions about the company I kept. "Oh, bloody hell, who died and made you my mother? It was interesting, talking with him. But it wasn't anything more than that. It gets kind of lonely, sometimes, all cooped up in this ship with no company, no one intelligent to talk to for months on end."

"I talk to you. And I'm far more intelligent that you deserve. Why would you need anything else? Much less a freak species of animal," the emphasis on the last word was sneering, "who brings you flowers? I heard you arrange to meet him again. Are you crazy? Did you hit your head when you dove in that pool?"

"No, I didn't hit my head. And you talk too damn much." I walked over to the console and for the first time since I'd been traveling, turned off the voice module, vowing not to turn it back on until I was ready to leave. If then.

It was quiet in the ship after that. But Romeo returned every day. And we talked as I swam and sunned myself. Sometimes I would close my eyes and try to imagine him as a humanoid male. It was easy. Frighteningly easy. And the computer was correct about one thing. He *was* hopelessly romantic. He would sing for me, quote me poetry. His knowledge of earth classics was surprising and when I questioned him about where he obtained it, he just shrugged. He'd always known it. Apparently it had been genetically programmed into his kind. Romeo was the perfect companion and I felt my normal reserve open under his kindness, his consideration. I'd never known a human male so eager to please, so thrilled to bring gifts and tokens.

The auto-shuttle had arrived with my parts and departed again. And still I stayed on the planet. Somehow I just couldn't face the thought of repairing the ship. I was enjoying my vacation, the first one I'd had in years. Or so I told myself. The truth was I was beginning to like this place. And its inhabitant.

One day, after I had my swim and was sunbathing, naked on the rocks as usual, Romeo showed up with a very large bottle tightly clutched in his talons. *We will have a party. I obtained this from a rex I know. I think you'll like it, Miranda.*

"What is it?"

Tequila. An Earth-type liquor. I thought perhaps it might make you happy.

I smiled at him. "I know what tequila is. The rexes make this?"

They are better with their forelegs than my kind. And clever about making things to drink and eat. Strange creatures, they are, but they serve a purpose.

"I see." I reached up and took the proffered bottle, pulled out its cork and took a long swallow. It burned all the way down and I choked. Romeo patted me on the back with his wing.

It is not good?"

"No, it's fine. Very good." I took another swig to prove it. "It's just that I haven't had anything this strong to drink in a long time. Have some?"

He cocked his head at me, his eyes intense as usual, but with a strange undercurrent of something I'd never seen before. *I may drink from the bottle with you?*

"How else could you have some?" I was missing some clue here that I should have gotten. But his pleasure at my wanting to share the tequila with him was obvious. "Please, have some."

He squatted down next to me, his back legs curled up underneath him. I held the bottle to his mouth and he grasped down tightly on the neck, tossed his head back and took a long drink.

Now it is your turn again. We must drink it all or the rex will be offended.

I took another drink and giggled. "I will be very drunk if we have to finish the bottle, Romeo. And I'll be no good for conversation."

Conversation is fine. But sometimes a shared silence is better.

We continued to pass the bottle back and forth. Each time he drank he asked my permission again, and each time when I granted it, his eyes would glow with an eagerness I didn't understand. But after half the bottle was gone, it didn't matter. When three quarters of it was gone, I began to drift away, falling into a delicious languor. Romeo began to sing to me again, a song I remembered from my dream so many weeks ago. And before I knew it, I was curled up under his wing and singing along with him.

The words were strange to me, with a ritualistic quality. Something about his being the last of his kind. And how he would die for his love. Romantic. Hopelessly romantic.

We continued to pass the bottle and my giggling stopped as the words of the song began to sink into me. It was so sad: him being the last of his kind, wanting to die for love and all, that I began to cry. He licked away my tears with his tongue and I shivered at his touch. So foreign and strange, yet so familiar and tender.

When the bottle was finally empty, he took it and flung it out into the lake. I hiccuped slightly. "It's all gone. Now what do we do?"

Now is the time. I will teach you to fly.

"Silly Romeo." I reached up and stroked the skin below his eye socket. "I have no wings. I can't fly. But I wish I could. It would be so lovely to fly with you."

And so you shall, Miranda, my love. It is our destiny. He flexed his wings and rose from the ground, grasping me beneath the arms as he rose. We soared over the lake, over the desert. I didn't look down, instead I closed my eyes and just drifted, losing track of time and distance, losing track of everything but the sound of his song.

Only when I felt him gently set me down did I open my eyes. We were in the midst of the distant mountain range. My ship was almost invisible, just a light glinting off a pebble a long way away and a long way down. It didn't matter. Nothing mattered but Romeo's song.

Which had stopped. I sat up, amazingly clear-headed, considering what we had just drunk. "Give my regards to the rexes next time you see them," I said with a smile, "that's wonderful tequila."

As I said, they have their uses. Come with me and I will show you another.

We entered into a cave set into one of the cliffs. "You live here?"

As much as it can be said I live anywhere, I suppose. When one has wings, one needn't stay in any one place for too long. And when one is alone the concept of home is an unknown. But I need not say it. It is a fact you yourself know quite well. He gave the odd gesture that served as his shrug, and brushed aside a curtain woven of reeds from a side opening. *Here is what I want you to see.*

Ever a gentleman, he stood back and allowed me to precede him. Prominently displayed in the center of the room was a wing-type device, very close in design to an Earth hangglider, except that the wings were curved and fluted much like Romeo's wings.

I walked over to it. "May I touch it? It looks very delicate."

You may do with it what you like. It is yours. And it is stronger than it appears.

I ran my hands over the leather of the wings. They were red, similar in color and texture to Romeo's skin. Too close to be anything but the real thing, I suspected. "It feels like you."

As it should. It was my father's.

I gave him a long glance. His father's, I wondered? As in, it belonged to his father? Or as in, the skin was his father's? I didn't want to ask.

"Does it work?"

Would you like to try it?

"Me?" My breath caught just a bit in my throat.

Fly? Without a ship under my control? Without any kind of safety features?

It is easy. I will help you. You do trust me, don't you? You do want to fly with me?

His voice was so confident, so relaxed, that any residual fear I might have felt flowed out of me. I looked at him and smiled. "I'd love to."

Good. He walked over to me, and enveloped me in a brief hug. We both shivered in the contact and I felt a surge of excitement spin through my body, as if his touch reactivated the liquor we had drunk. Then we carefully carried the glider out of the cave and onto the cliffs.

"So, what exactly do I do?"

Romeo showed me how to grip the glider, making sure that my wrists were wrapped securely in the thick leather straps. The mechanism was amazingly light and I gave him a doubtful look. "Now, you're sure this will hold me? I don't particularly want to go crashing down to the desert floor."

He looked at me reproachfully. *I will be with you, Miranda. Would I allow you to fall?*

"No. I suppose you wouldn't." We walked over to the edge of the cliff together. "Any last words of advice? Before I go hurtling off into the wild blue yonder?"

Romeo stroked my back with his wing. *Keep your wings high. Fly far and fast. And remember that I will always be with you. Always.*

Then he pushed me from the cliff. I barely had time to register the fact that he had, when my wings captured an updraft and I was flying. The blood was pounding in my veins, my eyes were tearing with the wind—but I was flying.

Do you like it? Out of the corner of my eye, I caught a glimpse of Romeo, flying to my right and slightly behind me.

"Oh, yes," I called over the wind, "it's wonderful." I experimented with the tilt of the wings and the shift of my body, discovering the control and the feel of the glider. He stayed with me, encouraging my efforts, congratulating my successes, correcting my mistakes. Soon, I felt at ease in the air, growing more confident with each minute. I laughed into the wind. "Romeo, race me to the ship."

I surged ahead of him, picking up speed. Felt him behind me, striving to catch up with me. Felt an overwhelming wash of emotion come from him and flood into my awareness.

I faltered slightly when I realized at last what this was. A mating flight. All the signs were there: the rituals, the courtship, the words and songs of love and romance, clues that would have been obvious had they come from a humanoid male.

Yet I had responded to him, more than I ever had to another human. Hell, I probably even loved him. And I laughed again. If he wanted a mating flight, he'd get it. But, I thought with a wicked smile, I wasn't going to make it easy.

"So go ahead and catch me, Romeo," I called tauntingly. "If you can." I veered sharply away from him, making a complete turn at a dizzying speed. And we played in the air, dancing the dance he wanted, while he sang his song for me. I would slow down and allow him to approach, then would glide away out of his grasp. The song in my mind grew more intense with each encounter, until eventually it began to take over my will, conquering any sense of self. Then I slowed and flew straight.

And Romeo caught me as I knew he would, as I wanted him to. He enveloped me with his wings, grasping me around the chest, working his way deep inside me. And oddly enough, I was inside him. We were one creature—not completely human, not completely dinosaur, but something new—gliding over the desert floor. And for the first time in my life I felt loved. Truly and completely loved.

Then we separated and both drifted to the ground. I

untangled my wrists from the glider straps and set it aside, lying myself down on the sand. I was laughing and crying and pulling in air in great gulps. "That was quite a race," I said when I caught my breath, "but I think it was a tie. We will have to try it again, sometime soon."

There will not be another time, I'm afraid. I thought you understood.

"Understood what?"

That I was the last of my kind. And that I would die for your love.

"Romeo? But you can't die."

I can and I will, my love. My kind searches for their one true love and when they find her they love her and only her. Then they must die. It is our way, the way we were made.

"The way you were made?" My voice rose indignantly. "Goddamned scientists. Messing about with lives and emotions they know nothing about. Playing God. How would they like it if they died after having sex? Bastards."

He gave a high-pitched cry. *Destiny cannot be changed, my love. But I will always be with you.*

And he died. There on the desert floor of that truly Godforsaken planet.

"Damn." I sat down next to his body, took his reptilian head onto my lap and stroked the skin on his face. "If I had known, I never would have flown with you. I didn't realize that the words of the song were true. Dammit, you stupid creature, you should have told me, warned me."

But I realized that he couldn't have told me and wouldn't have warned me. So I did the only thing I could do; I sang his song back to him, cradling his dead body in my arms, through the long cold night and into the next morning.

Mornin', mum.

I came out of my trancelike state and glared at the enormous tyrannosaurus rex standing over me.

"Morning." I gently displaced Romeo's head from my lap and stood up. "He's dead."

Aye, I know. We watched the flight. And a mighty flight it was, too. Inspirin', you might say. My brother's painting the picture of Romeo falling right now. And I'm here to help you.

This creature's high-pitched and nasal voice felt strange in my mind, where Romeo's had been for so long. And seemed so incongruous from a creature of his size and strength.

Aye, those bastard scientists had one helluva strange sense of humor. No wonder they all picked up and left. Must've been hard for 'em to live with the perversions they created. Good riddance, say we.

"I might say the same thing. You're here to help me. What do I need help with?"

Why the little 'un, of course.

"The little one?"

Romeo's son. He was the last of his kind until you came along. Now there will be another.

"Romeo has a son?"

The rex giggled slightly and shook his head. *These pteros, they're great with the ladies, great with the trappings and the words of love. But they ain't much on explanations.*"

I snorted. "I guess not. And as far as I can tell, neither are you."

You'll give birth to Romeo's son. Plain 'nuff for you?

"But, how can that be possible? We are different species, completely different creatures."

The rex waved his small forearms in the air. *Genes, strange combinations of DNA, mixin' of stuff that shouldn't be mixed. I can't say I understand myself. The brontos, now, they're the thinkers. They spend all their time alone trying to figure this kind of stuff out. They could explain it to you, if you wanted. But whatever the reason, it's a fact. You're pregnant with Romeo's son.*

I stared at him in shock for a while. Then I smiled.

A son. Romeo's son. "But how will I survive the birth?"

The rex clicked his tongue. *There's dangers of course, but the brontos can help. We got time to work around it. Unless, you wanna leave. Some do. Some go away and never come back. We don't wanna know what happens to the little 'uns in that case. It's not a nice universe out there, far as I can tell.*

"No, it's cold there and lonely. And there's never been anything out there for me. This is the only home I've ever known. I'll stay."

Thought you might. He walked over to Romeo's body, picked it up and slung it over his shoulder. *I'll take care of this here for you. The little 'un will eventually need a glider. And you might wanna be alone for a while. But when you want company, my brothers and me live in a cave over in the mountains. Fly by anytime.*

"Thank you. I will. But I'm not alone, you know. He promised."

The rex gave me a great big toothy grin and a wave, and shambled across the desert ground. I watched him for a while, then turned and headed back to my ship to gather what little I thought I'd need for my new life. And as I went I sang a song of love—bigger than species, bigger than life. I would want to teach the words to my son.

Deep inside I felt a spark and a tiny voice spoke in my mind. *Heathcliff. My name is Heathcliff.*

I smiled. No, I would never be alone.

FANGS FOR THE MEMORY
by Josepha Sherman

*Josepha Sherman wears many hats: short story
writer, novelist, nonfiction book writer, anthologist, and science fiction editor.*

"Yeah, we got a pretty rough deal," the dinosaur said,
belting back his third scotch.

"How so?" I was still nursing my second, keeping
one eye on my companion's fangs. "Seems to me that
. . . what . . . three million years or so is a pretty good
run for any species."

"Naw. We were just getting somewhere. I mean,
look at me. I mean, granted, great-great-whatever-
grandpa must have been pretty dumb, but hey, we
were evolving, going places." He wiggled one five-
clawed appendage at me. "Bigger braincases, opposable thumbs, the works. And just when it was all
getting good—*bam!*"

"Extinction?"

"Hell no! Do I look extinct to you?"

I backed up just a wary touch from those alarming
fangs. "Hardly."

"Hey, don't worry, pal! I may be a raptor, but I
don't eat sentients. Unless they ask for it."

"I'm not asking. But you have to admit that it's a
little . . . well . . . odd for all of you—almost all—to

just up and disappear! No 'asteroid from outer space causing nuclear winter and killing everybody off,' then?"

"Well, that did take care of most of the bigger guys, yeah. But the rest of us . . . Wanna push those beer nuts my way, pal?"

I did. He crunched one as though it was the skull of an enemy. I waited.

Sure enough, the dinosaur began, "It was all Great-Great-Great—well, let's just call him Great-Uncle Thrixix. Anyhow, it was all his fault. We had it good, lords of creation and all that, even after that blasted asteroid wiped out half the neighborhood. But Great-Uncle Thrixix, he wasn't happy. Never happy, that guy, unless he's taking someone else to the kill—figuratively speaking, of course."

"Of course."

"Great-Uncle Thrixix was one of those smooth talkers, could sell you anything. There was the time he sold a Rex—one of those big, stupid guys, all teeth and no room for brains, you know? Well, this was before the asteroid, natch. Great-Uncle Thrixix sold the Rex hunting rights to a herd of nice, tasty Iguanodons. Only it turned out, he didn't have the rights to those Iguanodons. Had to be a smooth talker to get out of that one."

"Ah . . . disappearance," I prodded.

"Right." He downed what was left of his drink, signalled to the barkeep for another. "So you got the picture about Great-Uncle Thrixix. And you won't be surprised to hear he got enough folks peeved at him that he was running for his life.

"Now's when things get strange," the dinosaur continued. "This was after the asteroid, understand, so everyone left's a little weirded-out. We got shamans, mages, whatever you wanna call them, same as your kind's got. Great-Uncle Thrixix, he wasn't what you'd call a religious raptor, but that many folks out to get you, you pick up religion pretty quick."

He paused, reminiscing. I prodded again, "And . . . ?"

"And it turned out the shaman was a bit of a con-raptor himself. He also had him some genuine, honest-to-blood magic, not much, but hey, there it was. He and Great-Uncle Thrixix, they put their heads together and came up with the greatest scam of all time.

"And that was: the Religion of Power! Great-Uncle Thrixix did his greatest sweet-talking deal yet, and got all his pursuers believing in it—*it* being the idea that they could con soft, fangless mammals into worshiping them."

"Ah, wait a minute. The mammals during the Age of Dinosaurs weren't exactly sentient."

"Yeah, yeah, I know. No one would have believed the scam, not with those little critters that passed for mammals back then. But remember, I said that the shaman had some real magic. He did some of this, some of that, some of who knows what—and he opened a doorway into another world, one where mammals had a pretty fair amount of brains and had the upper hand already.

"Until, that is, they got unexpected visitors. Who, of course, had paid Great-Uncle Thrixix and his shaman buddy plenty for the privilege of, shall we say, instant divinity. And escaping a world that was pretty cold and unpleasant. Hell, I'm just surprised anyone hesitated at all!"

"Five toes!" I said suddenly.

"Heh?"

"Five claws—dragons! They've got that tradition in this world. I bet it's in that one, too. They passed as oriental dragons!"

"You got it."

"But that still only accounts for a few of you," I protested.

"No, it doesn't, not when you look at what happened next. You ever hear of that whaddaya call it, that . . . ah, yeah, that conservation of matter bit?

Think about it. We got a *lot* of mass, particularly when you put a whole bunch of us together. And that put a lot of stress on that doorway, something Great-Uncle Thrixix and the shaman didn't stop to consider."

"Yes, but—"

"Wait, wait, there's more. One more thing they didn't consider—that world they were sending everyone into, that world turned out to have a lot of magic all its own. This world, we both know, didn't. Doesn't. So–o . . ."

"An explosion?"

"Yep. And when the dust, so to speak, had settled, most of my kind were either gone altogether or stuck over there in that other world—where, I might add, dragon-hunting quickly became the sport of the day."

I thought of the legend of Saint George and the dragon—no, *not* a good time to mention that!

The dinosaur was staring dourly into his drink. "So that's what happened. Never did find out what happened to Great-Uncle Thrixix or the shaman. Maybe the explosion got them, maybe someone took their heads, but I'll bet you anything they lived happily ever after." He paused, studying me. "Some of the magical guys from there got tossed over here as things balanced themselves out. But I'd guess you'd know about that part."

I nodded.

"Some of us," he continued, "survived the dragon hunters, did some more of that evolving bit, and figured out a way to get back here. Back home." He shrugged, a strange thing to see. "But what good is it? It's a mammal's world now. Soft, squishy guys all over the place—sorry, pal, no insult meant."

I waved it off.

"Yeah," he continued, "and everyone's so blasted *tolerant* now, so . . ."

He floundered for a word, and I supplied, "Politically Correct."

"Right, that's it! Politically Correct. Sure, folk are more accepting of magic here—because they don't have enough of it to bother them! They accept me, too, because, hey, you don't make fun of someone who looks like a—a freak. Everyone's so blasted *tolerant,*" he repeated in disgust. "Except, of course, a dinosaur still can't get himself a drink without having to listen to those stupid, 'a raptor walks into a bar' jokes."

"I hear jokes like that, too," I agreed. "Only mine involve Bloody Marys."

"Yeah. Figured you weren't really a human the minute I saw those sharp eye teeth. Kinda pale for one of your kind, too, aren't you? And I'll bet you don't care for that whaddaya call it, that daylight savings time, either."

It was my turn to shrug. "We are what we are." Tossing some money onto the bar, I got to my feet. "It's been interesting, my friend, but the night is growing late, and it's time for me to find myself some dinner."

"Yeah. Me, too. Assuming some idiot doesn't try some dragon-hunting in this world, too. Or that they don't all just Politically Correct me to death!"

I sighed. "What can I say? Life . . . sucks."

"It bites," he agreed.

And with that, we went our separate ways.

DOWN ON THE FARM
by Maureen F. McHugh

*Maureen F. McHugh, who has been nominated
for every major award in the field during her
relatively brief career, won the 1996 Hugo for
Best Short Story.*

The oviraptors are herded into the chute by Tiffin.
Tiffin is a black and white border collie, but she
doesn't have any problem transferring herding
instincts from sheep to dinosaurs. The oviraptors
click at each other when they're distressed and the
yard sounds like a geiger counter. It smells musky
and faintly of ammonia, the familiar oviraptor smell,
although they aren't dirty creatures. They groom like
cats. Or maybe more like pigeons, if the pigeons had
almost no feathers. I grab the oviraptor at the head of
the chute, hosting her into the air by the tail, and
swipe hormone gel across her cloaca and then let her
go. Ravished, she scuttles toward the egg house, hor-
monally activated to lay eggs for another month.

It's a strange way to make a living.

It helps to be quick, because the oviraptors are,
and their muzzles are more like beaks than soft
things, and they hurt when they get you. Funky
looking things: sort of like dwarf, leathery-skinned
ostriches with eyebrows and ridge crests of thin
feathers. People are always surprised at how birdlike

they are. Of course, the truth is that birds are really dinosaurlike.

It's not a moment when I want my cell phone to ring. "Sabiston Eggs," I say.

"Grace Sabiston?"

"Yeah?" I hold the phone between my chin and my ear, grab a brindle dinosaur tail, and haul it up into the air to swipe hormone gel on its ass.

"This is Bobby Kestler." Bobby Kestler is one of my distributors. He doesn't usually call me at 7:15 in the morning, but distributors, like farmers, start their days early. "Grace? I have to cancel my orders."

The next oviraptor screeches just then. "What did you say?" I ask, grimly holding up a squirming oviraptor. My right arm is really much stronger than it used to be but I'm getting bursitis. "You have to cancel an order?"

"No, he says, "all my orders. The FDA just put a moratorium on food products from genetically induced animals."

"Fuck," I say. "Bobby, they can't do that. What are they going to do about things like ever-ripe tomatoes? Tobacco mosaic resistant cantaloupe?"

"Vegetables aren't animals," Bobby says. "Look, I'm sorry, but I've got to make a bunch of calls."

"What about cows?" I say. "They genetically modify cows. They genetically modify everything."

"Genetic modification is one thing, creating species is another, at least according to the FDA."

"Hell, half the DNA in my oviraptors isn't even from dinosaurs, it's from chickens."

"Grace," Bobby says, exasperated, "I'm not the Goddamned FDA, argue with them." The connection clicks in my ear.

Tiffin is looking expectant. The line has stopped moving. For a workaholic border collie, this is a crisis. "Tiffin," I say and she cocks her head, "this is just the beginning."

*   *   *

Seven years ago I got a pair of oviraptors as pets. Their names were Fred and Wilma. I had a good job in the marketing department of a huge international corporation that made medical products like baby shampoo and telepresence surgical instruments, and I could afford to blow money on a couple of dinosaurs. They were so ugly they were cute. The male, Fred, was a brindle and the line of feathers on his eyeridges gave him a perpetually sardonic look. He and Wilma successfully bred a clutch of seven long, pale brown leathery eggs and I ended up with seven down-covered dinosaur chicks which I sold for $2200 a piece. Then my company moved most of its North American operations to Brazil and Ireland to save the cost of paying North American wages. I was out of a job, and the long-necked scaly things with their unexpected feathers on the eyeridges and crests were my bread and butter.

Needless to say, I couldn't live off of Fred and Wilma, so I bought some more females and a good breeding male who happened to be brindle. Sabiston Dinosaurs bred a lot of brindle oviraptors. A restaurant in Berkeley called *Allegro non Tropo* contacted me to find out if I knew a source of eggs for them, and then I went into the egg business. First in a little way, now in a medium-sized way. I'm not agribusiness. I'm not rows of gleaming combines. I'm just me and a bunch of oviraptors and some part-time help. And a lot of financing.

About mid-morning I call my lawyer, who says she really doesn't have the expertise for dealing with the FDA but she'll see who she can put on it. While I'm on the phone to my lawyer, *Allegro non Tropo* calls and leaves me a message asking me if I've heard about the FDA ban. While I am on the phone with Sarah at *Allegro non Tropo,* I get voice mail messages from a half-a-dozen other customers.

Eventually a guy named Becker Doogan calls me from a huge law firm called James, Daws, Riser, and

Clough. "I've just been talking to Freida Kostner," he says, "your attorney. I do Regulatory work and she told me about your dinosaurs."

I'm holding the phone to my ear and typing "Becker Doogan" into my system, which is filling my idle time while it's searching for information beyond that he is employed by James, Daws, Riser, and Clough to tell me that James, Daws, Riser, and Clough has offices in New York, L.A., Washington D.C., Miami Beach, Fla., Paris, Hong Kong, Riyadh, etc., etc. It also tells me that James, Daws, Riser, and Clough underwrite the PBS broadcasts of two news shows and a multimedia public broadcast called *Access* on the Net. "I don't think I can afford you," I say. "You know this is basically a chicken ranch."

"I thought it was dinosaurs," he says.

"Chickens are modern-day dinosaurs," I say. "All birds are. Every Thanksgiving, America sits down and carves up the Thanksgiving dinosaur."

"Makes you wonder if the stuffing is appropriate," he says.

Which makes me like him a little. A good thing because I've got a picture from James, Daws, and all showing a remarkably young and handsome man with glasses and Renaissance hair and a beryl drop earring. He's some sort of lawyerly cross between late release and dependable, and mostly he looks sort of like I imagine Benjamin Disraeli would look. I saw a mini-series on Benjamin Disraeli. I wonder if it was underwritten by James, Daws, and all the rest.

"I was thinking that AgriGene might be interested in funding some legal action with the FDA," he says. AgriGene holds the patent on my oviraptors. "How about if I check and get back to you?"

"Is contacting AgriGene considered billable hours?" I ask.

He looks pained. "No," he says, "I guess not."

"Contact 'em, then," I say. Why not?

* * *

"Ovi" means egg in Greek or Latin. Like "ova." "Raptor" means predator, like the dinosaurs in movies that hunt in packs. When the fossilized remains of the first one was discovered, it was close to a nest of fossil eggs. It had grasping little hands. The assumption it dined on eggs was obvious, but wrong. Given the way mine look, the sardonic expression was probably what led paleontologists astray. Actually, it turned out that the nest was an oviraptor nest and the oviraptor was probably protecting it. They can be protective little bastards. We don't collect eggs by sticking our hands underneath them. The crates are set up so the eggs slide down into a catch tray.

My oviraptors are a little less than a meter or so long. I have two kinds: the females I use for egg laying and the breeding pairs. Of the breeding pairs, only Wilma still lives in the house.

Wilma is mostly reddish brown, with black bars on her legs and tail. She has her own room, with her crate with its iguana light. Back when I got Fred and Wilma, everybody thought that oviraptors needed full spectrum light the way iguanas do. They don't, but Wilma is used to it. She's eight, which isn't old for an oviraptor.

My office is across from her room. Right now she sits on the window looking out into the backyard.

I cluck at her. She doesn't turn her head, she never does, but the quills of eyebrow feathers raise a little. When she's excited they stand way out and she rears on her hind legs and dances to look bigger. I know that oviraptors really don't domesticate. They don't have much forebrain. They're all r-brain, all reptile, all food/fight/wait reflexes. They're primitive. Dinosaurs. How much more primitive can you get?

Still, I think that Wilma likes me as much as an oviraptor can. I go into her room and she raises her head so that I can rub between her eyes. She watches the leaves moving in the trees, and then, blissfully, closes her eyes. Her skin is warm and smooth and pliable.

"Well," I say, "you saved me once, baby. I'd like it if you could save me again."

Wilma sits blissfully pleased but unlikely to save me from the FDA.

Wilma and the farm look unchanging. Wilma watches the trees and I start breeding oviraptors. They lay a clutch of eggs in about three weeks. I sell some of the eggs before they even hatch. People pay less for an egg than they do for a hatchling, but I have bills.

I sit in my office and stare at my accounts and try to scheme. I get a lot fewer calls than I used to. The fancy lawyer has never called me back. Late one afternoon I get a call.

"Ms. Sabiston? I'm Grace Kelly. I would like to discuss with you your oviraptors. Krishnamachari Importers is a growing member of the fashion industry and we believe we could be partners to our mutual benefit." Grace Kelly sounds as if she is from somewhere like Kansas or Utah.

My system sets off in search of Krishnamachari Importers and Grace Kelly. It's a smart system, which is good because I don't know that I could have spelled Krishnamachari on my own.

"You breed oviraptors, am I correct?" Grace Kelly asks.

"Some," I say. "Not much anymore."

"We are looking for someone who can supply us with the resources to make fashion accessories," she says. Krishnamachari Importers, my system informs me triumphantly, makes handbags, billfolds, daybooks, and shoes. A picture of Grace Kelly shows her to be little and Indonesian and nothing like the late Princess of Monaco.

"You mean oviraptor hides?" I ask.

"Yes, ma'am," she says. "Krishnamachari

Importers specializes in exotic fashion accessories. Ostrich skin, sharkskin, catfish skin. All farm raised, of course. Krishnamachari only uses renewable resources from vendors who do not exploit undeveloped or sensitive lands like wetlands and rain forests."

"Of course," I say, bemused. Why would someone name an Indonesian girl Grace Kelly?

"We realize that you are in an entirely different sort of business, and we are prepared to help you make changes." Grace Kelly says. "I'm sending you some promotional materials and a proposal, if you don't mind."

I don't mind.

"After you look them over, will you please give me a call and let me know if you are interested? Then perhaps we can find a mutual time to meet and discuss the proposal?"

"That would be fine," I say.

I am destroying some three hundred dozen eggs a day and dumping them in a wash at the back of my property. When the wind is blowing from the wrong direction the sulfurous smell of rotten dinosaur eggs feels almost palpable, a slick taste at the back of my throat. The local raccoons and coyotes believe I've opened a food court. I am terribly interested in talking to Grace Kelly.

So I find myself in a business suit from my closet. It's a five-year-old business suit, but I always tended toward conservative clothes. It is strange to be in the city. The city is so discordant. There is too much for the eye, and none of it is integrated. It is all noise and pattern on pattern, a green neon Thai restaurant sign next to a Victorian painted sign next to elaborate gilt curlicues announcing a law firm. The air stinks of water standing in puddles. The air smells nothing of earth.

Strange to catch my reflection in the office windows. A lot of the suits have velvet collars—that must be this year's fashion thing. They are fine looking. My olive looks a little drab, but my old Metropolitan Museum of Art pearl earrings do happen to coincide with the obsession with things Renaissance, so maybe I don't look too dated.

Grace Kelly comes down to the desk to meet me. She is small and slight, and I feel calico. She is wearing a delicate suit of Japanese medieval brocade, elaborate in blue and white, with a white cummerbund that breaks the suit visually almost like an obi would. This is a fashion accessory company, I remind myself. I am a farmer. If Grace Kelly finds me either dowdy or surprisingly well-turned-out for a farmer, she gives no indication.

"Ms. Sabiston," she says in her Idaho or Nebraska way, holding out her hand forthrightly.

"Call me Grace," I say, "please."

"Two Graces," she says. "Isn't that a coincidence?"

"It isn't a name you run into every day," I say. "That's a beautiful suit."

"Thank you," she says.

"I used to work downtown," I say. "Over on Fifth."

"What made you decide to go into dinosaur raising?" she asks.

"I was laid off," I say.

The elevator doors look like hammered brass. They take us up and open on a saffron-colored reception area where a brass Shiva dances in front of a rosewood screen and the air smells of fresh flowers. Faint Indian music plays. It is a beautiful place, of course. Grace Kelly's suit clashes a bit with the decor. Too much pattern and shimmer. I don't fit the decor any better.

My eyes are tired. My ears are tired. Even my nose is tired, and my head aches.

Grace Kelly's office is a gray cubicle, and she shimmers in it like a dragonfly on concrete. Across her desk in disarray are leather purses and daybooks. "I meant to have this all straightened up," she says.

My cubicle looked nothing like this. My cubicle was forest green and bone and burgundy, colors some decorator had said would never go out of style. It was small though, and I had a wall covered in those sticky notes. During the transition when the company was moving out of North America, I used to come to work and hives would break out on my belly and legs.

I feel itchy now.

The daybooks are lovely. There is something about the promise of a daybook: some belief that my life can be so neatly controlled. We had seminars on how to use our daybooks. Grace Kelly shows me a beautiful black ostrich hide daybook and I open it and the screen shimmers to life. There is almost nothing on this daybook. Mine was connected to my work station and had my addresses and appointments, my documents in progress. When I wrote in it, it converted my handwriting into an idealized version, Parkeresque. I would have liked it to be Spencerian hand, but I was embarrassed by my own pretentiousness.

Ostrich leather has little raised pinpoints, like pimples, where the feathers went in. Sharkskin is rough. There is a red leather sharkskin purse that makes me want to touch it. The supple sheen of catfish doesn't even feel like something natural.

Grace Kelly explains how the catfish is impregnated with a fibrous fabric. "Like tyvek," she says. "You know those parcel envelopes that you can't tear open? Not the brown paper ones, the other ones. They feel like paper but they aren't."

The catfish goes very well with my suit. It is a pale gray color that is hard to describe because it seems to partake of whatever other colors are around it.

She puts a piece of leather in my hands. "This is oviraptor," she says.

It is so soft it is almost spongy. The scale ridges are visible. The leather has been rendered a soft buckskin color. "Does it matter what color the oviraptor hides are?" I ask.

She shakes her head and her geometrically precise hair swings. "The tanning process takes care of all of that." I wish I had her hair. Mine never hangs straight and shines.

"A lot of mine are brindle," I explain.

"What's that?" she asks.

"Sort of tiger-striped. Sometimes you see bulldogs and Great Danes that are brindle. Sort of orangish-brown and black."

She nods politely.

"Do you like dogs?" I ask. Tiffin the border collie is sitting at home moping. Maybe even destroying things. Tiffin hates to have nothing to do.

"Oh, sure," she says. "But I live in an apartment. No pets."

No animals. Seems strange. On the other hand, I went years without having any animals and never thought about it. Tiffin isn't my dog, Tiffin is my employee. A cheap workaholic, but still.

We discuss the proposal. I keep thinking the words "sold my soul to the company store" which is melo-dramatic and foolish. The proposal would tie me up tight with Krishnamachari. They would pay for some of the capital improvements on my farm to make the transition from eggs to hides, and would work with me on establishing a tanner. Actually, they would have final approval over the tanner who would have to meet three sigma requirements for defects—

I used to do this. Not sell oviraptor hides, but deal with suppliers and three sigma defect tolerances, and establish relationships with vendors. It is in the manu-facturer's best interests to have the supplier in his hip pocket. Krishnamachari would want to tie me up in exclusive deals, so I couldn't sell to anyone else.

It was in my best interest to be as free as possible, so I could be as flexible as possible, but without financial help I didn't even know how I was going to weather the time it would take me to begin breeding the hides in earnest.

I should be discussing guaranteed minimums—I mean, what if I converted to this and no one wanted to buy dinosaur daybook covers? There I would be with a yard full of oviraptors and no orders again.

I can't sell eggs. I have to pay the bills or me and Tiffin the border collie could be out on the street.

Will herd for food.

When I was working in the city I loved it. I loved the hills and the restaurants and the feeling of being on the edge of the ocean—even though I don't know that I saw the ocean all that often. I saw the bay.

I took Grace Kelly's proposal and went over to Berkeley. Not to the restaurant that used to buy my eggs. Without income I couldn't really justify *Allegro non Tropo*. Truthfully, without income I couldn't really justify anything I was doing, but I wanted to go someplace and think. I went to my favorite bookstore and hung around for awhile and finally bought a magazine. The bookstore was quiet and small. Back outside the light reflected off the glass of the windows and all those styles and patterns and noise and all the meaningless movement hit me like weather, and I put my head down as if I was walking into a driving rain and went up the street to a coffee shop.

Walking into the coffee shop was . . . not what I expected. I remembered the coffee shop as an oasis. I remembered the coffee shop as a place where I could sit for hours and the city would wander in and out, filtered by the door to a manageable level of people in black and poet manques and graduate student-intellectuals.

The Indian cowbells on the doors rattle as I walk in and I start itching again. A couple of us used to come over here after work for a glass of wine, during the time that we were transitioning the company out of the country and ourselves out of jobs. The smell of the place—of ground coffee and people—brought back that feeling of dread and helplessness. The helplessness was

the awful part. It didn't matter whether I had done my
job badly or well. There I was, without a job.

I ordered a cafe mocha for too much money and sat
down. They were playing Brazilian jazz. There was a
stack of free papers on the windowsill. *Sendero. Zazz,
Free.* "Zazz" was some kind of music.

Tiffin and Wilma were sitting at home waiting for
me. Wilma didn't care, but Tiffin did. I want to be
home, so I go.

Grace Kelly and two men from Krishnamachari
come out to the farm. They are dressed in the city
equivalent of leisure wear: soft leather shoes, shorts,
loose tops of soft woven taupe for the men, printed
like Balinese batiks for Grace Kelly. "Tiffin," I say,
"don't jump." Tiffin obligingly does not leave muddy
paw prints on their city clothes. It's late in the
morning but I'm still wearing the work clothes I put
on at four, when it was cold and damp.

They want to see it all, despite the mud. I take them
into the hen house. It's a long, low building with rows
of cages for oviraptor females. The roof is mostly
skylights because they lay better if they get a lot of
light. The floors are concrete. The place positively
stinks of musky-ammonia oviraptor smell.

Weldon, the gray and black tease male, is standing near the door. Tease males get the run of the
place. Weldon rears up on his legs and looks threatening. "Weldon," I say, flapping my arms, "shooo!
Shhhhh! Shhhhh! Shhht!" Weldon dances backward a
couple of steps and then drops, hissing, to scuttle off.
The females are clicking madly, excited. The racket is
pretty intense.

"Did that one get out?" one of the men shouts to be
heard over the din.

"No," I shout. "Females lay better if there's a male
strutting around. Like chickens. Weldon is the tease."

"Do you name all your dinosaurs?" the other man
asks.

I laugh. "I have about three thousand. Weldon is named after the CEO that laid me off from my last job." I don't add that tease males never get any.

They exchange uncertain smiles.

Back out in the yard we talk about how it will all be changed. They are all consulting their daybooks. Grace Kelly's daybook is ostrich, the two men have sharkskin. I won't need Weldon anymore. I wonder if I could have a daybook cover made out of Weldon-hide.

They talk about how much it will cost to convert. Krishnamachari will own the pens and some of the equipment, and I will lease it from them. The land will still be mine. They are willing to buy unborn stock in order to provide me capital. They are willing to guarantee me three years' worth of minimum orders. I say that anything above those minimum orders will be at a separately negotiated price. They have to go back to the office and talk about that.

The dollars are huge. As much as I am already in debt now. Basically, my business will be worth about what I owe. It's all a gamble, of course. If it turns out that there's a steady market for dinosaur leather, then I'll make money. If fashionable women don't want to wear dinosaurs, then I won't. Like selling eggs.

The only difference is that a big chunk of my business will be leased from Krishnamachari. In effect, I'll be working for someone again. They are talking about a schedule for inspections. "If business gets big enough, we may have to have someone working here on site." I must look startled. "At least, maybe, part-time," he amends.

These are nice people. They do not mean to take over my life. It's just business. I used to write the documentation for things like this. I wrote procedures for purchasing. I would sit in Jim's office and he would tell me about how purchasing worked. One thing about being a technical writer, I got to work with all different departments. Funny, it never applied much to dinosaur farming until now. Dinosaur farming was never corporate before.

That is when the alarm starts to go off in my head, and I can't rid myself of the feeling that I am selling myself back into slavery.

So I turn them down.

Tiffin watches them drive off.

"I think I may have screwed up," I say. Tiffin cocks her head and listens to me.

"Will you be so trusting when we're homeless?" I ask.

Actually, Tiffin will. Tiffin leaves all the administrative stuff to me. "You're a specialist. Humans are generalists, right?" Tiffin just regards me attentively in case somewhere in all my chatter comes a word she recognizes like "down" or "cookie" or "cheese." Tiffin is something of a cheesehound. "Cheesehound," I say to her and she leaps to her feet.

We go back in the house to get some cheese and someone is calling. It's Becker Doogan from the huge law firm called James, Daws, Riser, and Clough. I bring him up on screen. "Ms. Sabiston," he says, "I'm calling with good news."

"How good," I say warily.

"AgriGen and the FDA have reached an agreement in lieu of AgriGen filing suit." He flicks his Renaissance mane over his shoulder. "Your dinosaurs are genetically enhanced animals, not genetically engineered."

"You mean they're legally chickens?" I ask.

He nods. "Rhode Island Reds, to be specific. You can sell all the eggs you want."

Deus ex machina. James, Daws, Riser, and Clough are lowered from the heavens wielding legal briefs and setting everything to right. "Can I get a copy of the ruling?" I ask.

"Sure. I'm sending one to your attorney, too." He is magnificently pleased with himself. "Congratulations. Are you roasting a dinosaur to celebrate?"

"I may settle for an omelet," I say. "Maybe I can ship you some eggs?"

He wrinkles his nose. "I don't think so."

"Do you ever get tired of working for other people?" I ask.

He thinks for a moment. "Well, yes. A lot, actually. I was thinking about starting my own firm, you know? But my wife and I, we just had a baby girl. And here I get benefits and if I work hard, eventually I'll make partner."

I understand. "Well thanks," I say. "Good luck to you and your family."

"Hey, Tiffin, you lazy bitch." Tiffin is waiting at the door. "After your cheese we've got a ton of work to do. We've got to gear this place back up again."

The world is an uncertain place. You can try to depend on other people and sometimes they can shield you from the world. I prefer to do it my way.

PETTING ZOO
by Gene Wolfe

There is a large body of critical opinion that holds Gene Wolfe, author of The Book of the New Sun, *to be the finest writer currently working in—or out of—the field.*

Roderick looked up at the sky. It was indeed blue, but almost cloudless. The air was hot and smelled of dust.

"Here, children. . ." The teaching cyborg was pointedly not addressing him. "—Tyranosaurus Rex. Rex was created by an inadequately socialized boy who employed six Build-a-Critter kits . . ."

Sixteen.

"—which he duped on his father's Copystuff. With that quantity of GroQik . . ."

It had taken a day over two weeks, two truckloads of pigs that he had charged to Mother's account, and various other things that had become vague. For the last week, he had let Rex go out at night to see what he could find, and people would—people were bound to—notice the missing cattle soon. Had probably noticed them already.

Rex had looked out through the barn window while he was mooring his airbike and said, "I'm tired of hiding all day."

And he himself had said . . .

"Let's go for a ride." One of the little girls had raised her hand.

From the other side of the token barrier that confined him, Rex himself spoke for the first time, saying, "You will, kid. She's not quite through yet." His voice was a sort of growling tenor now, clearly forced upward as high as he could make it so as to seem less threatening. Roderick pushed on his suit's A–C and shivered a little.

It had been cool, that day. Cool, with a little breeze he had fought the whole way over, keeping his airbike below the treetops and following groundtrucks when he could, pulled along by their wake.

Cold in the barn, then—cold and dusty—dust motes dancing in the sunbeams that stabbed between its old, bent, and battered aluminum panels.

Rex had crouched as he had before, but he was bigger now, bigger than ever, and his smooth reptilian skin had felt like glass, like ice under which oiled muscles stirred like snakes. He had fallen, and Rex had picked him up in the arms that looked so tiny on Rex but were bigger and stronger than a big man's arms, saying, "That's what these are for," and set him on Rex's shoulders with his legs—*his* legs—trying to wrap around Rex's thick, throbbing neck . . .

He had opened the big doors from inside, gone out almost crawling, and stood up.

It had not been the height. He had been higher on his airbike almost every day. It had not been his swift, swaying progress above the treetops—treetops arrayed in red, gold, and green so that it seemed that he followed Rex's floating head over a lawn deep in fallen leaves.

It had been—

He shrugged the thought away. There were no adequate words. Power? You bought it at a drugstore, a shiny little disk that would run your house-bot for three or four more years, or your drill forever. Mastery? It

was what people had held over dogs while private
ownership had still been legal.

Dogs had four fangs in front, and that was it, fangs
so small they did not even look dangerous. Rex had a
mouthful, every one as long as Roderick's arm, in a
mouth that could have chewed up an aircar.

No, it had not been the height. He had ridden over
woods—this wood among them—often. Had ridden
higher than this, yet heard the rustling of the leaves
below him, the sound of a brook, an invisible brook
of air. It had been the noise.

That was not right either, but it was closer than the
others. It had been the snapping of the limbs and the
crashing of the trees falling, or at least that had been a
lot of it—the sound of their progress, the shattering,
splintering wood. In part, at least, it had been the
noise.

"He did a great deal of damage," the teaching
cyborg was saying, as her female attendant nodded
confirmation. "Much worse, he terrified literally hundreds of persons. . . ."

Sitting on Rex's shoulders, he had been able to talk
almost directly into Rex's ear. "Roar."

And Rex had roared to shake the earth.

"Keep on roaring."

And Rex had.

The red and white cattle Rex ate sometimes, so
short-legged they could scarcely move, had run away
slowly only because they were too fat to run any
faster, and one had gotten stepped on. People had run
too, and Rex had kicked over a little pre-fab shed for
the fun of it, and a tractor-bot. He'd waded hip-deep
through the swamp without even slowing down and
had forded the river. There were fewer building
restrictions on the north side of the river, and the
people there had really run.

Had run except for one old man with a bushy mus-
tache, who had only stood and stared pop-eyed, too
old to run, Roderick thought, or maybe too scared. He

had looked down at the old man and waved; and their eyes had met, and suddenly—just as if the top of the old man's head had popped up so he could look around inside it—he had known what the old man was thinking.

Not guessed, known.

And the old man had been thinking that when he had been Roderick's age he had wanted to do exactly what Roderick was doing now. He had never been able to, and had never thought anybody would be. But somebody was. That kid up there in the polka-dot shirt was. So he, the old man, had been wrong about the whole world all his life. It was much more wonderful, this old world, than he, the old man, had ever supposed. So maybe there was hope after all. Some kind of a hope anyhow, in a world where things like this could go on, on a Monday right here in Libertyberg.

Before the old man could draw his breath to cheer, he had been gone, and there had been woods and cornfields. (Roderick's suit A–C shuddered and quit.) And after lots of corn, some kind of a big factory. Rex had stepped on its fence which sputtered and shot sparks without doing anything much, and then the aircar had started diving at them.

It had been red and fast, and Roderick remembered it as clearly as if he had seen it yesterday. It would dive, trying to hit Rex's head, and then the override would say, *My gosh, that's a great big dinosaur! You're trying to crash us into a great big dinosaur, you jerk!* The override would pull the aircar up and miss, and then it would give it back to the driver, and he would try the same thing all over.

Roderick had followed it with his eyes, especially after Rex started snapping at it, and the sky had been a wonderful cool blue with little white surgical-ball clouds strolling around in it. He had never seen a better sky—and he never would, because skies did not get any better than that one. After a while he had spotted the channel copter flying around up there and taking his picture to run on everybody's threedeevid, and had made faces at it.

Another child, a scrubbed little girl with long, straight privileged-looking yellow hair had her hand up. "Did he kill a whole lot of people?"

The teaching cyborg interrupted her own lecture. "Certainly not, since there were no people in North America during the Upper Cretaceous. Human evolution did not begin—"

"This one." The scrubbed little girl pointed to Rex. "Did he?"

Rex shook his head.

"That was not the point at issue," the teaching cyborg explained. "Disruption is disrupting, and he and his maker disrupted. He disrupted, I should say, and his maker still more, since Rex would not have been in existence to disrupt had he not been made in violation of societal standards. No one of sensitivity would have done what he did. Someone of sensitivity would have realized at once that their construction of a large dinosaur, however muted in coloration—"

Rex interrupted her. "I'm purple. It's just that it's gotten sort of dull lookin' now that I'm older. Looky here." He bent and slapped at his water trough with his disproportionately small hands. Dust ran from his hide in dark streaks, leaving it a faded mulberry.

"You are not purple," the teaching cyborg admonished Rex, "and you should not say you are. I would describe that shade as a mauve." She spoke to her female attendant. "Do you think that they would mind very much if I were to start over? I've lost my place, I fear."

"You mustn't interrupt her," the female attendant cautioned the little girl. "Early-Tertiary-in-the-Upper-Eocene-was-the-Moeritherium-the-size-of-a-tuber-but-more-like-a-hippopotamus."

"Yum," Rex mumbled. "Yum-yum!"

A small boy waved his hand wildly. "What do you feed him?"

"Tofu, mostly. It's good for him." The teaching cyborg looked at Rex as she spoke, clearly displeased at his thriving upon tofu. "He eats an airtruckload of it every day. Also a great deal of soy protein and bean curd."

"I'd like to eat the hippos," Rex told the small boy. "We go right past them every time I take you kids for a ride, and wow! Do they ever look yummy!"

"He's only joking," the teaching cyborg told the children. She caught her female attendant's left arm and held it up to see her watch. "I have a great deal more to tell you, children, but I'll have to do it while we're taking our ride, or we'll fall behind schedule."

She and her female attendant opened the gate to Rex's compound and went in, preceded, accompanied, and followed by small girls and boys. While most of the children gathered around him, stroking his rough thick hide with tentative fingers, the teaching cyborg and her female attendant wrestled a stepladder and a very large howdah of white pentastyrene Wickedwicker from behind Rex's sleeping shed. For five minutes or more they struggled to hook the howdah over his shoulders and fasten the Velcro cinch, obstructed by the well-intended assistance of four little boys.

Roderick joined them, lifted the howdah into place, and released and refastened the cinch—getting it tight enough that the howdah could not slip to one side.

"Thank you," the female attendant said. "Haven't I seen you here before?"

Roderick shook his head. "It's the first time I've ever come."

"Well, a lot of men do. I mean it's always just one man all by himself, but there's almost always one."

"He used to lie down so that we could put it on him," the teaching cyborg said severely, "and lie down again so that the children didn't have to use the ladder. Now he just sits."

"I'm too fat," Rex muttered. "It's all that good tofu I get."

One by one, the children climbed the ladder. The teaching cyborg's female attendant was standing beside it to catch each if he or she fell, cautioning each to grasp the railings, and urging each to belt himself or herself in once he or she had chosen a seat. The teaching cyborg and her female attendant boarded last of all. The teaching cyborg resumed her lecture, and Rex stood up with a groan and began yet again the slow walk around the zoo that he took a dozen times a day.

It had been a fall day, Roderick reminded himself, a fall day bright and clear, a more beautiful day than days ever were now. A stiff, bright wind had been blowing right through all the sunshine. He had worn jeans, a Peoria White Sox cap, and a polka-dot shirt. He had kept his airbike low where the wind wasn't quite so strong, had climbed on Rex's shoulders, and watched as Rex had taken down the bar that held the big doors shut. . . .

"Now," the teaching cyborg said, "are there any additional questions?" Roderick looked up just in time to see the corner of the white Wickedwicker howdah vanish behind Rex's sleeping shed.

"Yes." He raised his hand. "What became of the boy?"

"The government assumed responsibility for his nurturing and upbringing," the teaching cyborg explained. "He received sensitivity training and reeducation in societal values and has become a responsible citizen."

When the teaching cyborg, her female attendant, and all the children had gone, Rex said, "You know, I always wondered what happened to you."

Roderick mopped his perspiring forehead. "You knew who I was all the time, huh?"

"Sure."

There was a silence. Far away, as if from another time or another world, children spoke in excited voices and a lion roared. "Nothing happened to me," Roderick said; it was clearly necessary to say something. "I grew up, that's all."

"Those reeducation machines, they really burn it into you. That's what I heard."

"No, I grew up. That's all."

"I see. Can I ask why you keep lookin' at me like that?"

"I was just thinking."

"Thinkin' what?"

"Nothing." With iron fists, stone shoulders, and steel-shod feet, words broke down the doors of his heart and forced their way into his mouth. "Your kind used to rule the Earth."

"Yeah." Rex nodded. He turned away, leaving for Roderick his serpentine tail and wide, ridged back— both the color of a grape skin that has been chewed up and spit out into the dust. "Yeah," he mumbled. "You, too."

THE UGLY ONE
by Ann Marston

Ann Marston just made the leap from fan to pro with the sale of a major trilogy, the first two books of which are already in print.

From the beginning, she knew she was different. She was deformed, and she came from the egg smaller and weaker than her clutch-siblings. In their voracious birth-hunger, they would have killed and eaten her had their mother not placed the succulent carcass of a small leafgrazer beside the warm, sandy hollow of the nest. Her clutch-siblings turned blindly toward the scent of fresh blood and forgot her in their instinctive frenzy to feed.

Her mother studied her carefully. The Ugly One sensed her mother's regret as she looked at the infant with the unsightly bulge above her wide-set eyes where her head should have been sleek and flat, curving down gracefully into the back of the long, sinuous neck. The tribe could not afford to nurture a weakling or a deformed infant.

Her mother bent down. The Ugly One shrank back among the shards of leathery eggshell, terrified of the serrated rows of teeth in her mother's open jaw. But instead of snapping closed those terrible jaws, her

mother only nudged her gently away, forbidding
access to the carcass.

The Ugly One scrambled beneath the shelter of the
broken eggshells and waited. Her clutch-siblings finished eating. Their mother gathered them together
and led them to the safety of the low, rocky hills
where the tribe waited. When they had gone, The
Ugly One crept out and ate what remained of the leafgrazer's carcass.

So she lived. She found the tribe and lurked at its
fringes. She survived by scavenging until she learned
to hunt for herself. The tribe ignored her. Dimly, she
understood they tolerated her only because the larger
predators harvested the weak, the old, and the very
young. If something took The Ugly One, one more of
the tribe might live.

Only once did she come close to death from one of
the large predators who stalked the plains. She was
half-grown when the huge predator sent the tribe
fleeing in panic. She found herself scrambling through
the tall grasses ahead of the gigantic predator. He
stood easily the height of three of the tribe. The
ground beneath her trembled as his powerful back legs
hurled his bulk across the plain behind her.

Too late, she realized her blind panic had trapped
her on a sharp, v-shaped ridge above the place where
two rivers came together. The ground fell away from
the ridge on three sides in a steep, precipitous plunge
to the water below. She could not go forward and she
could not escape the terror behind her. The heavy
claws of her back feet scrabbled on the cliff edge as
she slid to a stop. She turned to face the predator. He
lunged forward for the kill.

Her heart thundering wildly in her chest, she saw
her only chance. When the predator was almost on
her, she darted through the narrow gap between his
left leg and the edge of the cliff.

The predator roared in frustration. He tried to stop
his lunge and twisted his huge body in an attempt to

follow her. His momentum carried him forward. He
overbalanced and plunged past her, tumbling helplessly over the cliff. His body bounced off the seamed
and weathered sandstone, spinning ponderously in the
air, until it landed, broken and bleeding, on the bank
of the river.

The Ugly One stood gasping for breath, hardly able
to believe she was safe.

The tribe gathered near the low hills. She sensed
their momentary surprise at seeing her. Then they
quickly ignored her as usual, as she took her place
just within their vision. She settled back and thought
again of the huge, broken body lying at the foot of the
cliff.

Something stirred murkily in her mind as she considered the predator's end. Slowly, laboriously, she
retraced the steps that had resulted in that marvel. She
wondered dimly if what had worked out of desperation might work with deliberate planning. She would
try it.

The ruse worked as well the second time. And the
third. She wanted to communicate her discovery to
the tribe, but they would not listen. Their minds were
caught up only in their continual cycle of hunt-feed-
rest. Finally, she gave up, realizing that, even if they
would listen, they would never understand.

The tribe had killed again, and the sounds of their
feasting carried clearly through the still night air. She
had reached her full growth now, and stood on the
stony verge of the deep freshwater slough, her back to
the sounds. She leaned back, using her tail for balance, her small forelegs pressed together across her
chest. The smell of fresh blood from the grazer's carcass drifted sharp and strong through the air. The
tribe would finish soon and, sated for the time being,
might leave enough of the carcass to ease the hunger
that always clamored in her belly.

The disk of the cold light climbed above the

horizon beyond the slough. She watched it idly. The cold light appeared when darkness covered the world and the tiny lights sparkled in the sky. Like the hot light that appeared during the day, the cold light always rose in front of her when she stood with her back to the low ridge of the hills, and descended into the far away, serrated mountains behind her. Surely the creature who pulled both lights into the sky must be stronger and larger than even Stalker, who led the tribe.

Behind her, the noises of feasting died down, and she sensed the contentment of the tribe settling into torpid rest. Carefully, she made her way across the open plain to the carcass. Enough remained to ease her hunger but not to appease it completely. Perhaps there would be more after the next kill.

She stripped the last shred of meat from the bones of the grazer, then gnawed the gristly bones themselves for the succulent marrow. When nothing was left, she went back to the slough to drink.

She didn't see the male until he was almost upon her. She spun to face him and froze, crouched and waiting. Startled, she recognized Stalker, the leader of the tribe.

He stopped a short distance from her. She knew then what he wanted. She was of an age to breed. Her female scent must have drawn him in spite of her deformity.

Excitement stirred in her belly. Instinctively, the tribe protected and fed gravid females. Deliberately, she turned her back to Stalker, glancing coyly at him over her shoulder as she presented herself to him.

When he was finished, Stalker led her back to the tribe and for the first time in her life she was part of it.

Now she had enough to eat. She grew strong and sleek while she carried her eggs. In the evening, sated after gorging herself on the kill the tribe provided for all the gravid females, she had time to watch the hot light sink behind the mountains and the cold light rise over the slough. She finally decided that some great and benevolent creature provided the lights for all the tribes—like Stalker and the others gave her food.

When her time came, she went to the same sandy hollow where she had been hatched and laid her eggs. Only three eggs, but she was young yet. There would be more. She left them only to hunt with the tribe, and came back to guard them and eat her kill.

The first two hatchlings were males, as sleek and well formed as their father. Anxiously, The Ugly One nuzzled the third egg while the males fed on the hopper carcass she'd left for them. As the hot light began its slow sink behind the mountains, a small female struggled out of the egg.

The Ugly One stood over the newly hatched infant, studying it the way her own mother had studied her. The female was also deformed exactly as she was. An ugly bulge spoiled the clean, smooth line of its brow. The Ugly One hesitated. She could sense the infant's fear as it cowered low among the eggshells. At last, she nudged the tiny female toward the meat.

Within the waxing and waning of the cold light, the two small males became indistinguishable from the other younglings wrangling over bones within the safety of the tribe. The young female, though, held herself aloof from the rest of the juveniles, and spent most of her time with her mother. For the first time in her life, The Ugly One experienced a contentment that went beyond the satisfaction of merely having a full belly and a safe place to sleep. She had companionship. The little one, whom she thought of as Searcher, was filled with lively curiosity. Her sprightly hum demanded answers and reasons, and she responded with wonder to the marvels The Ugly One pointed out to her.

The Ugly One stood on the stony verge of the slough. She had come for a drink in the cool before dawn. The cold light had already gone to its bed behind the mountains behind her. Overhead, the small lights streaked across the black sky in ever-increasing numbers. She drank her fill, then watched them curiously. Where were they going? What were they running from? They blazed brightly for an instant or two, then vanished. There was a new light in the sky, too. It was brighter and bigger than all the little lights, but not as big as the cold light. It was bigger this night than it had been the night before.

She sensed the presence of another and looked down to see Searcher standing beside her, imitating her posture, looking up. A tremor of fear went through the small body. The Ugly One soothed her easily. The small lights had often run across the sky, but no danger had ever followed them to the low hills.

The bright streaks faded as the sky brightened with the day. The Ugly One still watched. Even with the coming of the hot light, the new small light still gleamed faintly in the sky.

Searcher found something different to interest her curiosity along the shore of the slough. She darted away from the gnawed shoulder blade of a large grazer to the picked-clean bones of a swimmer, then bounded off to watch a crawler as big as her foot laboriously hauling its curled shell toward the water. The Ugly One was conscious of Searcher's delight with each new discovery. Her own curiosity and thirst for discovery flared anew with the little one's.

Not until she heard the rush of leathery wings did she realize the danger. A winged predator dived out of the sky at Searcher. The little one squealed in fear and darted across the stones. The winged-one thumped clumsily onto the stones, talons missing Searcher by only the length of her small tail. The predator swept one clawed wing out and tumbled the little one onto the stones, stunning her.

Even as the talon reached for the small body, The Ugly One knew she could not possibly reach the winged-one in time to save her daughter. In desperation, she kicked at the gnawed shoulder blade, aiming at the predator. She threw her body forward, thrusting with her powerful back legs.

The sharp, jagged edge of the shoulder blade caught the predator's wing just as it swept the wing and its small claws forward. The broken edge of the bone tore through the leathery wing. The predator screamed and turned to face The Ugly One, its long beak open showing the razor sharp teeth within. It hissed and Searcher whimpered.

The Ugly One was larger than the winged predator, but she knew those teeth and the vicious claws could kill her if she didn't make a quick kill first.

She lunged at the winged-one, twisting her head. Her teeth closed around its throat. It struggled violently in her grip. Its long, sharp talons raked down her side, opening the skin and drawing blood. The Ugly One ignored the pain and rose to her full height. The weight of the predator nearly toppled her forward, but she managed to hold it. She yanked her head back, then slammed the predator back down onto the stones. The flesh of its throat tore away between her teeth. The predator convulsed feebly for a moment, then lay still.

Searcher rose shakily to her feet and ran to The Ugly One. The Ugly One nervously sniffed her daughter to satisfy herself that she was all right.

The tribe sensed the kill. The juveniles bounded joyfully down to the slough to attack the carcass of the predator. The Ugly One herded Searcher to one side until gradually, the little one's terror abated.

A big light came blazing and streaking out of the sky, burning bright, the air behind it sizzling. The juveniles stopped feeding and looked up in astonishment. Terror slammed The Ugly One's heart against her ribs. She huddled protectively over Searcher, shivering with fear. She thought she could feel the heat of the light's passing.

It swooped over their heads, over the low hills, and was gone. The Ugly One didn't move. A cracking rumble, louder than the loudest thunder, shivered the air, and the ground beneath her feet bucked and rolled violently, knocking her to the stones. She curled her body around Searcher, aware only of the little one's gibbering fear.

Beyond the hills, a massive cloud of dust rose into the air, staining the sky as it spread on the wind. She looked down at Searcher, trying to sooth the little one's terror, sending waves of reassurance to her.

Gradually, Searcher became quiet. The Ugly One looked up. The new light, pale and malevolent, and bigger than ever, still gleamed in the blue of the sky. The Ugly One shivered, knowing nothing would ever be the same again.

THE LAND THAT GOD FORGOT
By Nicholas A. DiChario and Jack Nimersheim

Nicholas A. DiChario and Jack Nimersheim are good friends who are currently collaborating on their first novel together. Separately, they have been nominated for several prestigious awards.

SimSpace

Pope John Paul IV stood atop a ledge of ancient stone on the face of a great mountain, eye to eye with the dominant tyrannosaur of the river valley.

"God loves the world so much," said the Pope, "that He gave his only Son so that everyone who believes in Him will live forever."

The dinosaur snorted, not exactly a subtle response. She was a monster among monsters—fifty feet long at least, weighing a good seven or eight tons, her head the size of a luxury glider car. "Why should I want to be converted to your faith?" asked the dinosaur. She had a voice that worked like a drill on the Pope's eardrums. "What do I care if God, as you call him, sacrificed his son? Why should I bow to your king, when I and my ancestors have ruled here for more than a hundred million years, for as far as the eye can see?"

"There is more to the world than what meets the eye," said John Paul. "There are things within," he put his hand over his heart, "and there are things without," he looked up at the clear blue sky. The sun was hot and bright, the air as new and fresh as the fan-shaped leaves of the ginkgo. The Pope wore his plasticream body suit to protect him from diseases in this simulated prehistoric environment he now called home. The suit promised protection of a second kind, as well. The acrid odor it discharged presumably made him unappetizing to predators. He clutched his Holy Bible and prayed the suit would work.

The mountain ledge upon which John Paul stood exposed him to a breeze he would not have felt had he been down in the dense, teeming forest below, amidst the ferns and conifers and giant horsetails, where rushing river waters cut through towering trees as large and wide as the buildings of the New York City he'd left behind.

The Pope loved it here. Here, he led the life of a missionary, pure and simple. He'd learned how to enjoy peace and solitude. He knew what it was to be a small man, alone among giant beasts. But he had much work to do. God had sent him here to convert the dinosaurs to Christianity, to save their souls, and thus far this had proved an impossible task. Although most of the saurischians didn't mind listening to him, they balked at the spiritual commitment Christianity called for and seemed troubled by the concept of the Holy Trinity. The ornithischians didn't seem much interested in anything he had to say; they would make good followers, poor leaders. The raptors were savages, and John Paul feared that at any moment they might eat him for lunch, despite his plasticream suit and its forbidding aroma.

But underneath it all, John Paul felt that the other dinosaurs were simply waiting to see what Rexanne would do. Rexanne—John Paul's name for the beast, since dinosaurs didn't believe in names—was the largest of all the tyrannosaurs, a wise old female John Paul had come to think of as the mother of all monsters.

When Rexanne spoke, the others listened. The Pope knew if he could convert Queen Rex, he'd get them all.

Rexanne shifted her massive girth away from John Paul and looked down at the river, perhaps searching for more food. "You are a very strange little upright animal. You come here talking of religion. You wish us to supplicate ourselves to your invisible god. At first I was amused by your presence. Now you are beginning to annoy me. I wonder why I don't just ignore your stink and eat you."

The Pope shivered at the thought of those jaws closing around him. Rexanne had recently gorged herself on a flat-headed hardrosaur, but that didn't mean she was perfectly safe to be around. True, this was an SR scenario: simulated reality. But for all intents and purposes it was real. Once John Paul passed through the Gateway, there was no turning back. The unique patterns of his thoughts, the mathematical coordinates that defined the size and shape of his body, had been permanently transferred into Sim-Space. It was up to Pope John Paul IV to survive here on his own, to find his own food and shelter, and to use his own common sense to avert a meaningless death.

"Where do you think I came from?" said John Paul, "Or you, for that matter? How did we come into existence? How did this world get here? Whence came the plants, the water, the sky, the mountains? Haven't you ever wondered about these things?"

Rexanne shrugged, a comical gesture, given her stunted forearms and shoulders. "Why should I care?" she replied. "The water bathes me and quenches my thirst. The sky carries the winds that cool my hide. The plants help sustain the smaller animals I feed upon. And the mountains . . ." She gazed up at the rocky cliff rising like a colossal wall behind John Paul. "Well, the mountains exist. What does it matter how they came to be? What does it matter how you or I came to be, or where we came from?"

"But it does matter! It was God who created us, just as He created the world that sustains us. We are all God's children."

Rexanne turned and started to lumber away. John Paul was afraid he was losing her soul, and all those who might go with her. Their discussions had grown shorter, less frequent, of late. Too often she dismissed his intellectual challenges out of hand, as she was doing now. He did not want to fail God here in Sim-Space. The Almighty had suffered enough losses in the world he'd left behind.

"This is all coming to an end!" he shouted after her. He saw the great female stop and swing her enormous head back in his direction. If she had a weakness at all, he'd learned from their previous discussions, it was on this topic, perhaps *only* this topic. Her instincts spoke volumes he would never understand.

"You can feel it," he continued. "Things are changing. The world is pulling apart. Where once your ancestors could walk forever across the land, now great bodies of water interfere. The air is becoming colder—slowly, over the ages—but you can feel it in your bones, can't you?"

Cold black eyes stared back at him. For a moment, John Paul feared she might lash out and strike him down.

"Soon," said the Pope, "your hundred-million-year reign will come to an end. Perhaps you will not be able to adapt to the changing climate. Perhaps it will be something else that takes your kind—a catastrophe, a great hammer from the sky. Who knows? But a vast change *is* coming. And you—perhaps you alone—can feel its approach. Only the One, True God can save your kind, can spare you the destruction. God will be merciful if you open your hearts to Him. That's why I have come. I am God's messenger. I believe you know this in your heart, or you would have devoured me by now, even though I stink."

She turned from him then, and lumbered away. But

John Paul couldn't help thinking that perhaps all was not lost. There had been something in that last look of hers, something telling he'd not noticed before. Her reticence very well might have been a reflection of her crumbling resolve.

John Paul noticed his legs were trembling and lowered himself tentatively to the firm support of the mountain ledge. He sat there, shivering, and wiped the cool sweat from his brow. God, she was a terrifying beast. He held his Holy Bible to his chest. *Do not be afraid,* he told himself. *God is with you always.*

He thought, briefly, of the civilization he'd left behind, and the events that led him to this mission. He thought about his interview at SIMNet, just before he'd taken the leap into SimSpace. He'd been frightened that day, as well, but back then he'd fallen victim to a different kind of fear altogether:

Fear of the unknown . . .

New York City, Year 2212

The Pope felt uncomfortable, graceless, and nothing short of pedestrian in the khaki uniform SIMNet had provided him. He was used to his official vestments: the ornate robes and grand undergarments of his most Holy Vocation. He sat awkwardly in the chair beside the interviewer's desk, felt the plasti-cream body suit chafe his skin. The SIMNet prep team had told him it would take a day or two for the suit to adapt to his body, for the dinosaur repellent to achieve balance with his own unique chemistry. The discomfort, then, would disappear. Once this happened, the body suit—or, more correctly, its digitized reproduction in SimSpace—would last forever, as would the unappetizing odor it exuded. He would never have to change clothes again. "Functionwear," the prep team had called it, made specifically for simulated realities where clothing would not be readily available.

"I am Pope John Paul IV," he said to the young woman, "Vicar of Jesus Christ, Leader of the Roman Catholic Church." He spoke not out of conceit. These days so few people knew who he was, or what he stood for, that he felt compelled to explain his station.

The young woman on the other side of the desk tugged officiously at the lapels of her black vinyl business coat. She was neatly groomed, composed, and seemed infinitely more comfortable than Pope John Paul felt. She glanced at the Pope's file on her desktop vid display. "It's not me you need to convince," she said, clearly amused. "It's the dinosaurs."

John Paul did not even blink at the woman's insolence. He was used to it: the casual ridicule, something no other Pope in the history of the Catholic Church had been forced to endure. But John Paul held the unique position of being, in all likelihood, the last man who would ever hold this sacred office. Catholicism, after years of waning membership, a slow deterioration brought about by its weakened and quarreling factions, was collapsing. Pope John Paul IV, the first American Pope in the history of the Church, would be remembered as the man who oversaw its final demise. He knew this was not fair. No one man could be blamed for the fall of an empire. Still, he alone would bear the humiliation. John Paul wondered if God had done this purposely to an American, and if so, why?

"You have your job to do," said John Paul, "and I have mine." He sat back in his chair. The room, with its illuminated ceiling panels, was too bright for its cramped size. The walls were unadorned. No windows. He imagined a cross on the bare wall in front of him, with Jesus Christ gazing up toward the heavens, asking his Almighty Father for strength and courage. *"My God, my God, why hast thou forsaken me?"*

The woman shrugged. "Yeah, well, my job is to

inform you of the finality of your decision to enter SimSpace, and make sure you understand that, once you commit to the transference, there's no turning back."

"I have thought long and hard about it," said John Paul. "I understand the consequences of my actions."

"Right." Without looking up from the vid display, she pointed with her laser pen toward the ceiling panels. "And this is okay with God? I assume you've talked to Him about it?"

John Paul searched for the sarcasm behind the woman's words, but, surprisingly, found none. He no longer knew what people thought about his God, or his religion. Mostly, he decided, they knew nothing, and cared even less. It was easier for him to look upon their insults as ignorance. "I'll admit, His ways have been difficult for me to interpret as of late, but I can assure you I have talked to God recently, and of this decision I am certain."

"Good. I need to put that in my report. You *do* comprehend that this is not some VR game you're asking to participate in? You are about to enter SR—a real, live, albeit simulated, reality. Your entire brain and body patterns will be downloaded into an SR scenario of your personal design. Once this happens, you will be assimilated into the consciousness of Sim-Space forever. No second chances, John. You can't come back for a pack of gum or a string of rosary beads."

John? There was a time no one would have dared refer to him as other than "Your Holiness," or "Holy Father," or "Supreme Pontiff." The Pope closed his eyes and asked the Lord to bless him with tolerance. He reminded himself that he was just another emigrant to this woman, probably one of a hundred she'd interview this week. SimSpace was growing more popular by the day, with thousands of people deciding to abandon the uncertainties of the real world for the permanence of their own alternate realities. For most people, the thought of never being able to return to the world they'd left behind was a comfort. For Pope John Paul, given how the world had changed, it was a godsend.

The price was steep: everything a person owned in this reality, including the human body and all of its marketable parts, for a one-way trip to SimSpace. It would cost a rich man a hell of a lot more to enter SimSpace than it would a poor man, but it was all the same in the end. *They* were all the same in the end— equal in God's eyes—a basic truth of Christianity, death, and now, so it seemed, SimSpace.

"I won't have to come back for anything," John Paul said to the girl. "I need only my Holy Bible, and the inner strength God has given me."

The young woman leaned forward and stared at him for a moment. She looked almost pensive. "Can I ask you something, old man, off the record?"

Old man? The Pope sighed (he'd been doing a lot of that lately). "Certainly."

"Why this particular scenario? I mean, why would you want to convert the dinosaurs to Christianity?"

John Paul did not feel compelled to tell her everything. He saw no need to explain how God had appeared to him in a dream, a vision, and commanded him to enter SimSpace. *"Go to SimSpace, go to the dinosaurs, give them free will and the intelligence of Man, and we will start anew."*

No, he felt no need to tell anyone about that, not the SIMNet engineers who had created his prehistoric SR to the Lord's exact specifications, not even the few faithful followers of the Church who would remain in this world to fight, without his guidance, on God's behalf. Most Catholics already considered the American Pope a traitor, a coward for deserting his sinking ship. But God's instructions had been explicit. *"You must leave this world behind forever, John Paul, and go forth like a child into your new mission."*

Still, the question the woman had asked was a valid one. Why the dinosaurs? John Paul had pondered this same conundrum many times. He was no expert on SimSpace, but he knew that it was a cyber-universe as interconnected as it was disparate. A new frontier, a new world where the definition of Man himself, of *all* God's creations, took on unique and unusual proportions. Did some way exist to influence the collective consciousness within the infinite number of alternate possibilities in SimSpace? And if so, did this not imply that some common denominator, a central core, bound all of SimSpace together? That core, that link to the infinite, John Paul reasoned, must be God. There was no other answer. And God, thought the Pope, infallible as God was, for whatever reason, wanted a second chance in SimSpace.

"What is your name?" John Paul asked the young woman.

She looked taken aback. It was possible, the Pope realized, that no one she'd interviewed had ever asked her this question.

"Uron Rozna Berkley Hetia Davidson," she answered.

Not a Christian name among them. "Miss Davidson, there is a Latin phrase, *Gaudium et spes, luctus et angor hominum huius temporis.* It means, 'The joy and the hope, the grief and the anguish of the people of our time.' Through my sacred calling I accept responsibility for all of the people of our troubled times; and have committed my life to doing whatever I can to transform their grief, their anguish, into joy and hope. The actions I undertake now are designed to accomplish precisely that."

The woman shrugged. "Whatever."

The ennui of the unenlightened.

She instructed the report on her vid display to close itself out. "We're finished," she said as the image on her vid screen shimmered briefly, then faded to black. "This interview was mostly a formality. Your application has been processed and accepted. You've already passed the psychological evaluation. You're scheduled to enter SimSpace tomorrow afternoon at 3:30." The woman stood up and extended her hand across the desk. "Congratulations, John, and good luck."

"Thank you." John Paul politely accepted both the woman's hand and her good wishes, although he anticipated that success would not depend on anything quite so capricious as luck. He possessed faith, a much stronger and ultimately more reliable source of confidence.

SimSpace

It was late night. Exactly how late, John Paul wasn't sure; there were no clocks in his simulated reality. He'd just begun his evening prayers, having spent several hours earlier under the moonlight preaching to a surprisingly receptive group of sauropods, when an eerie glow in the southern sky illuminated the landscape. The glow was bright enough to transform night into day, to lure John Paul off his knees and draw him out of the small cave on the mountainside he called home.

He looked up at the nighttime sky and saw what might have been the very Sword of Almighty God cleaving the heavens—no, of course he knew better than that—the Pope recognized the phenomenon immediately for what it was, but the comet was so big, so brilliant, so *grand,* that he forgave himself this flash of divine illusion.

In New York, in 2212, deep-space probes and near-space orbital telescopes could have provided ample warning of the approaching threat. Interplanetary shuttles armed with plasma cannons would have been dispatched to avert it. In SimSpace, in a distant past that preceded modern civilization by sixty-five million years, disaster appeared unannounced, unanticipated, its catastrophic course unhindered by any intervention of human technology. In this time, in this place, God and God alone, controlled events, dictated destiny.

The comet sliced through the dark skies, moving from southwest to northeast, as large as the midday sun and almost as blinding to behold, leaving in its wake a trail of fiery tears. The friction generated by its great velocity ignited the molecules of the very atmosphere through which it streaked. He could not look at the blazing object directly. Nor did he want to. Man was not meant to stare into the eye of God's destruction.

Then the sonic boom hit. The explosion threatened to deafen him. A horrible sound. A terrifying sound. The sound of God's fury. It rumbled across his skin and rattled his bones, nearly causing him to lose his footing and tumble to his death. John Paul's trembling hand clutched at the cliff behind him. He almost dropped his Bible.

Instantly, an inferno erupted, a flash of Hell burning on Earth. Trees crackled and popped and burst into flames. Within seconds, it seemed, fires raged everywhere—above him on the unyielding stone, in tiny cracks and crevices where tenacious shrubs once burrowed—below him in the great forest where majestic trees once tried to reach up and embrace the stars—and upon the very ledge to which John Pope clung, heat searing his lungs, turning each breath he took into a shallow struggle for life.

"My God," he coughed, surveying the devastation. Then, in a painful shout, "My dinosaurs!"

The thought of all those beasts whose souls God had placed in his charge sent John Paul charging down the rocky path into the heart of the holocaust.

The dinosaurs thrashed madly through the forest. It was all he could do to escape being trampled. The heat became unbearable. How long would he be able to breathe the shrinking oxygen? He struggled to maintain his footing on the unstable ground. A triceratops mother and her pup rumbled past him, making the ground quake even more. Smaller creatures—troodon, saltopus, even the vicious velociraptor—hurtled by, alone or in small herds, oblivious to his presence. A huge tree crashed to the ground a few feet to John Paul's right, its leaves scorched, its bark blistered. A fiery branch struck him and brushed harmlessly off his plasticream suit. High above, unseen beyond the smoldering treetops, he heard the pterodactyls, their frightened screams the sound of a nightmares thrust suddenly, inexplicably, into reality. When the sky itself caught fire, there was no safe haven—not for *anyone*. . . .

Dear God, *she* was out there, out there somewhere—

"Rexanne!" John Paul screamed, before realizing the futility of it. This was his pet name for the tyrannosaur; it would mean nothing to her, even if she were able to hear him. "Rexanne!" he cried anyway, because he could not help himself. *"Please keep her safe, my Lord,"* he prayed silently. *"Why have you done this, Almighty Father? Why?"*

Why, indeed? It was happening again—prehistory repeating itself—just as so many paleontologists and astronomers and physicists had theorized it had in the real world. Why had God sent John Paul to this new world if He meant only to obliterate it?

"Rexanne!"

A tyrannosaur roared. It was a terrifying, ear-splitting shriek, rising above the stampede of dinosaurs, the fire, the havoc. John Paul knew that voice. When he'd first heard it so long ago, raging over a kill, the roar had been enough to freeze his blood. This time it liberated him. Queen Rex was close, very close.

He quickened his pace, sped across the scorched terrain toward the heart of the valley. His feet felt as if they were burning inside his boots. Then he spotted her. Rexanne lay alone among a nest of felled trees, her huge body bruised, broken, bloodied. Running toward her, John Paul searched for some expression in her black eyes, on her long, wide face. He thought he saw something there he'd never seen before. Not fear, not pain, but resignation. Her eyes glistened. Was she crying? The Pope could not remember if reptiles were capable of tears.

"Your god is very strong, little animal," said Rexanne, "to strike such a fierce blow against the Earth. Was he angry with us for not listening to your words? Is that why he struck us down?"

"No. The Lord is a God of love, not anger, not vengeance."

"I see," she said. Her voice sounded weak. "Still, he has thought to protect you. You are unharmed, while the world around you is dead or dying."

For the first time, John Paul took check of himself. It was true. He was not hurt. He'd not even suffered a scratch, while the comet had killed and burned everything in its wake. His functionwear, though durable, was not indestructible. He should have been incinerated, but the Lord had spared him. Why?

"This is it, isn't it?" she asked, her voice barely audible above the chaos that surrounded them. "This is the eternal doom you prophesied."

"No." John Paul shook his head. It could not end like this. John Paul had preached of the coming change, but it wasn't supposed to happen this way. *"Go to SimSpace, go to the dinosaurs,"* God had told him, *"give them free will and the intelligence of Man, and we will start anew."* This was supposed to have been a new beginning. Why would the Lord grant the dinosaurs a new existence, only to sentence them to the same senseless extermination all over again? It made no sense. What had John Paul accomplished in the service of the Lord, if all of this was destroyed?

"Take—take comfort in the Lord," he mumbled, a hollow platitude at best, one it troubled him greatly to say.

The tyrannosaur laughed; it seemed to pain her.

"You never stop trying, do you? Tell me, is there an explanation in your Good Book for this massacre?"

John Paul pressed the Bible to his chest. "An explanation? No. But there is a *reason* for it. There must be. There is a reason for everything He does. We must trust the Lord, have faith in Him. Only faith can save any of us, don't you see?"

The mammoth beast laughed a second time, although it was more of a gurgling in her chest. "Look around you, little animal. Is it not obvious that your god saves only you?"

"No, no, that's not true. Life will rise out of this annihilation."

"Your life, perhaps, not mine."

Then she choked, her face stiffened, and the great Queen Rex died.

When John Paul—once a seventeen-year-old student named Francis Edmonton—first heard God's summons to enter the priesthood, he answered the call without hesitation. Later, when the Almighty revealed to him his singular destiny, young Father Edmonton, the pastor of a small church in New Jersey, surrendered his parish to pursue a path that ultimately led to his becoming Vicar of Jesus Christ, Leader of the Roman Catholic Church. Finally, when God commanded him to abandon his Earthly duties and serve the creatures of SimSpace, Pope John Paul IV did not hesitate. Throughout his entire life, whenever God called, Francis Edmonton had been there for Him, ready and willing to serve.

Now he awaited further instructions, but God, it seemed, was not speaking to him.

It took weeks, months, for the fires to finally burn themselves out. Their fading however, did not restore the Lord's SimSpace scenario to the prehistoric paradise it once was. Rather, the world was supplanted by a sly sort of hell, a gray and desolate damnation. The comet's impact had lifted untold tons of dust into the atmosphere. This dust mingled with smoke and soot generated by the great fires to form thick clouds, stretching over the land a murky shroud through which little sunlight passed. Lacking sunlight to warm the atmosphere and drive the winds, the air grew still and cold. Lacking photosynthesis, the vegetation withered and died. How many ages passed like this? Pope John Paul could not say.

Time plodded silently on.

He built fires to warm him, and hunted with crude spears and traps for small animals: new kinds of animals with fur, the likes of which he'd never seen when the dinosaurs had walked the Earth. Often he would trod out upon the frozen streams, chisel holes into the ice, and, with vines he'd tied into tough nets, capture fish, none of which John Paul could identify. For the first time in his life, he grew a beard. When he was preaching to the dinosaurs he'd kept his face shaved with an obsidian knife, but now he'd learned to appreciate the shaggy patch of hair that helped warm his face. His functionwear adapted to the change in climate, and he survived the frigid weather with little discomfort.

Still, God did not speak to him.

John Paul sought consolation in the Bible and in prayer. It was the Pontiff's unique responsibility to open his heart to the entire world and voice a universal appeal for God's immense goodness to spring forth from the mystery of the Incarnate Word. He could not shirk these duties now. Quite the contrary. Within these very duties lay salvation.

He prayed for God to relieve the world's suffering. He prayed for the souls of his friends, the dead dinosaurs. "Why did you bring this terrible evil upon your children?" John Paul asked the Lord. "Is there any hope at all for this ravaged world?" He knew, of course, that there was always hope, and that there were always answers. The Pope was incapable of doubt. When he woke each morning to face another relentless day, he would shout into the cold, white tundra: *"Stat crux dum volvitur orbis!"* And his words would echo eerily back to him off the sterling mountains: "The Cross-cross-cross remains con-con-constant while the wor-wor-world turns-turns-turns."

But his own voice was the only one he heard. God's voice remained silent.

Then, one day, John Paul saw a miasaura working its way clumsily across a newly fallen snow. At least the beast looked like a miasaura—bipedal, stunted forearms, a tail extending almost straight out its backside, and just the hint of a spike showing atop its forehead. The animal was no larger than the Pope himself. Could it really be a dinosaur, after all this time? It must be, or a descendant, surely.

John Paul moved away from the small fire he'd been stoking and followed the beast at a good distance as it made its way down a shallow slope, toward a fast-running mountain stream of broken ice, where the Pope had often drawn water. The miasaura had an awkward strut, but adapted its gait in an almost comical way to the icy terrain. John Paul watched it step tentatively at the edge of the stream, and then extend its long neck out to take a drink.

Suddenly, two small, dark creatures leaped out from behind the rocks. They were two-legged and slightly hunched, with well-developed shoulders and arms. They rushed across the snow toward the dinosaur. The miasaura lifted its gaze, shrieked in fright, and tried to back quickly off the bank of the stream. The ground was slippery with water and ice, and it took the miasaura several attempts before it worked it's way clear and scrambled for the slope. By then the two dark creatures had overtaken the fleeing dinosaur. One of them tackled the beast's legs, while the other grabbed hold of its neck. The miasaura went down in the snow with a muffled *thud* and the two assailants fell upon their prey, howling in delight.

John Paul moved forward. The dark creatures—he'd never seen anything like them here in his simulated reality—were covered with fur. They were short and stout, with strong legs, muscular necks, and apelike heads. They stomped and beat on the miasaura for all they were worth.

At first, John Paul knew not what to do. This was the way of the world here, he understood, the hunter versus the hunted, the strong and the smart survived while those species unable to adapt became victims of natural selection. Then, suddenly, an anger emerged from deep within his soul—anger at this cruel world God had hurled him into, anger at the equally cruel turn God had done the dinosaurs, anger, perhaps, at God Himself.

"Stop!" the Pope screamed as loud as he could, and ran headlong down the slope.

The two fur-laden creatures snapped to attention. When they saw John Paul charging toward them, they yelped and scurried off toward the rocks from whence they'd come.

John Paul was winded by the time he reached the injured dinosaur. He knelt beside it. "Are you all right?" he gasped. "Say something. Can you hear me?"

The dinosaur didn't respond. Had John Paul really expected an answer? Yes. That surprised him. He'd expected the beast to be able to communicate with him, just like before, when the world was a tropical paradise and God had given dinosaurs the intelligence of Man. How many years ago was that? How many lifetimes had he spent here, alone?

The miasaura was barely alive. Its tail twitched, its arms and legs worked desperately to gain some purchase, to lift itself from the snow and make good its escape. But the dinosaur's body would not cooperate—broken ribs and crushed internal organs, undoubtedly. The snow was smeared with the miasaura's shocking-red blood. The beast cried, a pitiful squeal that reminded the Pope, of all crazy things, of the rats in the alleys and sewers of New York City.

John Paul looked out across the snow. The two dark creatures stared at him from the rocks. He stood up. "Damn you!" he hollered, shaking a fist at them. "Go away! Go away and never come back!" The two creatures stared at him, their eyes wide and unblinking.

Then, suddenly, the Pope's anger dissipated. He thought of Rexanne, and the final resignation she must have felt all those years ago when her era, the hundred-and-some-odd-million-year reign of the mighty dinosaurs, had come to an end. He glanced down at the dying beast at his feet, perhaps the last dinosaur descendant he would ever see, and understood, finally, after all this time, after all these ages passed, that the world to which God had banished him was, indeed, the land that God forgot.

He walked to the edge of the water and found a large chunk of sharp, icy bedrock. He carried it back to the fallen miasaura and stood over the whining beast. "If you want to kill something," he yelled to the two dark creatures watching him, "at least do it mercifully!" He raised the rock high above his head and brought it smashing down on the miasaura's skull. The skull cracked with surprisingly little blood, and the dinosaur's struggle ceased.

John Paul took the felled dinosaur by its tail and set off toward his cave, dragging the beast behind him over the ice and snow. For a while, the two dark creatures followed him. By the time he reached the warmth of his primitive home, they were gone.

That night, under the bright stars, the dinosaur meat crackled over John Paul's fire. The small apelike creatures came, as he suspected they would. There were more than two of them now—six, seven, eight, maybe a dozen.

As they inched closer, the dark creatures grunted and barked and hissed. They ran back and forth, bearing their fangs, making a great show of bravado. He could see, now, that some of them had come carrying large, sharp stones in their cupped hands. Quick learners, thought John Paul. Dexterous fingers. Rugged torsos. All of this would serve them well. They were built for survival.

Did they see him as competition? Had they come, with their new and more efficient weapons, to kill him? John Paul picked up his Bible, took a moment to feel the smooth leather in his hands, and raised the Holy Bible to his lips. If this was the end, he thought, so be it.

Then, another thought, a revelation, one he'd waited ages to have. Laying down his Bible, John Paul tore some meat off the stake and tossed it several feet away from the fire. "Come," he called to the creatures. "Join me for dinner."

Finally, one of the them, the leader of the pack no doubt, scampered forward, snatched the meat, and retreated back into the darkness. John Paul ripped more meat off the stake and tossed it out in front of him, closer to the fire. A few more brave ones shied into the warm glow of light and grabbed his offering. This went on for an hour or so, until the Pope had a small gathering of the furry apelike creatures sitting and eating in front of him. They chattered excitedly among themselves, swatted one another, cuddled next to the fire, and looked at John Paul every so often with eyes that held a hauntingly deeper sense of purpose than they seemed capable of.

"Thank you, God," John Paul whispered, when he was fairly certain the creatures weren't going to kill him.

He opened his Bible then, and began to read in a smooth, rhythmic voice:

"*In the beginning, God created the heaven and the earth. And the earth was without form, and void; and darkness was upon the face of the deep. And the Spirit of God moved upon the face of the waters.*'"

The dark creatures ignored him. Their physical needs outweighed any spiritual hunger they might possess. But someday, Pope John Paul knew, someday they *would* hear his voice, and begin to heed His Blessed Words. On that day, God's message would echo throughout all of SimSpace.

TERRIBLE MONKEY
by *Laura Resnick* and *Kathy Chwedyk*

Laura Resnick is a Campbell Award winner. Kathy Chwedyk is a romance novelist who has recently entered the science fiction field as well. Their story was inspired by the following paragraph:

"A single tooth from the Late Cretaceous of Montana has been identified as Purgatorious, and if this is correct, it shows that the first lemurlike animals, our most distant ancestors, were actually present on the earth with dinosaurs. It is certainly wrong to think of cave dwellers in the days of dinosaurs, but at least the oldest primates might have seen a dinosaur!"
—Dinosaur and Other Prehistoric Facts Finder, by Dr. Michael Benton

They call me Purga. Purga Torius. And danger is my business.

Let's get one thing straight from the beginning. I'm not a dino. Few creatures make the mistake of calling me one. And no one does it twice.

And while we're at it, let's get another thing straight, too.

That thing that Maia Saura uncovered while digging her nest last season? It didn't look like me. Not one damn bit. No matter *what* you've heard.

The whole thing began on a day much like any other day. I was underground, sitting out the heat. Napping in my burrow. Waiting for nightfall, when I could go out and forage. Ears sharply tuned, listening for the vibrations of any overweight dinos heading my way. Hey, one wrong footstep overhead, and it's good-bye Purga. A fellow's got to stay alert to stay alive. No second chances. Know what I mean?

I heard him coming even before I felt the vibrations.

Parasauro Lophus. No doubt about it. I knew him by the honking sound that the weird crest on his head always makes when he's agitated. Or trying to get a date.

He comes to my neck of the jungle every now and then. Sometimes he has a job for me. Sometimes he just likes the company. Either way, he usually forgets where my burrow is and winds up crashing around till he makes it cave in. He felt so bad about it last time, he tore up half the hillside trying to help me dig a new one.

No one ever said dinos were smart.

I decided to go topside and wait for him.

"Purga!" he called out, crashing through the jungle. "Oh,—Purrrrrrrrrrr—ga!"

Oh, great, I thought. Why not let every pterosaur in this hemisphere know where I live? Thanks, pal.

"Yo, Lophus!" I called back, keeping an eye out for Ptera Nodon overhead. She had a wing span almost as wide as Lophus was tall, and she was a whole lot smarter. And, unlike Lophus, she had a taste for fur. I shuddered just thinking about it.

"Purga? Is that you?" Lophus changed course and lumbered in my general direction.

In the end, he nearly trampled me beneath one of those big, clumsy feet.

"Oh! Sorry, Purga. I didn't see you!"

I hauled myself out of the puddle I'd jumped into to avoid being pulverized.

"Oh, well." I gave myself a shake. It wasn't the

first time Lophus hadn't seen me when I was right in front of him. I'm about the size of one of his nostrils. "What brings you down to this neighborhood, Lophus?"

"There's been some trouble out at the nesting range."

"I'm no midwife," I said. "*Danger* is my business, not—"

"But something strange is going on, Purga! And we think you're just the creature to deal with it."

"Why? What's happened?"

"Well, you'll never believe it when I tell you. At first, I didn't believe myself! Who would ever have supposed—"

"The facts, Lophus," I instructed. "Just the facts."

The crest on his head squawked with his agitation. "While nesting, Maia Saura . . . Do you know her?"

"Only to say hello to."

"Maia Saura uncovered . . . Oh, Purga! I think there may have been a murder!"

"She found a body?"

"Not exactly."

"What then?"

"Bones."

"Bones?"

"Bones."

I shrugged. "So someone got eaten there. It's not the first time—"

"No. This is different. It's no one we know."

"A stranger. So what? Pilgrimages, migrations, relocations . . . We see a lot of strangers passing through here."

"This one . . ." He shook his head. His crest hit a tree. It swayed violently. He didn't notice. "This one doesn't look like anyone we know. Anyone except maybe . . ."

"Yes? What are you trying to say?"

"You!"

"What?"

"It looks a little like you."

(This is how rumors get started.)

"It looks . . . like *me?*"

I could hear the fear in my own voice.

Zalambda . . .

"Well, more like you than like anyone else," Lophus replied.

Zalambda . . .

"You'd better show me where these bones are." I said nothing as Lophus led the way, but I felt sick.

Please, please, please don't let it be Zalambda.

Okay, okay, so she'd broken my heart. Stomped all over it. Left it in little pieces. And stolen my secret cache of insects when she walked out. But despite all that, there was and always would be only one female for me: Zalambda Lestes. Even now, as I followed Lophus through the jungle—occasionally falling headfirst into one of his massive footprints—I could see Zalambda in my mind's eye. The graceful curve of her snout. The wiggle of her little nose. The sheen of her fur. The elegant length of her tail. Her delicate round ears. Her fuzzy underbelly.

Ah, Zalambda, Zalambda . . . If I could go back and do it all over again. . . .

Aw, hell. Things would probably turn out the same way.

Dames. Can't live with 'em; can't feed 'em to the dinos.

We got to the nesting ground before dark. It was crowded. Very crowded. And not just with nesting mothers.

"What's going on here?" I demanded, sticking close to Lophus as he shoved his way past hordes of dinos that shouldn't have been there bothering Maia Saura and the rest of her herd.

"Thank goodness you're here!" said Silvi Saurus when she saw me.

Silvi was about as ugly as dinos get, but she had a good heart. She'd hired me the year before to track down her no-good mate, who'd run off and left her. I finally found him shacked up with a plesiosaur. Of the same sex.

Dinos.

"Silvi," I said. "Is it . . ." I faltered. My chest hurt. My tail twitched. "Is it Zalambda?"

"Zalambda?" She looked up—way, way, *way* up—at Lophus. "You didn't tell him?"

"Tell me what?" I demanded.

"The body. The bones. The . . . *skeleton.*"

"What about it?" I was getting impatient.

"It's big."

"How big?"

"Maybe . . . like, velociraptor-big. Maybe even bigger."

I glared at Lophus even as the vise around my chest loosened. *Not Zalambda.* "I thought you said this thing looked like me?"

"More like you than *me,*" he said.

"Or me," Silvi said.

"Or anyone else around here," Lophus added.

"Well, would you just shove a few more of these dinos out of the way and *show* me these bones?"

When we got to Maia's nest, she leaped up and came running toward me. I hid behind Silvi and waited for the ground to stop shaking.

"Sorry," Maia said contritely. "Didn't mean to scare you."

"I wasn't scared," I asserted. *"Danger* is my—"

"Yes, yes, I know. Come look at the skeleton."

Steno Nychosaurus was already there. A pretty smart fellow, as dinos go. And a reasonable size, too. It was nice to be able to look someone else right in the eye around here.

"Purga." He said.

"Steno."

"Glad you're here. Looks like we need your help."

"Where's the body?"

"No body. Just a—"

"Yes, I know. Just a skeleton."

"Can you get it out of here before I lay eggs?" Maia asked.

"Depends on what we're dealing with," I said.

"It's over here," Steno said. "Brace yourself."

"I don't need to brace myself. *Danger* is my—"

"Yes, yes, just look down there."

It was worse than I thought. Strange. *Bizarre*. Unfathomable.

Silvi hadn't been far off the mark, despite her poor eyesight. It was about the size of a velociraptor, maybe a little bigger. Nothing left of the flesh to help us identify it.

But clearly not a dino.

Two legs. Two arms—kind of long. A *huge* skull.

"Looks like it walked upright, whatever it was," I said, not letting Steno see how shaken I was. *Weird*.

"Maybe. Might have balanced itself on those long arms, at least some of the time."

"Maybe. Think it's been dead long?" I asked.

Steno looked me right in the eye. "I think it's been dead a long, long, *long* time, Purga."

"So you mean the killer . . ."

"If there was one. Might have been natural causes."

"If there's no killer, then why am *I* needed here?"

"Because it looks a little like y—"

"It does not!"

He blinked. I guess I sounded a little agitated. "We just thought it might be a distant relation—"

"No!"

"A *very* distant—"

"You're on the wrong track, Steno."

"But—"

"*Drop* it," I said.

"You won't like the rest."

"Give it to me straight."

"I'd better take you to him."

"Who?"

"Psitta."

"Who?"

"Psitta Cosaurus. He'll explain everything."

"Where are you going?" Maia cried as Steno started leading me away from the scene.

"The swamp," he said. "We need to meet with Psitta."

"But what about the skeleton?"

"Psitta doesn't want it moved," Steno said.

"What's it to him?" I asked, leaving Lophus behind to guard Maia and the bones.

"He'll tell you that himself," Steno said mysteriously.

Psitta was a dino from across the sea. He came over on the land bridge, just like Zalambda had. But this wasn't the moment for me to think about her.

Psitta was bigger than Steno, but smaller than Silvi. He was an ugly guy with a horny beak, a massive short snout, a heavy jaw, and a thick tail. One look at his face, and I could see that this was a driven dino.

"What brings you to our little corner of the world?" I asked, trying to put him at ease.

"I came looking for more specimens of Terrible Monkey."

He had a funny accent, like most foreigners, so I figured I'd misunderstood him. "Excuse me?"

"Terrible Monkey," he repeated. "The thing your friends have found in the nesting grounds."

"Terrible Monkey?"

He nodded. "That's what we're calling it."

"Where?"

"Back home."

"But how did . . ." Then it hit me. "There are *more* of these things?"

"We've found *plenty* more where I come from. We think . . ." He looked around and then lowered his voice. "We think there were quite a lot of them at one time."

"You're kidding me, right?"

"Millions and millions of them."

"Seriously?"

"They might even be distantly related to you," he said.

"But, uh . . . *distantly,* right?"

He chuckled. Sounds weird when a dino does it. They don't usually have much of a sense of humor. "Relax, Purga. This thing's been dead a long time."

"How long?"

"Longer than it would take a plesiosaur to grow legs."

"Wow." I considered this. "So what do we do now?"

"Collect the specimen."

"Terrible M . . . What did you call it?"

"Terrible Monkey." He nodded. "We collect it and study it. We find out just what these things were, and what this means to us all."

"Okay, Psitta. Just one thing."

"What?"

"Don't you or Steno tell anyone else you think I might be related to that thing. I don't want creatures thinking my ancestors looked like *that.* Could be bad for business."

"But isn't there *anything* you can tell us about it, Purga?" Steno asked. "We thought—"

"You thought wrong. I'm as baffled as anyone. And it *doesn't* look like me. Not one damn bit. Are we clear on that?"

"As you wish. But we may need your help on this, all the same."

"If there's no killer, no missing person, no stolen goods . . . What do you need *my* help for?"

I would soon be sorry I'd asked. Terrible Monkey was about to become the biggest controversy on the continent.

The next day, Psitta moved the bones to a cave so he could work on them without the dinos bothering him. When I found out what he had in mind for me, I was glad not to have an audience.

"You want to keep that hand? You better keep it to yourself," I said when he started getting touchy-feely with my back.

"Nothing personal. I'm just trying to figure out how these little bones go together."

"I need my head examined for going along with this. *Danger* is my—," I muttered.

"Yes, yes. Stand still," Psitta said as he carefully brushed one of the longer bones off with his tail. "This part is a little tricky . . ."

"You're not listening," I said. "This thing does *not* look like me."

"You can't turn your back on science."

"Watch me."

"All you have to do is stand in one place while I tie the bones together," he said. "By the time I'm done, you'll be famous. We'll *both* be famous."

"I don't want to be famous."

"Yeah?" said Psitta. I didn't like the smile on his face. "Tell *her*."

"Who, her?" I asked, annoyed now.

There she stood in the mouth of the cave. Her soft, shiny fur glowed with the fading sunlight. Her cute little snout was twitching with excitement.

Zalambda!

"Oh, Purga!" she cried happily, scurrying across the cave to brace her forepaws on my chest. It slammed my head back against the cave wall, and I saw stars. Or maybe it was just the usual effect Zalambda had on me. "I've missed you so much."

She brushed my face with her furry head. I was a goner.

"You moved!" Psitta said, looking cross.

"It's going to be wonderful," Zalambda went on, ignoring him. "We're going to be *rolling* in dead insects before this day is over."

"Uh, that sounds nice," I said, "but what are you—".

I noticed Psitta was giving her the high sign to clam up. I could have told him not to bother. Part of

Zalambda's charm was her enthusiasm. The dame really *loved* insects.

"Dinos will come from all over the continent to see you by the time Psitta is finished with his publicity campaign."

I glared at Psitta.

"*What* publicity campaign?"

"All you have to do," Zalambda went on, "is learn how to walk upright. You can do it, Purga! I *know* you can!"

I hated to disillusion her.

"Not a chance," I said. "I don't do tricks. *Danger* is my—"

"Yes, yes," Zalambda and Psitta said together as they dragged me out of the cave.

"Not even a dino is going to fall for this," I said. Psitta gave me a dirty look. I was trying too hard to keep from falling flat on my snout to be tactful.

"Sure they will." Zalambda was twitching all over with excitement. "All you have to do is walk upright a few steps! You can do it! I know you can!" She looked at me as if I were her hero.

The dame was my weakness. I could *fly* if it would make Zalambda happy. Walking upright was going to be more tricky. Psitta had tied a twig to the back of each of my legs to keep them straight. I'd been kissing the ground all day.

"Maybe we should cut off his tail, too," Psitta mused. "Might make it easier for him to stand upright. It seemed to work for the Terrible Monkey."

"Just kidding," he added when I glared at him.

Zalambda had a calculating look on her face that showed she was *thinking* about it. I knew I'd better come up with a distraction quick.

"Do we have to do this out in the open? If Ptera Nodon is out hunting, I can't run away all trussed up like this."

"I thought danger was your business," Psitta said. I

gave him a dirty look. "Those dinos are too big to get themselves into the cave. At least there's a lot of shade here in the jungle. Their eyesight isn't that good."

"Here they come!" Zalambda said.

A crowd of dinos stomped into the clearing and each one gave Zalambda a few dead insects. She sniffed them to make sure they were the real thing, and not pieces of bark before she put them in a little pile and guarded them jealously.

I managed to balance on my hind legs. I felt like every eye in the jungle was staring at me. It was embarrassing, having my belly hang out like that.

I waited for one of the dinos to snicker.

He wouldn't do it twice.

Psitta started the lecture.

"You see here," he said with a wave of his fore-arm toward me, "the surviving descendant of an ancient animal we call Terrible Monkey. As far as we can figure, Terrible Monkey lived a long, long time ago when the continent was new. Terrible Monkey's descendant is smaller, and its brain is not as developed."

The nerve of a *dino* making cracks about *my* brain.

In an aside to me, Psitta said, "Walk around a little, Purga. Give the customers their insects' worth."

I could hear a crunching sound coming from Zalambda's direction that told me she was snacking on her gross profit. Zalambda always binged when she was nervous.

I started to stomp around a little, careful to keep my balance. The fur around my face and tail had been trimmed away to make me look more like the little rock painting Psitta had drawn with berry juice. I was mortified.

I expected someone to yell, "That's just Purga Torius with his belly hanging out," but it didn't happen.

Then Psitta unveiled the skeleton which he had tied

together with strong grasses. The dinos gasped. I lurched over to stand beside it just like we rehearsed.

The skeleton towered over me. Gave me the *creeps*.

"Looks just like him," one of the dinos said, squinting at the painting and then at me with his beady little eyes.

I gave him a dirty look.

The dinos thumped their tails in appreciation before they filed out.

"Tell your friends!" Zalambda shouted after them. "Oh, Purga! You were wonderful!" Her eyes were shining.

"It's just the beginning!" said Psitta. "We're going to take this show on the road!"

Every show over the next few days was the same. Zalambda collected the dead insects. Psitta gave a lecture. I staggered around the clearing a little. Psitta unveiled the skeleton. The dinos thumped their tails. Then they left.

The crowds of dinos got so big, we were doing our show three times a day on the river bank. I didn't worry about Ptera Nodon much anymore. She had been hired by Psitta to drop little leaflets advertising our act all over the continent.

"Maybe we should start charging *three* insects admission," Zalambda said as she helped me tie my legs to the twigs one day before the show. I didn't answer. I had other things on my mind.

At a few of the shows yesterday I saw dinos at the edge of the crowd, just watching and scowling and muttering among themselves. Now the same dinos were back, all at the front and looking kinda mean.

When Zalambda went out front and tried to collect the admission charge, they didn't comply and she didn't argue. Most of them had *teeth* bigger than her.

As soon as Psitta started his lecture, one of the dinos forced himself to the front and knocked over the rock painting.

"Hey!" I shouted. The clumsy dino nearly knocked me over with his tail. Zalambda scurried out from under one of his big feet just in time to avoid being squashed. I had waved my forearms to warn her, overbalanced, and was now lying sideways in the mud of the river bank.

"We're closing you down," the dino announced.

"You can't do that! You're obstructing the cause of science," Psitta shouted, looking stern. He signaled Lophus. He was our bouncer.

Lophus just gave Psitta a puzzled look.

Dinos.

"Your theory about this *creature* is contrary to our religious beliefs," Psitta's heckler said. "In the beginning, The Great Lizard created the continent for the dinosaurs and their young to go forth and multiply. Dinosaurs are The Great Lizard's chosen creatures and the masters of all the Earth. But if what you say is true, the Terrible Monkey was the first creature to live here, and The Great Lizard, in his wisdom, would not have created the Earth for *that!*" The dino gave me a withering look.

I returned it.

"Our children have begun to question their parents. Some have begun to ask if The Great Lizard is a myth! A myth! I hereby confiscate that *thing* in the name of The Great Lizard!" He pointed to the skeleton.

"You can't suppress science!" Psitta sputtered.

"I hereby confiscate *that* thing, too." He pointed at *me!*

"Hey, wait a minute!" I said as one of the dinos grabbed me by my tail and started to drag me away.

It was humiliating. I bit the closest dino, but he couldn't feel it through his thick hide. The last thing I heard before my head smacked a rock was Zalambda's squeak of outrage as they took her and Psitta into custody.

We were all prisoners.

* * *

When I came to, I was in the nesting grounds, still trussed to my twigs, and tied hand and foot. I started squirming, trying to get free. Zalambda and Psitta were tied up nearby. The skeleton had come partially loose from its grass bindings. It reeled drunkenly in the wind. I was afraid the stupid thing was going to crash down on us.

I could hear the dinos talking. They were having a meeting.

"The heretics must die!" the fanatical dino shouted. He sounded like he was about to foam at the mouth. This was one scary dino.

"Yeah!" one of the dinos said, pointing at us. "They must die!"

"Go ahead and kill us! You can't suppress the truth!" Psitta shouted.

Foreigners.

"Stifle it, Psitta," I hissed. I could hear Zalambda's teeth chattering.

"This cult is spreading all over the continent," the leader continued. "Our children have already started defying us. The Great Lizard is a myth, they say. *Science* has proven it! Some have already begun to think that, that *thing* ruled the Earth."

I kept working at my bindings. I was almost free.

"What we need is a return to our traditional family values!" the dino proclaimed.

I could hear the other dinos thump their tails in approval. I rolled my eyes. What else what you expect from creatures with so much body and so little brain?

"Maia's nestlings are hatching," a dino said. He sounded as if he had been running.

"There," the leader boomed out. "The miracle of birth! Let's all go witness this hatching and reaffirm our beliefs. Round up all our young. They should witness this, too. Afterward we'll have a rally in support of our traditional family values."

"Traditional family values!" the dinos echoed.

They thumped their tails again. I coughed, because all of this tail thumping was kicking up a lot of dust.

"What about *them?*" one of them said, pointing at us.

"Bring them along," the dino leader said. "After the rally, we'll have a public execution as a warning to any heretic who dares to spread this blasphemy further."

Zalambda, Psitta, and I couldn't see Maia's eggs hatch because we were being guarded topside. The dinos rimmed the hole where Maia had laid her eggs. Psitta had dug deep to remove the bones and taken all the dirt away. It must have been a pain in the neck to lay her eggs in a pit, but that didn't stop Maia. Maia's family had laid their eggs in *that* spot in the nesting grounds as long as anyone could remember, and that was that.

For awhile all we could hear was the sound of cooing over the hatchlings. I was still squirming to get free, right under the snout of the guard.

I spit in the face of danger.

I had just about done it. Just a minute more, and . . .

But suddenly there was a commotion from the group. Maia and the last hatchling had been brought up from the hole, and everyone was staring at the little guy.

I peered at the gooey little fellow. He was disgusting. I could see he had a round object stuck to his slick hide. I glared at Psitta. He flushed pink from embarrassment.

It was a blue stone from the sea that Maia's mate had given her as a present when her first nestling was hatched many seasons ago.

It had been lost a long time, and it was buried deeper than the skeleton that supposedly dated from ancient times.

The skeleton had been *put* there. And I knew *who* had put it there.

Maia was cooing over the stone. The other dinos looked puzzled.

Well, you couldn't expect the dinos to catch on that it shouldn't have been *under* the place where Psitta claimed the skeleton had lain since ancient times right away.

"Psitta!" I said, glaring at him. "The skeleton is a fraud. *You* put it there!"

The fanatical dino heard me. He raised his snout to the skies in triumph.

"I knew it!" he shouted. "The Terrible Monkey was put in the ground by that evil scientist to shake our faith in The Great Lizard."

"Why did you have to tell them?" Zalambda said, bristling when I finally got loose and tried to help her get loose from her bonds. The dinos were not paying any attention to us now because they were busy stomping the skeleton to bits, so I aimed to get us out of here while the getting was good.

"I deal in the facts, ma'am," I told her glumly. "Just the facts."

Psitta lay there like a defeated log. Zalambda and I had to untie him. One of the dinos looked our way. I dared him with a steely eyed look to start something. But the dino only jeered at Psitta and moved on.

One of the younger dinos threw a piece of rotten fruit at us. Zalambda and I ducked, but Psitta didn't even flinch when it hit him flush on the snout. He just sat there with his shoulders bowed and globs of stinking fruit gunk running down his face.

Psitta was a broken dino.

"You call yourself a dino of science," I sneered when we were all back at Psitta's cave. Psitta was packing his stuff. Zalambda was sitting in a dark corner by the dead insects, making agitated crunching noises as she chewed.

"I *had* to do it," Psitta said. "I *know* there's a connection between you and the Terrible Monkey. The funding had almost run out, so I seeded the site to buy myself some more time. The evidence is here. It *has* to be here."

"Why *here?* Why not on the other side of the land bridge? There are *millions* of those things there, to hear you tell it. Or was that a lie, too?"

Psitta wrung his claws.

"There *are* millions of Terrible Monkey skeletons across the land bridge, but *you* are here. Without *you,* the Terrible Monkey's only living relative, my theory makes no sense. Now my reputation is ruined. Even if I find the evidence I need tomorrow, no one will believe me."

"Well, it's your own fault," I pointed out.

"If you hadn't told them, I might have had a little more time. I could see they weren't smart enough to catch the significance of Maia's blue stone *under* the skeleton. We could have all been famous. A little more time, and my reputation would have reached the land mass on the other side of the sea, and *nothing* that was found to contradict my theory on *this* side of the land bridge could have discredited me. Now I'm a laughing stock, and I can never go back there again."

"Suit yourself," I said.

"Don't look so smug," Psitta said. "*You* are disgraced, too."

"It will all blow over eventually," I said. "Who needs fame? Zalambda and I will be fine without it. Won't we, Zalambda?"

She didn't answer. I realized that I hadn't heard those agitated crunching sounds for quite some time. I felt a thud in the pit of my belly. Even before I looked in the corner and found all the dead insects gone, I knew what had happened.

Zalambda had cleaned out the dead insects and left me. Again.

Dames.

I went back to my burrow. I'm not going to show myself in public until the fur grows back on my face.

The case is closed. My affair with Zalambda is history. Psitta is a laughing stock on two continents.

But let's get one thing straight.

That thing Maia Saura uncovered while digging her nest last season? It didn't look like me. Not one damn bit. No matter *what* you've heard.

FIERCE EMBRACE
by Bud Sparhawk

Bud Sparhawk has been a mainstay at Analog *magazine for the past few years.*

The thick, steamy air was heavy with game scent as his slim figure weaved its way soundlessly through the brush. Somewhere ahead he could detect the sounds of something moving toward the river, something that might end his gnawing hunger.

Searching this near the crumbling edge of the cliff was dangerous during the rainy season. But his hunger had become overpowering, and the river bank was where he could most easily find the delicious, slow animals. He'd almost been killed just a few days earlier when the beast he'd been pursuing had been swallowed whole by an avalanche of thick red mud. It had barely missed him.

Hans Koenig was bursting with news of his find as he headed back to camp. The late summer sun beat down on his ever-present hat—only an idiot failed to take precautions in the sun-drenched Gobi desert.

But Mark Norvall, the head of the expedition, wasn't nearly as excited as Koenig. "A new tyrannosaur specimen is very interesting, Hans," he'd said sadly. "But we won't have time to excavate your specimen. Just cover it up, mark the site, and we'll try to get it on the work plan for next year's dig. It'll be a great draw for grants."

"At least let me get an estimate of what we've found," Koenig pleaded. "I've finished all of my assignments already and can spare the time."

Norvall rubbed his scruffy red beard. "All right, but I want those workers back on our sites tomorrow. We have obligations to our backers and time is getting short."

By mid-afternoon the diggers had exposed the top of a tyrannosaur skull and a nearby sharp edge of a shoulder blade. Koenig felt a thrill of discovery as he realized that this could mean that he might be standing over a complete tyrannosaur specimen, and a large one at that! "Let's dig around and see what else we can find," he ordered.

Two of the more careful diggers made an exploratory trench where he estimated the nose of the rex to be. There was the side of another skull less than a meter away and just a little deeper. He carefully troweled and brushed the packed sand away between the two. Just beneath the fore part of the original skull he found another bit of bone.

"Looks like the edges of a vertebra," Norvall said as he glanced over Koenig's shoulder. "Looks likes we've found another pair locked in mortal combat." There were several in this area. "What was it?"

Koenig dug furiously, exposing ever more of the other skull. It was a second, smaller tyrannosaur.

That night, after dinner, Koenig played with a pair of smooth white pebbles. He'd drawn two eyes and a slash of a mouth on each with soft pencil and was trying to position the two as the skulls were in the dig, using a bit of string he'd taped to each to represent their spines.

The only arrangement that made sense was for the larger one to be biting the neck of the smaller. He could imagine the scene as the larger one thrust its foot-long teeth deep into the other's flesh, severing the spine and rendering its victim helpless, later to be consumed. Damn, if he was right, this was a beautiful example of nature red and raw.

"I think," he suggested the next morning, "that this find is far more important than I first thought. We are definitely excavating a battle in progress!"

Norvall raised an eyebrow at that remark. "Great. That will be a nice touch to add to the grant request, Hans. Good thinking."

"So," Koenig asked impatiently. "Can I have the workers for another day? We really need to examine what we have in more detail."

Norvall looked annoyed. "I told you that it would have to wait until next year. Listen Hans, we've got four excavations going, three hundred specimens to pack, and only a week left before we have to leave. I'd love to help you, but we just don't have the resources. My earlier advice stands; fill it in and wait. Those two have been waiting for over a hundred million years, one more won't change anything."

Koenig exploded, allowing an uncharacteristic note of exasperation to show. "I don't want to wait! Don't you realize the significance of this dig? This isn't just the remains of a rex; we're excavating behavior—proof that will settle the predator/scavenger controversy. I can't just fill it in and leave it. Damn it, this is important!"

"I think that you are letting your argument with Quinn color your thinking. You need to be more rational about this," Norvall said calmly as he made another entry to his notes.

"Reggie Quinn and I merely disagree on whether tyrannosaur was a scavenger or a predator. It is not what I would call an argument."

"It's obvious that you *believe* strongly in the latter," Norvall said with peculiar emphasis. "I'm sorry, Hans. I just can't help you."

Koenig snorted. "All right, then. If you won't give me the workers I'll dig the damn site myself. I am not going to let this wait another year—it's too important!"

He dropped into a crouch as his ears picked up the faint sounds of the other's passage. They weren't the blundering crash of a large beast nor the panicky skittering of small game. No, these were the deliberate sounds of something wise to the hunt.

He tried to detect the direction the other was moving—was it going toward the river? Was it looking for a place to hide or was it, like him, seeking easy prey? Either way he'd best discover which before he committed himself. If it was a competitor then he would attack. He'd killed several rivals since he'd reached his full size and had driven off scores more. This was his territory and he would defend it.

The big argument he had with Regina Quinn started over Kelso's wild suppositions about the tyrannosaur being a scavenger. Doctor Quinn wanted to invite the man to speak at the forthcoming symposium and he did not.

"Look at the evidence he's presented," Reggie'd declared after she'd studied Kelso's papers. "It fits everything we've learned about the tyrannosaur."

"I can't understand how anybody as brilliant as you can believe that rex was a scavenger," he argued. "Kelso's trying to reduce one of the most magnificent creatures ever to roam the Earth to nothing more than a cretaceous vulture. His theory is patently ridiculous; all you have to do is look at the creature's dentation," he argued and flipped open a specimen case to withdraw a mock-up of a tooth. "This isn't something for nibbling on spoiled meat! The monster that owned this was a killer. This point could penetrate the toughest mesozoic hide. These sharp edges could cut through bone as if it were butter."

"A scavenger needs the same equipment," Reggie'd replied calmly as she clutched the recommendation to her chest. "All the better to tear a carcass apart."

"But what about the legs?" he shot back. "T-rex's muscular legs were built to give him the speed and power he needed to run his prey to ground."

"The same sorts of legs are needed so a tyrannosaur could be the first to reach a fresh carcass," Reggie'd countered. "And to outrun its enemies."

Koenig made no secret of what he thought of that and brandished the tooth as if it were some talisman. "What enemies? What would mess with something as fearsome as this? I tell you, your wild-assed guess that the tyrannosaur was some pre-tertiary garbage collector is ridiculous. Utterly ridiculous!"

"Nevertheless, I am going to recommend that the Board invite Kelso. I happen to think that he is correct in his assumptions and am going to support him."

Koenig swore. "You'll be the laughing stock of the faculty. I'd advised against publicly supporting him. Come on, Reggie, you must know better. Don't make a fool of yourself."

Reggie gave him an icy stare. "I *know* no such thing, *Doctor* Koenig. Kelso's views are just as valid as yours—which you would know if you bothered to read anyone else's papers with an unbiased eye. But no, all you want to do is carp whenever someone tries to upset your own views." The expression on her face told him that this wasn't just an argument about dinosaurs. It was probably their rotten relationship all over again.

"My views have a better basis than yours! Rex *was* a predator, the fiercest one ever! Kelso's views are just a silly saurian scenario." It was an nice alliteration, and damn effective in trivializing her point.

"I can see that we disagree on this as well," she said frostily. "Perhaps we should leave it at that. Oh, I almost forgot to tell you," she added with one hand on the doorknob, "I am going on sabbatical at the end of the semester. I've decided to take Prince up on his offer of developing an acoustical probe. It's a great opportunity for me."

"Fine, I wish you lots of luck with your old *friend*," Koenig replied frostily. "I believe the department and I can blunder along quite nicely without you."

"Blunder is the right word, Hans," Reggie sneered and slammed the door behind her.

The other's sounds suddenly stopped. He wondered if his quarry had heard his movements despite his best efforts to move silently.

Again, he wondered if this could be a rival, another hunter. The stealth with which it moved showed that it was experienced. An immature competitor would have made some mistake by now, as many of those he had killed had done. The young were too impatient, too uncoordinated to slip so quietly through the thick ropes of vegetation. Only an older, more experienced hunter would have the skill and patience this one exhibited.

He stood still, holding his breath, waiting, listening for the slightest sound that might betray the other's position.

In the morning he began to dig cautiously beside the spine, just beneath the upper jaw and, by the end of the day, he managed to uncover a bit of the lower jaw.

Koenig danced around the specimen tent as he bragged about his find. "I was right! This is exactly what I suspected; my rex was obviously biting the neck of his prey! We've found the proof we need!"

Norvall obviously didn't share his enthusiasm. "Fine, now that you have your proof can you help me with the more important work? I'll have the workers encase the lump you've excavated and drag it down the hill if you want. You can study it in depth when we get back to the States."

Koenig blanched. "We can't do that! No, I won't have the specimens destroyed by taking just a part of them. We need to excavate the entire site—both skeletons, the whole scenario."

Norvall snorted. "Listen, we have less than a week left. There just isn't enough time to do what you want, not with all of the other things we have to finish."

Koenig stood up, his voice rising to a shout. "Damn it, Mark; forget the rest! *This* is more important. Why can't you see that?" The arguments went on, Norvall insistent and Koenig unrelenting, into the night.

At 0100 hours, when the desert temperature had fallen precipitously, Norvall finally slammed his fist down on the camp table. "Let's end this once and for all! I am willing to let you waste your own time, but I doubt your granters will appreciate your fervor in pursuing some wild-hare of a theory."

"There's no way I can excavate the find by myself," Koenig protested. "You're killing me, Mark."

"Don't take this the wrong way, Hans, but maybe you could use a Quinn probe to explore the site," Norvall suggested hesitantly. "That's a lot easier than digging up a hundred cubic meters of sand and gravel."

"You know how I feel about this digital crap, Mark. Besides, even if I thought that would help, where could we get a probe?" Koenig responded hotly. "I doubt there's one within a thousand miles."

Norvall leaned back and grinned. "That's where you are wrong, my friend. I happen to know that there's one in Tatal Gol, up on the plateau."

"Tatal Gol?" Koenig replied dumbly. "That's only a little way from here."

Norvall nodded. "The British team has been sounding the Jurassic nests all summer. Unless I mis-

read their schedule, they're finishing up right about
now. If you'd like, I can shoot them a request."

Hans considered. "A probe might be the best way
in the time we have," he said cautiously. "Do you
really think they'd help us?"

Norvall smiled. "Certainly! Imaging the entire scenario would be a lot faster than digging it out by
hand, wouldn't it?"

"Yes, yes," Koenig agreed, trying to keep the rising
excitement from his voice. "Call them and ask."
There just might be a way to get his proof after all.

*For an instant he caught a glimpse of the one who
had so cleverly eluded him. It appeared to be huge
and carrying the long scars of past battles on her
flanks.*

*What was her purpose in penetrating this far into
territory he had marked and protected all these
months? Was she attempting to force him away, to
drive him from the rich game that populated this river
bed? No, he bellowed defiance; he would defend his
empire, his territory! He roared once again into the
pouring rain and stepped forward, all attempts at
stealth forgotten in his anger.*

Koenig impatiently watched the rising dust cloud
of the approaching convoy and raced to meet the lead
jeep as it screeched to a halt beside Norvall.

Regina Quinn stepped out of the jeep. "What are
you doing here?" she demanded as he approached.

"This is my dig. What are *you* doing *here?*" he
demanded as his head moved from Regina to Norvall
and back. "You knew," he exploded, shaking a finger
at Norvall. "You fucking knew she was coming,
didn't you?"

"And why didn't you tell me that Koenig was
here?" Regina shouted. "You could have warned me
before I made the commitment!"

Norvall put up his hands. "Listen you two, I

thought that you needed each other and didn't want your rather public disagreements to get in the way. Why don't you act professional and make the best of it. Who knows," he added with a wicked smile, "you might even find that you enjoy it."

"Fat chance," muttered Regina, glaring at Koenig.

"No way," said Koenig, fuming over Norvall's deception.

"Damn it, Mark, she'll use the images to prove her point," he said later, when they were in private. "She'll distort the truth until it is unrecognizable."

Norvall stroked his beard. "I doubt that, Hans. She's a good paleontologist and willing to help. I don't think you have much to fear. Besides, she's a pretty good-looking woman."

"What the hell does that have to do with anything? I've seen how she works, Mark. I'm afraid of what she will do."

"Make the best of it, Hans. Make the best of it," he advised. "Damn fine-looking woman," he murmured softly.

Hans had only been a scant two years ahead of Reggie when they first met, still ABD and loving the thrill of the chase, finding the odd fossil, uncovering the speck of bone, a hundreds-of-million-years-old shard that was a brief clue to the diversity of the late Mesozoic.

He'd been searching for the remains of the tiny, warm-blooded creatures that skittered between the toes of the dinosaur giants who ruled the Earth when he'd first met Reggie.

He hardly noticed her when she first arrived at their site in the Altay Mountains, having driven from Gilvent Uul in an open jeep. She was no beauty: dirty, tired, disheveled, and sunburned. He dismissed her as a lightweight—another novice who hadn't read her briefing papers.

She'd been assigned to help him find traces of the

multituberculates, marsupials, and placentals that co-existed with the early mammals and dinosaurs just prior to the great extinction. Doctor Prince, the expedition's leader, gave Reggie a dental pick and a loupe and showed her how to scrape the rocky matrix from these practically microscopic fossils because Koenig's clumsy fingers hadn't proven dexterous enough.

When Reggie wasn't busy digging and scraping, Doctor Leonard A. Prince, a.k.a. Lenny the leech, paid her particular attention. She seemed delighted to share the handsome doctor's company as well as his aversion to cold, lonely nights.

As the summer went on, she gradually took over more and more of Koenig's excavation work while he was relegated to the slathering and packing jobs. As a result it was her name that appeared below Prince's in the articles, not his. It was hardly professional behavior.

The Brits stayed for the evening meal and contributed a few of their leftover cans of beef to the larder. "Good stuff," they'd joked, "might even have a bit of the mad cow in there for excitement." They all laughed as Norvall nervously checked the dates, just to be sure.

As the shadows grew longer Koenig reflected on the strange twist of fate that had thrown them back together. Reggie's taken over Prince's development of the sonic probe, so much so that it was her name on it.

Koenig always thought using the probe was too easy. It reduced everything to digital form, images on a screen, and that distanced the user from the subject. Only careful and patient digging could unveil the valuable details that the probe missed, he thought.

But he could understand why many of the newer researchers preferred the timesaving gadget. Most hadn't the patience for the traditional dog work of pick and shovel, trowel and brush. No, they were more interested in examining the kill instead of participating in the hunt. More for quickly grasping the big picture than patiently extracting the tiny, revealing details. It would be just like Reggie to be at the forefront.

Then he smiled. In a way this would be poetic justice: to have Reggie help him prove Kelso wrong, to settle the argument that had seethed between them all these years. Yes, it would be amusing to watch her face when she realized that his much-vaunted theories were nothing more than a tissue of fabrication. *This* find would show those who denied rex's primacy the truth of the matter.

"Have you found any nests around here?" Regina asked casually as they sipped their strong, tepid tea. "It would be exciting if you've found examples of birdlike behaviors among more species."

"Ah yes, the bird-brain interpretation. Still trying to extend your oviraptor theory, I see," Koenig said.

Regina bristled. "Don't call it that! And, yes, I am. I'm nearly convinced that, since birds came from the dinosaur line, most of the dinosaurs had to originate those behaviors. Didn't you notice that most of the nests we've uncovered aren't much different from those made by today's birds. That's pretty solid evidence in my book."

"Not exactly conclusive evidence to me," Koenig argued. "More likely it's just another example of convergent development. Eggs need a nest so they won't roll away. Anything that lays eggs has to learn to build one—it isn't as if nests are complicated structures. Sorry, Reggie. A few isolated examples won't prove your case. Just because there were *some* egg-laying dinosaurs doesn't meant that they were *all* birdlike."

"But these oviraptor nests and all of the dinosaur eggs we're finding around here *are* darn strong evidence," she countered. "And if that is true, then the dinosaurs probably acted like birds in other respects, even sex. That would mean that they used the same techniques to fertilize their eggs." The traces of a nasty smile played around her lips. "Why, I wouldn't be surprised if your favorite tyrannosaur was more birdlike than you might think, with a nice little cloaca."

Koenig's face reddened. "What a bunch of bull! You might imagine an emasculated rex hopping about like some chirping sparrow, depositing a bit of sperm in an instant of coupling. I certainly can't!"

"Oh my, is that a scientific statement or just projection?" she asked calmly, with traces of her smile still lingering.

Koenig leaned forward and shook his finger in her face. "Something as magnificent as a rex would have had a monster's equipment. He would have made love that made the young mountains shake."

"Why do you always refer to the tyrannosaur as a 'he?' I think that's just sheer macho projection," she giggled. "Do you imagine yourself as a magnificent rex: the fearsome Doctor Koenig?"

"I don't remember anyone complaining when I make the mountains shake," Koenig grinned back.

"You probably wouldn't," Regina replied tartly. "You never bother to listen."

Koenig kept he smile on his face. "I'd hoped you'd changed, Reggie, but I see that you're still the castrating feminist."

Regina stood and stretched. "And I knew you wouldn't change, Hans. *You* still have to be the dominant one, don't you!"

It was another cold, lonely night in the Gobi.

Regina said no more than absolutely necessary as she set up the tripods for the probe the next morning. She was very particular about the placement of the thumpers—the sonic generators—moving them millimeters this way and centimeters that until Koenig thought that he would scream at the slow, deliberate pace of her work.

Finally Regina appeared to be satisfied and set the pick-up heads in place—one at the center and three arranged in a rough equilateral triangle around it. He helped her run the brightly colored leads from the various components back to the probe electronics on the jeep and patiently waited as she tested each with painstaking care.

The thumpers were designed to drive a low-frequency sound wave into the ground that would reflect from anything it encountered. The probe's processor converted the reflections into a digital file that could later be processed into a three-dimensional image. Unlike the explosive shocks used in an earlier era, this form of sonar did no damage to the specimens or the site.

"We'll move the pick-ups in one-meter intervals down the hill," she declared as the first image started to coalesce on the monochrome screen. "That will provide us with the differential views I'll need."

"Looks like a bunch of noise to me," Koenig said as he tried to make sense of the hash on the screen.

"Those are just the raw returns," she said absently as she adjusted a setting. "I'll process this into something more recognizable with the 3-D software on the laptop." The screen paint was complete. "Hey, look here. It looks like there's two heads and a backbone. Interesting configuration."

Koenig looked at the screen. "How can you make any sense of this garbage?"

Regina smiled. "Hang in there, Hans. We'll make a probe analyst out of you yet. Look here," She ran her finger around the shadowy spots she'd noted and watched as he traced the remainder. "Very good. All right, let's set up the next shot."

An hour later Regina silently watched the second hash-filled screen build. "That's disappointing."

Koenig peered over her shoulder. "What do you see?"

Regina waved her hand. "Bad image. Just rock reflections and noise. I think your specimens must be too deep for me to image."

"I can't see any difference," Koenig said as he tried to decipher the screen.

"I told you; it takes practice," she replied. "Listen, if you want to get a decent picture of this site, you're going to have to remove some more dirt. With these low-frequency bursts I can only see a few meters down."

"Why would they be any deeper than that?" Koenig wondered aloud. "I would think they'd lie parallel to the slope of the hill."

"That would normally be true," Regina answered. "But I suspect that the entire matrix is on a fold. This whole region has undergone some tremendous upheavals when those mountains appeared a few million years ago." She looked around and finally pointed at a place across the slope from where they were standing. "Listen, why don't we dig a little trench and see which way the sedimentary layers run. That might give us a better idea of the specimens' orientation."

Koenig groaned, but picked up a shovel and began to dig. So much for Norvall's declaration that the probe would eliminate any more digging.

By the end of the afternoon he had extended the trench to a one meter depth. "Just as you expected," he said as he pointed at the barely discernable stripes. "The sedimentary layer runs nearly vertical to the hillside."

Regina smiled. "I figured as much. We ran into the same thing last year when we worked the Khulsan sites."

Koenig looked at her. "You were with Chapman? I heard he did some good work. Lots of citations."

"He wouldn't have found a thing if it hadn't been

for my probe," Regina replied proudly. "Shovels are old technology, Hans, as you are probably learning."

Before he could answer Regina climbed into the ditch and peered closely at the exposed surface. "Looks like you'll need to scrape away another three meters if we are going to probe the lowest parts."

Koenig groaned. "I can't do that much excavation by myself and Norvall won't let me use the workers for this. I thought that your machine was worth using, but I guess I was wrong. Can't beat the old pick and shovel."

"Poor little dinosaur," Regina teased. "I guess I'll just pack up the probe and head back to civilization. Sorry, been nice seeing you again and all that." She dusted her hands and climbed back out of the ditch.

"Wait!" Koenig said and leaped out behind her. "Let me see what I can do. Maybe Norvall will relent. Maybe I can scrape off enough to let you get a half-decent image. Come on, Reggie, I *need* this!"

Regina cocked her head at him. "I've never seen you so passionate before. What is it about this find that has you so excited?" When he didn't answer, she added, "Well, I guess I *could* stay a few more days, if only to get a good look at whatever has you so worked up."

"Thanks Reggie. I appreciate that." He hesitated and then added; "You've no idea how anxious I am for you to see what we have here."

"Why, that's very nice," Regina replied, all unsuspecting.

He was frustrated by the way the large female danced away instead of rising to his challenge. She was never where he expected as he lunged to engage and destroy. He roared again and again in frustration and rage, knowing that his bellows were driving game from the area. But that didn't matter; he would feast on the haunch he would tear from this upstart, this intruder.

* * *

Regina was waiting at the breakfast table when Koenig sat down. "Why the hell didn't you tell me what we were looking for?" she demanded angrily and turned her laptop to face him. "You damn well know what this means!"

"Figured that if I kept quiet you'd provide an unbiased interpretation," he responded as he gazed at the amazingly crisp image rotating on the screen. It was amazing how clearly the skulls, shoulders, and backbones were depicted.

Regina tapped the laptop. "That's certainly a tyrannosaur, and under it is another one." Her pencil tip traced a bright line. "It looks like the one's dragging the other by the neck."

"*Biting* its neck," he corrected her.

Regina shook her head from side to side. "I think not."

Koenig blew out his breath in exasperation. "Why won't you admit that they were fighting?"

"Damn it, Hans, are you still blind to the possibility that I might be right? The rex could just as easily be dragging another tyrannosaur carcass. Cannibalism is another characteristic of a scavenger, you know."

"They're fighting," he argued. "This rex must have been attacking its rival when they were buried. Look at their relative sizes! The larger one must have been chomping on its rival's neck. Size really matters!"

Regina looked at him. "Size really matters," she repeated. "Yes, you would think that," she added nastily and pulled the laptop toward her.

"Just wait," Koenig promised, ignoring her crude remark. "When we get the rest you'll see how the lower limbs are positioned to tear the other's belly open."

"And I say that they're more likely be to one side because it was dragging the carcass," she added.

When they got to the site, Koenig dug another

trench in the gravel-filled sand. Regina sat in the jeep and watched.

By the end of the day, one meter deeper and fifteen fuzzy images later, there was still no resolution.

"You'll just have to scrape away more of the soil," Regina advised with barely hidden glee. "Good thing that you *love* your shovel."

The nearby insects suddenly stopped their incessant chirping, which meant that something had disturbed them. Strange that he had heard nothing despite his heightened state of alertness. He had the sinking feeling that he had suddenly become the prey instead of predator.

"There's an early storm coming," Norvall announced over breakfast. "Weather says it's due to cross the mountains in a day or two. We'll have to break camp tomorrow. These sand storms can bury our sites in a few hours, so we'd better be cautious."

"We'll need at least another week to finish up," Koenig said. "Unless you can give me some more help."

"He's right; this is very important, Doctor Norvall," Regina chimed in unexpectedly. "We really need to dig deeper so I can get some decent images."

"While I'm glad to hear you two finally agreeing on something, I just can't spare the help for your project. As it is, we'll need to work around the clock to get the remaining specimens loaded in time. No, I can't spare any resources to help you. We start breaking camp tomorrow. Do what you can by then."

The workers started breaking camp at the break of dawn and, by dinner time, had loaded the bulk of the supplies and all of the plaster-encased samples onto the trucks. "All right, you two," Norvall yelled as he came to where they were both digging furiously, side by side. "Time's up. Get your stuff onto the jeep. We need to get out of here."

Regina waved him away. "Go on ahead. We're going to try to get another couple of images before we leave." Koenig nodded agreement as he kept shoveling furiously.

"I can't believe you two. There's a bloody-be-damned front roaring down from the steppes and you two don't seem to care!"

Koenig tossed a shovel of sand at his feet. "If you'll give us some workers we'll be done in a day or two. And don't worry about us. We still have Reggie's jeep to carry our stuff."

"You'll have to deal with the mongols yourself," Norvall replied. "But I doubt if any of them are crazy enough to stay with you."

He was still muttering about damn fools and their obsessions as he slammed the door of his truck and led the convoy out of the campsite. A caravan of workers' camels followed the trucks.

"Well," Regina sighed as she rested on her shovel. "There they go. Come on, Hans; I think we can get three more shots in today, if we hurry."

"Right," Koenig replied, picked up his shovel, and motioned to the few workers who'd elected to stay for the bonuses he'd promised.

Dawn came dun-colored and windy. The workers were gathered in a worried knot around their camels and pointing to the north. In a brief burst of Mongolian they explained that the storm was coming and they had to get back. "The animals are nervous," their leader explained. "Very dangerous."

Koenig had to admit that the sky didn't look promising, but weather said they had at least another day before the storm hit. His attempts to explain weather's precise predictions fell on deaf ears.

Koenig and Reggie watched helplessly as the train of camels plodded away, carrying their workers to the lower plains, away from the coming storm. "Damn it, weather still gives us twenty-four hours. They could have stayed," he complained.

"Nothing you can do about it now. Come on, let's see what we can drag out of what we have."

Late that night, with only the whining of the laptop's drive and the jeep's generator to break the silence, they went over the images from the day's work. Regina swore at the repeated lack of definition in the hazy images. "We're still not deep enough, Hans. The fold turns straight down and there's a lot of slate that scatters the signals. We'll need to get the pick-ups at least two meters lower before I can produce a decent image."

"Can't you crank up the gain, use a stronger signal, or something?" Koenig asked plaintively. "As hard as this soil is packed, it'll take days to excavate that much!"

"I'm already teasing as much as I can out of this damn equipment," she explained patiently. "I can't perform miracles."

"We can't just let this go," he replied. "Come on Reggie, think! We've got to come up with something."

"We could dig a single deep hole," she suggested. "If we could get the pick-ups deep enough we might be able to get a partial image before the storm hits."

"Why can't we put the thumpers in the holes we've already dug?" he suggested. "That would give us a stronger signal, wouldn't it?"

"Good idea," she agreed quickly. "If we do both it just might work!"

The rush came quickly. He barely had time to catch a glimpse of the huge female as she charged toward him. He spun about and dropped into a defensive position.

The female raised up in attack, her head held high and her arms extended to grab him. He expected that she would use her hind claws to rake his unprotected

*belly and twisted to the side so that her claws would
strike the thick hide of his leg instead.*

*But the slashing blow never came. Instead her
gaping jaws opened wide and descended toward his
neck as he struggled to escape.*

The cool dawn breeze drove grains of sand into
their eyes and dumped cupfuls down their backs as
Koenig dug four deep holes in the deepest parts of the
excavations and Reggie repositioned her thumpers.

By the time she was finished the sand was blowing
so hard that the holes filled as fast as Koenig could
empty them. "We'd better position those pick-ups
soon," he advised as he glanced at the rapidly darkening sky. "It looks like weather was wrong."

"Let's just go with what we have," she replied.
"Half a loaf and all that." She carefully placed the
pick-ups in the holes, then raced to connect the leads
to the electronics on the jeep.

The windblown sand stung their skin as they hovered in the lee of the jeep. Regina quickly ran her
system checks and set the timers. In a few minutes the
returns began to be processed.

"Look there," she said, pointing at the hazy images
on the probe's screen. "That looks like the faint out-
lines of the pelvic region."

"I can't make any sense of it," Koenig replied.

"Look, there's a leg . . ." Regina began to explain
as the final line of detail was sketched on the phos-
phor. "Oh, my God!" She reached out to him as the
wind gusted. It hit so hard that it rocked the jeep.

"Get under the jeep! That will give us some protection!" Koenig shouted as he fumbled a tarp from the
jeep and wrapped it around them.

"What about my equipment," Regina shouted and
reached for her laptop.

"Come on, damn it!" Koenig shouted. "This storm is
going to get worse!" When Regina didn't immediately

respond, he grabbed her by the arm and pulled. "We can get that later. Come on!"

Regina twisted away from his grasp. She quickly removed the optical diskettes and shoved them into her pocket. The storm's intensity had grown remarkably quickly and it was now a blinding sand storm. She couldn't see because of the sand in her eyes and staggered around, disoriented, unsure of where she was.

"Down here!" Koenig shouted over the howling wind and pulled her to him, rolling them under the jeep, wrapping the two of them in the heavy canvas tarpaulin to shield them from the driving sand.

"Thanks. If you hadn't grabbed me I would have been lost," Regina remarked softly.

"You had the laptop," Koenig said too quickly. "Couldn't let you lose that."

"Still, I appreciate the effort," she said. The tightly wrapped tarp pressed them together, face to face.

"You realize that these images will probably destroy your stand," he said nervously. "They'll prove that I'm right."

"It could as easily go the other way, Hans."

Koenig smiled. "Yeah, but as soon as you process those last images we'll know for sure, won't we?"

"Perhaps," she admitted. "You know, we've never been this close," she remarked huskily and wiggled closer. "I'd no idea how nice it would be."

Her nose was scant millimeters from his own. He could feel her breath on his lips. He hesitated, unsure of how he was supposed to react. And then her lips found his and her tongue started doing its own excavations, raising emotions long buried. There was little he could do to escape.

Nor did he particularly want to.

"Are you going to publish a preliminary?" Regina asked, as she nibbled at his earlobe sometime later.

"If your images are halfway decent I certainly shall," he replied, trying to pull away from her fervent attentions. "This find is too significant to wait."

"But you'll have to wait until next year to do the excavation; isn't that right?" she said as she pressed her body against his. It wasn't a question.

"What are you saying?" he said harshly, trying to ignore his rising physical excitement. "You *are* going to let me use those images, aren't you?"

"We could share," she suggested as she pressed her lips to his. "You'd still get the citation, Hans."

Her kisses were warm and soft, and it had been a long, lonely summer, and she was so close, and there wasn't anything else to do, and . . .

"Promise me we'll share," she said as her hands slipped lower and lower.

"I promise," he said between gasps of breath. "Oh, yes!"

He was confused as the scent of the other reached his nostrils. Her smells were overpoweringly attractive and awakened strange sensations. They confused his senses and weakened his limbs. In a final spasm of panic, he tried to regain control of his muscles, but the heavy perfume clouded his mind, prevented him from thinking as she reached out and drew him into a fierce embrace.

They had a hard time digging out of the wall of sand that surrounded the jeep, but were finally able to wiggle themselves free.

The windward side of the jeep was worse for wear, sandblasted to bright metal where the paint was thinnest. Koenig shook his head as he looked at the site. The sand filled it completely, smoothing the surface until it looked no different from the rest of the landscape. Even the huge piles of soil they'd excavated had been blown away. Nothing remained of the tent and supplies.

"I'm afraid the probe is going to need some TLC," Regina remarked as she scooped handfuls of sand away. "There's grit everywhere."

"We still have the laptop, so let's process that last shot," he suggested. "Maybe we got lucky." While she was loading the data, he popped the bonnet of the jeep and began cleaning the sand off the engine.

"Oh, my God!" Regina exclaimed suddenly.

"What is it?" Koenig asked as he moved to her side to look at the image on the laptop's screen. "Oh." There was only one possible interpretation of the two embracing dinosaurs, wrapped in their stone tarpaulin, that rotated on the laptop's screen.

"Neither's dragging a carcass," he said, snickering.

"And they certainly aren't fighting," she giggled.

"Neither were we," Koenig sighed happily. "I guess we were wrong about the significance."

"These images are significant in other ways," Regina added and reached up to pull his submissive head down to kiss her dry, sandy lips. "And I'll even share the credit for them with you."

He was powerless to move as the huge female twisted him about and forced him under her. There was a new sensation building, a strange pressure that grew and grew as her belly pressed tightly against his. Somehow their legs were entangled, preventing him from using the claws on his feet to rip her belly, her upper limbs were holding his immobile as she nibbled and nuzzled his neck. The pressure rose to such an unbearable intensity that he hardly felt the encasing mud as the hillside crumbled.

FLIGHT
by *Michelle Sagara West*

Michelle Sagara West is a two-time Campbell Award nominee who has sold fantasy novels as both Michelle Sagara and Michelle West.

The first of the bones arrive in the mail—not an auspicious beginning. Not an expected one. Later, when he knew what they were, Peter Johnson would arrange for a safer method of delivery: He would rent a cube van from Hertz rentals and two young archaeology graduate students from the local University—who, he reasoned, knew how to pack fragile things with care—and he would drive all the way from Toronto to the house he had once shared with his mother and father, leaving his own wife and child in the safety of the house he had built for them.

But later came after the arrival of the first bone.

His wife brought it to him when he returned from his long day's work, her dark eyes glistening with unsatisfied curiosity. "The mailman brought you something," she said, and then smiled. "I called you to see if I could open it, but you were in a meeting. Not returning calls anymore?"

Nora always opened his mail, but she always phoned before she did it. After all, without permission it was an invasion of privacy, and if the permission was always perfunctory—what, in his life, did they not share?—it was also necessary.

Pert and pretty, she was a mail magpie, a gatherer of sealed and closed up information. If he'd once thought it odd or strange, it was at the dawn of time, when the romantic impulse was stronger than any other impulse in the world. Sense and reason being two.

"Sandra didn't give me the message. You should've called back."

"She sounded harried."

He smiled. "She was." He reached up, massaging the muscles in his neck that had knotted and twisted into something tense enough it felt like bone. "We all are."

"Well, open the package. Maybe it'll be a pleasant surprise."

A crash came hallward from the kitchen, and they both started guiltily at the sound of their son, eighteen months old, doing performance art with cutlery and aluminum pots and pans.

She rescued the kitchen. He retrieved the package from the dining room table.

It was wrapped in brown paper, across which his address was written in evenly made, impersonal letters, each the width of a black permanent marker. There was no return address—no indication that it had required a signature. As he often did in a case like this, he wondered, sliding a penknife through strands of thin rope that quartered the box, where it would have gone if the post office made a mistake.

And then he stopped wondering.

Wrapped in badly frayed cheesecloth and nestled in styrofoam peanuts was a slender bone the length of his forearm.

"Nora," he said, his voice quiet even to his ears. Then, when there was no welcome answer, louder. "Nora."

She came through the swinging door, child attached to her hip like a natural growth. "What is it?" Curiosity.

He lifted the bone; they'd been together so long he'd almost forgotten that there was anything he knew that she didn't. The bone, suspended in midair by nothing more than a suddenly trembling hand, glanced off her attention. "Peter?"

No. He drew a breath that filled his lungs like the first truly cold day of winter. There were some things, he thought, that she didn't know. That he had never told anyone except his mother. "My father," he said, his voice strangely rough in his own ears. "My father's dead."

"Uh, Peter—I may not have majored in human biology, but I'd say at a guess that there's no way that bone is human."

"Human? Of course not."

"Peter, are you all right?"

He started to answer as she drew close, but his son reached out for the bone—the ancient, fragile bone, a thing heavy with history and earth's secret. "Don't touch it!" he said, more harshly than he'd intended.

His son, no surprise, began to wail.

As he once had.

Much later, their child finally exhausted by the effort of keeping his parents awake, they lay in bed together, side by side, but without touching. The day's labor always weighed more heavily by day's end than at its beginning, and they often took moments of these, heavy with silence, in which to recover a sense of precarious balance.

It hadn't always been like this. Peter remembered, briefly, an earlier life, when they'd steal every minute they had between classes to be together. When touch was electricity and promise and fire that burned away the stain of the day. When had it changed?

As if she could hear his thoughts—and who knows, she might have been thinking them herself—Nora reached out and laid her palm against the flat of his chest.

"Do you want to talk about it?"

Did he?

"Peter?"

"I haven't seen my father in over thirty years," he told her, although this fact he was certain she remembered. "I'm not upset about his death."

"You don't even know for certain that he is dead."

"He is." The words were flat. The bone proved that. He started to tell her about it, and stopped, because to his thirty-five-year-old ears it sounded ridiculous. "The letter will come. Tomorrow, or the day after."

"Are you going to tell your mother about it?"

He nodded. But he knew, guiltily, that he wouldn't tell her until he got the solicitor's letter. He couldn't tell her about the bone itself.

She'd worry. Or she'd rail. Or she'd insist that it be sold or destroyed. And he wasn't—quite—ready to do that yet.

Midnight. Moon at nadir.

Good thing for electricity and lights. But his hand stopped on the switch and he stumbled over a small, four-wheeled metallic foot-trap as his hand found the dining room table in darkness. He thought he could see it glowing faintly where he had left it, some ancient repository of light. He touched its rough, pocked surface.

It's yours now. He could almost hear his father's distant voice. It offered him cold comfort, but memories frozen in time so long often did.

When I was four years old, he thought, as he lifted his hand from the bone's straight line to touch its rounded end, your father died. And someone came with a leather briefcase, like a doctor's case and summoned you off to the Midwest. You promised you would send for us once you'd settled his affairs. Do you remember?

As if a dead man could.

Death angered him because of its silence, but it was an old anger. It wasn't as if, live, his father had been more accessible.

And yet.

The letter took two days to come, but when it came it was thick and heavy. It jingled, but he expected that; he rounded the envelope slightly at the mouth, turned it upside down, and shook. A small key ring with three keys fell onto the table.

He read the covering letter carefully; it was written in syllable-heavy legalese, but it eventually made its point: His father, Peter Abrahms the second, had died, and the provisions in his will were simple enough: that all things were to be left to his son.

Finding his son proved more difficult for the attorneys in question—especially since his mother had legally changed his last name back to her maiden name. It had taken two months to track him down, through a web of relatives and old addresses. But persistence paid off—and, he thought ruefully, would probably continue to pay off as far as the lawyers were concerned, as he didn't imagine they were doing it for free.

He phoned his mother that evening, while Nora was chasing Gavin around his bedroom, trying to catch him for long enough to dump his sand-covered little body into the bath.

"Peter?"

"Mom." He paused. "I've just—I've just received word that Dad died. Two months ago," he added, as if it were relevant.

Her silence was long and heavy; although she'd made another life for herself, eventually, she bore the same scars that he did, a fact of life. "Did he—how do you know this?"

"I just received a letter from his solicitors."

Silence again.

He thought: *I should hang up now.* Because he knew what she would ask next. "Did he leave you anything?"

He didn't know how to answer her, and because he almost always answered her questions, she took his silence to mean what it did.

"Peter. *Did he leave you anything?*"

"Yes. The—the bird."

Her turn to offer silence, things unsaid. Memories, he was certain, of herself as a young woman with a son in a small house in Toronto, waiting for her husband to come back. And waiting. And waiting. "What are you going to do?" The question was curiously flat.

"I don't know."

"Don't go."

"Mother—I know what he did to us. Do you think I could do that to Nora and Gavin?" He felt a very real, if momentary anger.

She fanned it by laughing, and the laughter was dry and brittle as old bone. "Prove it, then. Don't go."

"I never said I was going anywhere," he replied, coldly. Because ice was a defense of sorts, and because he spoke the truth. But even if he hadn't said it, he knew it for truth.

So did she. "Peter. You can have his solicitors clear up his things."

"I can't. It's stipulated in the will. I go."

"Then walk away from it."

"Why?"

"Because you won't walk back."

"Mom—I have to go. Nora needs help with Gavin." He slid the receiver into its cradle and stood in the ringing silence.

As a child, he had had the usual fascination with dinosaurs. Picture books and small posters and plastic Royal Ontario Museum dinosaurs had been scattered across any free surface of his room; he knew their names, and their geologic eras, and their sizes.

"What is it," his mother would say fondly, ruffling his hair, "about dinosaurs?"

It was such a stupid question, he couldn't even come up with an answer for it; how could she *not* see it herself? His friends did, when he had them, but they liked the Tyrannosaurus Rex. He liked the Pteranodon. They argued about it all the time, even though, as he grew older, he realized that it was pointless. They liked the power of the killer, and he liked the power of flight over a barren, monster-rich land.

He remembered this as he finished his informal interviews. Two graduate students: a young man named Larry and a young woman named Janni—both children of colleagues. They were curious and excited when he told them that they would be packing bones. Much like the bone on the dining room table.

"How many?"

"A whole skeleton's worth."

They'd exchanged a glance, although they weren't, at that time, more than acquaintances. "We'll need to buy a bunch of stuff."

"Buy it then, and be ready; we leave in four days."

"Your mother called," Nora said, as he walked through the door. She was, he thought, concerned—but not for herself. "She's—I guess old relationships never quite die. I don't think I've heard her this upset."

"What did she say?" As if he couldn't guess.

Nora's lips turned down in a frown as she absently covered Gavin's head with her hand so that the corner of the table—the corner that was, unfortunately, at skull height—was no longer a danger. "She doesn't want to deal with your father's . . . estate."

"And?"

"She's worried about us."

"Are you?"

"Should I be?"

He walked past her, into the kitchen. But he didn't answer the question.

"Look, Peter—don't be so angry at your mother. I'd probably feel the same way if you just walked out of my life one day for no reason, and settled down in the middle of nowhere."

"Same way?"

"I wouldn't want Gavin to have anything to do with anyone who hurt him—and me—that badly."

"Well, I'm not my father. I'll be home."

"Promise?"

The drive out was long. He gave control of the wheel to Larry and Janni; they drove in shifts, finding uncomfortable sleep on the truck's single long bench when they weren't at the wheel. Larry and Janni seemed to recover well from their turns at the wheel, and they seemed to sleep only when he wasn't driving. Their pleasant, awkward, and earnest chatter, scattered with a little unacknowledged tension and an eagerness that age would certainly dull, was a quiet, even lovely, sound.

His first trip out had had no such pleasantries.

His mother drove, grim except when she forced herself to speak to her young son. Her face acquired lines, about then, that never really left it—a hardness that had nothing to do with youth, although at that time she was twenty-seven years old. He'd thought her beautiful then, but he, too, was preoccupied: He could not imagine why his father had left them. Everything had been so normal. There hadn't been that many fights, and his parents had seemed—to his admittedly naive eye—happier than the parents of many of his young friends.

But his parents' marriage had been the first one to crumble. And it had started, in many ways ended, on this road. Although the roads had been made new, although they wound their way west in slightly different turns, he knew that he was making a pilgrimage.

What he did not know was whether that pilgrimage was his father's, his mother's, or some strange combination of both—as he, born of both, was.

They stopped twice on their trip, and he thoughtfully arranged to have a separate bedroom for Janni, not so much from any old-fashioned impulse as from some desire to have friends who still spoke to him upon his return. But he noticed, with a certain wry smile, that after he'd closed his eyes and let his breathing fall into the regular intervals that were always a prelude to sleep, Larry carefully pushed his blankets aside and made the long, slow steps from bed to door.

He didn't actually think they would do anything foolish. But he knew they'd be up all night, talking about their specialties, their hopes for the future, theories that were bright and shiny and favored, music— things that had everything to do with a life, and were not a life in and of themselves.

And what, he thought wistfully, was a life? He rose as soon as he heard the door click shut. Thinking, as he planted his feet against the cool motel floor, that he'd been much like them, that he'd rushed into independence, that he'd been proud of his job, and his ability to work, and the house that he and Nora had bought.

Things changed, with Gavin.

He hated the thought, although it was true, because he knew where it was taking him. There were other things to think of. He turned to look at the box that held fate in the embrace of styrofoam and cotton, and he carefully lifted its lid.

That night, he dreamed of flying.

They came to the old homestead at dusk.

Dusk meant many things to Peter Johnson, but not here: Here, dusk was inextricably linked with a memory that rose as the sun set. He stepped out of the cab of the truck, stretching his legs and his arms, twisting his back to make sure that he still could. Then he reached into his pockets and pulled out the keys.

Larry and Janni jumped out of the opposite door, and Peter noticed, dimly, that Larry offered a hand down. It was charming, but distant. The old barn was waiting for them. Or perhaps the new barn; it looked weatherproof, solid, more like a miniature hangar than anything that housed living animals.

"Shouldn't we check out the house first?" Larry asked almost plaintively.

In reply, he handed Larry the key he thought should open the front door. He thought the younger man might take it, but Janni was determined to follow; her eyes were alight with the sun's fallen glow when he turned back to look at her face.

He led her on through grass that had been allowed to harden and grow to seed, knocking down weeds and stepping on thistles in the process.

"I think," he said, his voice rusty as if with disuse, "they're in here." And he lifted his key, found a lock for it, looked back to ask Larry, wordlessly, for help. Together they rolled the doors to the side and then looked into the darkness.

Larry muttered a soft curse. "Flashlights," he said, and turned back.

But Peter needed no light, not here, not in this building. The bones provided all the light that his eyes needed; they were glowing, faintly luminescent, as if beneath a thin, porous surface, the moon was held captive.

"Mr. Johnson?"

He said nothing at all, although he heard her voice. It wasn't until the boy arrived, with his battery-powered light, that the glow was lost.

Then, Janni and Larry understood his silent wonder, and he, watching them, felt a hint of jealousy, of possessiveness.

*   *   *

He phoned Nora when he got in, or he tried to. The phone was disconnected, of course. But it was the same phone that his father had when he and his mother had first arrived in their small car. The kitchen, dilapidated but clean in a way that suggested it had hardly been used these past thirty years, was the same; the living room small. There were two bedrooms in the square house, and a bathroom of sorts; the one bedroom had a bed, the other a desk and bookshelves. If the house had been at all attractive, it might have looked like a model house; as it was, it looked like a ghost house.

For Peter, it was.

It had not occurred to him—and it should have—that his father would have gotten rid of his bedroom; it stung, to see it gone, to see no small bed, no books, no plastic dinosaurs, although he'd left his father two when he and his mother had returned to Toronto almost empty-handed.

Larry and Janni would have to sleep in the living room, somewhere. Or perhaps he and Larry would, and Janni could have the room. The room.

It smelled of something faintly familiar, musty half-remembered and yet unknown. He crossed the room and lay down on the bed, thinking that he should get up, drive out, and find a phone. That he should call Nora, or at least call the telephone company to have them reconnect.

But he told himself, firmly, that he would not be staying for all that long, and that he'd have to go through all the trouble of disconnecting it when he left; at the rate the phone company charged for those services in these times, he'd have paid three months' worth of bills, or more, for a handful of days.

And Nora would understand.

Subdued and tired from their road trip, Janni and Larry separated in preparation for the morning. Peter waited them out, waited until he was convinced that the gentle snoring was genuine. Then he rose, like a child might.

Stopped at the threshold of his father's room, remembering his mother's face, the sight of it half-hidden by his father's back until she started to move. Until she started to pace. Until she balled her hands up in fists and struck him rapidly in the chest.

His father might have been made of stone, or something less. He said, "I'm sorry, Stephie, but you can't and won't understand. I told you you shouldn't have come."

He walked through their ghosts, scattering them boldly. But as he walked away, he remembered that his father had walked away, and he watched, wondering what it was that they had done wrong. That he had, if he were honest.

Still, Nora wasn't his mother, and she wasn't here. He quelled his unease, in this place that had grown four rooms too small and many acres too isolated. The door opened noiselessly and he stepped into a landscape cracked and blistered by the light of harsh and perfect stars, by the face of the watching moon. He thought that he had never seen moonlight so bright it cast shadows, but this moon was, and his shadow was long and slender as he approached the barn.

Hadn't he grown up asking, over and over again, why did you leave us? The night was pregnant with answers he meant to be midwife to.

No cars passed him by, no traffic. There was no city's light haze to mar the night. Instead he heard the patient chirp of crickets, loud as oceans breaking against the rock; he heard the muted sound of a bird, an owl he thought, although he didn't have to embarrass himself by actually catching a glimpse of whatever it was that made the noise. It took wing; he heard it, and the rush of air was so close, so strong, it took his breath away.

There was silence and crickets then.

A night like this had existed since the dawn of time, cold and clear and so crisp you cut yourself on a glimpse of it.

Peter Johnson brushed the hair out of his eyes and slid the barn doors open. And waiting inside were the fossilized bones. But they were no pile, no gathered mound of treasure upon which a different—a mythical—creature might sit; they had gathered and bunched in a shape, a whole shape, a thing of size and beauty that could not flex or extend itself in its cramped quarters.

And, as sightless eye sockets turned toward him, as a jawbone devoid of tongue, a neck without benefit of throat, moved, he noticed that one of the bones itself was missing. There, along the ridge of its wide, wide wingspan a gap as long as the length of his forearm.

It seemed to be waiting for him; he felt no danger at all as he approached it. Not even when it opened wide and engulfed him, swallowing him whole.

My god.

He dreamed of flight.

But this dream was, to all his other dreams, the sound to the echo it leaves behind. He could feel his wings, wide and strong, the rush of wind a strength, and the height of the fall a joy. Snap his jaws, and he could feel the unexpected crunch of this morning's sudden meal, the wetness of it as it bled and struggled.

He *was* the great predator, and he was not; he could feel its approbation, its guidance. Just as birds— lesser, ridiculous creatures—flew with their young, so too did the spirit of this ancient beast guide him into reality.

On the crags of the highest cliff he saw his kin, his gleaming perfect, leathered kin, their proud heads painted with their successful kills: the morning hunt. He was young and strong and full of himself, and he knew, as he landed and casually finished the kill itself, that it was almost his time.

He ate. It was like nothing he had ever eaten; it was like nothing he had ever imagined eating. It *was* food, it defined food. No knife and fork, here, no soft thing, no easy meal. He forgot about them. Forgot.

In the morning, they found him in the barn, his face against a conspicuously clean floor. Janni was clearly concerned, Larry better at hiding his. They helped him off the floor, and he was embarrassed to think that he needed help when he had been . . . so strong. The gravity weighed him down, made of his feet clumsy, heavy graceless things. A graduate student under either arm—and not in the manner of rather off-color jokes—he made his way back to his father's house.

I had a dream, he told himself.

And ignored the fact that, for the rest of the day, he felt no need to eat.

He could not bear to have them start their cleaning and packing, although he likewise couldn't bear to tell them that. So he offered them a different truth instead: "There's no food in the refrigerator. And if there were, it would rot; there's no electricity to the house." He frowned. The things you didn't plan for when you thought you were going, somehow, to go home. Taking his wallet out of his pants pocket, he pressed it between his palms, feeling warm leather. Thinking of dreams. "Take this," he said, "and buy a cooler and some ice. We'll need a few days' worth of nonperishables, but maybe tonight we can make a real dinner."

He went to the barn again. There, although it was daylight, a warm darkness reigned, and when the bird rose, he was waiting for it. On the ground, it was graceless; the lack of height robbed it of majesty. Or perhaps it wasn't the lack of height: It turned to him, wing splayed wide where a bone was missing, as if that bone were a key.

He knew where it was.

Turning, he quickly left the barn and made a mad dash for the house. To his great frustration, the key that he'd kept did not open the back door; when he looked at it closely, as if for the first time, he realized that it was, improbably enough, the key to a car. He cursed his graduate students then, because the house, unless he wished to smash the windows in—and he did consider it—was closed off from him until their return.

He walked back to the barn. And as if it knew that he had tried—as if intention counted for something— it opened the wide stretch of his wings in a sweeping embrace of wind and freedom and history.

You should have come alone.

He leaped.

This was freedom. Flight. The world fell away as he gained height; the prison of gravity shattered as his leathery wings carried him beyond the care of his old life. Here, exhilarated, he swept and spun, turning, the thermals all the fuel he needed. Beneath him: ocean. Forest. Rock, sprinkled with the glitter of primal snow. Above him nothing but sky, blue and endless, a crown into which sun had been placed.

His eyes were clear; he could see every movement of frond that spoke of skittering in the plants below, could see the awkward waves in water that spoke of fish schools. Today, he risked the water, his lungs taking air as his wings folded. His jaw was long and smooth, and it came up flecked with ocean spray as the glitter of scale caught his eye.

Food.

A flap of wings, and he forced his way up to the thermals again, and jumping from one to the other, returned to the crags that were his home.

She was there, at the peak of the crag, waiting for

him. He had only to offer her part of his kill—all of it,
there was more—and she might agree to let him court
her. He knew, as he reared up, spreading his wings in
prominent display, that she would take no other.

It was all so clear, so perfectly clear.

The noise sundered him from the realm, and it
enraged him, but he could not speak for a moment in
anything more than a roar. The roar said it all, but
once it left his lungs, it almost collapsed them in the
rush to be gone. His strength left, he stood before two
men who were both at least a decade older than he.

"Mr. Johnson?" one of them said.

It said something about them, that they didn't even
blink at the roar. He had the grace to redden. "Uh,
yes, uh, that's—I'm a—this is—" He ran a hand
through his hair. "Can I help you?"

They exchanged a look, and then the one with the
beard shrugged. "Young man, claims to be a graduate
student at the University of Toronto, was driving a
truck rented under your name."

"That would be Larry. He was with—"

"A young woman, yes. Jenny Simner."

"Janni."

"Pardon me. Janni," he said, taking a notebook out
of his pocket and glancing at the writing on the first
open page. They exchanged another glance, and then
the younger man said, "She's about two hours out of
here, in the country hospital. He's there as well, but
his injuries were relatively minor."

And because they seemed to expect it, and perhaps
because some small part of him recognized it as duty,
he asked them to take him to the hospital.

Larry was there, sitting quietly on a bench in a
small and rather plain waiting room. There were glass
doors; light came in, but as the sun fell, it grew darker
by degree until electricity was brighter than daylight.
Peter felt impatient, and couldn't really say why. He

sat down, and the weight of his presence, rather than the fact of it, caught the young man's attention. He was ashen.

The pain in his eyes surprised Peter. The hospital air grew crisper, cleaner for all that it smelled vaguely of urine and antiseptics. Awkward, he straightened his shoulders. Knowing that if he hadn't sent them to town, they'd be safe. "Are you—is there anything I can do?"

The boy's lips were tight, strained. He lifted his hands, rested his fingertips against his eyelids. "No. She's—she's in surgery. Yes."

Peter waited.

"You can call her parents."

He nodded. It was better to do something; he rose. For a moment he saw himself in the boy, saw the fears of his early life: Nora had been the only stability he'd dared to want after his father's flight, and he'd always been afraid that something would take her from him.

Something.

His hand was on the receiver before he realized that the police would have already made the call. There wasn't much to add yet; Janni was, as Larry had said, still in surgery.

You should have come alone.

His hands trembled. He looked at them and saw the fine-veined leather of wings. Flight. Freedom. Legacy.

You should have—

If the phone had been a dial phone, he wouldn't have made the call; his hands felt clumsy and foreign and he made the attempt six times before he managed to hit the zero key. The operator made the connection. Nora answered the phone.

"Peter?" She was breathless; she must have come running to catch the call before the answering machine did. "I was—I was worried. "I hadn't heard from you."

He smiled, a stretch of lips over teeth. "The phones are there—but they're disconnected. It's just over an hour to the nearest pay phone."

She laughed; he heard the relief color her tone. "I thought something might have happened."

"It did."

Silence.

"Larry and Janni had an accident with the truck. They're—he's fine. She's—she'll be fine. But we won't be coming back as soon as I'd thought."

"Oh, Peter—that's terrible. I mean, about Janni. Take care of them, and take care of yourself. But—but call me, okay?"

She sounded like his mother had, a life's distance away. "I'll call."

He went back to the bench that Larry sat on, and waited. Three hours later, the doctor came back: The news was good. He made the second phone call, to Janni's parents, the bearer of good news. Wondered briefly how police could handle being the bearer of bad news as often as he suddenly suspected they must be. He heard their voices thicken with relief; in relief, tears could fall that wouldn't fall otherwise. And he heard that relief as his own, as the relief of a parent for a child.

You should have come alone.

But he hadn't. "Come on, Larry. They're not going to let us see her until tomorrow morning. Let's go back and get some sleep."

"You ever tried to rent a car in this place?"

The police were kind enough to drop them off. They told him, with some tired curiosity, that his father owned a car that seldom saw use in a little garage half a mile away from the house itself. Peter had assumed it was a shed.

He put Larry to bed, as if Larry, at twenty-five, were his eighteen-month-old son. Larry offered less resistance. Sleep came before nightfall.

And before nightfall, Peter Johnson walked into the bedroom that had once been his father's. He stopped there only long enough to retrieve the sentinel: the wing's bone; the missing piece. At once, a rush of sweet air hit his face, carrying away the stress of the day and the night just past. He bit his lip, remembering.

Walk this path, he thought, and turned, his hand round the bone, his feet taking steps that were smaller than his stride allowed. It took forever to arrive at the barn, longer still to open the doors.

But when he did, the light poured out as if it were liquid and the barn a broken vessel. He heard the wind's song in the flapping folds of wings that were ancient long before his kind had dared to walk, naked and helpless, across the Earth's face.

This is what he saw as a young boy when he'd run out after his father into the darkness, leaving his mother to her bitterness, her dry silent tears, the terrible weight already settling into the lines of her face.

And he felt his desire, his visceral, terrible desire, to be *free*. Nora was half a country away, in the house that he paid for with endless days of drudgery and strain, in a city made putrid by traffic and industry. He had wanted them in his day. Had worked harder to get them—Nora, the house in the city, his *son*—than he had ever worked for anything. Too hard.

Why?

He lifted the bone as the creature blazed before him.

Touch it, he knew, and nothing but death could separate them again. In that world, *she* waited, uncomplicated by family and responsibility, unburdened by age.

And in this world, *she* waited.

He always thought to understand his father. He stood, his breath quickening as if with a life of its own, lifted the wing bone to his lips. Shade and shadow, his father's, crossed the light.

There's no place for you! Father's voice. Lips

contorted with rage and denial, eyes glassy with yearning for all the things that Peter could never provide him with—that Peter might actively deny him by existing. It was the last time he had seen his father's face, and he knew, as he saw it, that there was no love in it, no room for love in it. And what, after all, was love? He cried out, swung at the past with the bone as if it were a club, and the ghosts were made flesh by light and memory.

It's mine now! he shouted back, feeling the roar in his throat. *You were too old for it!* Nature's law.

And the creature roared, waiting.

He lifted the bone, tears streaming down his face, seeing for a moment past his desire to the skeletal face of the rival that had won. It was a tiny moment, a fraction of a second. And in that second, he could *hear* Nora's voice, and Gavin's, and Larry's and Janni's. His own voice.

Weeping, trembling with desire and with a terrible dread, Peter Johnson lifted the bone in both hands and snapped it across his knee.

The wind *roared* with anger and loss; keening, it swept him up in a terrible flight of his own. Wingless now, he flailed against its grip, matching the loss that he heard with a loss of his own. No more magic, now or ever.

No flight. No freedom.

He battled his way to the doors, clinging by dint of will and stiff fingers to the slats of the barn. He threw himself out into—stillness.

The moon cut the night like a scythe. He looked up into a sky that was cold and clear and undisturbed by light and man. He took a breath, took another, a deeper one. Then, in a single angry gesture, he wiped the tears that had started from his cheeks and went off in search of his father's car.

He drove into town, in the dead of night, and he found a pay phone.

Nora answered him.

Her voice wasn't the husky voice of his youthful desire; it wasn't even the strong voice of his youthful need. Sleep-laden and foggy, she whispered his name as if—as if he were beside her and not half a country away. It wasn't enough, and it was. He said, simply, "I walked out on my father's life tonight."

And she said, quietly, "Come home."

THE TEST OF TIME
By Ron Collins

Ron Collins has recently broken into print with a vengeance. This is his ninth sale.

Dr. Gregory Paul sat frozen with confusion as his assistant reached into the time machine's cockpit and keyed a new sequence into the control box.

"What the . . . ?" he said, unable to frame an appropriate question.

Randal Waterfield, his assistant, grinned and looked at him with wild eyes as he pulled the canopy's release mechanism. "Good-bye, Dr. Paul. Enjoy your trip—wherever you end up." Then he drew a handgun from his lab coat and calmly fired bullets into the input buffer until his gun clicked empty.

The time machine shuddered as its power system engaged and its canopy slid firmly into place. A panel of lights flashed Christmas-tree colors before his eyes. The Plexiglas-lined cockpit reflected Dr. Paul's face, his hair a dark wispy cloud over his lined forehead. Fear inched along his backbone, dancing upward like the ice-cold head of a charmed cobra. He focused on the shattered control box and realized this would be a one-way trip. Without the input buffer, he could never program the time machine to return.

Randal's smile was predatory, wickedly carnivorous. "Don't worry about your invention. I've got your drawings, and I'll make sure the world learns about it."

Lights flickered, and Dr. Paul's stomach lurched. The nylon straps holding him in the seat bit into his shoulders as the machine dropped through the air in sudden deadfall. Fewer than two seconds later, impact drove the breath out of his lungs and mashed the back of his head into the seat's soft cushion. The screech of tearing metal raked his ears, and a warm, dusty aroma wafted over the cockpit, mixing with lingering traces of stale gunpowder.

Outside the cockpit, everything was dark. The flashing lights blazed against the vacuous blackness, alternating in eerie silence. Dr. Paul unbuckled the restraints and rubbed his shoulders painfully. He peered outside but could see nothing through the reflections of his warning lights.

He slammed his open palm against the flat top of the control panel. "Damn Randal Waterfield! Damn him to hell!" He should have seen it coming. Only a fool would have missed the envy and greed that glittered in the young man's eyes.

Calming himself, he released the canopy. The covering raised with a hydraulic wheeze, thunking solidly into place.

Immediately, Dr. Paul smelled swamp gas as thick as pancake batter. His eyes teared. He gagged and covered his nose, but the arm of his lab coat did little to keep the smell from clogging his nostrils.

Dr. Paul stood and looked around, blinking his eyes clear and trying to adjust to the darkness. The moon was a thin sliver. Its early first quarter light painted a silver sheen over a landscape of harsh brush and gnarled trees, their branches twisting and hovering above the swamp like a witch's bony fingers preparing to snatch up an unsuspecting newt. A cottony mist coated the ground, obliterating the area's features. The sounds of insects gradually built, their raspy songs intertwining in the night air as if each frequency rose separately from the depths of the swamp. A cold breeze blew damply against him, and he shivered.

Where was he?

He stepped out of the machine, and his feet sank into semisolid ground.

A large splash came from all directions at once. The hair on the back of his neck stood up. Had that sound been the splash of a crocodile leaping into the murky swamp? No. A crocodile would merely slip quietly into the water with black, death-filled eyes drawn to a focus on its intended victim. Perhaps the sound was a swamp cat, a nocturnal predator who would wade through shallow water with its powerful forelegs, then drag its lifeless prey up into one of the low branches for its feast.

An insect flew past his ear with a solid sound—a hornet's drone rather than a housefly's buzz. Dr. Paul ducked, then crawled back into the time machine. He flipped the release mechanism again and shut the canopy. It shut with a satisfying click, placing a barrier between himself and the swamp.

A shiver ran through his bones, and he imagined ooze crawling over his skin.

He was used to feeling uncomfortable.

He knew all about conversations that stopped when he walked into rooms. He knew about whispers in the hallway and tittering laughter about his experiments. He knew about performance reviews with the department chairman, and wondering if the false secrets other people whispered of him would deprive him of the tenure his work so richly deserved. And he knew about peoples' eyes that grew hooded upon his arrival, about women who giggled at his comments then turned away to talk to anyone else in the room, about returning home alone with his embarrassment and his unspoken desires.

No one had ever accused Dr. Gregory Paul of being bold or decisive.

But in all his life, he had never known the fear he felt now: the kind that gripped him like a frozen glove clutching his heart. The kind that made him have to think to breathe. Though he had suffered numerous indignities, he had never before been in the outdoors like this. He had never camped out as a kid or even stayed out until dawn playing in the park like some of his high school classmates had done on occasion.

Gregory Paul, Professor of Physics, was truly alone and truly lost. He didn't know *where* he was. He didn't know *when* was—and in a sense, he even wondered *who* he was.

The flashing lights broke him of his stupor. It was too dark to see much of anything inside the cockpit, so he reached out and punched various shutdown buttons, each one dousing a set of blinking lights. The digital readout still functioned. He smiled sheepishly at himself. He had been so caught up in recent events that he hadn't even thought to look at it. Its cold blue numbers read -68,252,122. He stared at the number, letting it register in his mind.

With ice-cold clarity, Dr. Paul realized exactly *when* he was—sixty-eight million years in the past, right at the tail end of the Mesozoic era.

The night passed as slowly as evolution.

Sitting through darkness in the middle of this prehistoric swamp made him feel as if he were living amid a macabre collaboration between Bram Stoker and H.G. Wells.

The fog grew heavier as the night wore on, its tendrils reaching seductively upward as if to lure unwary travelers. Dr. Paul gazed over the swamp, not sleeping, and constantly seeing motion at the edge of his periphery that wasn't there when he looked straight at it. Once, he swore he saw an animal with a neck as thick as a telephone pole gliding though the mist. But it disappeared as rapidly as he had seen it.

When finally the sun rose, he was tired and frazzled. The dawning light showed the surrounding area to be a green and yellow mosaic, covered with razor grass and thicket, no direction much different than any other. From inside the cockpit, it appeared he had landed on partially solid ground, but open pools and marshy patches were everywhere.

He took stock of the time machine.

Everything seemed in reasonable shape with the exception of a few bent struts and, of course, the bullet-riddled input buffer. Dr. Paul opened the device and found a damaged circuit card whose memory chip had been shattered. On the positive side, all the solar energy collection and storage units made it safely through the trip, and the central control unit still functioned.

Of course, Dr. Paul thought, Randal couldn't have destroyed the mechanism that made the thing work or else he wouldn't have gotten rid of him. Dr. Paul cursed again. He was sitting in the middle of a prehistoric swampland with an operational time machine. But without a way to reprogram the system, Dr. Paul was stuck sixty-eight million years in the past.

The thought galled him. The boy was smarter than he looked, but certainly the most cowardly individual he had ever met. How much lower could one get than to steal the ideas of another person? It was the most despicable of all crimes, and Dr. Paul was embarrassed of himself, ashamed for falling victim to this young hoodlum. Now Randal would be free to develop the machine on his own. Whatever fame and respect Dr. Paul had worked so hard for over the past twenty-five years would be reaped by a devious young man whose scruples were lower than the magnitude of a neutron's charge.

His stomach growled.

What would Albert Einstein do at a time like this, he asked himself? Why, he would get off his butt and find something to eat. Then he would figure out how to get this tin can of a time machine to function again. That's what he would do.

With a fresh charge of determination, he released the canopy and stood up, scouting for an appropriate direction for his first venture into the world.

The area looked safer in daylight than it had in the nighttime. He decided to head toward a copse of trees that grew on a ridge. If nothing else, its height would make for a better observation tower than the time machine. Dr. Paul leaped out of the cockpit and sank up to his ankles in black muck that smelled like the university's chemistry building after a fire. He shut the cockpit once again and headed toward the ridge, picking his way through the firmest ground he could find.

There had to be something to eat in this world.

For the next few hours, Dr. Paul fought the swamp, striving to make it to the ridge. He struggled through water so thick and black it could have come from the inside of a barrel of crude oil. Small mangrovelike trees grew in dense clumps, their root systems twisting below the water. He tripped over them constantly, and the leaves and thorns of coarse brush stung painfully as they cut into him.

Insects were everywhere. Huge beetles with red chitinous legs and antennae twice the length of their bodies infested the brush, jumping at him as he passed by. Flying bugs with iridescent green and blue bodies landed on him with noticeable impacts. They clung to his pant legs and flew past his head. He imagined them looking at him through their segmented eyes, and his skin crawled. He finally broke a short branch off a tree to flip them away with.

As the sun climbed, the temperature rose until Dr. Paul thought he would boil in his own sweat. He wanted to take off his lab coat, but that would remove his primary defense against the insects.

The ground finally became dry enough to walk on. He rounded a thick copse of mangrove trees, only to come face-to-face with a reptile the size of a small school bus.

Each of them stared at the other, the dinosaur probably as surprised and possibly as frightened as Dr. Paul was.

It was a triceratops, or something as close to it as Dr. Paul could estimate. Its skin was leathery and mottled gray with green splotches. A horned shell rimmed its head, and a pair of curved spikes grew at dangerous angles. It stared at Dr. Paul with black eyes, apparently assessing whether he was a threat or merely an annoyance. The beast chewed once, a few strands of wet vegetation moving in the corner of its mouth.

Both moved at the same time. Dr. Paul turned to run, and the dinosaur lowered its head and charged directly at him.

The ground shook with each of the dinosaur's steps, and Dr. Paul's chest streaked with pain each time he breathed. He saw a large tree ahead and, glancing over his shoulder, he realized he may not have time to make it there. The triceratops growled, a bellow somewhere between the roar of a lion and the whistle of a freight train.

Dr. Paul's eyes widened and he raced faster, his stride lengthening, his muscles screaming in agony. He drew near the tree and leaped toward it, running up its trunk as he grasped the lowest limb and pulled himself upward. His fingers strained to keep hold, his skin ripping against the bark. As he climbed, the tree seemed to explode with activity. Several birds flew from the tree, squawking with wild calls and shrill whistles. Without looking down, Dr. Paul grasped the next limb, swinging upward like a baboon, praying his bleeding fingers would not lose their grip.

The triceratops stopped below the tree and struggled to peer upward. It snorted and pawed at the ground, then trudged angrily around the tree's base.

Realizing he was not going to be trampled into the Jurassic mud just yet, Dr. Paul sucked air in great gasps and tried to settle down. A black antlike insect crawled toward him, and he squashed it with his shoe.

Looking around, he realized the tree was heavily laden with small ovoid fruit. He picked one from the branch and squeezed it, his stomach tightening once again.

The fruit was firm, with a smooth skin. It had a fragrant, citrus smell, a cross between a pear and a tangerine. He stared at the fruit, trying to decide whether to chance eating it or not. The triceratops grunted again, turning away from the tree, its hide gleaming for an instant in the sun. The birds, if he could call them birds, that had half-flown, half-fallen from his tree called out, climbing awkwardly to new perches in different trees. There were no clouds above, and the sky was bigger and bluer than anything he had ever seen before.

He looked at the fruit and took a bite.

It crunched like an apple. Bitter juice flowed in his mouth, making him wince. But his stomach seemed to sing for joy at the prospect of being filled again, and he ate greedily. When he was done with that one, he grabbed another and another, until finally he was sated.

. . . Dr. Paul's assistant reached inside the cockpit and punched a few buttons. Shots rang out, slowly, slowly, each reverberating like a modulated laugh until it died out. Randal grinned and waved goodbye. . . .

. . . that grin stayed with Randal as he stepped to the podium. White teeth. Curled lips. Women loved him. The press snapped a thousand pictures. The

plaque read, Randal Waterfield, Nobel Prize for Science. . . .

. . . Linus Pauling retched in his grave. . . .

. . . the input buffer crumbled in Dr. Paul's hands. Useless. He punched the activation button, but of course nothing could happen without a reference. Outside the cockpit, a triceratops danced with a tyrannosaurus, both apparently waiting for Dr. Paul to fall out of . . .

. . . the tree.

He woke with a start.

Somehow, he had wedged himself into a nook between two branches and fallen asleep. He shook his head and immediately regretted it. His temple pounded with every movement from that point on. It was a headache that could kill an elephant, or, he thought, maybe a brachiosaurus would be a better allusion for this time period.

It was late afternoon, nearly dark. He had obviously slept most of the day. He cursed Randal Waterfield once again and crawled out of the tree. His joints ached with every movement, and his scabbed-over fingertips bled again. He felt groggy and slow. His tongue stuck to the roof of his mouth.

Dr. Paul looked at the fruit hanging from the tree. It must have drugged him, he thought. But there was no time to worry about it now. He gazed in the direction of his time machine, then glanced at the sun perched near the horizon. Less than an hour of daylight remained, not enough time to make it back to the machine.

He had to find shelter, and he had to find it fast.

Squinting his eyes, he examined the ridge as closely as he could, searching for anything that might serve his purpose.

Dr. Paul found a small cave and made a fire at its mouth. The flames were enough to keep him warm but fell short of calming his nerves.

Nighttime closed in on him, reaching icy fingers through the fire's warmth to touch his soul. Insects trilled with a steady, high-pitched hum, and various reptiles—everything from crocodiles to snakes, he imagined—groaned and cried in the darkness. He itched from bug bites, and his muscles ached from their exertion. He was tired; his afternoon of drugged sleep had done little to revive him. His fingers were cut and bruised. His lab coat was torn, and his shoes and pants were soaking wet.

It was too much.

He was going to die. Dr. Paul knew this for fact.

Everything here had the potential to kill. Beyond the obvious dinosaur problem, he could die of insect bites or poisonous food or plants. He could die of starvation or simple exposure to the elements. And if he managed to avoid these dangers, there were certainly Mesozoic bacteria that humans had never been exposed to before.

Everything he touched, breathed, ate, or looked at held some probability of destroying him.

Add to these the facts that if a human being were chosen for this trip, Dr. Paul would have graded out last in line; that all he understood was the university and his experiments; that he had no other talents of any appreciable merit; that his body was weak; that he was a forty-five-year-old professor who had never done anything practical in his entire life.

And now he had to survive in the Jurassic time period?

It was only a matter of time before his luck ran out and he became dinosaur food.

"Damn Randal Waterfield!" Gregory shouted at the top of his lungs. "Damn him to hell!"

His only way to survive would be to program the time machine to return. But without the input buffer, there was no method to alter the computer's date registers. And without a method to do that, the controller had no way to manage the process, no reference to arrive at.

Dr. Gregory Paul wasn't going anywhere.

He rubbed his hands together. There had to be another way. Throwing another armful of wood on the fire, he settled back into the cave, thinking. The time machine essentially did nothing but funnel a massive amount of energy into the right state to create a rift in time large enough to transmit a body through at a rate inversely proportional to its mass. The input buffer provided a manner for him to tell the control box what reference to use, and the control box measured energy as it was transferred, finally shutting down the whole process when the appropriate limit had been reached.

Simple, actually. Yes, a bit more complexity was thrown in to account for a specific passenger's mass, but these were small details. Anyone could have thought of it. Except, of course, he had been the only one to do so.

He smiled proudly despite himself.

Everyone had laughed at his ideas, but he had always known he would be successful. He trusted himself in this area, knowing in his bones he had been right. If only he had had such confidence in dealing with people. Maybe then he would have had friends, maybe even a wife and a child or two.

A bittersweet emotion passed through his mind. No, Dr. Gregory Paul would not be leaving any progeny.

Fitting, he thought, to die in such a lonely place and in such a lonely fashion.

He rubbed his forehead. The headache was beginning to wear off. If he were a bigger man, perhaps the effects of the fruit wouldn't have been so bad.

He paused.

If he were a bigger man. . .

Dr. Paul's heart raced. Something inside his brain

tingled, nagging at him in that way it did when he was onto an important idea but couldn't put it into words.

. . . a bigger man. . .

. . . more mass. . .

More mass would mean time would tear more slowly. The trip would unfold over minutes or hours rather than fractions of seconds. Enough mass, and it could even happen over days.

And if the event happened slowly enough . . .

Hours became days, and the days became weeks. Dr. Paul slept in his cave, waking every hour or so to throw more wood on the fire. He found a different fruit to eat, and he chipped a crude knife out of stone, allowing him to add an occasional lizard to his diet. He weathered storms so violent they moved the earth, found ways to outsmart monsters he had previously seen only in Japanese movies, and somehow managed to avoid eating anything that would kill him.

In the evenings he thought about Randal Waterfield, about the future, and about physics. With each day, he grew more certain it could be done. If he carried enough mass, he could control the time machine manually.

That's when he began to build the cage.

Dr. Paul ran through the swamp as fast as he could, wading through the brush with greater ease than he had the day of his arrival. He was stronger now, his body lean and tanned, his mind steeled to the harsh realities of life. The triceratops thundered along behind him sending water and swamp muck flying. His time machine and the huge bamboo cage were just ahead of him now.

The dinosaur halted, tiring once again of a futile chase.

Dr. Paul reached inside the tattered remains of his lab coat for another baseball-sized rock.

"Come and get me, you brainless coward!" he

shouted. Making sure he was far enough away, he tossed the stone at the dinosaur, striking it alongside its horny armor.

The triceratops roared its discomfort and charged at Dr. Paul once again.

Dr. Paul ran, scrambling up to the knoll where the cage and his time machine stood in close proximity. He scurried around the cage, making sure it stayed between himself and the charging dinosaur.

The triceratops entered the cage before it realized what it was doing. It was tired after its latest burst of energy, and the pile of mangrove fruit easily drew its attention.

Dr. Paul watched in silence as the dinosaur ate. His stone knife weighed heavily in his pocket. He removed it, hefting its weight in his palm, waiting anxiously.

A short while later, gorged on fresh fruit, the triceratops lay down and fell into a deep, drug-induced slumber.

Dr. Paul ran forward, his hands trembling. He cautiously entered the cage, hoping the anesthetic effect of the fruit would hold. Holding his breath, he cut into the beast and began packing the incisions with handfuls of the mangrove fruit.

If the beast outside the cave wasn't a Tyrannosaurus rex, it was the next best thing. Twenty feet from the tip of its nose to the end of its tail and showing a maw full of yellowed teeth, the animal peered through the crack in the cave. Its golden iris sparkled in the bright sunlight, and the smell of eight tons of carnivorous lizard filled the tight space Dr. Paul had squeezed himself into.

His heart pounded against his chest, and sweat pooled at his brow. His breathing came painfully slowly as he struggled to remain quiet, hoping if he remained still and silent for long enough, the T. rex would give up on him and discover the present he had left nearby.

The beast gave a guttural growl, half sniff, half complaint. It smelled the blood of the triceratops. It twisted around and strode boldly across the swampy marsh toward the tall bamboo cage.

The cage would never restrain the tyrannosaur but, of course, that wasn't its purpose.

Ignoring the time machine, the tyrannosaur stepped into the bamboo construct and ripped a huge chunk of flesh out of the triceratops. The smell of fresh meat momentarily overpowered the swamp gas. After swallowing the first mouthful, the T. rex took another bite.

With every mouthful, the T. rex ingested enough of the fruit to kill a human.

And the dinosaur kept eating.

Bite after bite.

Finally, the beast's movements slowed. It grunted and pushed at the carcass with its blood-covered nose. It blinked slowly, a nictitating membrane remaining to cover a majority of the eye.

Dr. Paul worried about the cage, hoping the T. rex wouldn't destroy it in the process of falling over.

The dinosaur laid its head on the bloody remains, looking like a satisfied cat falling asleep after a kill.

Dr. Paul stepped out of the cave and ran toward the time machine, wading through the water and the muck.

Reaching the time machine's side, he leaped inside and strapped himself to his seat and pushed the power buttons. While he waited patiently for them to show green, his gaze slipped to the dinosaurs. There was no way to tell how long the tyrannosaur would sleep, and no way to know how it would behave when it woke.

But that was an issue for another time.

He said a quick prayer, hoping he had placed the cage close enough to his machine.

Scanning the landscape for what he hoped was the

last time, he saw the swamp in all its beauty, and the Tyrannosaurus rex for all its wonder. Dr. Paul smiled almost as much in awe of himself as he was at the sight of the massive beast.

He had survived. A sense of pride washed over him and, in fact, Dr. Paul realized he was just the tiniest bit sad at the prospect of leaving. He had never felt so full of life, and the power of his emotions nearly brought him to tears. Taking a deep breath, he returned his attention to the time machine.

Green lights glowed from all the panels. Adrenalin surged through him like icicles in his veins. "Move 'em out, boys!" he said with a huge smile as he turned the makeshift dial he had fashioned using his belt buckle and excess wire elsewhere in the system. Power flowed through the control box.

Colors collided and merged. It grew dark, then light again. Dr. Paul's stomach looped around itself, just as it had the last time, but far more slowly. He laid his head against the rest and gripped the controller firmly in one hand, slowly turning the rate of change backward.

It worked! Adding the mass of two dinosaurs built up enough inertia to allow him to control the process manually. He didn't need the input buffer.

He made out shapes. Landscapes changed. There was a bright flash. Ice, then water. A mound of land rose. Animals occasionally flashed into view, lingering in his sight like the afterimage of a photographer's strobe. Trees. Plants. Dark clouds. Dr. Paul turned the dial to move more slowly and watched as the Earth grew up.

Years passed.

Storms clashed overhead. The smell of wildflowers. A creature hunched behind a rock, staring intently at game. Human. He reduced his rate of progress further, letting time sift slowly through the machine.

The birth of man.

Dr. Paul was filled with a sense of power so strong that he shuddered. It burned in his heart, a feeling of total awe.

The tyrannosaur grunted, breaking his mood.

He had little time for dalliances. Turning the dial, he raced through a hundred years, and another. Buildings made of wood sprang up, then buildings of concrete. Uncertain of the controller's sensitivity, he slowed the passage once again, trying to ensure he didn't miss the window of his own period.

Smokestacks littered the landscape, and men walked by in derby hats and canes. The first automobile rolled down a street. Bulldozers destroyed everything.

And then he was in his laboratory.

He slowed time's passage further. A year passed. A month. A young man with wild black hair, mussed in the style of Albert Einstein, walked into the large room. It was himself. He remembered entering the room for the first time. He had been full of dreams and ideas then. Anything was possible. He had left his youth behind and dreamed of an adult world where he could hold professorships at Cambridge or Oxford.

For an instant, he was tempted to shut the machine off and find out what would happen if two of the same entities shared a time.

But he had other things to take care of.

He slipped forward, a month every four or five seconds. Experiments and projects came and went. His laboratory changed, becoming more and more like he remembered it.

The dinosaur grumbled one again.

Randal Waterfield stepped into his lab for the first time.

Dr. Paul nearly choked on his hatred and his rage. He slowed the process down even further. Maybe an hour every second. His palms grew slippery with sweat and his muscles tightened despite his attempts to relax. This was as sensitive as the dial would get. He hoped it would be enough.

Randal Waterfield stepped through the doorway for the last time.

Dr. Paul watched himself enter and get into the time machine.

Holding the dial steady as long as he felt comfortable, he finally twisted it to a full stop, shutting everything down and bringing the time machine to a halt.

Colors flashed. Dr. Paul's stomach reeled. His vision swam, and he choked on bile for an instant.

The tyrannosaur raised his head, weaving slowly back and forth.

Dr. Paul gazed around his laboratory. Everything was just as he remembered. His desk, cluttered with notes. An old coffeemaker whose sides were stained brown from incessant dribbles. The stale smell of yellowed books. Posters. Einstein, Bohr, Pauling, Hawking. Dreams attached to each one. A window opened to the west, allowing a view of the setting sun.

And there, standing inside the bamboo cage with a waking Tyrannosaurus rex was Randal Waterfield, his gun still held in his hand. Randal's jaw gaped open, and he stared at Dr. Paul as if observing a ghost.

His timing had been perfect.

"Good afternoon, Randal. So glad to see you, too," he said with a huge smile on his face.

As if he suddenly became aware of the cage, Randal looked around. His face blanched at the sight of the bloody carcass and the woozy tyrannosaur.

"What the hell?"

Dr. Paul unbuckled himself and stepped out of the time machine, edging his way between the cage and the laboratory's wall. "They're friends of mine."

Randal stepped backward, retreating from the reptile. "How . . . ?"

"How did I program the input?"

Randal nodded.

"The physics of time travel are incredible, Randal. I've had plenty of time to think about them. And I discovered it just took a few wires, a homemade dial, and enough mass to keep from fluttering around in time like a feather on the breeze to let me control the process myself."

The T. rex pushed itself up, teetering slightly, but holding still. It opened its mouth, filling the room with its fetid breath. Randal cowered in the corner of the cage, trying to slip through the bamboo poles.

He wouldn't make it through, of course. Dr. Paul had designed them specifically to keep Randal in, spaced perfectly to leave room for an arm or a lower leg, but nothing else.

"Let me out," Randal pleaded. "This thing is going to kill me."

"Keep still, Randal," he said, trying to make his voice take on the same tone Randal's had a mere few minutes ago by Randal's own time. "Thanks in no little part to your help, I've learned a lot about dinosaurs. Sometimes they hunt as much through movement as they do anything else."

Dr. Paul grinned wryly and walked toward the door.

"In the meantime, I think I should report a Tyrannosaurus rex on the loose."

Randal gripped his gun as if just remembering it. He pointed it at Dr. Paul. "Move and I'll shoot."

Dr. Paul smiled, remembering the cold click and the smell of gunpowder from over a month ago. "You're out of bullets, remember?"

Then he walked out the door, striding down the hallway as if he owned the place. He was a different man now. He had lived with dinosaurs. He had seen time and witnessed the birth of humanity.

He could do anything. He would never be afraid again.

Behind him came a gigantic roar and a terrified scream.

The Tyrannosaurus rex, Dr. Paul knew, hunts by smell as much as by movement.

THINGS PRIMORDIAL

by *Batya Swift Yasgur and Barry N. Malzberg*

Batya Swift Yasgur is the winner of the Robert L. Fish Memorial Award. Campbell Memorial Award winner, Barry N. Malzberg has sold close to one hundred books and three hundred stories, and is a multiple Hugo and Nebula nominee.

So go find a hobby, I said, find something new to occupy your time. You were interested once in pre-historic monsters, those dinosaurs, right? So why don't you get a Hopper and bring one back to study. It will give you something to do. It's either that or the old men's club at midday. Which can be a wonderful diversion except that you seem so sick of it.

So what does he do this Sam, I will tell you what he does. He not only brings back a dinosaur, he keeps it, makes a special place for it on the outside. This is insanity.

Not dinosaur, Bertha, he says to me, correcting me as he always has, revealing his lack of trust. Making me hear the tired sound of his voice as if I'm not the one who is really tired. Not dinosaur. A Nanosaurus.

Nanosaurus, Shmanosaurus. Why does he have these strong and peculiar passions? Not only to view but to adopt which is so much more expensive. It costs five times to import a dinosaur what it costs simply to look at them, as I have explained to Sam over and again. Why can't he be reasonable? I say it

to him all the time, I say Sam, I say, I want you
should be more reasonable. From reason will come
kindness and from kindness will come some consideration for me. Don't go digging up the garden to make
a place for a dinosaur cage, making a fool of yourself
in your denim overalls like some youngster. If you
need a hobby, go play bridge at the club. Or use the
Hopper to look at showgirls in the Follies-Bérgère
two centuries ago. What do I care? What could you
do with any of them anyway?

Maybe if you used the Hopper to look at pleasant
things, not the Follies-Bérgère or dinosaurs, I could
join you in that, but I cannot be an animal keeper
here. You know my arthritis. I can't come out into the
garden with you, because the damp gets to me and
you know how it hurts to bend over. But no, you
don't care about me. All you care about it yourself.
So I've got to sit home and watch TV while my
friends have husbands who take them to the senior
center for lunch or the club for bridge. Myron is the
model husband; Sadie couldn't be happier. But what
do I get stuck with? A man who won't take me anywhere, a man who spends his life on his knees talking
to some kind of Nanosaurus in a garden when he
could at least be inside with the Hopper looking at all
kinds of creatures.

You don't understand, Bertha, he says. Looking at
creatures is for an old person, turning yourself into a
voyeur, looking through glass at what you can't
touch. Real life is touching, is pawing even. It is communion of some kind. Moses took the tablets down
from Sinai, remember. He didn't just settle for threats
and commandments.

And what are you going to do with this strange,
horrible little animal in a cage out in the garden? This
is what I ask him. This thing, Sam, that you are
keeping in a shed. It's slimy—dinosaurs are just big
lizards after all, and they're as reptile as the snake in

the Adam and Eve story, is what I always say—and it's ugly.

It's not slimy, Sam says. I have touched it; it is dry and scaly. Touch it Bertha and you'll see.

I should die first, I said, before I touch that thing. What kind of family sharing is this, petting a dinosaur? Besides, this isn't even a real animal. I always thought dinosaurs were supposed to be big. That's what they taught the kids in my day, when my Milton and Jonah were going to school.

(Oh, they should only know what their father has been up to, shaming me like this with this animal he takes with him everywhere. But Milton got really religious of all things; he's learning Orthodox at a Yeshiva in Israel even after I begged him not to go there with those terrible and violent Arabs, may their names be erased, and Jonah is married—not such a nice girl, too much of a go-getter if you ask me, and I told him so too, but he said Mama, he said, I love her and I said love, what's love? A newfangled American word, loyalty is what it's all about. Love is getting up together, doing laundry and paying taxes and changing diapers. Don't talk to me about love. Thank God I outgrew your idea of love long before Sam got involved with his Hopper. Anyway, I haven't heard from Jonah very much since the wedding, just a card around the New Year, and I always say to Sam I say, that girl ruined him just like I said she would. But at least Jonah has not gotten crazy religious like Milton, going around talking about primordial things and the canons of justice—the sacred texts and the meaning of the laws.

What was I talking? Does any of this have to do with the children or with Milton turning crazy religious or Jonah taking up with his go-getter? Why am I talking about children who are not such children— 38 and 33 if you ask me and still trying to start their lives in such crazy ways. With them, with the younger people now it is always a starting: a starting this and a starting that, but in our time we knew that it was finishing which really counted. The dinosaur. Or in this case, Sam's nanosaur.

The books which came with the Jurassic Hopper mostly show these monstrous animals, but you look at this one that Sam brought back to place in the cage, and it's really small. Rabbit-size. Just the size of Milton the day in nursery school when he put down his prayer book and said, I don't believe in any of this. Four years old and he didn't believe in any of it! Well, times have changed in the Milton category, that's all I can tell you, now with the tsitsis and yarmulke and special prayers for occasions I can't even pronounce. This baby-Milton-size Nanosaurus stands on its back legs almost to reach the top of the cage Sam built for him.

Do you understand my life, then? There is this horrible animal Sam scooped up from the past with the optional equipment and caged up in the garden shed outside in the back. He feeds it leaves and things, but it really likes animals not plants and that's not the worst of it. The worst of it is that Sam goes—he just takes the car at the risk of life and health because for driving conditions I think he can barely see—and he goes into town to the pet store and gets mice. It makes me shudder just to think of it. He takes these disgusting little animals by the tail and he feeds them to the dinosaur. I think they are still alive when he does it. Sam says no, they are really dead, they are sold dead like most of life is sold to us dead, but I do not believe him. I think that he is lying to me, and I do not have the courage to go and take a look for myself. It makes me throw up just to think about it, and do you think he cares?

When he brought the Hopper home, all that he cared about was staring into it and looking at all the animals in prehistoric times, and then when he found the Nanosaurus—look at this, he says, it's tiny, it's cute, it's like a Reform Rabbi, Bertha. It has all of the parts but none of the menace or conviction. All that he cared about was that animal itself. How it runs on its back legs—look, Bertha, he says rubbing his hands together in a self-satisfied-like way, like he had discovered the cure for cancer or something like that— look, Bertha, how short its front legs are and how long its tail is. It's shaped like a kangaroo, and the way it scampers it could be a Reform Rabbi running from the congregation on the day before Yom Kippur when he insisted that the place be open for the High Holy Days.

This is his sense of humor. This is the kind of thing which he finds amusing in his old age: bringing back dinosaurs and mocking what he does not understand. Not that I want to defend Reform Rabbis or any of that other part which has eaten Milton up in the land of Israel. Look here, I say, why don't you just give your Nanosaurus back to the Hopper, send it back to the past where it belongs. Or if you can't bear to let it go back to the past, then give it to a science center or a museum or a zoo or something and let us get back to a normal life. Come out of the garden and pay some attention to your wife. Spend your golden years with a person, not with a machine or some kind of crazed animal.

Be quiet, he says, and I know that he has eyes only for that Nanosaurus because we are conducting this very conversation out in the garden and he is leaning over the cage, staring and staring. You don't understand, you never understood me. This is the most terrifying manifestation, the most real evidence you could possibly imagine. It proves the reality of the ooze from which we all came. You too, Bertha. You are no less things primordial than any of the rest of us and Milton in Israel, too—if he would take the time to think about it.

I understood only too well, I say. I have spent my

lifetime understanding and we have come to the point where that creature of yours has got to go.

But how? That's the question. I mean, if I was dealing with a normal man, I could expect him to ship the animal away, right? Or at least make an effort in between all the times that he is out there talking to it to pay some attention to a wife who has spent all of her years doing nothing but being devoted to him and the children she gave him. He expresses his preferences very clearly.

There was a laziness in this man—what my mother warned me at the very start when she met him the first time—a certain disinclination. This was a man who would rather sit in one place and let things happen than take any real responsibility for his life. And she was right. One job in insurance, one company, practically one boss and one pension: that was Sam's life. In the evenings and on weekends maybe a little reading and two weeks in the mountains once a year. That was it and he had to be forced to do even that much.

But he isn't lazy with his nanosaur. He brought the animal from the past, selected that exclusive option, he says, and that means that he is responsible for the nanosaur in ways that he was never responsible for anything else. The nanosaur's presence is his sole creation. Cleaning out the cage, tying this leash around its neck. Soon I am afraid that he will be taking it out for walks around the neighborhood, and I do not know how I will be able to put up with that kind of mortification. The Nanosaurus can run really quickly in that cage, and sometimes Sam lets it run through the house really fast which it does just like a dog.

This behavior is getting tongues moving, believe me. Sadie who is not only a neighbor but a true, if nosy, friend called me up just yesterday and wanted to know where my husband got that toy animal. Did it come back from the past with the Hopper? She had heard about people doing things like this. More and more in development, Hoppers are getting rented to give people like Sam views of one part of history or the other, and sometimes animals are even being brought back. There are even rumors that people are being brought here, although that of course is completely illegal and a terrible crime, risking paradox which is something I do not pretend to understand.

Never mind, Sadie, I say. There is nothing to discuss. Sam has found a new hobby, that's all. Soon he will outgrow it the way he has outgrown so many other hobbies and go on to something else, maybe the clarinet or the older man's badminton group. I mean, what's the difference anyway what they do at this age? It's going to end up the same way pretty soon no matter what. Sadie agrees with this, of course. How can she disagree? It is a kind of simple wisdom and also has to do with accepting the truth.

But part of the Nanosaurus for Sam, I think, is not accepting the truth. It has to do with being involved outside himself and with a creature which he calls representative of the larger picture. It is only a matter of time until people begin to talk, until the Nanosaurus from the Hopper becomes a discussion topic at the Golden Age Arms, but long before that I will have to put my foot down.

Bad enough he has the thing, but to make a public spectacle of himself, I say no.

But and wouldn't you know, couldn't you have seen this coming from the start, Sam has to make a general statement about this. Had an interview with this reporter from the development newspaper about the Nanosaurus which got printed, and then the television station reporter came down and, against my advice, Sam spoke to him for a long time. Then, that not being enough, Sam got on the air in the garden with one of their remote broadcasts and had a little appearance on the evening news.

Sam on television, talking about this dinosaur and

how it's not your typical predator but a special, little-known, small kind of dinosaur. One who sneaked through all of the narrow spaces in the golden time of dinosaurs and survived by making no trouble, just as the Jews, for a while anyway, had been able to survive in this place or another place by making no trouble. Sam saying how this was a different kind of dinosaur and how he had read up on it after seeing it in the Hopper, and then, after the television, all of the calls coming in to the apartment—we have a listed number. In fact, soon enough there were all these old foolish ladies around him ooh-ing and ah-ing—disgusting, to try to get involved with a happily married man by acting like that. And their tongues hanging out around that animal like it was some kind of sacred Indian cow or sacrifice from God for Abraham, when the truth is that it is just a big, stupid, fast-moving rabbit from a long time ago.

So the decision has to be made; that animal is ruining our lives, our golden years. It's turning what used to be a perfectly good, if somewhat lazy and dull, old man into an idiot, and a perfectly good marriage into something so sad and lonely that I cry. Every single night in my room my pillow is soaking wet. I lie there thinking of Sam, not in his own bedroom but out there somewhere in the night, holding the paw of his Nanosaurus, and stroking its head, and I cry some more.

He should stop, knowing as he does how much pain it brings me. Things primordial! The only thing primordial around here is me and that man is putting me into a grave. For the first time in his life, the man shows passion and look what he shows it for.

This Nanosaurus, this thing: It has got to go. From where it came is not so important any more. The Hopper may indeed be part of the wonders of modern technology as Sam says, but I am not interested and I am not interested either in repossession or the heart of recovered darkness, as he also says. Sam has never

been clear as to why he had to bring this thing into
our lives, or what the expense of this optional treatment might be. All that he is clear about is that he has
brought it into the garden.

Evolutionary intervention, he says, the true conviction of our history. Here is something palpable, something that moves convincingly beyond all of those
mild devices with which you would shroud passion.
Now just don't push me any further, Bertha, don't ask
for any more explanation. Just know that this is for
the best, all of it. Just let it alone. For once in your
life, accept something and understand that it is larger
and more important than you. I found the Nanosaurus
in the garden, and I will tend to it and you will do
your part by letting me do the same. You can find
your entertainment and outlets otherwise, you always
did anyway.

So let him say this: What else is there for me to do?
There never was anything I could have done for this
man. He is stubborn, he will not be pushed, he must
have things his own way or not at all.

All on my own, thus, I evolve a plan. It is a plan
which comes from my own heart and is the only
possible way under the circumstances. What I do is
wait patiently inside the apartment watching television (no news programs though, no national news,
no local news) until at last Sam has finished his put-
tering around and his patting around, and the Nanosaurus has stopped with its running and its scamper,
until there are at last no more murmurs, no conversations with his creature. I wait until I have heard
Sam limp off to his bedroom where he will snore and
kick the sheets (we have had separate bedrooms—
both up North at the old place and in our Golden
Arms apartment—since the kids left a good ten years
ago. Milton was last of course, meaning that, praise
God, we did not have to answer their questions or
account for their looks or imagine any conversations
we might have had.)

And so having done this, having waited out all of his noises and craziness patiently, I go to the garden, that green and oily peculiar place adjacent to our condo, and there is the Nanosaurus in its cage, looking at me with great intensity.

We stare at one another, the Nanosaurus and I—the animal in its cage which was Sam's necessary idea because I would not, I would *not* have that thing running around the apartment, as right as it might have been for him. Get a cage, I insisted, and that must have been his own plan from the start because having it in a cage would mean that I had somehow consented to keeping it altogether. There was cunning to his plan, then, to go to the pet store and get a cage which otherwise and better could have fit a good-sized rabbit.

And there is the Nanosaur in that cage looking stupid as it always has, a single portable lamp, another of Sam's ideas, shining upon it. In the light now, it looks like a rat which Sam has said is not the case. He has made himself quite clear on this point. It is history, Sam has said. It cannot be compared with the present; we should not reduce history by making it a cartoon or cute version of where we are now. This nanosaur, it is primeval history, the primordial thing itself standing before us.

Which is one way of describing a large, scrambling, insulting, rabbitlike animal. When this creature sees me it makes a scuttling gesture, the sound of its little legs hitting the paper which Sam has used to line the bottom of the cage. It is as if it has always been waiting for me; it seems alert.

Dinosaur? I think. Nanosaurus? What is all of this business with prehistory? It is another means of escape, just like Milton and the stones in the great wall in Israel to which he has run away. No, it is not a prehistoric creature Sam has been sheltering there, it might be prehistoric to him, but the truth is that it is a clumsy, overgrown, oily rabbit. In fact, I decide, in the glaring, humming light, It is a rabbit. In the spokes of the casting light as I step before that bulb, the nanosaur could be anything at all but this is what I have named it.

And to name, as Milton once said, is to kill. I reach the knife inside the cage, holding the long, blunt handle carefully, admiring the reach of the knife. Not with Sam, perhaps, but in this instance, I have chosen well. One cut, one neat slice like working with a roast and the Nanosaurus will be a lump on the bottom of the cage. In the morning I can tell Sam that there has obviously been a Nanosaurus stalker lurking outside, and at last inside, the gates of the delightful Golden Arms. There will come an end to this and Sam will become again, for worse or worst, the man with whom I have lived all these years, but at least I will be able to understand him once more. That solution lies clearly before me.

But as I balance the knife to puncture the Nanosaurus to its deserved death, I hear a different scuttling, a whisk of movement within the cage and suddenly this lump of a creature which has turned, which has been staring at me, opens its eyes to a terrible luminosity—the luminosity of the prophets, of the light cast from stars—and it is staring at me now as if it were a shtetl Rabbi who had caught me fingering a rosary, caught me murmuring of the True Cross. Oh yes, I feel in the sudden and dark extension of its glance such a tremor as I have not known in thirty years; it passes through me as if another, a larger knife had been taken.

Then there is an enormous hand on my shoulders squeezing, another hand seizing my wrist and that wrist is clamped so hard that the knife falls, falls inside the cage where the nanosaur trembles in its sudden inflaming.

Bertha, says Sam behind me, of course it is Sam. I have always been waiting for this and now it is here; Bertha you should not have done this. You should not be doing this. This is a terrible mistake and it is one against which I warned you.

I try to turn. Let me go, Sam, I say. This has nothing to do with you. It is for me. You are hurting me. Sam, you must let me go now.

I did let you go, Sam says, I let you go a long time in the past. But I cannot do it this way. You are involving yourself with the prehistoric, he says. You are trying to control something you cannot understand. This Nanosaurus was not placed here to be my pet anymore than it was to simply inconvenience you, Bertha. This nanosaur has larger purposes, purposes which you cannot grasp at all, purposes which I can barely apprehend.

Larger purposes, I say, what are you talking about?

I am talking about things primordial, I am talking of the darkness of habit, the overwhelming scope of history, Sam says. And it is as if he were in Temple reading from the scrolls which he has not done since Jonah was Bar Mitzvah twenty years ago. I am talking of the incomprehensible. We must let the incomprehensible into our lives.

But it is, I say, Sam, it already is.

No, I mean other than that, Sam says. I have never seen him in such a condition; it is as if he himself were in the Hopper, as if I were looking at him in some distant, time-driven, time-extinguished jungle, Sam moving around slowly, burrowing through the vegetation of impossible soul. Bertha, we must admit the incomprehensible and only in that way will our lives themselves become understood.

Here, he says. Here, now. My Sam, my crazy lost Sam, insistent in the movement of his hand and in the light glinting from the fallen knife.

He pulls open the cage door.

The Nanosaurus pokes out its snout, then a further limb, then yet another limb, then inch by inch to emergence and then this thing, this strange and remarkable creature is upon me, inch by inch squirming through the garden and reaching toward my face. This is not tradition, this is the heavy, dark clamp of all circumstance descending upon us, Sam says. Think of Jonah's gallivanting, of Milton's strange hereticism.

And then something else which I do not understand either. In fact, Sam says many things but they are no longer words, they are sound, they are a stolen and discordant noise in a hundred languages which I cannot possibly understand. Oh, the Nanosaurus jumping like a dog, like a dinosaur, like an angry angel. Jumping as my riotous and damaged father under the ark, holding the shofar as if his were the hands of God. Raising the shofar toward himself; tekee-yah. Shouting and great darkness approach to overtake.

Get a hobby, I had said. Find something to do with yourself, maybe a Hopper if you don't want to leave the apartment, but it was nothing like this I had in mind. Take her over, take her alive, this time history wins and you roam the Earth, Sam says and my father the Rabbi drapes his cloak over me as the exploding sun must have draped the Jurassic. I sink, I rise. Sam has a lot more to add, no doubt, but I do not hear most of it. Custom has given way to the impossible, descending light.

FOREVER
by Robert J. Sawyer

Robert J. Sawyer won the 1995 Nebula Award for Best Novel.

Everything we know about dinosaurs comes from a skewed sample: the only specimens we have are of animals who happened to die at locations in which fossilization could occur; for instance, we have no fossils at all from areas that were mountainous during the Mesozoic.

Also, for us to find dinosaur fossils, the Mesozoic rocks have to be reexposed in the present day—assuming, of course, that the rocks still exist; some have been completely destroyed through subduction beneath the Earth's crust.

From any specific point in time—such as what we believe to be the final million years of the age of dinosaurs—we have at most only a few hundred square miles of exposed rock to work with. It's entirely possible that forms of dinosaurs wildly different from those we're familiar with did exist, and it's also quite reasonable to suppose that some of these forms persisted for many millions of years after the end of the Cretaceous.

But, of course, we'll never know for sure.
—Jacob Coin, Ph.D.
Keynote Address, A.D. 2018,
Annual Meeting of the
Society of Vertebrate Paleontology

Five planets could be seen with the naked eye: Sun-hugger, Silver, Red, High, and Slow; all five had been known since ancient times. In the two hundred years since the invention of the telescope, much had been discovered about them. Tiny Sunhugger and bright Silver went through phases, just like the Moon did; Red had visible surface features, although exactly what they were was still open to considerable debate. High was banded and had its own coterie of at least four moons, and Slow—Slow was the most beautiful of all, with a thin ring orbiting around its equator.

Almost a hundred years ago, Ixoor the Scaly had discovered a sixth planet—one that moved around the Sun at a more indolent pace than even Slow did; Slow took twenty-nine years to make an orbit, but Ixoor's World took an astonishing eighty-four.

Ixoor's World—yes, she had named it after herself, assuring her immortality. And ever since that discovery, the search had been on for more planets.

Cholo, an astronomer who lived in the capital city of Beskaltek, thought he'd found a new planet himself, about ten years ago. He'd been looking precisely where Raymer's law predicted an as-yet-undiscovered planet should exist, between the orbits of Red and High. But it soon became apparent that what Cholo had found was nothing more than a giant rock, an orbiting island. Others soon found additional rocks in approximately the same orbit. That made Cholo more determined than ever to continue scanning the heavens each night; he'd rather let a meatscooper swallow him whole than have his only claim to fame be the discovery of a boulder in space. . . .

He searched and searched and searched, hoping to discover a seventh planet. And, one night, he did find something previously uncatalogued in the sky. His tail bounced up and down in delight, and he found himself hissing "Cholo's World" softly over and over again—it had a glorious sound to it.

But, as he continued to plot the object's orbit over

many months, making notes with a claw dipped in ink
by the light of a lamp burning sea-serpent oil, it
became clear that it wasn't another planet at all.

Still, he had surely found his claim to immortality.

Assuming, of course, that anyone would be left
alive after the impact to remember his name.

"You're saying this flying mountain will hit the
Earth?" said Queen Kava, looking down her long
green-and-yellow muzzle at Cholo.

The Queen's office had a huge window over-
looking the courtyard. Cholo's gaze was momentarily
distracted by the sight of a large, furry winger gliding
by. He turned back to the queen. "I'm not completely
thirty-six thirty-sixths certain, Your Highness," he
said. "But, yes, I'd say it's highly likely."

Kava's tail, which, like all Shizoo tails, stuck
straight out behind her horizontally held body, was
resting on an intricately carved wooden mount. Her
chest, meanwhile, was supported from beneath by a
padded cradle. "And what will happen to the Earth
when this giant rock hits us?"

Cholo was standing freely; no one was allowed to
sit in the presence of the Queen. He tilted his torso
backward from the hips, letting the tip of his stiff tail
briefly touch the polished wooden floor of the throne
room. "Doubtless Your Highness has seen sketches of
the moon's surface, as observed through telescopes.
We believe those craters were made by the impacts of
similar minor planets, long ago."

"What if your flying rock hits one of our cities?"

"The city would be completely destroyed, of
course," said Cholo. "Fortunately, Shizoo civilization
only covers a tiny part of the globe. Anyway, odds are
that it will impact the ocean. But if it does hit on land,
the chances are minuscule that it will be in an inhab-
ited area."

The Shizoo lived in an archipelago of equatorial
islands. Although many kinds of small animals

existed on the islands, the greatest beasts—wild shieldhorns, meatscoopers, the larger types of shovel-bills—were not found here. Whenever the Shizoo had tried to establish a colony on the mainland, disaster ensued. Even those who had never ventured from the islands knew of the damage a lone meatscooper or a marauding pack of terrorclaws could inflict.

A nictitating membrane passed in front of Kava's golden eyes. "Then we have nothing to worry about," she said.

"If it hits the land," replied Cholo, "yes, we are probably safe. But if it hits the ocean, the waves it kicks up may overwhelm our islands. We have to be prepared for that."

Queen Kava's jaw dropped in astonishment, revealing her curved, serrated teeth.

Cholo predicted they had many months before the flying mountain would crash into the Earth. During that time, the Shizoo built embankments along the perimeters of their islands. Stones had to be imported from the mainland—Shizoo usually built with wood, but something stronger would be needed to withstand the waves.

There was much resistance at first. The tiny dot, visible only in a telescope, seemed so insignificant. How could it pose a threat to the proud and ancient Shizoo race?

But the dot grew. Eventually, it become visible with the naked eye. It swelled in size, night after night. On the last night it was seen, it had grown to rival the apparent diameter of the Moon.

Cholo had no way to know for sure when the impact would occur. Indeed, he harbored a faint hope that the asteroid would disintegrate and vaporize in the atmosphere—he was sure that friction with the air was what caused shooting stars to streak across the firmament. But, of course, Cholo's rock was too big for that.

The sound of the asteroid's impact was heard early in the morning—a great thunderclap, off in the distance. But Cholo knew sound took time to travel—it would take three-quarters of a day for a sound to travel halfway around the world.

Most of the adult population had stayed up, unable to sleep. When the sound did come, some of the Shizoo hissed in contempt. A big noise; that was all. Hardly anything to worry about. Cholo had panicked everyone for no good reason; perhaps his tail should be cut off in punishment. . . .

But within a few days, Cholo was vindicated—in the worst possible way.

The storms came first—great, gale-force winds that knocked down trees and blew apart huts. Cholo had been outdoors when the first high winds hit; he saw wingers crumple in the sky, and barely made it to shelter himself, entering a strongly built wooden shop.

A domesticated shieldhorn had been wandering down the same dirt road Cholo had been on; it dug in its four feet and tipped its head back so that its neck shield wouldn't catch the wind. But five of its babies had been following along behind it, and Cholo saw them go flying into the air like so many leaves. The shieldhorn opened her mouth and was doubtless bellowing her outrage, but not even the cry of a great crested shovelbill would have been audible over the roar of this storm.

The wind was followed by giant waves which barreled in toward the Shizoo islands; just as Cholo had feared, the asteroid had apparently hit the ocean.

The waves hammered the islands. On Elbar, the embankments gave way, and most of the population was swept out to sea. Much damage was done to the other islands, too, but—thank the Eggmother!—overall, casualties were surprisingly light.

It was half-a-month before the seas returned to normal; it was even longer before the heavens completely cleared. The sunsets were spectacular, stained red as though a giant meatscooper had ripped open the bowel of the sky.

"You have done the Shizoo people a great service," said Queen Kava. "Without your warning, we would all be dead." The monarch was wearing a golden necklace; it was the only adornment on her yellowish-gray hide. "I wish to reward you."

Cholo, whose own hide was solid gray, tilted his head backward, exposing the underside of his neck in supplication. "Your thanks is reward enough." He paused, then lowered his head. "However . . ."

Kava clicked the claws on her left hand against those on her right. "Yes?"

"I wish to go in search of the impact site."

The waves had come from the west. Dekalt—the continent the Shizoo referred to as "the mainland"— was to the east. There was a land mass to the west, as well, but it was more than five times as far away. Shizoo boats had sailed there from time to time; fewer than half ever returned. There was no telling how far away the impact site was, or if there would be anything to see; the crater might be completely submerged, but Cholo hoped its rim might stick up above the waves.

Queen Kava flexed her claws in surprise. "We are recovering from the worst natural disaster in our history, Cholo. I need every able body here and every ship for making supply runs to the mainland." She fell silent, then: "But if this is what you want . . ."

"It is."

Kava let air out in a protracted hiss. "It's not really a suitable reward. Yes, you may have the use of a ship; I won't deny you that. But while on your voyage, think of what you really want—something lasting, something of value."

"Thank you, Your Highness," said Cholo. "Thank you."

Kava disengaged her tail from the wooden mount, stepped away from her chest cradle, and walked over to the astronomer, placing the back of a hand, her claws bent up and away, gently on his shoulder. "Travel safely, Cholo."

They sailed for almost two months without finding any sign of the impact site. Cholo had tried to determine the correct heading based on the apparent direction from which the huge waves had come plus his knowledge of the asteroid's path through the sky, but either he had miscalculated, or the ocean really had covered over all evidence of the impact. Still, they had come this far; he figured they might as well push on to the western continent.

The ship deployed its anchor about thirty-six body-lengths from the shore, and Cholo and two others rowed in aboard a small boat. The beach was covered with debris obviously washed in by giant waves—mountains of seaweed, millions of shells, coral, drift-wood, several dead sea serpents, and more. Cholo had a hard time walking over all the material; he almost lost his balance several times.

The scouting party continued on, past the beach. The forest was charred and blackened—a huge fire had raged through here recently, leaving burnt-out trunks and a thick layer of ash underfoot. The asteroid would have heated up enormously coming through the atmosphere; even if it did hit the ocean, the air temperature might well have risen enough to set vegetation ablaze. Still, there were already signs of recovery: In a few places, new shoots were poking up through the ash.

Cholo and his team hiked for thousands of body-lengths. The crew had been looking forward to being on solid ground again, but there was no joy in their footsteps, no jaunty bouncing of tails; this burned-out landscape was oppressive.

Finally, they came to a river; its waters had apparently held back the expanding fire. On the opposite side, Cholo could see trees and fields of flowers. He looked at Garsk, the captain of the sailing ship. Garsk bobbed from her hips in agreement. The river was wide, but not raging. Cholo, Garsk, and three others entered its waters, their tails undulating from side to side, their legs and arms paddling until they reached the opposite shore.

As Cholo clambered up the river's far bank and out onto dry land, he startled a small animal that had been lurking in the underbrush.

It was a tiny mammal, a disgusting ball of fur.

Cholo had grown sick of sea serpent and fish on the long voyage; he was hoping to find something worth killing, something worth eating.

After about a twelfth of a day spent exploring, Cholo came across a giant shieldhorn skull protruding from the ground. At first he thought it was a victim of the recent catastrophe, but closer examination revealed the skull was ancient—hundreds, if not thousands, of years old. Shizoo legend said that long ago great herds of shieldhorns had roamed this continent, their footfalls like thunder, their facial spears glaring in the sunlight, but no one in living memory had seen such a herd; the numbers had long been diminishing.

Cholo and Garsk continued to search.

They saw small mammals.

They saw birds.

But nowhere did they see any greater beasts. At least, none that were still alive.

At one point, Cholo discovered the body of a meatscooper. From its warty snout to the tip of its tail, it measured more than four times as long as Cholo himself. When he approached the body, birds lifted into the air from it, and clouds of insects briefly dispersed. The stench of rotting meat was overpowering; the giant had been dead for a month or more. And yet there were hundreds of stoneweights worth of flesh still on the bones. If there had been any mid-sized scavengers left alive in the area, they would have long since picked the skeleton clean.

"So much death," said Garsk, her voice full of sadness.

Cholo bobbed in agreement, contemplating his own mortality.

Months later, Cholo at last returned to Queen Kava's chambers.

"And you found no great beasts at all?" asked the Queen.

"None."

"But there are lots of them left on the mainland," said Kava. "While you were away, countless trips were made there to find wood and supplies to repair our cities."

" 'Lots' is a relative term, Your Highness. If the legends are to believed—not to mention the fossil record—great beasts of all types were much more plentiful long ago. Their numbers have been thinning for some time. Perhaps, on the eastern continent, the aftermath of the asteroid was the gizzard stone that burst the thunderbeast's belly, finishing them off."

"Even the great may fall," said the Queen.

Cholo was quiet for a time, his own nictitating membranes dancing up and down. Finally, he spoke: "Queen Kava, before I left, you promised me another reward—whatever I wanted—for saving the Shizoo people."

"I did, yes."

"Well, I've decided what I'd like. . . ."

The unveiling took place at noon six months later, in the large square outside the palace. The artist was Jozaza—the same Jozaza who had assured her own immortality through her stunning frieze on the palace wall depicting the Eggmother's six hunts.

Only a small crowd gathered for the ceremony, but that didn't bother Cholo. This wasn't for today—it was for the ages. It was for immortality.

Queen Kava herself made a short speech—there were many reasons why Kava was popular, and her brevity was certainly one of them. Then Jozaza came forward. As she turned around to face the audience, her tail swept through a wide arc. She made a much longer speech; Cholo was growing restless, hopping from foot to foot.

Finally the moment came. Jozaza bobbed her torso at four of her assistants. They each took hold of part of the giant leather sheet, and, on the count of three, they pulled it aside, revealing the statue.

It was made of white marble veined with gold that glistened in the sunlight. The statue was almost five times life size, rivaling the biggest meatscooper's length. The resemblance to Cholo was uncanny—it was him down to the very life; no one could mistake it for anyone else. Still, to assure that the statue fulfilled its purpose for generations to come, Cholo's name was carved into its base, along with a description of what he'd done for the Shizoo people.

Cholo stared up at the giant sculpture; the white stone was almost painfully bright in the glare of the sun.

A statue in his honor—a statue bigger than any other anywhere in the world. His nictitating membranes danced up and down.

He *would* be remembered. Not just now, not just tomorrow. He would be remembered for all time. A million years from now—nay, a hundred million hence, the Shizoo people would still know his name, still recall his deeds.

He would be remembered forever.

THE GLYPTODON'S QUADRILLE
by *Karen Haber*

Karen Haber is the author of a STAR TREK VOYAGER novel, Bless the Beasts *and recently completed a science fiction trilogy for DAW Books, ending with* Sister Blood. *Her short fiction appears in many anthologies.*

Alison Davies pushed her shopping cart along the broad aisle at Entire Foods and scanned the unbleached pasta shelf with expert focus. She wanted the large succulent strands of bucatini—monster spaghetti—but there didn't seem to be any so she settled for whole wheat linguine instead.

A soothing orchestral rendering of the Jefferson Airplane song, "White Rabbit," was playing over the store's excellent stereo system and Alison hummed along. Already sitting in the cart were quart bottles of pure spring water, a carton of fertilized eggs, returnable, glass gallon jugs of nonhomogenized milk, and recycled paper bags filled with oat bran and unbleached flour. Still on her list were sun-dried apricots (organically grown, of course), and cold-pressed safflower oil.

She bought a bottle of elderberry wine and paused by the frozen organic pizza case. Tonight was the second anniversary of her relationship with her boyfriend, Matthew Tyler. He loved pizza, especially with anchovies. But all of those additives and salt

were an affront to Alison's delicate palate. She
paused, read the ingredients on a vegetarian pizza,
saw that there were preservatives in the tomato sauce,
and returned it to its shelf. Matthew would just have
to make do with tofu skins braised with garlic and
leeks. That was much better for him, anyway.

While standing in line she cast a cold eye over the
contents of her fellow shoppers' carts. Didn't that
woman over there know that the guava juice she
planned to buy was filled with refined sugars? And
that short thin man over there who had three tubs of
Ralph's Oldtyme Yogurte. Surely he knew that
Ralph's cows had been fed hormones! Alison wondered why people didn't look out for their own best
interests more carefully. It took constant vigilance to
keep the modern world from forcing its pollutants
upon you.

She paid for her groceries, loaded them onto her
bicycle, and pedaled off. As she sped down Ashby
Avenue, past row upon row of stopped traffic, she
couldn't help feeling smug. At least she was moving.
These gas hogs were sitting, breathing one another's
poison fumes as their stress levels climbed.

Back at her sunny, groundfloor apartment—with
garden privileges—she parked her bike and plucked a
ripe tomato from her lovingly tended vine. She would
make a huge vegetarian feast for Matthew. They had
tickets to the Pre-Early Music concert that evening at
the Third Congregational Church. It would be a perfect night.

The remains of the meal lay upon the table. Alison
had given Matthew his anniversary gift—a subscrip-
tion to *Garbage, the Magazine for Serious Recyclers*.
Now, as he watched, she unwrapped his gift to her.
Under the mud-colored recycled paper was a gray
velvet gift box. She opened it. Honeyed depths
glinted with micaceous flakes, calling to Alison's
mind the myth of the god Zeus turning himself into a

shower of gold in order to penetrate the reluctant nymph Danae. Within the box lay a piece of fossilized amber the size of her thumb.

"Oh, Matthew, how beautiful!" Alison cried.

Her boyfriend's long face reddened with pleasure, at least the portion visible around his dark beard. "I thought amber was a good choice for you for an anniversary present," he said. "A natural piece of the Earth—with an ancient insect in the middle."

Alison hugged and kissed him in sheer delight. "From the last time that the world was perfect. Those must have been the days: no pollutants, no additives, no humans." She kissed him again.

Matthew's blush deepened. "It's hard to believe that it's been two years since we met at that Earth First sit-in."

"I'll never forget how you chained yourself to that giant Sequoia." Alison tossed a hank of her long blonde hair over her shoulder and studied his gift to her. It sat neatly within her palm, was warm to the touch and surprisingly light—almost weightless. And at its heart resided a remarkable elongated insect whose limbs seemed to have far too many joints.

She rubbed it, hard against her cheek. A spark leaped, crackling, from the fossilized pine resin.

"What the hell?" Matthew cried.

Alison laughed. "Just making sure that it's genuine. Real amber, when rubbed, emits an electrical charge."

Matthew's smile evaporated. "Genuine! Do you really think that I'd give you a piece of fake amber, Ally?"

"Not knowingly. But there's plenty of fake amber on the market. After all, it feels exactly like plastic. I just wanted to be sure that you hadn't been taken."

"Oh. Guess it's a good thing I've got an amateur gemologist for a girlfriend." Obviously mollified, he lifted a glass of wine from the table and took a sip. The candlelight sparkled in the wine's yellow depths. "Nice not having the lights on."

Alison leaned over to kiss him one more time, then settled her homespun skirt around her ankles. "You know how I feel about electric lights."

"About technology in general." He held up his glass. "To us."

"We're a couple of old hippies, no getting around it."

They clinked glasses and swallowed generous mouthfuls of wine.

"Thank Gaia for the University: It employs an entire generation of Woodstock refugees." Matthew took another sip. "And thank Gaia—and your father—for your trust fund."

Despite the gaiety of the occasion, Alison felt nettled by his comment. "I'm not some spoiled rich girl, if that's what you mean," she said sharply. "And I'm no refugee from the sixties, mouthing empty slogans. I've kept the faith. I grow my own vegetables, spin my own cloth—"

"Too bad you can't shear your own sheep!"

"I would if the Berkeley city council would let me keep them in the yard." She nodded, smug with self-righteousness. "That way I'd have all the fertilizer I needed. You know I only eat natural foods, sleep on unbleached, undyed cotton, won't use any toxic chemicals in the house, won't have a television, and don't own a car."

Matthew held up his hands in surrender. "Yeah, yeah, yeah. You don't have to make a speech. Of course, *some* of us lesser mortals live too far from work to walk. But I guess I should be grateful you deign to ride in my old heap." There was a mordant touch to his comment that further annoyed her. She finished her glass. Why, she wondered, was Matthew so obtuse about her concerns? She hated the modern age and he knew it. But before she could say more the wind-up mantle clock struck the hour seven times. "Gods," she said, "we'll be late for the concert."

Matthew drained his glass. "We can get high in the car."

They were halfway to the church when Matthew's old Volkswagen beetle sputtered, coughed, and gave up the ghost. Even worse, clouds were darkening the horizon: An unseasonable storm was brewing. But a kindly retired professor helped Matthew and Alison push the car to the curb just beyond Dwight and Sacramento. They left it in a spot marked for handicapped parking, but they didn't know what else to do. Then their rescuer gave them a lift to the concert.

"I just love Berkeley," Alison said. "Don't you?"

The concert was a charming collection of plainsong and medieval ballads. For a while, Alison could pretend that she had left the twentieth century far far behind.

As they left the church, a streak of lightning crossed the sky.

"No rain," Matthew said. "Weird."

When they got back to Dwight Way, his VW beetle was gone. Matthew cursed loudly. "Goddamned Berkeley. Another towing bill. I can't afford this. Why couldn't the cops have left it where it was? It wasn't hurting anybody, was it?"

Alison patted his arm. "I'll go halvies with you on the tow bill."

Matthew brightened slightly. "Thanks."

It took them the rest of the evening to rescue the car from the sullen tow-driver. All the while, lightning crackled overhead. It was past midnight when they got back to Alison's apartment.

"Some anniversary," Matthew sighed. "I'm ready for bed."

"Me, too."

But before turning in she couldn't resist admiring his gift once more. Alison held the amber teardrop up so that it caught the candlelight, casting golden shadows against the wall like a tiny lantern.

A piece of ancient resin from a long-extinct pine tree in which some hapless bug had become trapped and was thereby immortalized.

Not for the first time Alison wondered about the whimsies of human nature that turned dead insects into ornaments.

She rubbed it hard against her one more time and felt the slight spark. But a second later she felt a sharper shock, as though she had touched an ungrounded electric cord. A crack of thunder shook the house. The lights flickered and the telephone began to ring. Alison picked up the receiver.

"Hello?"

There was no answer. But before she could react, a third shock sent her plunging into darkness.

Alison awoke . . . elsewhere. She was no longer in her snug little apartment on Sacramento Street. Her room, her bed, Matthew—all were gone. Gone, too, was the neat blue two-story apartment building. Sacramento Street was gone as well. No cars, no trucks, no buses, no bicycles. She was sitting, alone, in a meadow of high dense grass.

She stood, smoothing her skirt. The grass came nearly to her waist. It was bright, acid green, with chartreuse tassels. Although Alison prided herself on her knowledge of native grasses, this was no kind that she could identify. Probably some aggressive European superhybrid, she thought, squeezing out the hapless local competition.

The air was very warm. Her hair was already beginning to frizz from the humidity. She could make out distant hills on the horizon. The sun was high overhead and a deep orange-gold. The sky itself had an odd orange cast to it.

Palm trees of a peculiar sort dotted the edge of the grass field. They looked like ferns growing out of giant pine cones. Alison hated palms: They had no business in Northern California.

A dragonfly the size of a hawk buzzed past, fluttering at shoulder level for one heart-pounding moment before darting away. Its huge, multi-faceted eyes were iridescent blue-green.

Alison decided that perhaps she was no longer in Northern California.

There was not one sign of civilization anywhere to be seen.

How wonderful, Alison thought. She took in a deep lungful of unspoiled air and let it out slowly, savoring the odd pungent flavors. It didn't matter where she was. This was a treat. Besides, sooner or later she would find something that would orient her.

The grass rippled around her. There were things moving past her.

They looked like large—huge, really—red caterpillars. In fact, despite their size and color, they reminded Alison of the tomato worms that plagued her crop every year. They were each at least three feet long. If these were tomato worms, she wanted to see the monster tomatoes they must live on.

Thorny treetrunks as vast as Egyptian stone columns thrust into the sky crowned by strange spiraling whorls of spiked leaves. On the forest floor, a dense growth of small furry pink toadstools nestled at the base of giant purple leaves. A distant escarpment of dark rock—lava?—rippled across the horizon.

Fantastic, she thought. *It's like some kind of primeval landscape. Maybe it* is *a primeval landscape. What else could it be? I must have gone back into the past, somehow.*

She hugged herself in delight. Her prayers for a simpler life had been answered. If only Matthew could be here to see it.

Something croaked urgently in a nearby copse of trees. An answering croak came from a stand of horsetails. A huge head thrust up above the ferns, duck-billed, with tiny yellow eyes and a huge hatchet-like crest that curved along the top of its head. Mottled green and brown scales covered its glistening hide. Lizardlike eyes flicked over her and dismissed her as unimportant. The thing—could it really be a dinosaur?—scrambled into the horsetails and disappeared.

A squat, low-slung animal munched contentedly upon a low-growing bush with spiny leaves. It had red and black striations across its leathery golden shell. Alison felt a strange urge to pet it. "I don't know where I am," she said. "But you look mighty like a turtle to me."

Something whizzed through the air and at first she thought it was the dragonfly come back again. But to her amazement it appeared to be a bird. Not a winged reptile but a bird, with recognizeable wings, spotted blue plumage, and a beaklike structure. Before Alison could get a closer look, it gave a wild, raucous cry and darted away, skimming over the tree tops.

Alison walked slowly, staring around her in enchantment. *I don't know how I got here,* she thought. *But I hope I can stay for a long, long time.*

Now she came upon an area of battered vegetation, treetrunks leaning drunkenly this way and that, gnawed boughs hanging by a bark thread, leaf-stalks bent and broken, leaving a litter of huge leaves upon the forest floor.

Something big had passed this way.

Alison walked more cautiously now. Whatever had knocked those trees askew could most likely flatten her without a moment's hesitation—or notice.

She moved out into a clearing. Ahead was a slope. At its base sat a sulfurous lake fringed by huge black tree ferns and green horsetail reeds. On a slight rise beyond the lake stood two strange creatures: squarely built and reminiscent of rhinoceroses, all pebbly hides and jutting jaws. Their heads, however, fanned out to form large dishlike shields behind their ears, and sprouting along the perimeters of those shield were dagger-sharp horns in a riot of colors. Despite their ferocious appearance the beasts were mildly—almost daintily—cropping up ferns and chewing away like cattle.

Alison took a step toward the scene, but stopped as she felt an odd vibration, something almost subliminal. At first she thought it was just a muscle spasm and waited for it to pass. But her entire leg began quivering, and then the other one joined in.

The trees shivered and groaned. Several winged creatures launched themselves into the sky with forlorn cries.

Boom! Boom!

Something was making quite a commotion. Something big, very big, with long jagged teeth. It wasn't big enough to be a Tyrannosaurus Rex but it was big enough, with a massive block of a head and huge mouth. It stampeded the smaller creatures before it, snapping hungrily at them as they ran for their lives.

The horned animals on the hillside confronted the thing, refusing to give way. They swiped clumsily at its broad chest with their many horns, roaring defiantly.

The predator yielded before them. Obviously those horns were as sharp as they looked.

Alison decided that a tactful withdrawal was in order.

But the beast had noticed her movement and turned its huge head in her direction. Grinning horribly, the thing issued a roar of challenge.

It was ridiculously big, would dwarf an elephant, a giraffe, maybe even a whale. Alison couldn't imagine anything that large moving, let along running. Its massive legs were the size of bridge stanchions.

The dinosaur took a step toward her.

She pulled back.

The dinosaur followed. It was coming after her. *Her.*

She began to run.

Panting, her heart pounding, Alison ran as she had

never run before, until she felt that her lungs would explode. And yet the huge ungainly dinosaur was gaining on her. The ground shook as it got closer. She could smell the beast's disgusting musty reek, hear its wheezing exhalations.

She couldn't outrun it. A shelter, that's what she needed, and quickly.

Those rocks, beyond the trees. There were crannies there that were too small for that beast but they might just fit a human.

The thing roared. It sounded like a freight train bearing down on her. Alison tripped over a vine, stumbled, and fell to the ground.

Get up, a thin, high voice in her head screamed. *Getupgetupgetup!*

Somehow she was on her feet again and moving, running like a mouse before a cat.

She made it to the cover of the trees.

The thing bashed in after her. Trunks cracked and fell, splintered by the force of the beast as it rammed its way between trees.

Alison dashed out into the open and cut over a patch of pebbly ground. Her chest felt like it was on fire. Each breath burned its way in and out of her overtaxed lungs.

Boom! Bam! The beast's steps echoed behind her. She understood now why the dinosaurs had been called Thunder Lizards.

There: the rocks. She might just be able to reach them. Alison sprinted between two boulders, slipped under an overhang, and wedged herself deep in the declivity. Shaking, she crouched in the tiny space with her head in her arms.

Her pursuer circled the boulders but couldn't follow her into the small space between them. Roaring in what Alison took to be frustration, it made a swipe at the entrance to her refuge. But its mouth was too large to fit in the opening.

Slowly, trumpeting its fury, it retreated.

Alison exhaled noisily and rested her head against the cool stone.

A strange scratching noise caught her attention. It reminded her of a mouse working patiently on a piece of drywall. She craned her neck and looked behind her.

Reddish eyes glinted in the darkness. Many reddish eyes.

Not a mouse, no.

A spider, a giant spider, shared her hiding place, clinging to the back wall of the tiny cave. Its fleshy limbs were covered with coarse dark hair and its mandibles snapped open and shut.

"Oh, shit!"

Alison jumped out of the cave.

The spider lunged after her.

Without thinking she kicked at the thing. Her L.L. Bean Tundra-Trekker laceups—guaranteed good to thirty degrees below zero—pinned the spider to the ground, imprinting a good portion of its body with the boot sole's distinctive waffle pattern. Bright green blood spurted out onto the sandy ground. Alison shuddered at the sight.

Oh, God, she thought. *What if I've just killed the ancestor of an entire genus of arachnids?* she wondered. *What if, because of me, a whole species of plant or flower can't be fertilized? I'd get kicked out of the Sierra Club for sure.*

The concern plunged her spirits to the depths of her being. Oh, shameful, horrible, how could she have taken an innocent life like that? She was a danger to the future of the planet. Perhaps she should just allow herself to starve to death—or to be eaten by a predator. At least she'd be contributing to the local ecosystem that way.

That same high thin voice that had screamed inside her brain before now told her to get over it; One dead spider, more or less, wouldn't upset the entire ecobalance of all time to come.

Alison decided to listen to herself. She felt a faint rumbling of her own stomach and realized that she was hungry.

That was a problem. Just what, exactly, was she supposed to eat here in this ancient, unfamiliar place?

She was a vegetarian. She didn't—wouldn't—eat meat, especially lizard meat. She might be able to eat fish—after all, she liked sushi. But did fish exist in these sulfurous seas? And how could she catch them?

For that matter, what about fruit? Nuts? She wasn't certain about berries either, but she hadn't seen any nearby.

Was there anything, anything at all in this vast and untrammeled age that could support the life of one lone mostly-herbivorous member of *Homo sapiens*?

The grumblings in her stomach came faster and louder. Alison searched the area with increased attention.

There, up ahead, were some large trees with leaves that looked oddly familiar. Alison wracked her memory and finally came up with sassafras as a likely possibility. She could make tea from that, if she could find fresh water. And over there, horsetails, she knew, could help strengthen bones and be used on the skin.

She reached out and broke the tassled head off a clump of high grass, and sniffed it experimentally. It had a faint chivelike odor.

In the shade of a tree fern, a creature that was either a rodent the size of a cat or an extremely small horse munched contentedly on a hunk of the stuff, pausing now and then to blink its colorless eyes at her.

How could this grass possibly be poisonous? she thought. Without stopping to consider it further, she took a bite. It was bland, rather tasteless with a slight bitter edge. She swallowed and waited. Her body seemed to tolerate it well.

I'd better get used to this, she thought. *I might be here a long time.*

She felt a momentary chill and her spirits plummeted. Was she actually feeling nostalgia for the twentieth century, with all of its noise, pollution, and senseless bustle? Nonsense. She was in paradise. She would just have to get used to it.

Besides, she needed to lose weight anyway.

The sun, already reddish, was getting low in the sky. Alison knew that she would have to seek shelter for the night.

A hollowed treetrunk seemed like a possible shelter until she saw that it was surrounded by footprints— footprints with clawprints. No thanks.

The open ground was clearly no good. Could she climb a tree and sleep on a limb? What if she fell?

Finally Alison found a small cubbyhole—a crack really—in a stand of greenish rock. It was empty, defensible, and enclosed by several larger rocks that would keep predators away. She checked it carefully for any other residents and found that it was empty. Grateful for small miracles, she crawled into it and fell asleep.

She awoke to howling winds, slashing rain, and deafening peals of thunder. The rest of the night she spent huddled, soaked to the skin, in her would-be shelter.

In the morning, at the first sign of the sun, Alison crept out to find a world transformed.

Giant orange slugs lay all around her, languidly waving their fleshy antennae.

"Oh, gross!" Alison jumped to her feet and got away from the vile things.

She felt something odd at the back of her head and reached her hand up.

A slug had gotten tangled in her hair.

"Aughh!" Gagging, she pulled it out and tossed it into the underbrush. Her hand, where she had touched the thing, burned faintly and then went completely numb.

Giant, poisonous orange slugs. In her hair. *Wonderful.*

When she had finished trembling, she decided to wash the slug residue off her hands and face. The only water source she knew of was the ocherous lake. She trundled cautiously down to the shore and stared at it. The scent was not encouraging.

Despite its swamplike odor, she decided it was safe to wash with, and she scooped some up in her hands to splash over her face.

The yellow water churned and bubbled. Alison jumped backwards.

A beast reared up, streaming water down its knobby reddish hide. It had a frilly baroque crest atop its rounded head that ended in a row of spikes along its ridged back.

Alison moved closer.

The thing saw her and hastily submerged.

Alison waited. The thing didn't reemerge. Didn't it need oxygen? Suddenly it appeared at the far side of the lake, and two others beside it. A family? Did these things have any concept of family?

The water boiled again and something else emerged, six to ten feet long with a giraffelike neck snaking out over the stream, its elongated jaws dipping in now and again to scoop up some morsel of aquatic plant life.

Its eyes flickered redly. Its neck suddenly elongated in a terrifying way. Its open jaws were aimed straight at her face.

Alison backed away quickly.

It's probably a plant-eater, she told herself. *Harmless. An eater of grubs. Probably just had a nice feast on some trilobytelike thing.*

That high thin voice in her head reminded her that it had teeth, and those teeth had been inches away from her nose.

A plant-eater, nothing more. Nevertheless she

moved to higher, safer ground. At least, it seemed safer there.

She shivered in the air. She was getting cold now. A fire would feel good. But how could she make one? Rub two sticks together? She gathered up some likely looking branches and tried to decide if she should strip the bark off of them.

Off, she decided. But it was a tedious process to peel the thin layers free. Finally she had two naked sticks. She began rubbing.

Five minutes later, her hands beginning to ache, she was still rubbing.

After five more minutes she gave up in frustration. Perhaps the sun would dry her off and warm her up.

Her hands were nearly raw form her exertions. Alison was suddenly unexpectedly nostalgic for her spirulina-enriched handcream from BodyStuff. And she was getting sunburned, too. But PABA wouldn't be invented for hundreds of centuries. Thousands, maybe.

To buck up her spirits, Alison gave herself a little lecture: "All of these creatures here have a right to exist. I'm a stranger here, a stranger in a strange land. I've got to learn how to survive here."

Her guts began to churn. Perhaps, she thought, that grass hadn't agreed with her after all.

After several hours of wretched illness, Alison felt somewhat better. The spasms had stopped, and there was nothing left in her stomach to come up. But she was wracked by thirst. She had to find water that was drinkable.

Fresh potable water. Yes. That was her goal now.

She sneezed once, twice, felt an itching in her throat, and thought, miserably, that cold medicine wouldn't be invented for a goodly number of centuries either.

She braided her hair and tied it behind her neck with some plaited fibers of the tall grass.

She got hungrier and thirstier, but still she couldn't

find anything that looked safe to eat or drink. Finally, nearly delirious, she found a fleshy leaf that had tiny, round pink globules dotting its perimeter.

Like pricklypear fruits, she thought. She popped one into her mouth. It gushed a sweet, cool liquid that soothed her fiery throat. She ate another, and another.

Suddenly sleepy, she curled into a ball at the foot of the plant and, oblivious to danger, slipped into a doze.

She was disturbed by what sounded like an altercation between several animals.

Looking up muzzily, she saw a procession of animals approaching. Foremost was a turtlelike creature with an enormous shell. It bowed. "How do you do?" it said. "I'm a Glyptodon. What are you?"

"I'm a mammal," Alison said.

"Do you live under the sea?"

"Uh, not much, anymore."

"Then perhaps you were never introduced to a plesiosaur. . . ."

"Never."

"So you can have no idea what a delightful thing a Glyptodon Quadrille can be." It paused, ducked its head shyly, and said, "I, would be delighted to demonstrate."

"How kind," Alison said. "What sort of dance is your quadrille?"

"Well," it said. "You form a line by the seashore. Two lines. Phobosuchus—mind those teeth!—and Hadrosaurs, Zalambdalestes, on the right, with the Ornithomimus and Hypacrosaurus, Deltatheridium, and related multituberculates, on the left.

"You advance twice . . ." said a rather pushy Phobosuchus, "change partners three times,"

The Glyptodon cut him off. "Throw the Mosauruses—or any other water-dwellers—as far out to sea as you can. And swim after them."

"Swim after them?" Alison said.

"Of course. In you go, turn a somersault, and come back to land. Nothing could be simpler."

"It must be a very pretty dance," Alison said politely.

"Would you like to see a little of it?" asked the Glyptodon.

"Of course."

The Glyptodon turned to the Phobosuchus in great excitement. "Let's do the first figure. We can do it without the Mosauruses, you know." He struck a dramatic pose and began to sing, very badly:

"Will you walk a little faster?" said the lordly Iguanadon.

"There's a Tylosaurus right behind us, and he's treading on my horn.

"See how eagerly the Hesperornis and Glyptodons all advance!

"They are waiting on the shingle—will you come and join the dance?

"Will you, won't you, will you, won't you, will you join the dance?

"Will you, won't you, will you, won't you, won't you join the dance?"

As the Glyptodon sang, the other dinosaurs capered and snorted, some doing a sort of cha-cha, others attempting the prehistoric version of a cakewalk.

Even as Alison watched, she noticed something peculiar. The dinosaurs, all of them, were getting smaller, they were shrinking down to eye-level, and now they were shrinking to toy size. The landscape, too. It took her a moment to fully realize that the dinosaurs were unchanged. She, not they, had done the changing. She had gotten enormous. She was at least sixty feet tall and growing fast, with no end in sight.

But look, she thought. *That tiresome Gorgosaurus has snuck up on that sweet little Glyptodon and is trying to eat him.* What a bully. She would settle his hash. She could sweep him aside like a bowling pin.

Another snatch of song, yodeled by the Gorgosaurus himself, wafted up to her, just barely audible:

"You can really have no notion how delightful it will be,

When they take us up and throw us, like Mosauruses, out to sea!"

It reached hungrily for the Glyptodon.

Alison decided that she would throw *him* out to sea and see how delighted he was by that, the toothy bastard.

But wait, Was he growing? Getting larger?

No.

She was shrinking. Shrinking, getting smaller and smaller, coming down from her lofty height until the Gorgosaurus, grinning with ugly malice, could grasp her with his tiny withered front claws.

He swung her back and forth, singing, "There is another shore you know, upon the other side."

She could smell the blood on his breath, see his horribly sharp teeth. He swung her, to and fro, to and fro—

"Alison? Ally, can you hear me?" The voice was remarkably familiar.

She was being swung, gently, to and fro. At least, so it seemed.

Alison opened her eyes.

Matthew was kneeling, holding her awkwardly, swaying back and forth. The dinosaurs were gone. She was in her own apartment.

She raised her head. "What happened?"

"I dunno. I must have been asleep. There was this crash and the phone started ringing. Then all of the lights went out."

"I think I remember. . . ."

"I realized you weren't in bed so I waited for a minute, but you didn't come back. So I went to look for you and I found you on the floor, out cold."

Alison felt something hard under her left knee and twisted around to look down. It was the telephone receiver.

Suddenly she remembered. A storm. Lightning. A powerful electric shock that had knocked her . . . back in time? No. No, she had been rendered unconscious. She had dreamed the entire thing, her trip to the Mesozoic. Thank Gaia.

"A power surge must have come over the phone line," she said. "I think I was nearly electrocuted."

Matthew hugged her against him, hard. "Do you feel all right?" he whispered.

"I think so."

"The power will probably be out for a while."

Alison felt tears welling up in her eyes. Suddenly she desperately wanted bright lights. Loud music. All the comforts of civilization. Nothing here had sharp teeth or smelled like blood. There was safe water. Shelter from storms. Stoves.

Matthew stared at her, obviously concerned. "Are you sure that you feel all right?"

"Yes, fine."

"Can I get you anything? Do you want a glass of water? Some wine? Milk?"

"What I really want," she said slowly, "is a hot bath. Yes, a long, hot bath. And I'm starved, Matthew. I could eat a Tyrannosaurus."

"I think there's some gluten loaf in the refrigerator."

"No, no. I don't want that. You know what I'd like?" She smiled slowly. "A nice, big pizza covered with anchovies. And hamburger."

"Hamburger? Anchovies?" Matthew's eyes got wider. "How will we get something like that at this hour?"

"Call Domenico's and ask them to deliver. They're open all night."

"Are you *sure* you're okay?"

"Never better." She hugged him tightly. "Oh, Matthew, I never realized before just how wonderful the twentieth century is."

(With apologies to Lewis Carroll)

STOMPING MAD

by *Kristine Kathryn Rusch*

Kristine Kathryn Rusch, Campbell Award winner, and Hugo and Nebula nominee, is the former editor of The Magazine of Fantasy and Science Fiction *and is now a full-time writer.*

She called herself the Martha Stewart of Science Fiction, and she looked the part: homecoming-queen pretty with a touch of maliciousness behind the eyes, a fakely tolerant acceptance of everyone fannish, and an ability to throw the best room party at any given Worldcon in any given year.

So when a body was found in her party suite, the case came to me. Folks in fandom call me the Sam Spade of Science Fiction, but I'm actually more like the Nero Wolfe: a man who prefers good food and good conversation, a man who is huge, both in his appetite and in his education. I don't go out much, except to science fiction conventions (a world in and of themselves) and to dinner with the rare comrade. I surround myself with books, computers, and televisions. I do not have orchids or an Archie Goodwin, but I do possess a sharp eye for detail and a critical understanding of the dark side of human nature.

I have, in the past, solved over a dozen cases, ranging from finding the source of a doomsday virus that threatened to shut down the world's largest fan database to discovering who had stolen the Best Artist Hugo two hours before the award ceremony. My reputation had grown during the last British Fantasy Convention when I—an American—worked with Scotland Yard to recover a diamond worth £1,000,000 that a "big name fan" had forgotten to put in the hotel's safe.

But I had never faced a more convoluted criminal mind until that Friday afternoon at the First Annual Jurassic Parkathon, a media convention held in Anaheim.

The convention was officially called Dinocon I because Crichton's people, or Spielberg's people, or some studio's people wouldn't give permission to use the Jurassic Park name with a non-sanctioned project. I normally don't get involved with a media con, especially one held in Anaheim, but this one had a million-dollar budget and a state-of-the-art computer system, and I simply couldn't resist the challenge.

So I was in Ops with most of the folks running the con when the call came through. Ops, for those of you who've never seen one, is a hotel function room with most of the furniture removed, replaced with tables covered with computer equipment, too many chairs, and tons of print-out paper. Most of the people working Ops look haggard and stressed by the time the convention starts, and many of them are ready to collapse by the time it's over. So we really didn't need to hear some security person, young by the sound of him, on the two-way radio:

"Hey, ah, we got a, um, Situation X, here."

Everyone in Ops snapped to attention. The actual term was a File X—always a pun, everything a pun—and it was only supposed to be used for an extreme emergency.

"Copy that," Doris, a muscular woman the size of Stallone, said. She headed security, and had at every major con I'd ever worked on. Security is important at sf conventions, perhaps *the* most important thing, because these cons, as most of you know, aren't your simple suit-tie-and-briefcase affair. The big conventions have three levels: the fans, most of whom dress in costume (some medieval barbarians, some Captain Kirk, some space aliens); the pros, most of whom write, act, or somehow work in the science fiction field; and the dealers, most of whom sell sf paraphernalia—books, videos, posters, and the ubiquitous Bajoran earrings. Media cons had more earrings, videos, and actors, and fewer books, writers, and intellectual discussions. Behind it all is the con-com, the army of people who run the entire shebang and put out any and all fires along the way. Security deals with most of those: from regular hotel guests who are scared by the werewolf in the elevator to the teenagers who've stayed up all night playing the card game *Magic* and who suddenly think it fun to pull the fire alarm on the second floor.

Never, in my twenty years of fandom, have we gotten a call for this kind emergency, and never have I heard a security person sound so scared.

"It's in room 4708. Can someone come here?" The security kid's voice cracked, confirming my suspicion: He was a volunteer, and he was eighteen at most.

"What's the nature of the emergency?" Doris asked.

"I don't think you want me to describe it on an open channel," the kid said.

"All right, be right there," Doris said, and left.

We mused about the "Situation" X for a moment. "Maybe," Ruth, the con chair, said, "he saw a fur bikini for the first time."

"It's the masquerade tonight," John said behind her, and we all laughed. He probably saw a costume, got scared, and decided to call it in. We'd all had that happen before.

"Or maybe it's pea soup," said Ben, and I, being

most senior on the staff, groaned. I remembered that one, which had now eased into fannish legend. Just after *The Exorcist* came out, some fans in Baltimore held a room party and served pea soup along with the usual potato chips, cheese, and beer. After midnight, when the crowd got really drunk, someone had the brilliant idea of imitating Linda Blair in the famous vomit sequence. Of course, everyone had to do it, and by the time security arrived, a sea of pea soup was running down the corridor like the Blob without the assistance of the special effects people.

"Please, ghod, anything but that," I said.

At that moment, the phone rang. Ruth answered and handed it to me, her tired face filled with confusion and surprise. "It's Doris," she said. "For you."

I slid my chair back and grabbed the phone, feeling as confused as Ruth looked. Doris could have radioed me. That would have been procedure. Maybe something was really up in 4708.

"Yeah?" I said.

"Spade," she said—my fannish friends had called me Spade since I solved the first case almost twelve years before—"you've gotta come up here. Now."

"What's going on?" I asked.

"An absolute disaster," she said, and hung up.

"Why didn't she use the radio?" Ruth asked.

I shrugged. "I guess she didn't want anyone else wandering up to the room." I eased myself out of my special chair, the one that I insist a con-com bring to every convention if they want my services, and with a push of a button, shut down the financial files on Dinocon's main computer. Then I made my way slowly—because I never hurry—to the fourth floor of the main convention hotel.

Dinocon had 8,000 registered attendees, and it was only Friday afternoon. The convention was scheduled to go through Sunday, and another 2,000 people were expected at the door on Saturday. Most of these folks were already crowding the halls, having conversations with friends they hadn't seen for a while, and trying to discover where that night's parties would be held. I squeezed my way through—negotiating packed hall- ways was never easy for a man of my bulk—and made it to the elevator in time to nab the last spot. No one complained, though, as I squooshed people toward the back. Part of that was my con-com badge—regular con attendees knew better than to harass a person in a con-com badge—and part of it was my reputation.

"Hey, Spade!" someone yelled from the back. "You get a piece of that diamond?"

"I don't charge for my services," I said in a gently chiding voice. I made my money years ago as an early employee of Microsoft. I took all my bonuses in stock and then retired at the age of thirty-one, not as rich as Bill Gates, but rich enough.

"He's a gentleman detective," someone else said from the back, and the entire elevator chuckled.

"Imagine," I said as the doors opened on four, "a gentleman—and a scholar."

I got off, but not before I heard more giggling as the doors closed. Fannish humor was not the stuff of stand-up routines, but it was usually full of sweet, if not always socially adept, affection.

The room 4708 was on what had been designated by the hotel as a party floor. On these floors, it was okay to have loud conversation all night, to serve beer in rooms, and to talk in the hallways. Other floors, the nonparty floors, were for people who actually wanted to sleep during the con, something I hadn't done in the last thirteen conventions I had attended.

Photocopied 8"x11" signs were taped onto the wall- paper, most of them announcing bid parties for other conventions. The signs on 4708 looked professionally done on slick glossy paper. They announced the first annual Literature Con to be held in an ancient Hilton an hour outside of Manhattan. I stared at the signs for a moment frowning. Anyone with half a brain knew that most of Dinocon's attendees weren't likely to attend a literature con, especially one held all the way across the country. But the posters had another draw besides their slick appearance.

Food.

Come to our bid party, the sign read, *and dine to your heart's content. Award-winning chocolates, Lucinda's World Famous Chili, and gourmet dishes from the farthest reaches of the Solar System. Come to the party of the convention. You'll talk about it for the next three lifetimes.*

Curiouser and curiouser. Lucinda was Lucinda Danielle Stanhope, also known as the Martha Stewart of Science Fiction. Lucinda hated media cons, thinking that they ruined "pure" science fiction. Pure science fiction, to her, was anything beautifully written with long treatises on science. She thought plot-driven fiction an abomination, and sf in movies and television beneath her notice.

Although she might have changed that opinion, since her current boyfriend, who had started as Science Fiction's answer to James Joyce, had gotten a job as a story consultant for a major studio. ("A guy has to make a buck," he said to me at the last Worldcon. "Besides, since *Independence Day,* everyone is hot for sf properties.")

She might have changed her opinion, but I doubted it.

I had known Lucinda for a long time. She and I had had a run-in at Con Diego (called Con Digeo by its attendees because of all the typos in the program book) several years back and I had tried, unsuccessfully, to avoid her ever since. Our conversations from that day on had consisted of only two words, uttered in passing.

Asshole, she'd say.

Bitch, I'd respond.

I sighed, squared my shoulders, and braced myself for the verbal onslaught as I knocked on the door.

Doris answered. She looked grim and shaky. She motioned me inside and closed the door.

The suite smelled of fresh bread, chili, and something foul: something I had never smelled before and wasn't sure I wanted to smell again. We stood in an entry that led to the bathroom on the left, a main room just before me, and a bedroom on the right. The security kid, so skinny he was skeletal and a shade of green I'd never seen outside of a blacklight poster, leaned against a faux Louis the Fourteenth table. He had a hand over his mouth and was taking deep breaths, as if to calm his stomach.

"What is it?" I asked.

Doris pointed toward the main room. I lumbered in, cautiously, not sure what to expect. A chocolate pterodactyl hung from the ceiling and flower arrangements that looked vaguely prehistoric stood on every end table, along with cute little origami triceratops heads. A human-sized tyrannosaurus rex made entirely out of cheese stood on a circular mirror stand in the center of the room. Crockpots filled with chili bubbled on a table leaning against the wall dividing the main room from the bathroom.

"What—?" I started to ask again, and then I saw her.

She was sprawled on the floor, her left hand resting on the glass double doors leading out to the patio. The doors were closed. I cautiously made my way around the cheese dinosaur and the main table, still in the middle of preparations for the night's party, and stopped near her apron-clad torso.

There was no doubt it was Lucinda. She wore a linen pantsuit beneath that apron, and in her right hand she held an apple partially julienned into a stegosaurus. It was her head that was the problem.

It had been stomped flat, crushed into unrecognizability. More gray matter than I would have expected spattered the teal carpet, mixed with more blood than I had ever seen in my life. I swallowed twice, hard, not wanting to repeat the pea soup episode and contaminate the crime scene. Then I cautiously made my way back into the foyer.

"You call the cops?" I asked.

"No!" Doris said. "They'd shut us down."

"Damn straight they'd shut us down," I said. "We have a murderer on the loose here."

The kid moaned and headed toward the bathroom.

I grabbed his arm. "Uh-uh," I said. "Puke in the public restroom. You don't want to contaminate a crime scene."

"Too late," he mumbled, yanked free, and stumbled into the bathroom, kicking the door closed behind him.

"Poor kid," Doris said. "I'm amazed he has any stomach left."

"Listen, Doris, we gotta call the cops." I covered my hand with my sleeve and reached for the black rotary dial on the faux Louis the Fourteenth.

Doris put her hand on mine, forcing the receiver down. "It's Friday afternoon," she said. "Think about what that means."

Eight thousand attendees, all of whom would demand refunds. The hotel, which would sue for breach of contract. The reputation, which would shut down all Los Angeles area conventions for the foreseeable future, not to mention all media cons, not to mention all conventions held in this hotel chain forever.

Millions of dollars, all because Lucinda made someone stomping mad.

"Can't we at least wait until tomorrow?" Doris asked.

Retching sounds echoed from the bathroom. My stomach rolled in sympathy.

"Tomorrow?" I asked. "Don't you remember the party signs that are up all over this convention. For tonight? In this room?"

"Can't we change them to tomorrow night?" she asked. "Then we won't have to refund, and we won't be in breach of contract."

But we would still have the reputation problem, along with another one. "Tampering with a crime scene is illegal, Doris," I said softly.

"Can't you solve this?" she asked. "Can't you solve this before the cops get here?"

"I've never done a murder investigation before, Doris," I said.

"Please," she asked. "If we can give them a suspect, they won't shut us down, and Ruth and I can handle the p.r. problem, at least long enough to save the con."

"You don't care that a woman has been trampled in her own hotel room?"

Doris crossed her muscular arms. "You really need to ask me that, Spade? I wouldn't be so rude as to ask you."

She could have, though. Because I was upset. Lucinda had her points. She made a mean chocolate soufflé, and she knew more about fannish foods than anyone I had ever met. She also had her moments: The charity auction she ran for literacy at Orycon in the early '90s brought in $5,000 more than usual because she browbeat the attendees into spending more money. And she got them to do it by having them buy signed books.

Sometimes I found myself in complete agreement with Lucinda's arguments.

And that terrified me.

I stared at Doris.

"Will you help us?" she asked.

I sighed. "I won't tamper with the crime scene, and I will meet with the police when they arrive. You will call them from this room, and you will make sure that no one else enters here. You'll also keep the kid from talking to anyone but me. If I happen to solve this thing before the police arrive, fine. But I won't go any farther than that. I'm not going to let some murderer run loose because you want to hold a media con honoring one of the lamest movies of all time."

"The special effects were cool." The kid had opened the door to the bathroom. He was now chalk white.

"But the plot sucked," I said. Then I nodded at Doris. "Call. I'm going to snoop a bit. And don't leave until I tell you to. Got that?"

She nodded and reached for the phone. I stopped her. "Cover your hands with your sleeves. And don't touch anything besides that receiver."

She glared at me, but followed my instructions. I prowled into the bedroom, deciding to talk to the kid after his breath cleared up.

Lucinda, not surprisingly, was a neat freak. She had arrived and unpacked, her clothing hanging on her hangers in the walk-in closet. Each item was separated by tissue paper, and her hats were in boxes on the shelf above. Her shoes were lined up below in neat little rows beneath the matching clothes. She had two wigs on the dressing table, one studded with little plastic dinosaurs—the clear, brightly colored kind that bartenders used to put in drinks in the mid-sixties. A silver lamé dress hung from the plant hook in the ceiling. Lucinda had planned to go all out on this party, and it surprised me. She had to be doing a favor for someone. Media cons were beneath her—and while she enjoyed fannish cooking, she hated fannish clothing.

I got back into the foyer as Doris hung up the phone. "I didn't tell them it was a murder," she said.

I mentally shook my head. That would be her problem when the cops arrived. It would be better for all of us if I had some idea what had happened.

"Okay, kid," I said to the security boy, "come into my office and talk to me. And don't touch anything."

The kid's color still hadn't returned. He followed me into Lucinda's bedroom and started to close the door.

"Don't touch," I said. We went deep into the bowels of the room, and stopped near the bed. I knew that Doris would have trouble hearing us from this spot because I had had trouble hearing her on the phone.

"What's your name?" I asked.

"Chad," he said. I raised a single eyebrow, Spock-like. I had never met a kid who worked con security named Chad. Or at least, a kid who worked con security who would admit to being named Chad.

"Okay," I said, "I need to know: What made you come to this room in the first place?"

He wiped his mouth with the back of his hand. That stomach of his was amazingly weak. "I was by the flyer table—that was my post—when these fans came down the stairs and told me they'd heard a huge pounding on the fourth floor. They took me to their room on three and I heard it too, like something really heavy was going to crash through the floor. Then I came up here. The door was open, and I let myself in. It was really quiet. I called out to see if anyone was here, and then I saw the food. I went in to grab a snack and—"

He burped, then covered his mouth, swallowing hard. "Sorry," he said.

"It's all right," I said. "Do you know who these fans were?"

"Not by name," he said. "But they have the room below this one."

And were probably preparing for another party since the room below also had to be a suite. I rubbed my chin in proper detective fashion. I had a conundrum. I need to talk to those fans, but I didn't want to leave Doris alone in the room. Nor did I want anyone else to know what had happened to Lucinda.

Then I realized it didn't matter. Doris had been in the room without me already. I had investigated, and I knew how things looked. I had seen everything but the bathroom, and that could be remedied.

I took the kid back to the foyer. "Wait here," I said and peered into the bathroom. The kid had already contaminated the crime scene—several times—but there didn't seem to be much to see. The bathtub was still maid-spotless and the counter had Lucinda's makeup and nothing else. The toilet seat was up, one of the towels was askew, and otherwise everything looked fine. It didn't even smell as bad as I thought it would.

"Okay," I said as I emerged. "Let's find those fans. You wait here, Doris, and don't touch anything."

"Don't worry," she said, looking faintly annoyed at the suggestion.

The kid and I slipped into the hallway. The con was filling up. Two women wearing belly dancer skirts and midriff tops conversed about the proper navel jewel. Five teenage boys compared tattoos. Three grown men, in Klingon boots and armor, adjusted each other's forehead ridges.

The kid and I took the stairs.

The third floor was filled with people in dinosaur costumes. Some were cheap Halloween masks, while others were full-bore papermaché or plastic. The costumes looked heavy, they looked hot, and they smelled of glue. I stared at them, mostly at the feet, wondering what kind of pressure a person would need to drive those hard plastic soles through a skull and crush it.

Then we were in front of 3708. The kid knocked on the door. His hand was shaking.

It was opened by a slender woman whose black hair formed perfect Louisa May Alcott ringlets around her face. She wore a lavender satin shirt with purple satin pants, and the outfit somehow looked perfect on her. Her convention badge was clipped to a tiny piece of cardboard inside her shirt's high pocket, so as not to ruin the satin.

"Hi," she said, looking a bit confused.

"Security," the kid said, glancing at me. "Remember? You asked about the big stomping?"

"Oh, yeah." She was staring at me. Her eyes were lavender, like the shirt. I'd never seen eyes like that in person before. Only in photographs of Elizabeth Taylor. "Who're you?"

"I'm from Ops," I said. "Mind if we come in?"

"Why?" She was asking the kid.

"Because when I went upstairs," he said, "I found—"

I kicked him. He shut up.

"He found that he had a few more questions to ask you," I said. "Mind if we come in."

"No," she said. "I guess not."

She got out of our way, and we stepped into the foyer. It exactly matched the suite above, only here the carpet was brown. Two men sat in the suite's living room. They looked vaguely familiar. They stood as they saw us come in.

"Something wrong?" the first one asked.

He was tall and muscular—that fakey kind of muscles that comes from too much health club and too much low-fat food. His shirt was unbuttoned below the navel, revealing a washboard stomach, and his bare feet looked manicured. His companion wore ripped jeans and a *Star Trek* T-shirt, but unless I missed my guess, his hair had been permed.

Interesting look, for fans. It looked a little too Hollywood, a little too put together, for my tastes. Maybe these folks were slumming.

"You guys with the convention?" I asked.

"What's this all about?" T-Shirt asked. He had his hands on his hips. Same fakey muscles, and he didn't look as if he had ever cracked a book. But, I reminded myself, this was a media con. Folks here didn't have to crack books, even though most of them did.

"Of course we're with the convention," the woman said, and tugged gently on her badge as if to prove it.

"What's your interest?" I asked. "Filking?"

"Excuse me," Manicured asked. His face flamed and he looked insulted.

"Fill-king," the kid said, "not fucking."

Interesting comment, I thought, but I didn't look at

him. "Pipe down, Chad," I said. "What are you guys doing at the con?"

"Anyone can come," the woman said, apparently realizing that my questions had more importance than the guys were giving them credit for. "Right?"

"Of course," I said, "but usually people have special reasons for attending. What are yours?"

"We like dinosaurs," T-Shirt said.

"Fascinating," I said in my best Spock voice. No one laughed, even though most fans usually did. My best Spock voice was pretty damn good. "So what's your favorite dinosaur? A plugosaurus or a brontodacdyl?"

"All of 'em," T-Shirt said.

"Hmmm," I said. "Hear you had some noise problems."

"Yeah, man, sounded like weird pounding upstairs," Manicured said. "Like someone was trying to punch a hole in the floor."

"Sounds serious," I said. "Will someone move that chair over here?" I pointed to a square wooden chair that seemed to be the sturdiest thing in the room. T-Shirt moved the chair to the place I pointed to, right next to the balcony doors.

"Spot me, Chad, will you?" I asked as I climbed up.

"Ah, um, ah, you might want me to do that," he said.

"No need," I said, even though the chair was groaning under my weight. I reached up and removed the ceiling panel. Gobs of dust and dirt rained on me, and I had to clear a spider web, but after that I had a pretty good glimpse of the space between the ceiling and the floor above.

"Looks normal," I said, and to my surprise, it did. I put the tile back. "You guys are safe."

"That's it?" the woman asked. "That's all? It sounded wretched up there."

"It was," Chad said. I braced myself on his shoulder and squeezed as I got down. It shut him up again.

"That's it," I said cheerfully. "I hope you have a good con."

"Ah, thanks," T-Shirt said. He was frowning at me.

The kid and I left. The dino costumes flooded the hall. The newer ones looked even more realistic than the earlier ones. Especially the Spielbergian velociraptors. All terrifyingly icky except for the guy wearing blue jeans and a tie-dyed brontosaurus head. And the inevitable tot dressed as Barney.

One glance at the elevator told me we weren't going back to the fourth floor that way. Too crowded. It also meant the cops wouldn't come up very quickly when they arrived.

"Where to now?" the kid asked.

I didn't answer. I was feeling pretty annoyed with him. Pretty annoyed with the whole thing, really. I wanted to get back to my Ops computer with its lovely numbers and forget I had ever gotten involved with this detecting business.

Even if I was good at it.

We took the stairs and I was puffing by the time we reached the fourth floor. I hadn't had this much exercise in weeks. And I was moving faster than I liked.

Most of the dino costumes were on the third floor. Regular con-goers littered the fourth. None of them looked like the three-ringers downstairs.

I "shave-and-a-haircut" knocked on 4708. Doris answered immediately. "What took you so long?"

I didn't answer. As I came in, I asked, "Did Lucinda know I was coming to Dinocon?"

"How should I know?" Doris asked.

I glared at her.

She sighed, exasperated. "Probably. If she was looking. You would have been hard to miss since your name was in the con-com listing in all the progress reports. Why?"

I had my suspicions. I made my way back into the suite's main room.

"Hey!" the kid said. "What're you doing?"

His voice had gotten increasingly shrill. I ignored him. I made my way to the body, and, just as I remembered, the floor didn't sag under my considerable weight.

I knelt beside the body. The gray matter and blood were drying in a perfect arch.

"Hey!" the kid yelled. "You said no tampering."

"Grab him, Doris," I said through my teeth. He was getting on my nerves. This whole thing was.

I grabbed the right wrist, dislodging the julienned stegosaurus, and felt—plastic. Soft, lifelike, fake plastic.

"Bitch," I mumbled. I half expected the crushed dummy to mumble "asshole" in return. Then, louder, I said, "Doris, did you call 911?"

She didn't answer. I turned. She was frowning at me. "Doris?"

She flushed. "No," she said. "I called the regular line. I wanted to give you as much time as possible."

Her caution had worked to our advantage. "Call and cancel," I said. "Then break that kid's arm if he doesn't tell you where Lucinda is."

"Lucinda—!"

"Just do it." First time I'd ever understood the sense of a Nike ad.

She twisted the kid's arm up behind his back. Within seconds, he was screaming, "Executive suite! Executive suite!"

I got up and walked over to him. "Key," I said.

He handed me a specially marked executive floor key. "Come on, Doris," I said. "Keep a good grip on this kid and commandeer us an elevator."

She did exactly as she was told.

On the way up, I explained the whole thing, and the kid wisely said nothing, confirming all my suspicions. I was trying to contain my anger, because this thing had just become personal.

And to think I would have mourned the bitch if that had truly been her on the floor below.

You see, the plan was simple: The execution was hard. Lucky for Lucinda that her boyfriend had his new job in Hollywood and even luckier for her that most special effects guys are also sf nerds. Ironic that she needed media people to tamper with a media con. But Lucinda had always been a bit dim when it came to irony.

And, apparently, detail, at least non–food-related detail.

First there was the fannish clothing. No matter what kind of theme party Lucinda gave, she never, ever dressed in fannish clothes. No wigs decorated with little plastic dinosaurs, no silver lamé dress. She might have consented to work a media con, but she would never have given up her stylishly proper clothing. She planned the perfect media party, all right, down to the clothes, forgetting that she would never, ever wear those clothes because, of course, she didn't plan to.

But that wasn't the only detail that bothered me. The three "fans" on the floor below had been extras in a straight-to-video sf release that I'd been watching at home a few nights before the con. I would have made them as non-skiffy folk anyway. All science fiction fans—media and lit alike—know the difference between a real dinosaur and a made-up one.

And then there was Chad, clearly another actor for hire. Except he overdid the vomit bit, and the bathroom smelled as if the maid had just left. Lucinda probably hadn't counted on the strength of my sniffer.

But she had counted on me. In fact, I had been the center of her plan. Without me, it wouldn't have worked. She knew that I knew better than to tamper with a crime scene, no matter how great the temptation. She knew that I had a healthy respect for the authorities and that I would insist on cops being present.

And she knew that the cops would see this for the hoax it was. She would appear at the right moment, blame the convention for overreacting to her little party, piss off the cops just enough to get the whole con shut down. The hotel chain would have been angry, the attendees would have demanded refunds, and the whole cascade effect that Doris had foreseen when she first saw that body would have occurred. Media cons, not just in LA, but all over the country would have suffered, and possibly died.

Lucinda's little stunt would have caused more damage than the murder. It was sabotage, served cold.

When we reached the executive suite, Doris made the kid open the door. Lucinda saw him, stood up, and cooed. She was dressed for her act in a white sheath that accented her lightly tanned skin and golden hair.

When she saw us, her eyes widened.

"You bitch," Doris said, blowing my line and letting go of the kid. He started to back away, but I shoved him forward and closed the door behind us.

"Back off, Doris," I said. "She's mine. There won't be any cops, Lucinda. You won't ruin this convention."

"I'm going to see that you're banned from cons forever. I'm going to make sure that your name is taken out of the Fannish Directory. I'm going to—"

"For what? For a little party I planned to throw for some friends?" Lucinda asked. "Don't you think it rather cute? I do."

"You—"

Doris lunged for her, and I caught her, staggering a bit under her power. The kid bee-lined for the bathroom, fear making his intentions real this time.

"Go to Ops," I said to Doris. "Tell them everything is fine. I can take it from here."

"I'm going to get you," Doris said, but she listened to me. She knew as well as I did that strange things happened at sf conventions, and that there was no proving malicious intent here.

Knowing about it was something else.

"Misunderstandings are so tragic, Doris," Lucinda said, blinking her blue eyes guilelessly.

Doris growled and disappeared out the door. I stood in front of Lucinda. "Media cons aren't your style."

She smiled. It was sweet as rhubarb pie. "They're not yours either."

"I don't see anything wrong with people having fun. I'm a bit more open-minded than you, Lucinda. I believe people can enjoy reading and watching movies. I believe there's room in fandom for both."

"You're so naive," she said. "These cons are so anti-literature. They appeal only to the ignorant. People who don't understand real science, or real science fiction."

"I think people who think they guard pure science fiction may not understand real science or real science fiction either," I said pointedly.

"Good god," she said, "a philosophical discussion when I have a party to finish."

"It seems strange to me that you'd put on a party here, Lucinda."

She shrugged. "I thought I'd give these people the opportunity to come to a lit-con and see what they were missing."

"So kind of you," I said.

She smoothed her dress. "We all do what we can in the circumstances provided."

At that moment, I almost told her what tripped her up. I almost told her that it was her lack of scientific knowledge, her lack of understanding of forensic science that had destroyed her. First, the splatter had been too pretty, too uniform. Second, and more importantly, the type of force it took to stomp out someone's brains would have caused damage to the plywood floor. Damage someone of my weight would have felt in loose boards or groaning wood.

But I didn't. Why give her the ammunition? She might try again someday.

"Am I excused?" she asked brightly.

"There is no excuse for you, Lucinda," I said in my best fannish manner, and moved out of her way.

The bane of the nonlicensed investigator is that we have no real authority. We can't arrest. Worse yet, people with authority often look down their noses at us.

So we are forced to take some matters into our own hands.

Lucinda, misguided as she was, was clever. Who could prove that the panic the kid, Doris, and I felt was anything more than a product of our own imaginations? She would say that she had planned a perfect party, and we had nearly ruined it.

In fact, that night, she did carry off the party with full aplomb. She did change the victim from her clone to that of a lawyer, in keeping with *Jurassic Park* (the movie) tradition, and she did pour ice in the bathtub, but those were the only changes she made. The party was the hit of the convention, and became the talk of sf—both media- and literature-oriented—for years to come. It was, in its own way, the Woodstock of science fiction. Eventually everyone who was anyone claimed they had been there, even if they had been clear across the country at the time.

Everyone who was anyone except me.

You see, I was in Ops, checking the computer records. We had an unexplained power failure just as I was transferring Lucinda's credit card information from her con file into an active file so that we could bill her account. Unfortunately, the accident caused blips in her credit record that cascaded down the system and destroyed her credit rating for the next year. She had to defend and deny and repair, all of which took time away from cons and con parties, and fandom.

And somehow she got it in her pretty little head that this would happen again if she ever attempted to sabotage—even accidentally—a major convention again.

Misunderstandings are so tragic.

But we all do what we can in the circumstances provided.

ARBUTHNOT
by Malcolm Beckett

This is Malcolm Beckett's seventh professional sale.

Twice-dead animals smell just as rotten as any others. The only thing that was special about Arbuthnot, now, was the skin that stretched the length of the corridor and wrapped seventeen layers thick around the skinny drum that ran all the way from the old Captain's cabin to the airlock. Theory said that, after Arbuthnot was separated from all this epidermis, the offal (*"Good* word!" muttered Eratosthenes) would slide right out the opened lock, and then, so would the skin, on its plastic drum, to be preserved for a second time in the great out-of-doors along with the ten months' feed that the gigantic rest-of-Arbuthnot would make. But this out-of-doors had no air at all in it.

Theory was right—it was his theory, after all—but both doors would have to be open for at least several minutes, in order to get the long skin outside intact. How the *hell* was he going to accomplish that?

Eratosthenes slipped sideways in a mound of intestine mixed with blood and a few other fluids that he didn't really want to name or acknowledge. His left foot hit the stainless steel of the passageway wall, and he sighed in relief, though a little prematurely. The right foot had been little more secure than the left, and now, it, too began to slide. He tried a laugh, as he went down, and thought he had got away with nothing but a bruise, but he was going to have to take it a lot easier. If he hurt himself badly, he might as well just push himself out the door along with Arbuthnot—he would probably be just as dead, though still breathing.

There was no one else on board. Eratosthenes had fired his last employee eighteen months before, off Deimos Station—for teasing Arbuthnot, as it happened—and there was no one left to rescue an injured Eratosthenes Gwynthorpe.

The corridor swam a little as he rose, but nothing was broken. He would have known if anything was broken. He would have been a lot happier if he'd been able to use the gravitators, but then the air system would have been overloaded with the fluids and odors from his old friend.

"Arbuthnot, believe me, I wouldn't be doing this if I didn't really need the money." And the meat. But he didn't say that.

He had always sworn that Arbuthnot was just as important as he was; that the huge reptile would get the same treatment as would Eratosthenes himself, should he be the first to die.

He had never mentioned aloud that he was pretty sure Arbuthnot would eat him, if the circumstances should permit. Arbuthnot would eat anything.

He tripped again, and caught himself.

"Damn! My *shoe!*"

A year ago, he had lost the right of a pair of Port Glenn walking shoes. Arbuthnot had just looked innocent. Or shocked. One or the other.

"Damn overblown walrus. You are my *shoe*. What kind of friend was that, Arbuthnot? Why just the one? You wanted me to look high and low, always hoping I might not have to cut off the other foot to get my money's worth out of that pair—*pair*, Arbuthnot!— *pair* of expensive Martian shoes? I swear, Arbuthnot, you knew. . . ."

But Arbuthnot hadn't known. Arbuthnot had just been being Arbuthnot—a normal, undistinguished plesiosaur.

GWYNTHORPE'S SHOWS! it said on the outside of the ship. To the best of Eratosthenes' knowledge, no one had ever read the sign on the outside of the battered *Olduvai*. In fact, during a gig near Titan, one old man, having missed it altogether, had asked him was that not a strange sort of name, and what was the nationality of his wife.

He chuckled again, and began looping the already deteriorating esophagus about his arm. No good. It was too strong to loop small enough to carry comfortably. Why had he wanted the esophagus, anyway? It wasn't in any way remarkable. Except for its length. Oh, that was it! He stumbled again, but caught himself. To pretend that this was the trachea and voicebox of the famous singing dinosaur. To have two to exhibit. Every little bit helps.

Olduvai Gwynthorpe, indeed. What a name to burden a woman with. And who, named Olduvai, would have married a man named Eratosthenes Gwynthorpe, anyway?

Arbuthnot had sung his way through four planets and six moons and asteroids. He had, at one time, been the most famous singing creature in the Solar System. For a quarter of an hour, anyway, during the news.

Absently, he reached out to pat Arbuthnot. Then, remembering, found himself thrown again into a depression. Grief, yes, and fear, too. What would become of the show, and of him, without a plesiosaur to sing for their supper?

It was Eratosthenes who had discovered that plesiosaurs sang. Others had known that they could make sounds, of course. It had even been speculated that they would sound a little like big, fat, giant birds, but it had taken Eratosthenes Gwynthorpe to find out the truth.

And the truth was that the plesiosaurs—but *not* the shorter-necked pliosaurs—had been the superparrots of the entire lifetime of the Earth.

Well, until Humanity and lipsynch came along. He chuckled again. For no lipsyncher in the short, awful history of kareoke had ever made a noise. And no parrot—*"And no human being, dammit!"*—had ever sung as sweet as Arbuthnot.

The beast had been stupid. He could admit that, now. Dumb as a stump, his dear old Dad would have said, and only half as sharp. But oh, he could sing!

He had acquired Arbuthnot in the usual way.

In those days, and perhaps again, soon, he had hung around the "Deliveries" entrances to the gene labs a lot. Not for anything specific, but just because, and just because it had paid off three times in the past. Eratosthenes still had the other three beasts.

Sure enough, after only a week and a half of hanging about, the back door of the place—*Baylor Pale-ontological Revivification Research Establishment,* it had said, on the wall that faced Houston—had rolled up, taking about a quarter of an hour to do it, he had thought. (But then, he had been very excited.) And out had rolled the expected little cart, this one a con-verted forklift, dragging the usual long rope, which was pulling gently at the neck of—a living plesiosaur.

Only the ten generations of carnies in his blood had prevented him from screaming with joy and racing about the compound of the place with his hat in his hand and a prayer on his lips.

Instead, he had waited for the man with the gun. (*Pardon,* he thought—*pardon me—weapon. Not gun.*)

Sure enough, within five minutes, out he came. This one was wearing a hat, and squinting up at the Moon, just because the Sun was not out at night, as if he were a big-game hunter. Some hunter. He would stalk his prey one yard and blow off its head with a hundred rounds of automatic fire.

Eratosthenes went into his act.

"Say! Wassat?" The trick was not to appear too dumb, and not to appear too drunk, but just a little of each.

"Who's there?" And, as usual, the shooter raised his gun a little, though he probably didn't really shoot intruders to hamburger with that thing.

"Just me." (Small hic.) "'What's that,' I said?" He raised his voice a tad toward the end of the second sentence. Might as well get them afraid he'd alert the neighbors. The gene people did not like the neighbors to know just when they shot an experiment to death in their courtyard. The gun would be muffled somehow, when the time came.

The plesiosaur, out of luck, out of water, and dying already, whipped its head around, having heard Eratosthenes.

Just a minute . . . Arbuthnot. Be right with you. He always named them on the spot, and as soon as he knew their names.

He was convinced that most animals were telepathic. This one quieted. Others had not. No proof, then, but Eratosthenes believed.

"Shut up, you'll wake the neighborhood!" somebody hissed. "Look, what do you *want?*"

"Oh, I was passing. Saw something strange when I stopped for a piss." It never hurt to be just a little shocking. Then they paid less attention to anything but the shocking thing about you. "Tell me what it is and I'll finish up and go." He turned toward the fence, and reached for his fly.

"Plesiosaur. It's a plesiosaur," said a young woman at the edge of the small crowd of onlookers.

The man with the gun was looking upward at the head, swinging druggedly at the top of the—*oh, wonderful!*—neck. "My God . . ." he muttered.

"What's wrong, Doctor?" asked Eratosthenes.

"Oh, nothing. Just . . . there's a hell of a lot of it, out here."

"Yeah, there is. Hey, you ain't going to waste it all, are you?"

"What do you mean?"

"Well . . . a hundred dogs could eat well for a year on that thing. That . . . *plastisaur*."

"Plesiosaur. No, no, we mustn't make a profit. We'll take care of it."

"Oh? How? Thassa lotta tons, Doc!" Generally speaking, Doctors of the sciences do not like the nickname "Doc." He wanted this one irritated enough to be off base, but not enough to act too smart.

Not for another minute, anyway.

"Yeah . . . lot of tons. Ms. Smitherman, how far is it to the ocean, again? And how big is the vehicle you've got?"

"Far. Not big enough," said a pleasant female voice. It sounded respectful, but not necessarily of the Doc.

"Hey, *I* know!" said Eratosthenes, excitedly, as if he had just had a wonderful idea. As slightly-drunken-but-intelligent-men-with-huge-trucks-who-happen-to-be-stopped-where-you're-about-to-kill-your-pleiosaur usually do.

"What?" asked the Doc, not thinking at all. "If it's any good . . . well, *hell,* anything's got to be better than carting this around the city all night in a tiny truck. And how are we going to get it *in?*"

Eratosthenes had found that genetic revivifiers had rarely considered reality quite enough. Mostly, they thought about flies and amber—small things that one could carry in a pocket. But flies in amber give rise to bigger things. . . .

"Why don't *I* cart it away for you? I'll take care of the body. Don't worry about that! Hey, why not? I'm in the animal-feeding business!"

And so he was, sort of, and so it went.

Finally; "All right, all right, just show me your animal handling license. . . ."

Eratosthenes did, and, if the man was surprised that it was endorsed at the breeder-level for all classes of animals, and, in fact, was probably a higher-grade license than his own, he said nothing.

"And how are *you* going to carry this thing away? And how will you carry it to whatever you carry it in?" He sounded as if he wanted to add, "Smarty-pants!"

Eratosthenes just grinned. He had been handed a hundred dollar bill to carry away the "animal feed," and he was content. He never cared how much, just so long as it was he who was paid, and not the other way 'round. He just pointed upward.

He had already triggered the tender's computer, and she was settling in on auto. Right in the middle of the compound.

"In that."

"*Hey!* I thought this was . . ."

"Yeah, I know. You thought you were doing something illegal with the experiment that got too big for the project budget to feed anymore."

"Well . . . yes."

He grinned, and called the plesiosaur.

There are some people in every age who can call a strange, drug-drunk plesiosaur from across a wide compound in the dark of a wet Houston summer night and have some expectation that the animal will respond. Eratosthenes Gwynthorpe was one of a minuscule number at the peak of *that* group who can name an animal, call the name, and turn away, confident that, if it is not too injured, it will follow.

"Ar*buth*not!" he called softly, and walked to his ship's tender, the plesiosaur lurching happily after him. The night was getting wetter, and Arbuthnot smelled the temperature-controlled transport-tank inside the ship.

A year and a half later, a small party turned out for

Arbuthnot's first show. Usually, Eratosthenes didn't bother with the people who had supplied his animals. Enough that they had revived the beasts' DNA from the dead—never mind the mistreatment the beasts sometimes got.

But Arbuthnot had been treated well right up to his scheduled execution. So the Doc and assistants were present when Eratosthenes pulled him out onto the stage that was also the tender's loading-ramp, using a small airport tug.

"Looks as if we might have missed out on a good deal," opined the Doc to one of them.

Just then, Eratosthenes quieted the crowd, and raised a hand before Arbuthnot.

"What's it going to do? Sing?" asked the Doc.

Eratosthenes nodded, and grinned.

Arbuthnot opened his mouth, and raised the serpent-neck, pointing his face to the Permian sky he had never seen, and did what he had been trained, over eighteen months, to do.

"Just for you, Doc," said Eratosthenes.

Arbuthnot's voice was a clear baritone bell across the valley where Eratosthenes had decreed he make his debut. His diction left a little to the imagination, once in a while, but this . . . this was a classy parrot. He rolled his tones from wall to wall of the valley, and the song, always rich, gained from the power and warmth of the perfect voice that sang it.

"I'll take you home again . . . Kathleen . . ."

Never mind that he only knew three songs; Arbuthnot had had fifteen encores, that first night. Later, when the people from La Scala came to see for themselves . . .

Eratosthenes stuffed the last of the internal organs into the air lock, cycled it for the last time, and watched the autosluice begin to shower the corridor, where he had begun, seven hours before. He was about done. Whatever had killed Arbuthnot after eighteen years, it was not affecting him, and probably couldn't live in humans.

He was done.

He flipped a toggle at the side of the air lock hatch, and muttered instructions. Sound filled the corridor with the presence that had stunned and won worlds. The last of Arbuthnot that would not go into making a stuffed image of him puffed out the side of the huge ship. The hide, which would, was safely out of sight, stowed in a long locker that had originally been the travel-home of a Martian serpent-worm who could hibernate in vacuum for sixteen months.

Eratosthenes stood very still, and tried to pretend that it was sweat that was rolling down his face. He listened, for a second, in the stillness of the suddenly silent vessel, to the water lapping gently in the gigantic empty tank that he had made long ago for his friend.

And watched Arbuthnot drift away, with strains of song floating after him.

"... *across the ocean far and wide.* ..."

WALKABOUT ENCOUNTER
by Kent Brewster

Kent Brewster is the publisher of Speculations, *a magazine aimed at helping hopeful science fiction writers.*

After three hands of days working his cautious way south along the narrow strip of beach dividing the jungle from the sea, Nush Kankits had come to believe that surviving Egg—and quickening a few of his own, as a result—might be possible after all.

Each evening saw the Steering Star higher into the sky; each morning brought a new taste of fresh, tiny game from the reefs and rocks along the way. Fish, crab, and rock-hugging delicacies kept him fed well enough, if blandly. He wasn't tempted to poke his snout into the bush in search of something meatier, not until he found the strange tracks in the sand.

Someone was wearing shoes on Egg's sacred beach.

Blunt, round-toed shoes, to be exact, with a curious repeating pattern carved into the bottom of each, almost as if the wearer was proud to announce his presence. At first they seemed huge against his own dainty four-toed impressions, twice as long and half again as wide.

But no, they were flat and shallow. And whatever

made them had a plodding stride, clearly shorter than his own.

Here the tracks veered under the tide's most recent sweep, there they stopped at a tossed-apart pile of seaweed, and further along they looped back into the forest, seemingly unaware or uncaring of any danger. Nush could think of only a few possibilities: The track-maker carried heavy weapons, or had armed friends waiting somewhere in the bush. Or both.

Any answer was unacceptable. Nush, like untold generations of seekers before him, had been stripped bare and put ashore, to live or die on his own. The thought that someone was cheating—and passing his criminal seed along to a new generation—sent a shiver down the length of him from crest to tail. Dropping his trail-rack, a crude thing lashed together of driftwood and ill-tanned hides, he unlimbered his blowgun and counted available darts. Six were ready, a bare hand and a half, all tipped with shellfish toxins that—in theory—would bring down a Big One many times his weight.

Not really believing that he'd made the decision so quickly, Nush edged into the hip-high creepers, looking for further evidence of intrusion. His scalp tightened, bringing his crest fully erect over each ear-hole and focusing the sounds of the jungle—peeps, warbles, and groans, punctuated with the occasional far-off grumble or crash of something Big moving about—to an almost painful clarity.

There. Off to the right, down a thinly-marked game trail. Something sounded . . . wrong. Nush detected a constant buzz at the extreme low range of audibility, feeling it more in his gullet than his head. And—yes. Broken stems marked the way, along with another oblong track in the mud.

The jungle seemed to flow around and squeeze itself shut behind him; after a few cautious paces down the trail, he turned to look back and could see no sign that he was anywhere near its edge. Only the trail—over downed trees and through hacked-apart curtains of viny underbrush—gave him any reason to continue. The trail, and the sound, a crackling hum that made his skin crawl. No insect-hive or waterfall made a noise like that. It had to be machinery, corrupting the carefully preserved heart of Egg by its very presence.

The clearing was perfectly round, a magic circle where the jungle was simply . . . not. In a flash of insight Nush saw that it had to have been created in an instant; the lopped-off halves of trees and severed branches leaned in around its edges, masking the fact that its surface—hard and unnaturally dry—was a half-step higher than the ground around it.

On the platform was a pair of brightly colored tents—one large, one small—and the bled-out carcasses of three small-to-medium-sized Big Ones. A black-wheeled vehicle bigger than either tent had a tangle of chains ending in bloody loops at one end; the gap in the jungle at the other side of the clearing looked to be just about the right size for it.

In the center of the circle squatted a four-legged machine, the source of the vibration that threatened to shake Nush loose from his teeth. And over the machine's complicated head—a fist-sized knot of metal that Nush's eyes refused to bring into focus—hung a miracle.

Something had captured blue-white fire the color of summer lightning, bent it into a ring big enough to drive a longneck through, and hung it in midair, motionless except for tiny, fitful sparks and flares around its edges. A long metal ramp wide enough for the four-wheeled vechicle stuck through the hole and touched the ground; it crawled with eerie blue sparks where it touched the surface of the discontinuity.

And through the hole in the sky, through a distorting ripple like clear water, was visible—

—someplace else.

The sky was flat and light blue, the ground gray

and hard. The forest was entirely absent. The other place was desert, studded with an occasional dark spiky-looking thing that might have been a tree.

All senses at full alert—the machine emitted a burned gassy smell that made his head swim, while the tips of his toes tingled from the vibration of the ground against his claws—Nush took three cautious steps into the circle. Readying his blowgun, he moved towards the cover of the nearest Big One, an ancient threehorn whose spiked rill towered over his head even in death's stillness. Some sort of heavy, fast-repeating weapon had made a neat line of fist-sized holes across its leathery flank; one had let the beast's heart-blood out in a sudden fountain, judging from the size of the stain.

And that was all. No other bite or scratch marred the Big One's corpse. The other two—a longneck calf almost the size of the threehorn and a half-grown Eater that made Nush shudder even in death—bore similar marks: grievous damage, sloppily applied, to the widest, easiest target.

The Eater seemed to have survived several passes of the terror-weapon. Momentarily paralyzed by his thinking-half, Nush tried to visualize its final charge. It must have been facing away in the beginning, crouched over carrion, perhaps, for the series that stitched its flanks and tail. And here two wound-lines intersected with a particularly deep hole at one of its shoulders, entirely removing an arm—

—*crack!*

Nush jumped straight up, a bodylength or more above the ground. Time slowed to a crawl as he reached the apex of his leap and the other part of his being took over. He had more than enough time to twist in midair, sight a brown blur that might have been his assailant, and put a dart into flight before he landed. And rolled right—

—*crakka-crack! Crakka-crakka-crakka-crack!*

—behind the threehorn's corpse, which shuddered with the impact of every shot.

Then came silence, and strange groaning noises. Time returned to its normal pace; in midstream the noises jumped to a much higher pitch, the sounds of animals fighting. Risking his life, Nush dropped to the ground and cautiously peered through the tiny, dark hole formed by the hook of the threehorn's beak and the ground.

Three figures stood at the edge of the clearing, pulling the long stick-shaped noise-weapon back and forth between them. A fourth spasmed on its back, the stub end of Nush's dart quivering in what had to be its neck.

Nush's crest stiffened once more. Everything about them, head to foot, was wrong.

Nush's people came in a wide range of shapes and colors; none but the deathly ill, however, was ever that pale. Even in the great cities none wore so many clothes; these creatures were covered from neck to toes in lumpy cloth and leather. None of Nush's kind had tiny, flat-faced heads covered with filthy black hair, grotesquely swollen shoulders, and clawless five-fingered hands on arms that nearly reached their knees, which—Nush noted with a ripple of nausea— bent the wrong way. And all had tails for balance; these strangers did not. It caused them to stand unnaturally straight, giving them the illusion of extreme size from the front and allowing their silhouettes to almost disappear from perception when they turned sideways.

Above all, however, Nush's people were silent. Noise was the mark of the animal. And these animals were by far the noisiest—from the sound of their weapons to what had to be their speech—that Nush had ever seen.

Animals. They were clearly animals. And even if they weren't, it was obvious enough that none had ever completed the trek that separated the People from the rest of the species of Egg.

Then three things happened at the same time. The hair-creature on the ground curled into a ball and expelled the contents of its stomach. The ones fighting over the weapon stopped and bent to its aid. And behind them, a fourth hair-creature stepped cautiously out of the tent.

This one was different. Smaller and paler than any of the rest, it wore no clothing. Its head-hair was lighter in color and many times longer than the rest, pulled back from its face into something approaching a crest. Its hands were tightly bound in front of it with white rope. It was hurt; blood as red as Nush's flowed freely from its snout, one of its eyes was nearly swollen shut in the center of a purple bruise that covered half of its face, and the body language it used—hands pressed to its middle, holding the pain inside—was universal.

It made no sound audible over the background hum. Locking its eyes on the dark hair-creatures, it backed cautiously away, toward the jungle.

Nush's target made a liquid sound and died. The hair-creature that had been straddling it and pushing on its chest made a loud noise, an animal howl. The one on its left touched it gently and received a sharp backhand blow across its face; although clawless, their overmuscled arms could nevertheless inflict serious damage.

The third hair-creature sat back on its haunches with a totally unnatural motion that looked to Nush like both its legs had been broken. And then it saw the pale one, jumped back to its feet, and charged.

Nush, unthinking once more, acted. Popping back up over the threehorn's neck, he put a poison dart squarely between the charging hair-creature's shoulder blades. It staggered and dropped; the heavy dart must have hit something vital.

The grieving hair-creature who had thrown the

punch acted nearly as quickly as Nush. While the other was still falling, it scooped up the noise-weapon, rolled to its feet, and crabbed sideways to the point where it had a clear shot down the alley between the longneck calf and the threehorn. The weapon spoke again: *crakka-crakka-crack!* Gobbets of threehorn flesh leaped around Nush's ears as he zigzagged his way back around, hoping for a straight line to the jungle—

—but the other hair-creature blocked his way, fumbling with a smaller weapon. Another heartbeat would have been time enough to for Nush to reload; instead, he turned and ran straight up the side of the dead longneck, his claws tearing toeholds into the blubbery mass. Both hair-creatures bellowed and tried to follow; neither was equipped with enough traction.

Both opened fire.

The larger weapon cracked and jumped in the hands of its wielder; the smaller made much louder noises, spaced further apart. Hot bits of angry death thudded into the longneck's flank and screamed past Nush's ears. One creased his side, tracing an ice-cold line just under his right armpit and shattering the delicate cane barrel of his blowgun. His hand stung; flinging away his darts and the remains of the weapon revealed many sharp splinters in his palm.

Time slowed to a crawl again.

The jungle seemed to lean in as Nush hit the ground running, claws churning up puffs of black dust that seemed to hang in midair. Across the clearing he could see the startled face of the pale hair-creature, hanging in the dimness just across the line of demarcation, unable to look away. The gate-machine hummed its song of madness; as he drew closer it felt like stinging insects crawling beneath his skin.

The repeating weapon sounded behind him, its report dragged down to the low thudding sound of an Eater charging across hard-packed earth. The first round nicked Nush's crest; unable to change course more than a few degrees, he nevertheless managed to lean to the right, trying, perhaps, to draw fire away from the pale one in the jungle.

The second round took him high in the fleshy part of his left arm, further altering his direction towards the center of the circle. The third and fourth shots slammed into a square red tank strapped to the back of the four-wheeled vehicle, triggering a greasy orange explosion that threw Nush to the ground.

And the fifth hit the gate-machine, which spat fire and began to die.

The magic circle wavered in the air like the surface of a pond in a rainstorm; the blue-white discharge that surrounded it took on a red glow and began to inch further out along the metal ramp.

The hair-creature howled, dropped its weapon and ran for the gate. The ramp buckled beneath its weight; the glow Nush had taken for discharge was apparently heat, instead. Moving with a respectable amount of speed for a being with such short legs, the hair-creature hit the gate in midair, penetrating the surface with a flash brighter than any Nush had yet seen.

The gate-machine spat smoke and fat red sparks. The ring of fire began to open and shut, fluctuating wildly, ranging in size from the span of Nush's outstretched arms to double its previous width, digging a larger smoking gash into the dirt with every expansion.

The other hair-creature hesitated just a bit too long.

Apparently it could see its partner through the gate; it made howling language-sounds, shaking its head. Finally it charged up the ramp, trying to meet the hole at its widest aperture.

It failed. The gate snapped down to smallest size just as the last hair-creature tried to enter. An intense white flash and the smell of burned meat followed; after his vision cleared, Nush saw only the torn-off end of the metal ramp, the machine, now silent, and the lower two-thirds of the hair-creature's body. A few paces away lay the smaller thunder-weapon, still clutched in a struck-off hand, the wrist-stump cauterized and bloodless.

Time sped up to its normal pace once more, and Nush became aware that his arm *hurt*. Not daring to look—was it still there? He could only think of the hair-creature's missing appendage—he raised his other hand and cautiously investigated. A bite-sized chunk had been torn out of the fleshy part of his arm, missing the bone.

Nush's ears rang in the sudden silence. His scalp relaxed, allowing his chest to slump and the sensations of pain to start chasing themselves up his arms and legs and into his brain. He felt dizzy and weak, and not just from loss of blood. The hair-creatures and their sky-gate were something . . . big. Much bigger than something as trivial as cheating on walkabout; they were clearly people, and yet not People—

The small one was moving, Nush realized. Slowly. Around the edge of the circle, toward the smaller tent that hadn't opened.

Rising painfully to intercept it, he had a chance to examine an alien artifact up close for the first time. The tent was a round pyramid of bright red cloth, held rigid by some impossibly light combination of flexible rods and the tension of the material itself. Flimsy metal stakes held it fast to the ground. And the opening was . . . strange. A sliding fastener of some kind brought two rows of tiny metal teeth into close alignment; it seemed unbelievably complicated for so simple a purpose.

Inside the tent was another hair-creature, dead. This one had been stripped of clothing, bound, gagged, and butchered with something very sharp; the coppery smell of its blood filled the tiny enclosure. Nush's stomach growled in spite of him; he suddenly identified hunger as the source of some of his weakness. Sickened, he backed out of the tent—

—and very nearly ran into the pale hair-creature,

who had managed to recover the smaller thunder-weapon, divest it of its late owner's hand, and aim it squarely between his eyes. Silently, and quickly, with its hands still bound.

Its eyelids fluttered, squeezing clear fluid down past its still-bleeding snout. Its face spasmed; Nush could see small white teeth grinding inside its mouth, none with enough of a point to damage anything. But still no sounds emerged.

The motion of the weapon-barrel was enough; Nush raised both hands in what he hoped was a universal gesture of submission and took two sliding steps sideways. The pale one advanced to the tent and snatched a quick look inside. Then another, twice as long.

Then it dropped the weapon and fell to its knees, its face working, more fluid falling from its eyes.

It recoiled from Nush's touch but relaxed when it saw what he was doing. Four or five quick sawing motions with his thumb-claws loosened the knots enough to allow it to free itself from its bindings. Rubbing at its reddened wrists, it stared at Nush with what he later came to know as a speculative look in its eyes. It brought a hand up to one of its pink, shell-shaped ears and touched something Nush hadn't noticed before, a tiny device the exact color of its skin.

And then it began to speak.

Not the grunts and roars of its animal captors. And not the ordered speech of Nush's kind. But speech nonetheless, elegant flowing gestures, its hands dancing like birds. Nush's jaw dropped. He understood none of it, but the creature was clearly trying to communicate.

Nuance would have to wait. Without the pervasive machine-hum warning the indigenous life away, the local scavengers—Eaters, claw-packs, and worse—would quickly close on the rich scent of dead flesh. Nush held both hands up in front of him and waved for attention. The pale one stopped speaking and watched, another sign—in Nush's estimation—of intelligence.

First things first. Nush brought a fist to his breast-bone, and then made the one-handed sign of walking feet, toward the narrow gap he'd entered the clearing through. "I go." Then he repeated the sequence, this time indicating both himself and the stranger, made walking feet with both hands, and finished with the spread-hand sign of inquiry. "We go?"

The pale hair-creature shook its head, a gesture Nush couldn't identify. It pointed towards the tent containing the dead one, tapped itself, and made walking feet in the direction of the torn-off metal ramp. Then it lurched to its feet and hobbled back to the gate-machine. Clearly, it wanted to go home.

But a few heartbeats later it became apparent that the gate-machine was beyond repair. At the pale one's touch it made a grinding sound, a tiny blue spark, and a thick cloud of dense black smoke. The pale one hissed and jumped away, bringing one singed hand to its mouth. Then it sat and began to make more water from its eyes.

"We go?" Nush repeated the question. The light in the clearing was beginning to take on the dull green glow of dusk; the last thing he wanted was to find himself alone in the dark with no cover, atop a mountain of fresh carrion. Night-feeders would track the smell of fresh blood from his wounded arm; immediate immersion in salt water—in a pool sheltered from sea-Eaters, of course—was his only chance at continued existance.

Regaining the relative safety of the beach seemed more important to Nush than the issue of proscribed clothing and artifacts. He even found himself holding the pale one's trail-rack—a cunning arrangement of light metal and tough cloth—as it pulled on a pair of shoes and a loose garment that seemed to Nush to be far too large for it. Clutching a thin piece of the gate-machine—green, with tiny golden loops, whorls, and beads attached to its sides—it nodded, apparently an affirmative, and added verbal confirmation. "We go."

The twilit jungle seemed to grasp at the pair of them with every clinging tendril and patch of sticky mud at its disposal. The game trail Nush had followed in from the beach was invisible after a few paces; trusting his instincts, however, he led his new trail-partner toward the good salt scent of the ocean.

When they finally found it, the beach bore no track, friend or foe. It was as if Nush had never left it, except for his wounds, which throbbed and stiffened more with every heartbeat, and the pale hair-creature that shivered by his side.

The sun had already dropped below the ocean's blank horizon; this was always a critical time for Nush to sight the Steering Star and assess his daily progress. Clearly visible as a disk, it shone brighter than the full moon, hanging a tiny bit higher in the sky than it had the evening before.

"There." Nush made exaggerated sweeping gestures. "We go there." The pale one's eyes flicked upward, dropped to the ground once more—

—and jumped back up to the glaring white beacon of the Steering Star. Its mouth fell open and Nush heard a barely vocalized sound, a shallow grunt. Shrugging its trail-rack loose, the pale one fumbled at the pack's fastenings, eyes still locked on the sky. Finding what it wanted, it brought a linked pair of small black tubes up to its eyes and focused on the blazing sky-pearl. Another faint sound emerged from the pale one, this one seeming to come from the center of its body.

When it finally brought the far-seer down, more clear fluid stained its cheeks.

"May I?" Another gesture seemed to be universal; trembling, the pale one placed the tiny instrument into Nush's outstretched hand. Although the tubes were set too close together for him to use both at once, peering through a single side brought him an excellent view of the Steering Star in all its glory.

The main body was a sphere of rock, Nush knew, nearly invisible beneath the layers of metal construction—living space, sun-stealers, far-speakers, docking arms, and uncountable numbers of sky-ships—built by a thousand thousand generations of his kind. The Star—and dozens more like it, coming in waves over the aeons—could have been the death of Nush's people; instead, his ancestors had put aside their differences to capture it, hang it over the face of Egg, and use it as the first true step toward the stars.

The lower surface of the Steering Star held Nush's attention the longest. Although he knew it was invisible from any distance even to the assisted eye, the tether that stretched between Egg and its guardian was definitely there, somewhere.

Someday soon, Nush planned to cross that bridge of air and spider-silk, to learn the full range of his ancestors' power. They lived a very long time, he'd heard, and traveled far and wide. But they always returned home, to found the next generation upon the fragile shell of Egg. And those few hatchlings of each new clutch who proved strong, wise, and bold enough had their chance to join their number, and eventually return to have children of their own.

There. The Steering Star began to fade; the fringe of Egg's shadow had begin its nightly sweep. He offered the far-seer back to his pale companion; he preferred to watch the Star enter darkness with his own eyes.

"We go . . . there?" The pale one waved aside the instrument, pointing again at the Steering Star.

The key to the puzzle lay,—thin, green and shell-fragile,—strung on a thong around the hair-creature's neck. For a bare instant Nush thought about skimming the thing out into the ocean, biting out its owner's throat, and continuing on its journey alone. A return to normalcy seemed almost overpoweringly attractive, even if it killed him. At least he'd die by rules he understood.

But no. Nush had spent most of his life building and testing his own equipment, in preparation for his trek. He knew the look of something handmade; the heart of the gate-machine had all the individuality of a brick. It was clearly a machine-made thing itself, and that meant that there were others. Many others.

And, of all his ancestor's glorious triumphs in the skies over Egg and hundreds of other Egglike worlds, he'd never heard of anything that would make a hole in the air big enough to drive a longneck through.

A new word was needed. Nush brought both hands up, simultaneously tapped his chest and that of the other, and drew his hands together in the space between them.

"Yes. We go there. We go . . . together."

Rx
by Barbara Delaplace

Barbara Delaplace is a two-time Campbell Award nominee, and a winner of the HOMer Award.

It wasn't easy being a wimp.

Tony White could vouch for the fact, having been one all his life. And as a consequence, he considered himself an expert. All through school he'd been teased by the guys, giggled at by the girls. As he grew older, he became resigned to remarks like, "Grow some hair on your chest first—then maybe you'll be man enough to make the team" (invariably followed by hoots of laughter) and "But, Tony, I think of you as a *friend*—let's not spoil it" (invariably followed by a peck on the cheek). Because he was used to it, he didn't expect much more out of life, and he was resigned to a boring existence working his way up through the hierarchy of the graveyard shift at the All-Nite Groceteria Megastore—We Stay Open Twenty-Four Hours A Day For Your Convenience.

All that changed the day he met Theresa.

She was everything he'd ever wanted in a woman: gentle, pretty in a quiet way, a laugh that lifted his spirits every time he heard it. She was the vision of his dreams, and he knew it the moment they met. "Hi,

Tony, my name is Theresa," were her first words to him. What man could resist?

He shook her proffered hand and stammered, "It's nice to meet you," in reply. The fact that as he did so he dropped a five pound bag of Uncle Ben's Long Grain Converted which split open in a cascade of white grains across the toes of her shoes didn't seem to bother her. She just smiled sympathetically as Bowden, the nighttime manager, scowled at him.

"Clean up that mess, goddammit," Bowden growled, and led her off to met the rest of the staff.

Alas, as promising as their initial meeting was, she didn't return his ardor. Indeed, she seemed unaware of it entirely. She was open and friendly with him— just as she was to everyone else on the staff. She was quite willing to go to coffee with him—but all too ready to invite along others who needed a caffeine jolt as well. This had a dampening effect on his planned heart-to-heart conversations, in which he intended to Reveal All. Tony despaired of getting her to pay more than generic attention to him. Until one evening, when he saw a possibility on his way to work.

Normally, he paid little attention to the shops he passed on the short walk from his apartment to the grocery store, but today the reflection of the setting sun in the window of the old shop flashed in his eyes, making him blink. When he glanced again at the window, he noticed the sign written both in English and Chinese characters. Of course he couldn't read the ideographs, but the other half of the sign said: "Improve your health and vitality. Finest, most effective traditional preparations available. Enjoy life and love."

Hmmm, thought Tony. *I wonder if . . .* Then he shook his head. *Nah, that's crazy.* He continued on his way to work.

But all through his shift, the idea nagged at him. He'd heard people setting great store by acupuncture, and one of his aunts swore that ever since she'd started feeding her second husband ginseng tea, he'd become a regular Don Juan between the sheets. Maybe he could find something in the little shop that would help him become more attractive to Theresa?

He was interrupted in his meditations by a shout as he restocked shelves. "Hey, Tony! Hurry up, man—it's nearly time to go Bowling for Turkeys!" Roger's voice came from the Frozen Foods section.

Tony stacked another half-dozen Cheerios boxes neatly on the shelf. "Be right there as soon as I'm through in Cereals!" he shouted back to Roger. His voice echoed across the empty aisles of the grocery store. Business wasn't heavy at 2:45 A.M. on a Monday morning, even in an open-24-hours-for-your-convenience grocery megastore. He liked it that way.

"Better hurry! Old man Bowden's just gone off for his lunch break."

Supervisor Bowden's 'lunch breaks' were legendary among the store's night staff, involving as they did lengthy visits to the Parched Parakeet Bar down the block. When the cat was away, misdemeanors like "Bowling for Turkeys" were the rule of the night. Tony was the night shift champion.

"Theresa's gonna bowl with us. So get it in gear, White!"

"Coming!" The possibilities inherent in coaching Theresa in how to bowl using everyday grocery store stock such as frozen turkeys and two-liter soda bottles made his heart quicken. Who needed dumb old Chinese herbal tea? Tony stacked faster.

Unfortunately, it wasn't Tony who instructed Theresa in the finer points of handling an awkward and heavy frozen bird. Roger was making a definite play for Theresa's attentions. And in Tony's opinion, he was far too solicitous about showing her how to hold the turkey so that it could be rolled along the floor toward a careful six-pin arrangement of soda bottles.

"Now, your hand's smaller than mine, and more delicate," Roger was saying with a smirk. "So I think you'll get better control if you use a large Cornish game hen."

Despair flooded Tony's heart as he saw how she laughed and looked up at Roger with warmth in her eyes. "I'll get one for you, Theresa," he said quickly.

"Oh, thank you, Tony—that's sweet of you." Now her smile was directed at him. He felt ten feet tall, and shrugged off the black look Roger was also directing at him as he headed toward Frozen Foods to find the perfect game hen for Theresa's delicate hand.

A rival! The situation was clearly desperate and called for desperate measures. Even though he knew he was grasping at straws, he decided he had to take a chance and visit the little Chinese shop. Maybe there was something to the ancient Oriental wisdom after all—modern science didn't know everything. This was too important just to leave to mere chance. This was a matter of love.

The old man behind the counter introduced himself as Chin Soong Li. "What can I do for you, my son? You look far too young to be troubled by a bad liver or rheumatism." He smiled gently.

Tony looked at him. He wasn't sure what he had expected when he entered the old shop, but somehow it seemed odd to hear perfect English spoken by an elderly Chinese man dressed in the silk robe and felt slippers of traditional garb. He looked around at the dimly lit shop, hoping he could browse for a few minutes and get up his nerve.

But alas, there was no help there. The floor and counters were crowded with jars and crates. Each was filled with herbs, strange animal parts, grasses, and flowers that he'd never seen before: all dried or powdered or preserved in some way—and each was labeled in Chinese. The shelves were filled with boxes of pills and vials of liquids, similarly labeled.

The old man cleared his throat, bringing Tony back to the present. He took a breath—the air was rich with strange odors, pungent, sweet, earthy, tangy, musky—and screwed up his courage. "Oh, I'm sorry—Mr. Chin, was it?" The old man inclined his head in response. "I . . . well, it's like this . . . I want to . . ." Tony stammered to a halt. What on earth was he going to say?

"My son, I understand. You've met the most wonderful girl in the world and you want some potion from the mystic East that will help you attract her attention. Am I correct?"

Tony's jaw dropped. "How did you know?"

Mr. Chin looked amused. "Infirmities of the body are for the old. With the young, it is always matters of the heart."

"You're right. She's wonderful but she treats me like one of the gang. And Roger—" he stopped short and blushed a little.

"Ah, so you have a rival upon which she looks with more favor?"

Tony replied, "Yes. I know it sounds crazy, but do you have something, a pill or something that I can take that'll make—" Again he stopped short.

"That will make her love you? Alas, my son, nothing in this shop can do that."

Tony's shoulders slumped and the hope went out of his face. It had been childish of him to think he'd find a magic love potion. "Thank you anyway for your time." He turned away to the door.

The older man looked at the younger with compassion. How well he'd known that despair in his youth. "Wait, my son." He paused, considering. "All is not lost." Tony turned back, his face brightening. "Sit down. Tell me all about yourself, and about this woman of your dreams. I may be able to create a preparation especially for you that will help. . . ."

Tony talked for a long time to Mr. Chin. He was a very sympathetic listener.

* * *

He almost ran all the way to the shop. Today was the day when it would be ready! Then Theresa would pay attention to him!

Tony entered the shop, and stopped short. Chin Soong Li wasn't behind the counter. Instead, there was a young man, someone he'd never seen before. His buzz-cut black hair was adorned with a Cubs baseball cap, and he was snapping his gum in time to the pulsing bass beat of the rap music playing on the boom box on the counter.

"Hey, man, can I help you?" he asked with a friendly grin.

Tony eyed him doubtfully and replied, "Uh . . . I don't know. Where's Mr. Chin?"

"He passed away. I'm his grandson. I'm Dave Chin."

"Oh. I'm sorry. My condolences to you and your family."

Dave nodded. "Thanks. He was so old, I guess it shouldn't have surprised us, but we all felt like he'd go on forever."

Tony paused, confused. What was he to do now? Dave certainly didn't have the aura of vast knowledge that the white-haired, serene Mr. Chin had. How did he know this guy knew anything at all about the ancient preparations the old man undoubtedly used in his formulations?

While Tony pondered, Dave casually blew a huge bubble, popped it, and began chewing again with the ease of a long-time Dubble Bubble addict. Then, showing more perception than Tony had expected, he said, "Hey don't worry. Grandfather was training me in the business—it was all arranged that I'd take over the shop for him. I'm really interested in folk medicines and homeopathy and all that stuff."

"Well . . . I was consulting your grandfather about a . . . a personal problem. He was the only one who could help me." How much should he tell him? Tony had no intention of baring his soul to a guy like this.

"Good—I like challenges."

Dave's response slightly disconcerted him, but Tony abruptly decided to continue. What choice did he have? Besides, he'd seen Roger eyeing Theresa speculatively at work last night when he thought Tony wasn't looking. "Look, your grandfather was making something up for me."

"What was he making up? A song?" Dave grinned at his own joke.

Tony rolled his eyes. "No, a—a prescription. Isn't there something ready for me? Something with my name on it? Tony White."

"No problem, dude. Let me go check in the back." Bopping in time to the music, Dave boogied through a beaded curtain into the shadowy storage area.

Tony wondered what he'd got himself into. Chin Soong Li had questioned him carefully for a long time, and pondered even longer before saying he thought he could prepare something that would help Tony. And he'd made no promises about miraculous cures. "It's important that you have confidence in yourself, my son. That will work best of all." Perhaps he'd be better off trying to get over Theresa. . . .

"There you go. Uncle Dave's Magic Pills, guaranteed to cure what ails you. Take one daily before meals."

Lost in his pondering, Tony hadn't noticed that Dave had returned, plunking down a dusty bottle made of old greenish glass. He looked doubtfully at the bottle, then at Dave. " 'Uncle Dave's'? I thought your grandfather was making this for me?"

"Hey, he did, he did. I just finished it up. Final polish and all that."

"Are you sure this'll work?"

"Absolutely, man. Inside a month you won't recognize yourself."

Dave Chin turned out to be absolutely correct.

* * *

He'd been taking the pills for about a week when Theresa asked him during their lunch break, "Tony, are you feeling okay?"

Thrilled by the concern in her voice, he barely thought about what she'd asked. "I'm feeling great, thanks! Why?"

"You just look awfully pale, that's all."

"Maybe he's pining for an unrequited love," hooted Roger.

Tony put down his barely touched sandwich and glared at him. "I'm fine, thanks." He was just considering using Roger as one of the pins in Bowling for Turkeys, when Bowden strode in.

"All right, you slackers—you've had your half-hour. Back to work!"

Tony packed away his uneaten lunch with a sigh. Funny, but he wasn't really hungry anyway.

It was a few days later, while he was shaving, when he realized that Theresa was right—his reflection in the bathroom mirror *was* looking awfully pale. Almost dead white, in fact. And there was no doubt about it, his appetite was poor; about the only thing that tempted him was rare steak, the bloodier the better. *I wonder if those pills are doing this to me?* They certainly didn't seem to be doing much toward their intended purpose: Theresa was friendly but nothing more—as usual. *This wasn't what I paid for,* he thought. He inspected his reflection again. *Looking pretty wimpy, there, White. Even more insubstantial than usual.* He decided to give it another couple of days, and go complain to Dave Chin if things didn't improve.

He nearly didn't make it. He stepped out into the bright sunny day—and howled in pain as his exposed skin reacted to the sunlight as though it were a branding iron. He ducked back into the safe shadowy

building and stared at his arms in disbelieve—there
was smoke rising from them? The skin was badly
blistered and cracked.

It's those pills. It's got to be those pills. He'd wait
until the sun went down, but he was giving Mr.
Boombox Chin a visit tonight.

"I'm allergic to sunlight. *Really* allergic. My skin
cracks and burns if sunlight falls on it. Look!" He
thrust out his arm—and had the second shock of the
day. The skin showed no sign of damage at all. It
seemed to have healed in just a few hours. "It was all
burned and blistered this afternoon. I don't get it." He
stared at his other arm. It, too, seemed fully healed.

Dave was unimpressed. "Allergic to sunlight? Man,
what are you, a vampire?"

"Oh, yeah, right—" Tony began hotly, then stopped
as he caught sight of the mirror on the wall behind
Dave's back which was reflecting Dave all right. *But
there was no reflection of himself.* Suddenly he had
the awful feeling Dave had hit on the truth. "I think
you might be right."

"Hey, *cool!*"

Tony stopped, nonplussed. "Uh, 'cool'?"

"Oh, yeah. Grandfather hinted that he had some
really weird dudes for customers, but he wouldn't
give me any details. Said there'd be time enough for
that later. Only, well." Dave shrugged ruefully. "So
what clued you in? Did you develop an allergy for
garlic?" He grinned at his own joke. Tony decided
Dave was easily amused.

"Not quite. Look, Chin, this is the result of those
pills you gave me."

"No way, dude. Grandfather had that formulation
all written down. I just finished putting it together."

"Yeah? Well you must've misread the directions."

Stung, Dave stood up. "Not a chance. I'll go get the
recipe and double check it." He stomped through the
bead curtain, leaving the strands swinging and

clashing together in his wake. Tony heard him rummaging among shelves for a few minutes, then he returned.

"Now look," he said, throwing down a large piece of rice paper covered with ink brush writing. "See, this ideograph stands for bear gallbladder," he pointed, "and this one for ginseng, and this one for—" He stopped, peered more closely at the sheet, and then flushed scarlet. "Man, these old brush characters sure are hard to read. One little slip and . . ."

"And I turn into a vampire? Swell. Some traditional healer you're going to make."

"So there were a few little side effects."

"Side effects! You call *that*—Tony pointed at the mirror—a side effect!"

Dave turned, and his jaw dropped. "Oh, wow."

"That's the best you can do? 'Wow'? What about me? I can't stay like this!"

"So you become a night owl." Dave shrugged. "No big deal."

This guy's incredible, Tony thought to himself. "Look, moron, even in a town like this, there are some things you can't do at night—"

Dave cackled gleefully. "I'll *bet.*"

"—like get a driver's license, for instance, or go to a job interview," Tony finished crushingly. He groaned to himself. *Why am I talking to this boob? He obviously hasn't got a clue.*

"Oh. I hadn't thought of that." Dave paused, pondering the implications.

"So what am I supposed to do? Beside stop taking those pills you gave me? How do I know I'll go back to normal?" *How do I know Theresa will ever look at me again?* Fate was manifestly unfair, Tony thought. His destiny was in the hands of a teeny-bopper who thought the best that music had to offer was Vanilla Ice. "You've got to do something."

Dave pondered further, then reached under the counter and hauled out an old leather-bound book.

"Let me look something up." He thumbed through the pages for several minutes."

Tony glanced at his watch. "Look, I'm due at work in fifteen minutes. I'll be back after my shift is over. You'd better have a cure all ready for me to pick up by then."

"Hey, that'll be like, what, four in the morning," Dave protested.

"So stay up late. Otherwise, I may just start exhibiting some vampire side effects that could prove unhealthy for you." Tony licked his lips as he stared meaningfully at Dave's neck.

Dave looked uneasy. "Okay, okay, so I stay up late. Come back after work."

Tony nodded and turned away. Come to think of it, he *was* kind of hungry—he stopped himself abruptly. *Dave better come through or things could get a lot rougher for both of us.* He went out the door.

Dave did indeed have something for him when he returned in the wee small hours of the morning. "Just rub this ointment into your skin twice a day for the next two weeks. You'll be a new man."

Tony took the ointment with guarded optimism. "I don't want to be a new man; I just want to go back to being the old one again."

"Trust me," said Dave. "It'll put color back into your cheeks and grow hair on your chest."

Once again, Dave turned out to be absolutely correct.

It was early on a slow Wednesday morning while they were bowling (old man Bowden was drinking his lunch down at the Parakeet again) that it happened. Tony was having a lousy game—he had bowled nothing but spares. To make matters worse, everyone else could do no wrong. Mark from the Seafood Department made strikes every time he got his hands on the turkey. Even Roger, not normally the best of the after-midnight athletic league, had just cleaned up a four-six split and was fighting it out with one of the guys from Produce for second place. And to top it all off, Tony had a killer headache that even Excedrin PM couldn't handle. About the only thing that made the entire situation bearable was that Theresa was absent—she'd phoned in to say she'd come down with a twenty-four-hour virus—and wasn't there to see his humiliation.

He'd just left another split when his headache suddenly flared up so viciously that he nearly collapsed. His fellow sporting enthusiasts gathered around him in concern.

"Geez, Tony, you look awful," said Mark from Seafood. "Maybe you should go lie down."

"Yeah," chimed in Roger. "Come on, I'll help you into the back." He solicitously draped his arm around Tony and heaved him to his feet. Tony's stomach nearly heaved with him, but he managed to control it and stumbled along, clinging to Roger's shoulder. The beat-up sofa in the stockroom had never seemed so far away, or so welcome when he finally collapsed on it.

"Thanks, Roger. I'll lie here for a while."

"You do that, buddy. I'll cover for you if Bowden comes back."

"You're a pal, Rog." He leaned back and closed his eyes. Roger switched off the lights as he quietly left the room.

But the quiet darkness didn't prove as soothing as he'd hoped. The headache refused to go away. He felt feverish and his body started to ache all over. *"I'm coming down with something—wonder if it's that twenty-four-hour bug that got Theresa?"* he wondered, as he shifted restlessly. He tried focusing mentally on a cool pool of water, hoping the image would help soothe his body.

When his arm started to itch, he didn't pay much attention at first. He rubbed at it absently, then noticed how stubbly the skin felt. *Bet it's that oint-ment Dave gave me. He probably put poison ivy extract in it instead of witch hazel or something like that. 'Those ideographs are so hard to read'. Hah.* He'd been applying the skin cream faithfully for a week now, but it didn't seem terribly effective; he was still extremely sensitive to sunlight, and only went outdoors on cloudy days.

Then he realized the stubble was getting longer. He looked at his arm more closely. Even in the dim gloom of the room, he could clearly see the coarse hair was growing thicker and thicker. (It wasn't until later that he realized just how clearly he was able to see, as though the lack of light no longer mattered.)

And his hands! The nails had lengthened and thick-ened until they were almost claws!

He jumped up from the sofa and lunged for the washroom with a fluid grace of movement that—at any other time—would have thrilled him. The cracked mirror on the wall showed a horrifying, beas-tial image: his ears had become pointed, his face was covered with fur, and as his mouth opened in a gasp of shock, he saw his teeth had become pointed fangs.

He'd become a werewolf!

And someone—Roger, he could tell from the walk—was coming down the aisle to the back of the store. He'd be here in a matter of seconds.

Tony ran to the loading bay door. It was locked as always when not in use, but he gave it a mighty shove and it flew open with a crash. Roger, hearing the noise, came into the stockroom at a dead run, calling his name. Tony glanced back at him, then gathered himself and made a thirty-foot leap from the loading dock into the alleyway. He loped away into the night, Roger's bewildered shout echoing behind him.

He blessed the fact that he lived so close to work. He managed to cover the short distance without run-ning into anyone, the streets being deserted at 3:30 A.M.

It wasn't until he reached the safety of his apartment and locked the door behind him that he calmed down slightly.

The room seemed awfully bright, even though there were no lights on. He decided to close the drapes, just in case anyone happened to glance in. As he crossed the room, he realized why the room seemed so well-lit: It was—of course—the night of the full moon.

There was no doubt at all in his mind. It was time to pay Dave Chin another visit. *Thank goodness the moon's only full one night a month*, he thought. He could visit him tomorrow night.

"You said that ointment would put hair on my chest. I want you to know that it did indeed do that. And it gave me unbelievable vitality. More than I knew what to do with."

Dave looked proud. "See, what'd I tell you, man? You want the best, you come to the best." He slapped his knees in time to the bass beat of the boom box.

Tony continued, "You know what else? It put hair *everywhere* on my body. It did it last night. Do you know what was special about last night, Dave?"

Dave looked blankly at him. "Barry Manilow's birthday, maybe?"

Tony wouldn't be diverted. "It was the full moon, Dave, baby. Full moon, hair all over my body—are you getting the picture? I turned into a werewolf."

Dave's eyes grew wide. "Oh, *wow!* The call of the wild and all that. Tell me, how did it feel having your animal nature take over?"

"It wasn't cool at all. It hurt like hell, and I nearly trashed my apartment before the sun came up. To say nothing of making my coworkers wonder just what the deal was when I bolted out the back door of the store." His tone became very patient. "Tell me, Dave, are you *sure* you read that old recipe of your grandfather's right? You didn't, maybe, by any chance mistake the character for 'wolfsbane' as the character for 'ginseng,' hmm?"

Dave blushed. It made for a nice contrast with his dark hair, Tony thought. "Look, a mistake like that can happen to anybody—I was just a little out of practice, that's all. Besides, think how you could terrorize your boss and all that—dynamite!"

"You don't understand. I don't *want* to be a werewolf—any more than I wanted to be a vampire. I just want to be your average, dull, boring guy, okay? I just want to be able to go bowling, and work at the grocery store, and maybe, now and then, take a girl out on a date. Mr. Normal, not Mr. Excitement. Get the picture? Otherwise I trash *this* place next time the moon is full. I'm *real* strong during the full moon."

"Okay, okay. So you want me to make something up for you?"

"Now that's a darn good question, Dave. Right now, I can't go out at night during the full moon. And I can't go out during the day, either, because I'm still reacting to sunlight. What's left for me, do you suppose? Do you think I can find a girl who's only interested in going out when there's no sun and no moon in the sky? It sort of limits our options, wouldn't you say?"

"Listen, man, I understand how you feel—"

"Somehow I doubt that."

"—And I want you to know I feel bad about how things have turned out. Just to show you there's no bad feelings about this—"

"The hell there isn't!"

"—I'll make up something that'll neutralize all the side effects you're still suffering. Come back in a couple days and I'll have it ready for you. Oh, yeah, and stop using the ointment, okay? Don't want you to turn into a walking commercial for Nair." He laughed in appreciation of his own wit.

Tony growled at him and slammed the door as he left the shop.

* * *

Theresa was back at work, looking a little wan and pale. Tony told her she looked like she was on the mend, and she perked up slightly. "Thanks, Tony—that's sweet of you to say so."

His heart jumped up in his chest and he searched for something, anything, to keep the conversation going. "You know, I wonder if I didn't have the same bug as you yesterday. Really sudden, killer headache, aches and pains through all my joints." *Superhuman strength, sudden hair aquisition—yeah, there's a lot of* that *going around.*

She suddenly looked grim and said, "Oh, I don't think so. I get this every month. I've given up on regular doctors—I'm trying a homeopath now. He said he'd have a prescription ready for me tomorrow. I hope it works." She paused, then said thoughtfully, "Though you know, your symptoms *do* sound rather like mine." She shrugged. "Well, if his prescription works, I'll let you know. This bug is really limiting my social life. I mean, who wants to go out with someone who gets sick once a month?"

Tony nodded sympathetically. He'd heard about female "troubles." Then gathering up all his courage, he replied, "I would. Why don't we go take in a late late late show after work? Not tonight," he added hastily, noting again how tired and drawn she looked, "I mean, I'm still feeling kind of rocky and I'll bet you are, too, but how about tomorrow?"

She brightened and said, "I'd like that, Tony. Why don't we? It'll give me something to get well for."

His heart soared. "Gee, that's just . . . just *great!*"

She smiled impishly at him, and suddenly, to his shock, stood up on tiptoe and gave him a peck on the cheek. "I'm looking forward to it already."

"White!" Bowden's bellow cut through the rose-colored haze surrounding Tony. "I've got a dozen cases of T-bones sitting here on the loading dock.

When they're on the loading dock, they're not out
where the customers can buy them. Get in here!"

"Coming!" Tony shouted back. He waved at
Theresa as he headed toward the back of the store. It
seemed to him his feet didn't touch the ground once.

The next day's shift seemed endless to Tony, especially with Theresa smiling sweetly at him every time
their paths crossed during the night. She even sat with
him during the lunch break, to Roger's evident disap-
pointment. *Take that, you Romeo!* Tony thought
smugly.

"So what movie do you want to see?" he asked her
after the shift was over.

"Well, they're showing 'Casablanca' again, and
that's one of my favorites."

"Really? Mine, too!" Tony would have said this
about 'Attack of the Killer Tomatoes', but in fact he
really did enjoy the old Bogart film. "Casablanca it
is." He helped her on with her coat.

"If we hurry, we can make the next show—oh,
dear." Theresa's face suddenly fell.

Tony was alarmed. *Oh, please, not after everything's been going so well,* he prayed under his
breath. "What's wrong?" He strove to keep his tone
concerned but light.

"I forgot, I have to pick up my prescription
tonight."

"At this time of the morning?" He was relieved but
puzzled. "What drugstore around here is open at this
hour?"

"Oh, it's not a drugstore. Remember, I told you I
had a homeopath treating me? He has his own little
shop only a block from here. He offered to stay open
for me, when I explained how late I worked. He said
he liked working at night—no one complained about
how loud he played rap."

A homeopath only a block from here? Who played
rap music? An awful suspicion entered Tony's mind.

"Theresa, is this place by any chance a Chinese traditional medicine shop? Dave Chin, proprietor?"

"Why, yes—how did you know?" She looked puzzled.

"You shouldn't be going to him. He's a complete idiot."

Theresa frowned. "Now just a minute, Tony. What do you know about Dave? He was very nice to me."

I'll just bet he was, Tony thought. A pretty girl like Theresa, he'd haul out all the stops to impress her. Any guy with normal urges would. "He inherited the business from his grandfather, who really *did* know what he was doing. I was going to old Mr. Chin for a—a skin condition. Dave screwed up on the formulation and only made it worse. I wouldn't trust him an inch."

"An accident can happen to anyone, Tony."

"Funny, that's just what he said to me at the time."

"One mistake is hardly grounds for calling him a quack." Theresa's tone was taking on a definite chill.

She had him there. He couldn't really explain any further without getting into all sorts of, well, hairy details. And he didn't want to lose the chance of spending a few hours with her. "You're right, it doesn't." Which was true as far as it went. "Look, why don't we pick up your prescription on the way to the movie theater—it's not far out of the way." No way was he letting her deal with Dave alone.

Theresa agreed, though with some reserve in her tone. She buttoned her coat, and shrugging into his jacket, Tony followed her out the door.

He made a determined effort to be cheerful during their walk to the shop, so that by the time they arrived, the atmosphere between them was almost restored to its original friendliness. He even opened the door of the shop for her, wincing as the blast of the boom box punched through the peaceful night.

"Theresa, it's great to see you!" Dave's greeting

was effusive. "And Tony, too! I didn't realize you two knew one another! This is great. I've got it ready for you both."

"Us both?" Theresa exchanged surprised looks with Tony. "Tony, I thought you said—"

"I decided to give him one more chance," Tony quickly said, eyeing Dave balefully.

"Well, hey, it's not often you get *two* customers who are werewolves. Made it a lot easier for me—I just made up a double batch." He placed two small bottles of purple liquid on the counter.

Theresa turned scarlet and glared at Dave. "Dave, dear, I thought this was going to be our little secret," she said sweetly, her fists clenched until the knuckles turned white. "There aren't too many men who want to go out with a she-wolf, even in this day of women's liberation." She turned anguished eyes to Tony. "I didn't want you to find out, Tony. I was hoping this prescription would cure me, and then I could just be a normal woman and able to go out with normal guys like you." Her eyes filled with tears, and Tony felt his heart swell with sympathy.

Dave looked surprised. "But, Theresa, when I saw the two of you together, I just assumed you knew about each other. I mean, Tony was in here just the other night—"

Tony took Theresa's face in his hands. "Theresa, it's all right, really it is. I know *exaclty* what you're going through. Do you understand?"

She looked at him with sudden comprehension. "He said—"

"—*two* werewolves," he finished for her. "We really *did* come down with the same twenty-four-hour bug on the night of the full moon."

"Oh, Tony!" She threw her arms around him, and for a moment, he knew what Paradise was like.

Dave cleared his throat. "Um . . . are you two love-birds interested in my medicine or not? I mean, I went to all the trouble of looking up Grandfather's recipe and everything."

Tony eyed him with deep suspicion. "How carefully did you follow it?"

"Man, I swear, I triple-checked each and every character. I even got Grandmother to translate it for me as a cross-check."

Tony looked at Theresa. "What do you think?"

"I'm tired of being a werewolf. What could be worse than turning into a monster every month?"

Turning into one every night, he thought to himself, but didn't say it aloud. He felt much the way she did.

"All it'll take is one dose, and you'll be changed for good," said Dave.

"Oh, what the hell. Here, Theresa." He handed her one of the little bottles and took the other for himself. They uncorked them together. "Down the hatch."

They each upended a vial and swallowed together.

Tony lowered his head and looked at Dave, nonplussed. "Grape?"

Dave looked abashed. "My favorite flavor. Who says traditional medicines have to taste bad?"

"When do we find out if we're cured?" asked Theresa anxiously.

"Wait for the next full moon—nothing will happen. I guarantee it," said Dave, confidently.

"You'd better be right, Chin—or we'll pay you a visit that very night. Together." Tony looked steadily at him for a moment. "Come on, Theresa, or we'll miss the movie."

On the philsophy that at least they had a month's worth of hope, they spent every moment they could together. Tony had never been so happy, and Theresa seemed as happy as he was. By mutual agreement, they didn't discuss anything about their mutual condition. But they did agree to call in sick the night of the full moon and spend it together at Tony's place.

The night came. They watched the silver orb rise high in the sky, and, anxiously, watched each other. "How do you feel?" asked Tony, when he couldn't stand it any longer.

"Well, it might be all in my mind, but I feel great," replied Theresa. "*Really* great. I feel full of energy, the way I did when, well, you know."

Tony nodded. The one thing he remembered with anything like pleasure from his transformation was the feeling of vitality that flowed through him once he'd completely changed form. He'd never felt so— alive.

His thoughts were interrupted by a horrified gasp from Theresa. "Tony!"

"What?" He didn't want to go look in the mirror.

"You're—your skin is turning to scales!" She looked frantically at her own hands. Tony could see the scales gradually appearing, covering her beautiful milky skin.

Then they gasped in unison, as each felt a tremendous pressure, a stretching, as if their bodies were clay being molded by giant hands into new forms. This wasn't like before—there was no pain. But it felt awful all the same. Tony watched in horror as Theresa's jaw elongated and her forehead flattened, becoming lizardlike. He knew from the anguish mirrored in her eyes that he too was altering, changing. Even as he watched, her eyes became yellow with catlike slitted pupils. A feeling of hopelessness filled him as the changes continued to pull at them. They twisted and writhed together, united in awful transformation, for what seemed like an endless time, until at last their bodies quieted and they lay still.

Tony raised his head, which felt strangely out of balance. No wonder. If he looked like Theresa— and a glance down at his body confirmed that he did—they had transformed yet again. This time into dinosaurs. Some sort of predatory dinosaur, judging by his fang-filled jaws and the huge talons on his front and back feet.

He looked around. He could see in the dark as easily as he could when he'd transformed into a were-wolf, only better. Instantly he realized why: He could now see into the infrared. Warm objects glowed with color. He sprang to his feet. Physically, he felt superb: strong, flexible, ready for anything.

Tony? He heard Theresa's voice, and turned to her. She, too, was on her feet, and feeling as exhilarated and confused as he was.

He stopped. Now how did he know *that?*

The same way I know how you're *feeling.* Again Theresa's voice rang—in his mind! His jaw dropped. Somehow, in turning into six-foot versions of *Tyrannosaurus Rex,* they'd also become telepathic!

The emotions that poured through their minds were a thrilling, frightening, exciting torrent—a shared torrent. It was a perfect communion of the spirit. Now Tony knew exactly how she felt about him, and the feeling was glorious. And he could feel Theresa's astonished delight at knowing how *he* felt about *her.*

They were closer now than they ever could hope to be in human form. Their mental communion almost made up for their grotesque physical shape-change.

Almost.

Are you thinking what I'm thinking? Tony asked Theresa.

You know I am, she replied coyly. And he could feel the predatory twinkle in her mind. She turned to face him.

He turned full face toward here. *Are you sure you're up for this?*

Absolutely. Her mental voice was full of confident certainty. *We're only going to be this way for one night a month. We certainly don't want to waste it.*

He smiled. They were of one mind.

They swung their powerful tails in unison. The plaster of the wall cracked and crumbled to bits. Together, they crashed through the opening.

They were going to pay a little visit to Dave.

EVOLUTIONARY GAME
by Robyn Herrington

This is Robyn Herrington's first professional sale.

The room was filled to capacity by members of the press—beyond capacity, C'Nar noted with excitement and pride. He could see heads in hues of green and brown vying for position in the corridor beyond the conference room, and could smell the anticipation.

"We don't have much time before the Game," the Game Master muttered. He was an impressive specimen for an old Albertosaurus, rising almost to C'Nar's chest.

"My name is Kalorn," the Game Master said into the speaker phone, though to the last one, they knew. "I have been the Keeper of the Game since its development, shortly after the Great Return. First used as training for our soldiers, the Game's tradition has been one of honing our skills which we had neglected for too long." Kalorn paused dramatically, lifted his patchy brown head and repositioned his glasses on the sagging skin of his heavily scarred snout. C'Nar wondered if Kalorn had any idea how old he really looked.

"Until now, the Game had provided entertainment for our young, as well as providing them with an important tool to educate them about our past." He took the glasses from his eyes and wiped them quickly. "Today, the Game—our link from our now to our then—will be played for the last time." The Game Master's last words came out in an undignified rush, and his voice broke. Again he paused, his aged, bowed shoulders rising and falling dramatically in a deep breath. "I now open the floor to questions. You—front row."

A small troodon stood, recorder positioned on her shoulder. "Thank you, honored Game Master. My name is T'mpeka. I represent our people in the southern province."

The silence in the room was momentarily replaced with the unbidden surprise of those gathered. Even C'Nar's mouth opened, and he felt his focus sharpen.

"You made quite a journey to be with us today," the Game Master said, visibly impressed.

"Yes, sir, I did. But it was worth the journey, to be here on this day."

The Game Master inclined his head, gratified that this youthful sauropod had some measure of politeness. So many of the young, even C'Nar the Magnificent, forgot what the Game was, what it represented, and put aside the basic tenets of civilized behavior in favor of the boisterous, rude state they'd seen displayed by the Humans.

"I have two questions," T'mpeka said. "The second question is to you both. How much did the S.R.I. influence the decision to stop the Game?"

Kalorn's hands closed over the edge of the podium. "And your first question?"

"Is to you, Game Master Kalorn," T'mpeka answered. "Your position is to keep the Game ongoing. Why? What purpose will it serve? When the last Human dies, surely we don't need reminders of their infestation."

Kalorn's knuckles paled as he gripped the podium tighter. "Long ago," he said, "our people's history was passed from clan head to clan head, a verbal history that reminded us of our evolution and growth. Now, we have machines that can record and play back those events, and I believe, down to my last cell, that we *must* maintain the Game to teach the young of our struggle to regain this world, and to remind *us* of our actions. We did not take this world easily. We marched in victory over the bones of our fallen as well as our foes. We *must* remember them."

"But the Game kills dinosaurs," T'mpeka put in. "Can you justify *that?*"

Kalorn sniffed. "Yes. There is no battle without casualties. If we forget that, then . . ."

Kalorn's voice trailed off, his sentence unfinished as C'Nar pushed his way to the stone podium. He knocked the Game Master aside, and barely acknowledged his ignorant action with a quick lowering of his snout. He grabbed the speaker phone, turned to the Game Master and said, "Thank you, Kalorn. I'm sure we all found your discourse *most* interesting." Then he faced the media and said, "The S.R.I. are a bunch of mewling babies who need a political platform to feel important. We all know there is only one true and pure race, and we are *it!*" He bobbed his head from side to side, thanking the audience for their applause. It didn't come, and C'Nar growled. Kalorn tapped him in the chest and indicated for him to move aside. Which he did. Reluctantly.

"Females, Males." Kalorn began formally. C'Nar yawned, his mouth opening wide to display his impressive array of teeth, the stench of his breath filling the air around the stage. His yowl temporarily overpowered the speaker phone, and its squeal joined his yawn. Kalorn scowled at C'Nar, his dry upper lip rising to show his still sharp incisors.

"Sorry," C'Nar mumbled, lowering his head just a touch.

Kalorn adjusted his stance, pulling himself straighter. He threw back his shoulders and said, "The Society for Racial Integrity is . . ." he struggled for a polite phase, "*somewhat* misguided. As C'Nar has said, we are an intelligent race, and no one need remind us of that. Soon, we will be the only intelligent race on this planet." The room was filled with the buzz of whispers. He noticed the heads bowed together, the hushed exchanges at his suggestion of another intelligent race. He quickly continued, his voice loud and strong. "There has never been a purer race. The intervention and continual petitioning by members of the S.R.I. *did* heavily influence the Council of Representatives, but I will maintain the position that erasing the Game is erasing an important era of our history." He raised his head higher, and thumped the podium. "What will our children learn, now? And what of our children to come? They will not know of our struggle. And they *should*. Next question." He pointed midway down the room, not even certain what raised talon belonged with whom.

An Albertosaurus rose quickly to his feet, and with distaste, Kalorn recognized him as the young Kane, one of the wave of dinosaurs that had adopted Human names. The S.R.I. was after them, too.

"Kane," Kalorn said. "Your question?"

"For C'Nar," Kane said. "When did you first play the Game, and when did you know you were the greatest Game player that ever lived?"

Kalorn coughed indelicately, and Kane's eyes widened. He lowered his head and added, "After Game Master Kalorn, of course."

C'Nar seized center stage, gripping the podium so hard that the sandstone edge crumbled. "Of course," he said, giving Kalorn a small, toothy smile. "I played the Game when I began going to Temple. I was seven, and the Game was then part of the Teachings." C'Nar grinned as well as any Tyrannosaurus could. "I knew, right away, that I was destined to be great. My kill ratio, that very first time, was ninety-eight percent."

Another appreciative murmur traveled through the crowd of media representatives. C'Nar's grin widened, and as he caught Kalorn in an unblinking gaze, he bent low over the speaker phone. "And I've *been* great ever since."

Kalorn didn't back down. He met C'Nar's gaze. "True enough," he said quietly to the larger dinosaur. "But you still haven't matched my record."

C'Nar's answer was threatening in return. "I will today, old one. Match it *and* beat it. I want your title, old one. I want the mantle of Game Master on my strong *young* shoulders."

"Next question," Kalorn said loudly, eyes still locked with C'Nar. He was forced, by his position, to look away first, and he felt his cheeks flush with anger at the impudence of the tyrannosaur.

"The next . . ." Kalorn stopped as the back of the room started to rumble. He watched as dinosaurs parted, creating a small aisle down which Minister Chedwan could walk, unhindered.

"I yield the stage to Minister Chedwan," Kalorn said.

C'Nar lashed the stage with his tail, knowing what the arrival of the Minister signaled. He opened and closed his claws, flexing the muscles of his hand. He tilted his head from side to side, noting with pride that his shoulders weren't tight at all. He was ready for this. He was more than ready.

The minister, remarkably large for a stenonychosaurus, held on to the podium, then took his hands away when he realized the stone was hopelessly cracked. He folded his hands before him and said reverently, "Females, Males—the time has come. The last known living specimen of Humankind died quietly in the conservatory's medical clinic, one hour ago."

Members of the audience not equipped with recorders scribbled the information down.

"Minister Chedwan," someone yelled, "did it die peacefully, or was it, ah, *helped* in its journey to the next world?"

Minister Chedwan fixed the dinosaurs with a steady glare. "He died in his sleep, without assistance." The last word came out viciously. Chedwan then looked from Kalorn, who'd grown pale around his face, to C'Nar and said, "Let the Game begin."

The arena was full. Despite not knowing the time or the date of the actual game in advance, tickets had sold out in a matter of hours. Four huge screens had been placed, one on each side of the arena, affording everyone a good view.

In the center of the arena was the game platform. Kalorn stood to one side of the raised stage, looking at the chair. It was made of woven metal, uncomfortable, but formed to fit and support the large tyrannosaur body. It was anchored to the floor by iron bolts and girders. Even at that, Kalorn wondered if it would be secure enough. The helmet and game unit were positioned above the chair, and would be slipped on C'Nar's head when the time came.

The house lights dimmed. The time *had* come. A deeply mournful musical crescendo filled the air. Four small sauropods entered, carrying urns that billowed fragrant smoke, and the fans began to chant. . . .

"C'Nar! C'Nar! C'Nar!"

C'Nar followed, arms raised high, already the champion, already proclaiming final victory. He wanted the robe of Game Master, a robe which Kalorn believed C'Nar would never earn. He was skilled,no disputing that. But there was more to the Game than points and levels of difficulty. There was the history, educating others. C'Nar wanted none of that responsibility.

And Kalorn had learned the truth about Humanity through the Game, had come to understand that a race both intelligent and sentient had been brutally wiped out. But C'Nar neither cared about knowledge, nor cared to learn. All he sought was the adulation of the crowd.

And damn them all, they gave it to him.

The music stopped when C'Nar ascended the platform. Some lesser gaming official handed C'Nar the speaker phone, then hurriedly backed away, body half bent over in total supplication. Kalorn felt a little ill.

"The time you have waited for is finally here!" C'Nar bellowed. C'Nar waited again for applause, and this time, he got it. A rousing cheer went up, followed by thunderous stamping of feet. The sound echoed around the arena—hollow. Loud. Even Kalorn grudgingly stamped one wrinkled foot a time or two. He could not help but marvel at C'Nar's presence on stage—how he commanded his audience.

C'Nar signaled for silence. "As tradition dictates, I now must hand the speaker phone to the honorable Kalorn, who will perform his last duties as Game Master. Then I will prove beyond any doubt that *I* have the right to that title. Now listen as Kalorn recites—and possibly bores us with—the story of the Great Return." As Kalorn reached for the speaker phone, C'Nar added menacingly, "And he *will* keep it short."

A chuckle rippled around the arena. Normally, Kalorn would have been outraged, but he held his place and his tongue. He took the speaker phone and said, "Thank you, great C'Nar. Females and Males, listen to the story of the Great Return."

The lights dimmed again, and the four screens began to show pictures.

"There was a time," Kalorn began, "many, many years ago, when our people first landed on this world. It was lush, and food was bountiful." The screens showed dinosaurs traveling in herds across grassy plains, showed herbivores partially submerged in water. "Though the planet was beautiful, we knew we could not all stay. A colony remained to settle this new world, to make ready for our return." Lights flashed through the arena, temporarily blinding the crowd, followed by the sound of thunder. "But the planet did not welcome our people, would not sustain us as so many other worlds had. When we returned, after too long an absence, we found the planet littered with sprawling cities, infested with a race called Humans. And our kind? Gone. All gone."

The sound of dinosaurs shifting uneasily in their seats added to the background music coming from the screens. They showed a dinosaur skeleton on display from what had been called a museum. "The bones of our kind were desecrated for the amusement of Humans. Our holy ground, where the footsteps of our forbearers lay, were turned into havens where the Humans gathered. Though fascinated by us, they did not respect us." Kalorn signaled for an attending dinosaur to hand him a glass of water. He took a quick drink, then continued. "And so, we chose to take our planet back. The fighting was intense, furious. At first, we suffered great losses, for we had given too much of our time to matters of the mind, to technology—and not enough time to hone the skills all dinosaurs are born with. So the Game was developed to teach us how to take back that which we had lost. It taught us to fight."

A few dinosaurs stamped as the screens displayed pictures of dinosaurs, armoured in metal, firing huge laser cannons, charring Humans where they stood.

"The Humans deployed their nuclear weapons, poisoning our planet, killing our valiant soldiers, and killing many of their own kind in the process. And so, we waited, patiently orbiting our world, working on ways to nullify the poisons. Those ways were developed quickly, and before two solar cycles had passed, we were able to reclaim our world."

The sound of stamping grew louder. Kalorn had to yell to make himself heard. "The remaining Humans found that they could not survive against us, and within another cycle, the world was ours!"

The arena exploded into growls and howls, dinosaurs bellowing. Kalorn lowered the speaker phone, giving them time to feel the pride they'd earned.

C'Nar walked to stand beside Kalorn and said, "Are you just about done, old one?"

"The . . ." Kalorn faltered as C'Nar's breath overwhelmed him. "The Game reminds us of our struggle; the Game Master, a title not easily won. And I have held the title for too many years—many years more than most of you have lived."

"What are you doing?" C'Nar hissed. "This isn't part of your speech!"

Kalorn ignored him. "Here and now, I resign my title as Game Master, giving it gladly to C'Nar." Kalorn looked up, fixing the Tyrannosaur with a rock-steady glare. He exposed his teeth in a smile. "May he enjoy it for the length of this final game, for the title will have little actual meaning after the Game is gone."

C'Nar drew his shoulders together and leaned forward, eyes glaring. "But it *is* a title, and was *your* title. You will be nothing, old one, while I will be the idol of our people. I should kill you right now."

Kalorn nodded. "Perhaps you should. But you won't. It would damage the reputation of C'Nar the Magnificent, the reputation you have worked so hard to cultivate. You," he said, "will play the Game, and you will win. You will have your precious title, and it will ultimately mean nothing. You, C'Nar, will never have the life I have had, will never know what I know, and you will be the lesser being because of it. You will die a meaningless figure, a footnote in history." He patted the Tyrannosaur on the thigh. "Go on, now. Play your Game. Your fans are waiting."

C'Nar growled, and worked his way into the game chair, his thick tail sliding into the slot cut in the back of the seat. He huffed, furious that the old Albertosaurus had cheapened the greatest day of his life.

"Prepare the player," Kalorn said. Four dinosaurs scurried across the stage, attaching electrodes to six places on C'Nar's skull. Kalorn nodded in satisfaction and said, "Lower the Game."

As the helmet slid into place, the last thing C'Nar saw was Kalorn's face, mouth twisted in a smirk. He closed his eyes, willing the former Game Master's face from his mind. He took two deep breaths and let them out slowly, steadying himself, readying himself.

"Let the Game begin," Kalorn said, stepping back to one side of the platform. "Level one."

It was silly, really, Kalorn thought, to have C'Nar go through the preliminary levels. The Tyrannosaur knew the game by heart, could easily fight his way through the banks of Human armaments, could deflect the crude missiles with his shielded body armour. The explosions were nothing but an inconvenience, causing the electrodes to deliver only the slightest of shocks.

It wasn't until the seventh level that C'Nar began to hesitate in his moves. Probably no one but Kalorn even noticed the split second between action and reaction.

There, thought Kalorn. *There he should have employed a direct attack. The group had no weapons—he could have wiped them out in a few tail-sweeps. He's not thinking clearly. C'Nar the Magnificent is getting tired.*

But C'Nar made it through that level, and the crowd went wild. Very few of them ever made it past level six, and they had just seen C'Nar the Magnificent devour the last Human on level seven.

Level eight. Kalorn had lost his battle on this level, barely surviving the encounter. The Game lasers had seared across the game helmet, mirroring the wound

he received as he played. He aborted, then, unable to
finish. He'd lasted five minutes. Now, as the atten-
dants activated the lasers, he wondered how long
C'Nar would last. Less than five minutes, he hoped.

At four minutes, Kalorn began to feel uneasy. Until
now, a part of him believed that C'Nar wouldn't be
better than he had been. Despite the public adoration,
despite the media coverage, despite the times he'd
seen C'Nar play, a small part of Kalorn was saddened
that this young, brash Tyrannosaurus was better than
he had ever been. He sighed as the clock pushed
near—then past—the five minute mark. C'Nar
howled as he took a blow to the midsection. The
lasers sliced through his belly, though not deeply. The
injuries weren't life threatening. Kalorn watched as
blood seeped from under the helmet, and remembered
how he, too, had bled from the eyes. Then C'Nar
howled in conquest, level eight finished.

"Level nine," announced Kalorn. "Lasers to
seventy-five percent power."

The screens showed wave after wave of coordi-
nated attacks. Blood from his belly wound and from
his eyes pooled around C'Nar's feet. To Kalorn's
mind, C'Nar had already won.

"Stop the Game," he said.

C'Nar swung with one fist. "NO!"

"NO!" chanted the audience, "NO! NO! NO!"

Reluctantly, Kalorn gave in. "Continue," he said,
and C'Nar completed the level without taking any
more hits.

"Level ten," were the next words Kalorn said.
"Time limit of ten minutes. Lasers to lethal." He
rested on his tail, looking at the screen, waiting for
the all-out attack.

It happened quickly, more quickly than Kalorn
remembered. Missiles launched at C'Nar from all
sides. The dinosaur reacted just as quickly, finding
cover behind the battered remains of an old Human
building. The building was destroyed, but C'Nar still

stood. Only now, a small, bright red gash cut across his chest.

C'Nar roared.

Kalorn hid his hands within the folds of his cloak, talons crossed.

Next came the aerial attacks: more bombs, more missiles. C'Nar fended these off too, swinging left and right with his long, wide laser cannons. He fired rapidly and with deadly accuracy, blowing the small Human aircraft from the sky.

The injury had not slowed him at all. It had infuriated him.

At six minutes, the final ground assault began. Humans in lumbering armored vehicles crept toward C'Nar. They spat fire at him, gassed him. C'Nar pushed forward, ignoring the flames, ignoring the stinging fumes, and crushed one tank after the other.

Seven minutes. Only the forces on foot remained. They had nowhere to go in the city, trapped in a man-made gully, tall buildings offering them no way out. C'Nar began to stalk them.

Eight minutes, and only one platoon of Humans remained. They'd made their way to a partially standing bridge, had taken cover under it. In his chair, C'Nar howled in victory. He leaped onto the crumbling roadway, landing with his full weight on the weakest point. The bridge collapsed. C'Nar stood in the rubble while the audience cheered, looking before and behind, making certain that no Humans . . .

Wait. One scrambled from the wreckage, clawing his way on his hands and feet. C'Nar spied him easily. He took slow, deliberate steps as the Human stumbled, zig-zagging to the left and the right, his last feeble attempts at escape.

C'Nar bent over, took the Human's head in his teeth, and nipped it neatly off. At eight minutes and forty-five seconds, the game was over. C'Nar had won. Kill level: one hundred percent.

With one smooth move, C'Nar swept the helmet

from his head. He stood as the arena erupted into a frenzy of stomping feet and shouting voices: "C'Nar! C'Nar! C'Nar!"

Then C'Nar shrugged into his Game Master robes, allowing them to settle on his broad shoulders. He ran his hands over the soft material, crossed the stage to Kalorn, and offered him his hand.

Kalorn gazed at C'Nar, barely recognizing him as the Tyrannosaur that had started the game. He seemed larger than life, now, even more menacing. And Kalorn knew that this is what the Humans saw as the dinosaurs reclaimed what they believed to be theirs.

The Humans. So much about C'Nar reflected everything that Kalorn found despicable in the Humans: his arrogance, his ignorance, his readiness to display force when clearer-thinking dinosaurs would have chosen a more reasonable way. C'Nar would never have what Kalorn had, what he'd come to see in the Humans: compassion, reason, a deep racial pride that was based on more than a score in a game. With dread, Kalorn knew that more than the last Human had died. He was witnessing the end of his way of life.

C'Nar was before him, hand outstretched, waiting.

As Kalorn took it, C'Nar pulled him close, swept a leg under the old Game Master so that he fell on to his back. Then C'Nar raised his huge foot and planted it on Kalorn's chest. He bent over as far as he could, spittle dripping from his mouth, his eyes wild. "To hell with tradition, old man. The numbers are all that count."

And somehow Kalorn knew that the torch had not only been passed, but would consume in flames the world he had hoped to build.

THERE GOES THE NEIGHBORHOOD
by Melanie Rawn

Melanie Rawn is the best-selling author of many DAW novels.

"A little more—almost got it—there! That's the last of 'em." The specialist growled his satisfaction as he tossed away another triangular piece of metal. Carefully rubbing a cramp from his arms, and wishing they were longer so he wouldn't have to bend over so far (murder on his spine), he nodded to his patient. "Go have a nice long soak and take it easy on that leg for a few days."

"*Easy?*" she inquired acidly. "And where's my dinner going to come from while I'm wallowing in a mud bath and limping with every step and—"

"Your meals will be brought to you. It's all arranged. The food may not be what you're used to, but it won't do you any harm to eat lightly for a while."

An explosive "Hmph!" rattled the frond of an inoffensive nearby fern, and baleful green eyes regarded the specialist. "Are you telling me I'm too fat?"

"Not at all, merely that in your condition you need to be careful about what you eat, and especially where you go."

She resettled her shoulders and stood up, favoring one leg. "I'd like to see *you* outrun an attack while pregnant! Males!"

"Yes, yes," he rumbled soothingly. "I understand. Of course you're in a delicate state. Go have that soak now, and in a few days you'll feel just fine."

When she was gone, he glanced at the array of projectiles he'd just removed from her leg: metal tips, broken off from long wooden shafts. His collection included similar types made of wood barbed with chipped and sharpened stone, an assortment of heavier weapons that were easier to pull out but did more damage, all manner of straight and curved and pronged things (some with ropes), and even a few of those pestilential metal objects that were nearly impossible to dig out of flesh. Those wounds were hell to treat, but if he was careful and the tiny objects hadn't torn into anything vital, the patient usually survived. Scarred for life, of course, but scarred was better than dead.

Shoving aside a thick curtain of leafy vines, he called out, "Next!" An adolescent tottered toward him from the waiting area, whimpering softly, a metal shaft in his shoulder. "Doesn't look too bad. You be very brave for me, now, and I'll have this out in no time."

Afterward, he bolted down a snack, trying to remember the last time he'd eaten a fresh meal. He'd been so busy lately—winter being the worst season, attracting visitors who wilted in spring and summer. Unwanted and unwelcome, they came without warning, inflicted casual damage that he and his colleagues tried to heal, and vanished. He hated them. Everyone did.

"Next!" he called again, and another patient came through the vine curtain. She had a spear stuck in her back. "How'd you get this?" he demanded.

"Protecting my children," she replied tearfully. "These horrible strangers—they've no respect. You

aren't even safe around your own home anymore, no
matter how well you think you've guarded yourself
and your little ones—mine are safe, praise the Lore of
Accumulated Wisdom, but my friend lost three and
her sister lost five, and to hear them calling for their
stolen babies is enough to break your heart."

Abruptly furious, he threw back his head and bellowed, "This is absolutely the limit!"

Ferns trembled. Vines rattled. Flowers dropped
dead from their stems. And his patient cringed.

"I'm not yelling at *you,*" he said quickly, calming
himself. He was usually careful, but sometimes things
just got the better of him and his essential nature
broke through his professional restraint.

"Just—just please don't do it again," she quavered.

"I won't," he assured her, and got to work. But she
trembled throughout the treatment. He couldn't blame
her. Though he had taken his oath of healing in front
of hundreds, and had spent six sun-circles practicing
his craft with diligence and skill, even the stoutest of
heart could not but shudder when a Tyrannosaurus
Rex got pissed off.

As he slowly worked the spear from her back, he
muttered, "Goddamned tourists."

"I tell you it's intolerable!" he raged at the next
staff meeting, pacing the moonlit forest floor. "They
arrive out of nowhere to gawk at us, tromp through
our nests, steal our eggs and even our children, shoot
us full of holes, poison us senseless while they drain
our blood—"

A colleague from across the valley nodded, a not-
quite-complete set of incisors glistening silver-white.
"Not to mention taking teeth as a souvenir," he lisped.

"And the flat-faced runtlings even try their luck at
combat! With the Stegs, the Trikes—even *us!*"

Because they stood upright, because they were tall
enough to reach the back of the biggest patient,
because they were possessed of strong jaws that could

yank spears and such from flesh, because they had long claws with which to probe wounds, because as predators they had brainpower superior to others and had quickly learned this new and necessary craft—for all these reasons, selected T Rexes had decided that some of their kind should forswear shredding anything that came into their path and use their advantages to save the injured who could be saved. These Chosen ones still hunted on occasion, of course—and for some it took tremendous restraint to treat a wounded Brach without salivating. But theirs was a larger duty, and they performed it proudly.

Still, enough was enough.

"We have no peace or quiet—"

"And no privacy! Do you know they were in my sector to watch the mating season? Hundreds of the repulsive little things! Half the males were so upset they couldn't—"

"And half the females laid curdled eggs." The Elder, who had taken his oath fully twelve sun-circles ago, nodded. "Yes, that's happened before, and it will happen again."

"It's a scandal. It's indecent."

"It has to stop!"

"But what can we do?"

Not one of them had any answer. The scrawny poachers appeared out of nowhere, carrying all manner of instruments and devices and weapons. They did what they had come to do—sometimes nonviolently, never nonintrusively—and vanished. There had been tales about Folk vanishing with them, but no one in this region had believed it until a very young Rex, barely come into his serious teeth, disappeared. Two moons later his frantic mother found him wandering aimlessly through a swamp, glazed of eye and dazed of mind. When a few good meals had restored him, he told a remarkable story.

"The runty ones—they come from the next moon, and the moon after that, and—"

"Do you mean they come from *there?*" his mother cried, pointing to the silver circle overhead.

"No, no, the *next moon.* There is that moon up there in the sky, and then it gets eaten, and it grows again, and there is another moon, do you see? They come from *that* moon—the moon that will come after this one is devoured! And the one after that, and—"

"*Which* one after *what?* My poor baby, you've been through a horrible shock, you don't know what youre saying—come and rest, and Mother will hunt you something nice and fresh and bloody."

But the Elder had understood. And now he said, "Whatever afterward they come from, they just keep on coming. We managed to kill quite a few of them in my young day, but nowadays they are too many and too clever for us to mass against them in battle. *We* do not hunt in packs, in any case. And some of the Folk . . ." He paused delicately.

"Some of the Folk, popularly known as Leaf-Chewers," said a colleague, with a snort of disgust that shook the leaves off a nearby tree, "are too stupid to find their own tails."

"But what can we *do?*" someone else asked plaintively (for a T Rex).

"Look at what they've driven us to—we, with our proud and bloody heritage, reduced to this! Every one of us Chosen—ha!" Another explosive snort denuded a bush. "Chosen to jerk wood and stone and metal and who knows what else out of the Folk—forbidden to sample even the most succulent morsel of Allo hide when it's right there in front of—"

"Calm yourself," the Elder commanded. "We are strong, and smart, and physically equipped for the work. Think of it as self-interest. Would you have these runtlings so decimate the Folk that there's nothing left to hunt?"

"They're well on the way to it," one of them said glumly. "What with their weapons, and stealing eggs, and unnerving everybody during mating seasons—"

"We have to *do* something."

"Yes," the Elder sighed. "But what?"

Before the next moon was eaten, more visitors came. Not like the others who were small, furry on top, flat of muzzle, and entirely revolting to look at. These new visitors were tall as the top of a Diplo sailfin, and decently constructed with tails, the proper number of toes, and nicely articulated horny crests. They arrived, however, in the same kind of noisy, smelly, metal cave the others sometimes used, and the Folk scattered when a Ptero on sentinel duty screeched a warning.

"From the sky?" the Elder asked, blinking incredulously at the winged one's report. "None of them have ever arrived from the sky before!"

"Well, these did," panted the Ptero.

"Maybe they're different," mused the Elder.

"You mean maybe they won't loose those *things* at me?" the scout wailed. "Or haul me down out of the air, and throw a net around me, and spread out my wings until they cramp, and—"

"Stop whining," scolded the Elder. He didn't like Pteros; impossible to catch, and scrawny eating if you did. "You're still in one piece, which is more than can be said for plenty of others. Come, show me where their metal cave is. I want to look at these new visitors."

And so it was the Elder who was the first to know that these were not as the others were. In fact, that night he told the hastily called staff meeting that they said they were of the Folk themselves, and called the Elder "cousin."

"What? Impossible!"

"They're here to torment us just like those runty, flat-faced menaces—"

"Oh, shit! More tourists!"

"No," said the Elder. And then he told them a very curious tale.

When he had finished, a stunned silence rang through the forest. He waited, and waited some more, but no one said a word.

"The Cousins," he said at last, "have made an offer. What say you to it?"

One of them cleared his throat. "You tell us they can keep those miserable little menaces away?"

"So they claim. Has anyone seen or heard of any runtlings today?"

"None. But that doesn't prove anything. It's getting on for spring, and you know the hotter it gets, the fewer of them come."

"If they can keep the runtlings away for a day," said another, "surely they can do it forever!"

But the Elder shook his head. "They have arranged it—somehow—so that we can have peace until six moons are eaten to darkness. We must decide."

Another silence, and then someone burst out, "I can't believe it! I *don't* believe it! Those foul furry-headed things, outlive *us?*"

"I agree! This is *our* world!"

"Theirs, as well," the Elder replied sadly. "The Cousins say that they will do something called 'evolve'—which seems to be something like the development of an egg's softness into a hatchling's bones." Suddenly spiteful, he exclaimed, "If I knew which of these pesky little furry things they evolved from, I'd make it my mission in life to hunt down and eat every damned one of them!"

"Stand in line," a colleague said bitterly.

"I've been on constant duty so long," another mourned, "I'm not sure I remember *how* to hunt any-more."

"If we accept their offer," the Elder said, "you would have no duty other than to hunt. Think of it—we, the proudest of the proud, could be true once again to our heritage—"

"And leave this world to *them?* This is a hard thing, a very hard thing."

."They know that. Go to your homes, talk to the Folk. Ask what they think. We meet here again when the moon is half-eaten."

The offer was accepted. What else could they do?

So word went forth to all the Folk, spread to the farthest reaches of the land by those with wings: *Come, gather in the place we show you, and be free.*

The Pteros returned to the Elder, reporting mixed reactions.

"Count me in. I've a notion to live out my remaining time in peace and quiet."

"What about my children? It's much too far for them to walk."

"Show me where, tell me when, and I'm outta here."

"I'm not tromping all that way for nothing."

"I'm not tromping all that way for *anything.*"

"I'll come—as long as I get a guarantee that every Longtooth in a day's walk won't try to eat me."

"I'll stay and fight. This is my home and hunting ground, and if they think they can take it away—"

"Anyone who doesn't join us," growled a tired Ptero to the Elder, "is too stupid to know an egg from a stone."

And so when the day came, and six moons had been devoured, and the black sky shone only with stars, more of the Folk than had ever gathered in one place before were gathered at a place the Cousins showed them. Allos and Brachs, Stegs and Trikes, Raptors and Diplos and T Rexes, and all other manner of Folk came, and eyed each other warily, and huddled together in groups of their kind for protection.

But each and every one of the millions that walked and swam and flew forgot ancient enmities when the Cousins arrived.

They came not in a small metal cave, as they had before and as the runtlings sometimes did, but in a huge, incredible, terrifying, magnificent *thing* that hovered above the sea. It made a sound like a thousand feet thundering, and a wind like a million tails lashing. It was covered in colored stars. Nothing in Lore or Legend prepared them for the sight of this, their rescue.

All night it took, and all day, and all night again for the Folk to pass between the monstrous jaws. Within, all was miraculous, massive. Food was plentiful for the Leaf-Chewers; for the Longteeth, fresh meat (but no hunting allowed). Those who needed water to live in were provided it; for those who preferred sand underfoot, or forest, or swamp, these were available too. The only unhappiness was amongst those with wings, for as big as this sky might seem to the ground-bound—crowded as they were against each other, and envious of the avians—this sky was cramped to anything that could fly.

When all were settled, and the toothless muzzle closed, the Cousins warned everyone to stay calm and hang on tight. Then there came a greater roar than was ever heard, and a lurch that tumbled thousands, and a brilliant light brighter than any sun—some screamed, some fainted, and some few collapsed and died of the shock.

And thus did the Folk leave.

On the bridge of the great starship, the Cousin in charge and his second-in-command watched as the launch-fires receded.

"Course set for Cadence Central, sir. That's quite a hole we've left behind."

"Not as big as the one on Fratzinor Two—remember? Now, *that* was a crater!"

"I remember it, sir." He forbore to remind his captain that once they'd returned to their own time, the Endangered Kin Search-and-Rescue Authority had nearly brought them all up on charges for unnecessary damage to the planet. Damned bleeding-heart, tree-gnawing herbivores.

"But this was a pretty good one, all the same." Suddenly the captain bared his teeth in a ferocious grin, tail twitching with glee. "The best part is, the humans will think so too! 'Meteor crater'—*ha!* All they'll ever know is that everybody vanished—and they'll never figure out why!"

HOW DOG GEORGE SLEW THE DINOSAUR, AND OTHER SONGS THE YELLOW CUR SANG TO THE MOON

by Alan Rodgers

Alan Rodgers, former editor of Night Cry, *is now a full-time horror and fantasy writer.*

There is a tale that the dogs tell among themselves in the language that no man understands. They tell it to frighten wild-eyed young pups and tame the insolent among the cur: It is the tale of the Dogsnatcher, and there are dogs who say it is true.

Wise hounds know better, or think they do. The Dogsnatcher is a myth, a cautionary parable; nothing like that monster ever truly walked the world of men and dog.

So they say.

But I know a dog who felt his touch, and afterward that dog spoke to me as few men and dogs speak to one another.

He told me of a terrible white dragon who swallows dogs alive and whole—a canophage dinosaur come fallen out of time to haunt the dark heart of the city.

This monster waits hungry at the center of all urban blight, feeding itself on strays as it grows fat to menace and devour all modernity.

I believe my friend because he spoke in that true tongue that can carry neither lies nor misinformation.

I also know what I have seen—I know the
Dogsnatcher is real because I've seen his shadow
looming on the precinct wall.

No man who ever saw that sight could doubt it.
Mark me and take care: The day will come you'll see
it, too.

This is the Tale of the Dogsnatcher, as I heard it
from my friend I will not name.

My friend set eyes upon him on a cold and empty
night—a night when mindful men did not linger, but
hurried through the shadows, uneasy to be about;
when yardbound dogs whined and yowled before the
doorways of their masters, pleading for admittance,
eager to curl themselves to sleep at the feet of arm-
chairs and cabinets; a night when the cats wailed high
upon their fences, shrill and loud and long.

It was an evil night, and my friend was far, far from
home, lost among the feral dogs of the city. He knew
that lot too well, for he had spent his youth among
them and the coyote of the hills. He tarried with them
now and then by day, but always in the end he would
return to me, good and faithful, no matter what company he might sometimes keep.

He did not return to me that night. He surely should
have—but that afternoon he and his company of ban-
dits took a game of harrying a sanitation vehicle, yap-
ping and vexing the driver and the crew for hours as it
led them far afield. They didn't question the destina-
tion of their game, but they surely should have questioned it—for it led them deep into the city.

The city is no place for dogs. Its cobble-hard
bowels forbid them by their nature; its alleyways
entrap them; its hydrants call to them like sirens
enticing them to doom.

But my friend and his company hardly noticed
where they were. There was only the game—the
vexation of the driver; the sweet scent of the truck's

exhaust; the snarling epithets rolling off the tongues of the crew.

As the sanitation truck led them deeper and deeper now into their doom.

Now they reached the inmost moldered quarter of the city, and hardly noticed where they were—until, abruptly, the truck turned into a fenced lot, parked, and went dead for the evening.

Leaving my friend and his dubious companions alone in the dark and quiet of the nighttime city that terrible night of rain.

That was when the dismal nature of the night and their surroundings finally settled into their canine hearts. Just before the rain started—not far from where they first caught scent of the dogsnatcher.

The trouble started there at the edge of the fenced lot, as the dogs fell to arguing among themselves about the surest way from where they were to where they ought to be. My friend yipped of the south, and the largest of his companions gestured east as though he were a pointer and not a feral mongrel—and as he pointed, great, fat, cold hide-soaking wallops of rain began to fall. Rain and hail—hard sharp beads of hail that matted in their fur, stinging with their intensity.

A yellow dog howled at the suddenness of it, and the companions took up his cry—all of them bristling end to end as they sang the forlorn melody of the moon.

"No time," the big would-be pointer growled when the song was done. "There is no time to waste. If we do not hurry to our lairs, the cold will have us all, it will have us each and every one."

The yellow dog allowed as this was so, and began to sing of it. He would have sung all night if the mangy wolf-mix dog hadn't caught the scent.

"Quiet!" the wolf-mix dog snapped. "I have the scent of it!"

His yips were full of terror rage, the kind of angry growl one hears escape the throat of a cornered cur.

My friend had never seen the wolf-mix dog with his tail between his legs before, but there it was, plain as scent, pulled under in submission—

"Scent?" the little brown one asked. "There is nothing but the smell of rain."

The pack ignored him. All of them knew the story of the cat that had scratched the little brown one's nose while he lay dozing—without the cur ever catching wind of it.

"What do you smell?" my friend asked. "I do not have the scent that frightens you."

"The monster," said the mangy wolf-mix dog, blinking away a flea that worried at the corner of his eye. *The Dogsnatcher.*

Silence from the pack—till now the yellow dog whined in fear, shivered twice, and peed itself.

"You know that scent?" my friend asked. "You've lived to tell of it?"

No dog lives to tell the tale of the dogsnatcher's spoor—but the wolf-mix was only a dog so long as he took a collar or ran in a dog pack; there were days when it was more rightly a wolf or a coyote.

"What I've seen and smelled are mine," said the wolf-mix. "Pee on your own tree, cur."

This was a challenge, strictly speaking—but it wasn't worth the trouble of an answer. My friend looked away, sniffed the air. "South?" he asked.

Howls of misery and despair drifted toward them from the near distance in the west.

"South," said the big would-be pointer, and they were off, running hard and quickly among the nose-blind streets of the inmost city.

Three long blocks they ran, fast and hard and steady—and then my friend caught scent of the dragon, and screamed in mortal terror the way dogs will when they know their death is on them.

"We've gone the wrong way!" he shrieked. *"Run for your lives!"*

And the pack scattered hither and yon, lost in the dark heart of the city.

My friend found a hiding place in the basement of an abandoned building, and watched the thundering monster pace the streets and alleyways. Each time it passed, the howling despair grew closer and more melancholy, and finally it came to my friend why that was.

The Dogsnatcher fills the streets and alleys with the sound of cur despair because it swallows them whole and digests them still alive!

My friend whined in terror when that came to him. But frightened as he was, he did not leave his fear to master him.

Just the opposite, in fact. When he heard the song of the yellow dog, bellowing in agony within the dragon's bowels, he eased up through the shadows at the front of the basement to peer through the building's crumbling façade, where he could spy on the monster.

And saw the terrible white dragon that swallows dogs alive and whole. Saw the man who is his servant, and how that manling rides within the Dogsnatcher's maw impudent and fearless, too dull to realize the terrible peril that surrounds him. . . .

Saw the *Dogsnatcher.*

This is the measure of my friend: where most dogs would recoil at the sight of such a monster, turning tail to run screaming away, my friend heard the death-song of the yellow dog and found himself possessed of preternatural audacity.

He saw the Dogsnatcher and bounded out of the shadows, charging the reptilian monster.

"Disgorge them!" he barked, leaping at the monster's leviathan throat. The monster effected not to notice—for the time it took my friend to find purchase and begin clawing and tearing at the dragon's steely-ashen hide. "Disgorge them, dragon, or you will die!"

The dragon roared defiantly, enraged, and then it bolted—surging through an alleyway as it flung its great head to and fro, trying to dislodge my friend. Down in the creature's maw the servile manling shrieked obscenities at my friend, threatening to disembowel him and scatter his entrails to the four corners of the Earth—

As the dragon lurched and bucked, trying to throw my friend into the alley wall—

And there, standing on the skull of the monster, high above its eyes, my brave friend finally lost heart.

He braced himself on all fours, digging his claws into the monster's steely hide, raised head to the moon and shrieked a yowling prayer of terror, begging mercy from the moon.

And in his fear he peed himself.

That may've saved him. For it was that yowling cry that I heard from half a mile away, in the margins of the blight where I'd been searching for him till that moment.

And even more important, my friend's unintending void spattered down the monster's carapace, and into its maw—choking the dragon, blinding his manling toady. The dragon wretched and sputtered, and its struggles lost all semblance of control—till now the monster screamed like a bird of infinite proportion—

And rammed the precinct wall.

As it rammed the wall the creature lost its balance and tumbled onto its side, tearing into a hydrant that split a long gash through the monster's gullet.

As the fallen dragon bellowed out its rage, it breathed explosive fire that shattered its own skull.

In the terrible moments that followed, three dozen half-digested dogs make good their feeble escape from the belly of the fiery beast. My friend, thrown clear of the monster in its final tumult, limped away terrified, to hide among the shadows of the city.

I found him an hour later—there in that heart of deepest blight. I came around a corner in my aging Pinto and he saw me. Yipped three times and staggered into sight—as I saw the shadow of the beast upon the precinct wall.

And gasped. And knew in my own heart that terror that stalks the misbegotten in the dark heart of the city where a dog can know no rest. Knew in that instant how it lured them and hunted them, and how it will snatch a dog if it is able, and when it does it draws him to his doom.

"Good boy," I said.

And opened the Pinto's door to welcome my friend home.

THE FEATHERED MASTODON
by David Gerrold

Best-selling author and TV writer David Gerrold is the winner of the 1995 Nebula and Hugo Awards for Best Novelette.

Okay, I hereby publicly apologize for pushing Mike Resnick into the La Brea Tar Pits. I did it. I'm sorry.

I won't try to excuse it by saying it was poor impulse control on my part—after all I did smack him with two feather pillows, and the fact that I'd brought the pillows along was clear proof that the stunt was premeditated. So I plead guilty for that and I apologize.

But I'm not going to give the money back. If the purchasing agent at the Page Museum was stupid enough to believe my story about having cloned a feathered mastodon, then that's his fault and his employer's responsibility.

But I do want to apologize to Bantam Books for spoiling their traditional Worldcon dinner excursion. They'd rented a big bus, filled it with beer, and schlepped all of their most-willing writers—those who hadn't found other obligations with other publishers—off on the science fiction version of a magical mystery tour. Tom Duprec has already told me that I'm not likely to be invited back, and that's probably punishment enough, I guess.

Tom also told me how much it cost to have the emergency vehicle called—they had to call in one of those extra-huge cranes that they use for lifting box-cars to hoist Resnick out of the sticky black oil. He looked like a giant fudgsicle—or a Godzilla turd—and while he was hanging there, all gooey and dripping and glumphing unintelligible threats, that's when I slit open the feather pillows and whacked him with them.

It was expensive, but—what the hell, even though I've apologized, I have to admit it was worth it. But Tom says they're going to take it out of my royalties. Like that's a threat. Maybe if they'd sell some books, I could get some royalties once in a while.

But I'm not worried. Even though the SFWA Defense Fund turned down my requests for legal aid, there are enough other former contributors to Resnick anthologies who have sent me generous checks—enough that I should be able to mount a credible defense. Just contributing a story to a Resnick anthology goes a long way toward proving temporary insanity.

Okay, yes, he deserved it—there's no question that he had it coming. He shouldn't have said what he said. He shouldn't have said it on camera. And most of all, he shouldn't have sent me a videotape of him saying it in front of an audience of three thousand people.

The only reason I'm apologizing now is that I didn't know about his skin condition and how, when the oil and the tar seeped through his skin, it would render him sterile and impotent—kind of a chemical castration.

While all the behind-the-back jokes about Resnick's new career as a harem guard, and how he's now in demand for the soprano lead in *La Castrata* have been funny in their own sick way, the fact is I'm really starting to feel bad about all this. The doctors say it's unlikely that Resnick will ever grow another follicle of hair anywhere on his entire body—some kind of interaction with the pollutants in the tar—and since he has to wear those rubber pants because of the resultant incontinence problem, he looks sort of like a three-hundred-pound baby. And they say he cries a lot, too. Especially when the male nurses come to change him.

So, okay, I guess I'm not a very nice person. And this particular fraternity-level prank only proves that I'm not to be trusted out in public without a keeper. A simple pie in the face would have made the point just as easily and probably would have been a lot funnier too. But Resnick started it, so he deserves some of the blame. That remark about how "recombinant DNA splicing explains Gerrold's nose" *hurt.*

The thing is—Resnick should have known better.

It's no secret. Science fiction writers gossip. They talk about the stuff they've seen. Pournelle's been inside the space shuttle, Benford gets guided tours of particle smashers, Ben Bova got an advance peek at the—oops, not supposed to mention that one yet. But you get the idea. Where do you think we *really* get all our ideas? We hang out every year at the annual meeting of the American Association for the Advancement of Science—and hope for invitations to the real labs. And then we get drunk at the conventions and brag about what we've seen. I got invited to a tour of Intel's new fabrication plant. Ellison got to see a building demolished with a new small explosive named after him. Roddenberry once got a free tour of the whiskey museum in Edinborough.

In this case, I know that the research papers haven't been published yet; there aren't any articles yet in *Scientific American* or *Discover* magazine—only a few weird articles in the *National Enquirer* about potatoes with real eyes and hairless mice with purple mohawks. Oh, wait—there was that one thing in *Discover,* but it was in their April issue, and everybody thought it was another one of their silly April Fool's jokes like the particle the size of a bowling ball or the naked ice-borer that grabbed penguins from underneath.

But the fact is, they have been doing some serious gene-splicing work at—well, never mind. I could tell you, but then I'd have to hunt you down and kill you. Everyone who reads this. And that would seriously decimate the population of science fiction readers. Or maybe not. How many people read Resnick anthologies anyway? Not that many. The loss would hardly be noticed.

But anyway, I was invited up to a place in Marin County. It's funded by a couple of famous movie directors, you figure it out. This goes back more than fifteen years, when they first decided they wanted to do a dinosaur movie—only at that time nobody, not even Stan Winston's guys, could figure out how to coordinate all the separate machines necessary to create an illusion of real motion. The was when computers were still as big as refrigerators and cost more than Ferraris.

So that's when the dinosaur-cloning project really began. They thought they'd make their movie with real dinosaurs. And maybe even open a park, too—which is where they got the idea for the movie that did get made.

It wasn't done with amber—although that's sexier because it films better. It was really done by processing coal. Coal is really a compressed peat bog. And peat bogs are really good at preserving dead things—every so often somebody finds an ancient mummy in a bog. Well, sometimes they find dinosaur bones in coal—so if you process the coal immediately around the dinosaur bones, you get chains of DNA.

Most of it is damaged, of course. DNA doesn't last for eighty million years. But if you collate all the different chains, you can put them together and pretty much approximate what was there in the first place, and then you can plug them into ostrich eggs and see what you get. Mostly, you get deformed ostrich embryos. So that was pretty much a dead end. It used up a lot of money, but the movies were paying for the research, and it was tax-deductible too, so the thing just chugged away, burning dollars and coal at the same rate.

But after a while, the guys in the lab coats decided to try something else. They thought, "Hey, why don't we back-breed from existing species of birds and reptiles until we match the dino DNA?" And so they started down that path with high hopes. That was another good way to use up millions of dollars a year. Pocket change.

Somehow, the back-breeding project took a side-turn. I think it was the time that they were trying to do all those weird fantasy movies. The Henson people were good with the puppets. The Winston people were getting better with the machines. The computers were getting smaller. But it still wasn't enough—and meanwhile, the guys in the labs had gotten a little stir-crazy—

Oh yeah, I should explain that. Because the whole thing was being done in such incredible secrecy, they had built this little city off in the hills north of the bay; the cover story was that it was a movie production facility—and they even built a real recording studio there as a kind of false front. But underneath it were the real labs. And because the work was so secret, the scientists and all the technicians were literally confined to the site. They were allowed to see their families only on Thanksgiving and Christmas. It was like being sent to Antarctica, but without the snow.

So, yeah—they got cabin fever. And they got crazy. It happens.

When I was in college—USC Film School, although I try not to admit it—one of the animation professors told us of a "tradition" at animation studios. Pornographic cartoons. Each animator would (on his own time) add a scene. The next animator would pick it up where the last guy left off. Back in the days of wild fraternity parties and pornographic movies—before VCRs—some of these animated films were floating around town. I remember one with a farmer and a donkey and . . . well, never mind. I also remember the instructor sighing wistfully. "Ours were good, but they were never as good as the ones coming out of Disney. Now those guys were great." I don't think any of the Disney stuff ever got off the lot though. I never saw any of it. I wonder sometimes if Walt did. I'd be surprised if he didn't.

Anyway, that's what started happening at Project Back-Breed. The DNA Team started mixing genes just to see what would happen. They weren't having any luck with anything else: They hadn't licked the viability problem, nothing lived, so they got desperate just to see if they could make *something* that would survive.

That's where the hairy chicken came from. They actually created a small flock of hairy chickens. They looked like furry bowling balls. They were hysterical to see—clucking around the yard like big fat tribbles. (That's why I got to see them. Otherwise, I'd never have been allowed near the place.) Two of them were fertile, so they were able to breed several generations by the time of my visit. All colors—blonde, brown, red, white, black, even one with a weird purplish tinge. They were pretty good eating too. They tasted like chicken. Of course.

After the hairy chicken, the DNA Team decided to try going the other way, to see if they could put feathers on a mammal. That was about the time someone had the bright idea of injecting an elephant with frozen mammoth sperm. They're always finding dead mammoths frozen in the Siberian glaciers, and it's not that hard to chip some sperm out of the ice, defrost it, do a testtube fertilization and inject it into an unsuspecting elephant cow. The technology has been used on horses, pigs, sheep, cattle, dogs, mice, gorillas, chimps, and even humans. So why not elephants? What's the worse that could happen, right?

Right, Somehow, the chicken DNA crossed the information highway.

Eventually, they tracked it back to a software error. This file and that file got crossed, so this DNA pattern got mixed with that DNA pattern—and the project was so big by that time and there was so much going on that nobody even noticed that this sample and that sample were from two different experiments, two different species—because that's what they were doing anyway, so it was just one more set of genes to be spliced—and the compatibility problem got knocked down as a matter of routine—and eventually, the samples got processed and put into the pipeline and chugged along until—well, that's how they ended up with the feathered mammoth. Cute little thing.

Of course the cow that delivered it practically died from the shock—but after a dose of Prozac large enough to make New York polite, she cheered up and nursed the little guy as if he were her own calf—which he was, but he had this weird yellow down all over him. At first, everybody thought it was just normal fur, but when the first feathers started appearing six weeks later—let me tell you, there were a lot of questions asked and there were a lot of red faces, too—but that could have been from the other experiment, the one about genetically redesigning already-living creatures. One of the retro-viruses had escaped, recombined, mutated, and become airborne, and now half the team was evolving into Native Americans. So the red faces were normal by then.

Fortunately for everybody, there were a lot of cinematic possibilities in weird animals. That was about the time Paramount was going to send Kirk and Spock to the Genesis planet, and they were looking for a cheap source of weird creatures as a way of keeping the special effects budget down, so they pumped some new money into the whole thing; two or three of the other studios also came aboard then, and in short order the guys in Marin were turning out all kinds of little monsters. Hairy chickens of all sizes—they were clumsy and unstable and a strong wind could knock them over and blow them like tumbleweeds—and that's how you saw them in *Critters.* And there was an ostrich with scales—supposed to look like a deinonychus, but ultimately unconvincing. I think the Corman people finally used it in a dog called *Carnosaur.* Carnivorous rabbits for *Lepus II.* Unmade. A green cat. (That one sold for nearly two million—but the cat died before the script went into turnaround. Pity, the merchandising on it would have been phenomenal. They were all set to breed a million green cats in time for Christmas.)

And, of course, the feathered mammoth. They were going to use him in something with Arnold Schwarzenegger, another Conan picture, I think, *Conan in Atlantis,* but it didn't happen either. The studio sunk it. Nobody really likes working with animals, children, or Martians. They always use the Martian's best take. (But that's another story, the one about the Martians. When Resnick publishes *Alternate Martians,* I'll tell it. If they let him edit any more of these. I doubt it after this one, but who knows—they say it's good work-therapy at the outpatient clinic, so who am I to piss in his oatmeal? We all wish him a speedy recovery. Well, most of us do. Well, his family anyway. I think.)

But eventually—finally—they did manage to back-breed some real dinosaurs. Sort of.

The problem was they were working with frog and lizard and bird eggs, so the dinosaurs they got were small. Miniature. The size of Dinky toys. That's what they called them at the farm. Dinky Dinos. Stegasaurs as cute as hamsters. Hadrosaurs that looked like parakeets. A T Rex the size of a crow. It took a lot of really skillful trick photography to make them look full size for the movie. (I hear they're going to start selling the Dinky Dinos in pet stores next year, simultaneous with the release of the sequel. That'll be interesting when Daddy brings home a little T Rex as a birthday present for little Jill.)

What you didn't hear about—what nobody heard about—were the raptors. Three of them escaped.

At first nobody on the farm worried about it. There was a chronic problem with rats in the feedstock, so they had brought in terriers and later on, a few wild tomcats had joined the menagerie too, and that had kept the problem manageable—sort of. The cats killed as many lizards and birds as they did rats—so the guys at the farm figured the pussies and the pooches would probably kill the raptors too, thinking they were just some kind of lizard-bird. Only it didn't happen that way.

First, the rats disappeared. And the mice. And the gophers and the skunks and the badgers ("Badgers? Badgers? We don' need no steenkeen' badgers!") and the rabbits and the weasels and the foxes and the coyotes and everything else small enough to be brought down by a pack of land-piranhas. And of course, the pooches and the pussies, too.

By that time, the raptors were numbering nearly thirty. They traveled in packs—five or seven to a group. At any given time, they were between four and six packs of them roaming the grounds of the farm, chirruping and cooing like demented pigeons, their little heads bobbing back and forth, turning this way and that, their tails lashing frantically. They were brightly colored—the males were green or blue, with yellow flares of color down their backs and bright red stippling around their heads and forearms. The females were drab gray-green. The females traveled together, the males kept apart from them, except during mating season—when it wasn't safe to get out of your car unless you were wearing heavy boots.

It wasn't until the raptors started bringing down the

newborn calves that the farm guys realized the problem was out of control; they brought in some tropical quarantine experts who laid out slabs of meat laced with poison cocktails. That got half of them; the other half got smarter. So they tried traps. And retroviruses. And hunter-killer droids—that was another nightmare. The software mutated—remember the law of unintended consequences? The ex-terminators (formerly terminators, now just ex-terminators) shot at anything that moved—or even looked like it was thinking about moving. Finally, they cut power to the feed lines and the ex-terminators ran out of juice after two or three more weeks. Meanwhile, they still had a raptor problem.

They finally got them with pheromones. They put out lures that smelled like female raptors in heat and all the males couldn't help themseles, they came sniffing around the lures and tumbled through trap doors into little tar pits where they died like dire wolves and sabre-toothed cats and mastodons in prehistoric Los Angeles. (LA needs more tar pits. There are still too many sabre-toothed lawyers and dire agents and studio mammoths staggering around the countryside.)

That should have been the end of it, but it wasn't. By this time, the guys upstairs were so pissed, they were ready to shut the whole operation down. The DNA Team had to get rid of the remaining raptors, so they donated them to the San Francisco Zoo. Oh, that was smart. On the one hand, there are no rats in San Francisco any more. On the other hand, there are no stray animals either. You have to keep your cat in the house, and it's not safe to walk your Chihuahua.

All of which has nothing to do with Resnick directly, except that he was supposed to be part of the solution, not part of the precipitate. Instead, he ended up in the pits. Down in the mouth . . . and all his other orifices as well.

See, Resnick had been doing this whole series of

anthologies—*Alternate Nightmares, Alternate Sexes, Alternate Bicycles*—whatever he thought would sell. And he had sold one called *Alternate Dinosaurs* or something like that. Who keeps track? And the publisher had decided that it would be fun to do some kind of tie-in with all the dinosaur movies, but they couldn't afford much of a licensing fee and the only one they could link up with was that dreadful turkey Fox was making—*The Feathered Mastodon*. In fact, that's what it was about—a dreadful turkey—and the mammoth was playing the lead.

And so they sent Resnick out West to have his picture taken with the critter, and there they were, the two of them, side by side—and I was there, too, with my kid and my video camera, and I forgot that everything I said while taping would be heard on the tape, so when I sent Resnick a copy of the tape, he could hear me saying clearly, "The family resemblance is astonishing. They both have the same birthmark in the shape of an Edsel."

I guess Resnick felt he had to get even. So there he was at the secret convention of trufans, held in Moscow, Idaho every February, and he was still smarting over the tape I'd just sent him, and that's when he said what he said, and that's why I pushed him in the tar and smacked him with the pillows. And then, while no one was looking, also injected him with a cocktail of kangaroo, frog, and lizard DNA, with a chaser of growth hormone.

Things should start hopping around the Resnick household *real soon now*. I'd move out of the state if I were you. In the meantime, I've sold an anthology called *Alternate Resnicks*. Watch for it in the bookstores next fall.

DRAWING OUT LEVIATHAN
By Susan Shwartz

Susan Shwartz, short story writer, novelist, and anthologist, has been nominated for numerous Hugo and Nebula awards.

Canst thou draw out Leviathan with an hook? Or his tongue with a cord which thou lettest down? (Job 41:1)

Even before the Anakim appeared, giants roved the fertile earth and brown waters. They lived long, slow lives between the two wide rivers that carved the young land into a crescent enriched by regular floods. In the summer, Leviathan and her mate Behemoth bathed their flanks in the warm rivers. Juicy reeds and sweet grasses sprang out of the black mud for the nibbling any time they cared to wade toward the shore, bend long, slender necks, and scoop up a meal.

In the winter, the rivers were crisp and cool. Winter was for sleeping through the long, slow nights and into the pale mornings, dreaming of the ancient memories of their kind. But Leviathan also dreamed of the Spring, when women would bring fat babies to the riverbank once more, to show them giants like herself, floating in the water.

As Spring warmed toward Summer, the sun seemed to glow a brighter yellow, baking the bank where she had buried her eggs as the women baked their bread in mud ovens. On the great day when they hatched, the two-legged mothers gathered up the broken shells for bowls and scrapers.

Leviathan looked forward to several joyous months while the children of both kinds played together. On land, the two-legged children took the lead. In the water, they followed Leviathan and Behemoth's offspring, grasping their long, agile tails and supple necks for their first forays into the water under the careful eyes of mothers of both species. The children seemed to fear Behemoth as they feared their own fathers, but, from time to time, some brave child would bring Leviathan a special mouthful of sweet grass. She would incline her neck to receive it, a bow of thanks. And, on very rare occasions, when a child had been especially good, she would let herself sink down into the water. Then, a watchful parent might lift a laughing child up onto her back for a ride, cautioning it all the while never to throw rocks or to pull the tail-feathers of the winged creatures that hovered about Leviathan and groomed her, keeping her free of tiny bugs that crawled and flew. The different peoples spoke voice to voice or mind to mind, for, in those days, speech was not sundered.

In the evenings, the oldest men of the tribe would come out to the riverbank and sing. Some of them were very old, perhaps as ancient as her own long-lived kindred. Also, like her kindred, the human elders had possessed memories of the most ancient days when no moon shone in the sky and clouds hid the face of the sun and the being that humans called God walked in the twilight.

The world, her human kindred said, had changed much. Now, it possessed a moon that turned her vast flanks to silver every evening. How the humans exclaimed when they saw her scales glitter. How they marveled at her and made songs of praise for Leviathan and her mate Behemoth. *Behold now Behemoth, which I made with thee, he eateth grass as an ox. Lo now, his strength is in his loins, and his force is in the navel of his belly. He moveth his tail like a cedar; the sinews of his stones are wrapped together.*

"*Canst thou put an hook into his nose?*" the sages asked, those ancient men with impressive names like Enoch, Methusaleh, and Lamech. The very thought seemed laughable. Leviathan and Behemoth were their valued neighbors, and, with the exception of Cain, who would think to turn on neighbors? "*Or bore his jaw through with a thorn? Shall the companions make a banquet of him, shall they part him among the merchants? Canst thou fill his skin with barbed irons? Or his head with fish spears? Lay thine hand upon him, remember the battle, do no more.*"

The songs, like the friendships between child and child, were a sacred covenant between mankind—that race that made names as readily as artifacts—and her long-lived, slow-moving kindred. For generations, as it seemed, she and her sisters and their mates stood belly-deep in the rich brown waters, thinking their long, slow thoughts and watching the children of two races grow.

And then the Anakim arrived. This new kindred was different, she and her family agreed in the first conclave they had held from time almost out of mind. They waded into the river which buoyed up their enormous weight, comforting them, and swiveled their long necks, glancing as they spoke, from one to another until they had reached their laborious consensus.

For one thing, this new tribe called themselves the sons of God. That was a strange, stark name, not like Enoch or Methusaleh, with whom generations of her people had grown up. Still, it was in this God's name that the sons of men had always praised her kind, and it was the name of whatever creature it was who had invited Enoch and Methusaleh to walk with Him. The old men had not seemed afraid before they left; and thus, if Leviathan and Behemoth thought of God at all, it was as their friends' protector.

Another thing that troubled Leviathan was that the Anakim were all men. This should not have been a bar to their welcome; the women who dwelt between the two rivers were comely and warm, as the Anakim soon found. They hastened to pick the strongest and cleverest of the females, those with the reddest lips.

The Anakim's speech was different, fast, and harsh, and imperious. They demanded first choice of everything and the best of everything: from mates to the reeds and fish of the river. The children born to these new men and the mates they had appropriated were larger, hardier, rougher than the gentle race Leviathan had come to love. As these children grew, they seemed to stride over the earth as if they had the right to shoulder anyone else out of the way. That extended, too, to her kindred: When she saw one of this new breed of children staring down an adolescent Behemoth thrice his size, she nudged her son away and placed her own massive bulk between him and the human child.

Above all, the Anakim never had enough, and nothing ever came quickly enough when they called. Their haste stirred up the pools where Leviathan preferred to drink, muddying the water. Then, there was the day that all the reeds disappeared. Now, the daughters of men crafted things called paper and baskets and hats, but those were all tasks they had not performed before. The Anakim sat constantly in judgment on the work and its quality. Their demands and the fear of them ended the lazy afternoons by the water. Even the children had no time to play.

Perhaps, Leviathan thought, it was because the Anakim moved and spoke faster. It was easier for anyone to listen, bend the neck, then edge away. Leviathan knew it was the Anakim who had upset the balance of a life that had pleased many for generations. But she and her kind were slow-moving, slow of speech, slow to decide and plan. Too slow.

How long was it until she realized that nest after nest of her own children and all of her sisters had bent the neck and edged away? She and her mate Behemoth stood alone in the swamps. Even the praise songs brought them by Lamech and his young son, a fine boy much like the children of ages past, had changed. *"Who can open the doors of his face?"* they sang. *"His teeth are terrible round about. His scales are his pride, shut up together as with a close seal. One is so near to another, that no air can come between them. They are joined one to another, they stick together, that they cannot be sundered."*

It hurt to think that humans might think of Behemoth as a fighter.

In long, leisurely conversation, her mate and she agreed: The children of the Anakim were mighty men, men of renown (that there were no women of renown seemed not to cross the Anakim's acquisitive, haughty minds) who spoke at length about bringing other tribes to join them and ease their labor.

Now it was they who called themselves giants in the Earth: It was an easy enough claim to make, because the children of Leviathan had been growing fewer and fewer. Had humans noted their own numbers declining, they might have found that of concern enough to fear and take action again. Leviathan's breed, content with their long lives, drowsed in the water, dreaming their long dreams that wandered back and forth in time. If barriers to dreams rose on either side of time, why, those, too, would pass in the fullness of things. They trusted. They loved. They remembered. This was their life, and the remnant dwelling by the rivers did not care to go beyond it.

In those days, too, of the Anakim's pride, the sons and daughters of man seemed to rise up and pass away like grass. Their long, long lives became a thing of the past: Enoch and Methusaleh had lived almost two human hands' of years longer than the sons and daughters of the Anakim and, sad to say, Leviathan's old friends.

Except, of course, for the family of Lamech. They were, Leviathan recalled, the last of the original tribe that had settled near Leviathan's people on the river-banks not long after the gates of Eden had closed to them. Like Leviathan, they remembered the old ways.

As soon as Noah was of an age to leave his mother, Lamech brought him to see Leviathan, and he was enthralled. He would come down, every afternoon, to the riverside and squat on the shore, watching her. He dared come into the water with her latest brood. She smiled within herself years later when she saw him walking out by the trees with a tall, vigorous young woman. Sure enough, in the fullness of time, three small children followed their father to the river to meet her and her mate. They did not even fear Behe-moth, who consented to bear them on his back.

In Lamech's son, Noah, Leviathan and her mate agreed one night, the old race might be reborn.

Shouts, not the dawn, woke them the next morning. Some time ago, the children of the Anakim had enslaved beasts to carry them. Now they raced past the water, brandishing pointed wands and singing incomprehensible boasting songs.

They rode their beasts down the riverbank, and Leviathan's heart froze as if she had waded belly-deep into the river at midwinter. Their path would take them to where the sand and mud could be heaped up into a mound to cover a clutch of eggs while the sun blazed down until first the mud, then the shells beneath it hardened until the growing infants cracked shells and mound wide open.

She swung her head around and nudged Behemoth awake. She reared up, trumpeting her distress for her mate and for humans such as Noah and his young sons to hear. And then she and her mate pursued the children of the Anakim, regretting for the first time that they were ponderous and slow of foot.

Shouts came from the hatching ground. She knew Noah's voice, had heard it mature from baby wails and gurgles to the bass of an adult male, teaching his children. "You don't want to do this!" he told the children of the Anakim. "They are our neighbors!"

"What fools you are, with monsters for your neighbors!" laughed the Anakim.

They and their sons laughed again as Leviathan and her mate lumbered up. In days gone by, they might have called tens of them, maybe fifty to their aid, making the earth shake with the thunder of their tread. Now, there were but two. Such speed as they built up was slow to dissipate; their motion carried them beyond the hatching ground—the hatching ground that was; for the children of the Anakim had hacked open the mound, pierced the hardening shells, and extracted the half-formed bodies of what she knew, deep within her, might well have been her last clutch.

Several built a firepit, buried a few unbroken eggs within it, and kindled flame. They would eat her young!

Leviathan trumpeted distress. Behemoth, her gentle mate Behemoth, bellowed in rage, and then he reared, towering over the Anakim by fifty cubits.

"The sword of him that layeth at him cannot hold the spear, the dart, nor the habergeon," the ancient praise songs went. *"He esteemeth iron as straw and brass as rotten wood. The arrow cannot make him flee; slingstones are turned with him into stubble. Darts are counted as stubble; he laugheth at the shaking of a spear. Sharp stones are under him: he spreadeth sharp-pointed things upon the mire. He maketh the deep to boil like a pot; he maketh the sea like a pot of ointment. He maketh a path to shine after him; one would think the deep to be hoary. Upon earth there is not his like, who is made without fear."*

Thus the praise songs ran, but they did not daunt these children of pride. As Leviathan's mate Behemoth reared up over the ruins of his family, the children of the Anakim rode at him screaming. They hurled their lances into his underbelly where years of river water had softened his scales. Behemoth screamed denial, twisting his neck in agony, forbidding Leviathan to lumber to his aid. He tried to rear again, then toppled heavily, pinning riders and beasts beneath him. The others hacked at him until he moved no more.

They rode at Leviathan, shaking their spears, dark now with Behemoth's life. The ancient truce was broken.

Why leave even one? She challenged them. The Anakim crushed beneath Behemoth's weight did not move: so, like her mate, they could be killed.

Noah placed himself between her and the riders. "Go back!" he commanded. Light wreathed him about and he seemed like an ancient of days, his grandfather, as Leviathan recalled before that strange creature he called God took him to walk with him in parts unknown. How could God be Methusaleh's and Enoch's friend, yet the father of these murderers?

For a moment, Noah too seemed a giant in the Earth. His beard looked like cloud, and his eyes flashed with the lightning. Rain fell upon the earth, dousing the cookfire they had kindled to seethe or roast Leviathan's last eggs.

She was alone now. What use was there to dig out those eggs and try to save them? With no one to help her, she was the last.

Her long neck drooped. She turned her face aside. She wandered far away from the water that had been her home for so many generations. It did not matter where.

She found the world different than she had expected. It was, for one thing, far larger and filled with humans. Mounds made of stone or heaped of the

living mud of the river dotted the earth, as many as
there were reeds upon the river bank. While her breed
had dreamed, the Anakim had bred into a race as
mighty in people as it was in crime.

Up and down upon the earth, Leviathan wandered.
The ancient truce between man and Leviathan was
not just broken: It had been forgotten. Man hunted
man as if for sport. Man treated man—or woman or
child—worse than the brute beasts of the field.

When a child hurled a rock at one of the winged
creatures who still hovered about her and groomed
her for the things that buzzed and crawled, Leviathan
knew that the evil brought by the Anakim had spread
past all endurance.

In all her wanderings she found no foothold where
the old ways held. Ultimately, she raised her head,
sniffed the air, and made her ponderous way back to
the riverbanks where the willows stood. Past them lay
the hatching ground that, so long ago, the sons of
Anakim had profaned.

Her murdered eggs were long since gone. The
ground was smoothed over where they had lain.
Nearby, however, towered a mound bigger than any
nest in all her memories. Leviathan edged cautiously
over to it. How long and how broad it was! Such a
mound might cover not eggs, but a creature as great
as herself.

Her memories stirred, and understanding came to
her: The mound covered her mate—honor such as the
sons of men gave their fathers' bodies, cast aside,
when their fathers went to walk with God.

Noah and his sons must have buried Behemoth as
they would have done for one of their own.

Behemoth's bones might lie in that mound, but his
essence was long gone. Leviathan wandered back
past the willows, and into the river and sank down
into its shoals. The warm brown water comforted her
haunches. The sky, overcast, eased her eyes. Her
vision was not as clear as it had been in days gone by.

Unlike the humans, she had no power to weep. Never before, had she felt that to be a loss.

Now, she felt herself being watched. Well enough. Perhaps some fluke of the water would heap mud over her body as it had over Behemoth's.

"Surely the mountains bring him forth food, where all the beasts of the field play. He lieth under the shady trees, in the covert of the reed and ferns. The shady trees cover him with their shadow; the willows of the brook compass him about."

The exultation of the praise song whose words Leviathan had not heard for many years brought her head up, then around, before sorrow bowed her shapely neck. Her winged ones ceased to groom her and chirped their sympathy.

"Great mother, do you know me?"

How strange it was after all these years to meet speech and thought that were not sundered from her. It was like old times. The eyes she gazed into were not ancient, like those of her kind, but they were old enough and steadfast, and familiar.

"You must be Lamech's son," Leviathan said slowly. "Little Noah. No, that cannot be right. Did my last children really swim with your . . . your sons?"

"I have but three: Shem, Ham, and Japheth. They built that mound for Behemoth, you know," he said.

She inclined her head, a stately gesture from far sunnier days.

"I would be glad to thank them. I remember them as goodly lads."

Three was a small clutch for Leviathan or, in these troubled days, for the sons of man. Still, Leviathan thought, three who lived . . . They might have children who would ride upon her back; but they would never again sport in the water with the younglings of her kind.

"I had thought," Leviathan mused, "that our speech was sundered. But you and I speak voice to voice or mind to mind. How can that be?"

"God favors me," Noah said. Even as a child, he had favored the bold move, the brave declaration. As a boy, it had won him standing with the Anakim. As a man, it had almost gotten him killed defending Leviathan.

Noah looked beyond the river bank at Behemoth's mound. His eyes were troubled. "I would have advice of you, who remembers my father and grandfather."

"What small wisdom I have is yours," Leviathan said with the exquisite courtesy of ancient times.

"I have sons and daughters, and a mighty task to perform if they are to live."

"What is it?" Leviathan asked. What was Noah's task to her? Still, his family had always been her friends. And his sons had buried Behemoth as if he were one of their own.

"A great burden has been laid upon me. I was walking in the cool of the evening, and God came, as long ago, he came to Adam and told me, 'The end of all flesh is come before me; for the earth is filled with violence through them; and, behold, I will destroy them with the earth.' "

"I have seen the violence," Leviathan agreed. "But an entire world, to be cast aside like a broken tree?"

The Anakim had to be the source of all this trouble, with their pride and their enslaved beasts and their sharp, deadly lances. Once again, she longed for the power to weep.

"Must all the creatures perish?" she asked.

Noah's gaze went strange, and he trembled. Enoch had looked like that when God had summoned him, and Methusaleh in his turn.

Noah drew himself up and summoned memory. " 'I will destroy man whom I have created from the face of the earth; both man, and beast, and the creeping thing, and the fowls of the air, for it repenteth me that I have made them.' "

Leviathan sank down into the water, letting it lap about her neck.

"But you," she said, "you and your children surely merit better.

"You were kind to me. You tried to stop the Anakim. You buried Behemoth."

"We have," said Noah, "a chance. If we fulfill the Lord's commandments exactly and speedily. A mighty rain is coming to destroy the earth."

Leviathan glanced down at the brown water that had sustained her for so long. When she looked back up, Noah's gaze was filled with pain. "I cannot imagine it, can you?" he asked. "All this vast world turned to water, even to the mountain peaks, and no foothold anywhere?"

Leviathan's long neck bent; her head lowered until her eyes were level with Noah's. He seemed to sway, too. She let him lean against her side. The mother rivers lapped them both.

"It is so many commands, so many words," he sighed. "Each morning when I wake, new words rouse me. They dance in my head, each one a picture of tasks I must perform before the skies open. I have been commanded to make an ark of gopher wood three hundred cubits long, fifty cubits broad, and thirty cubits high, with rooms within and doors and a window to the outer air."

"An ark?" Leviathan asked, testing the new word as if it were a strange type of plant she tasted for the first time. "You and your family are but few. What need have you of so vast an ark?" They would find the world a lonely place if the floods ever receded—just Noah and his family and no other creatures.

None of her kind would live, she thought. She glanced at Behemoth's mound. She had accepted long ago that her race would not survive. She simply had not expected to see the whole world end, too.

"I am commanded to take two of every sort of creature with me, male and female, to keep them alive."

"Then take these," Leviathan commanded. She nodded at the winged ones who had groomed and companioned her all these long years of exile. "That's right, little ones. Go with the man. He will not let wicked children throw stones at you."

The birds left her. They circled once, then flew to land on Noah's shoulders.

"Take care of them," Leviathan asked. "I give you all I have left to give."

Now Noah shook his head. "There is another thing I need."

"What is that?"

Noah's turned and pointed to Behemoth's tomb. "I told you how the new words thrust themselves into my thoughts?" His hands came up and he gestured. "Words like 'keel' and 'prow,' shapes like the place where ribs and breastbones join. It is not enough to have the words, or even the pictures in my head. If I am to build, I must see."

"So you would dig up Behemoth's bones to observe how he is made," Leviathan said. "I remember the words of the old song.

His bones are as strong pieces of brass; his bones are like bars of iron.

He is the chief of the ways of God.' "

"You buried him as one of your own," Leviathan asked. "Does not your kind account despoiling graves a profanation?"

Noah nodded, much as her own kind used to when faced with a hateful choice. "But I have no other way to learn before the rains come."

Leviathan looked up at the sky, already overcast and darkening. How many clouds would it take to make rain enough to turn the earth into a river? How long did Noah have? She remembered sunlight and laughing children slipping from her hatchlings' backs, to be prodded back into safety by her or by her sisters. She remembered a man who stood, shouting, between her and the death wrought by the Anakim. She thought of Noah's three strong sons heaping mud over the body of her mate. Behemoth had once carried those boys upon his back. He would not begrudge them any knowledge they could gain.

She inclined her head. "You may," she said.

Something else needed saying. It took her time to find it. Noah waited until the slow words came.

"Thank you for Behemoth's burial."

Leviathan left him then, walking at what would have been a mourner's pace for Noah. What he did with Behemoth's cast-asides was nothing she wished to see.

More buildings had grown up beside the rivers; more ground was filled with rows of plants too orderly to be natural and too well-guarded to be of interest to her. Armed men rode out toward her, as if challenging her or warding her off. She let herself be driven toward where she had made up her mind to go—the curve in the river where she could put great rocks at her back and stare out onto the water, revisiting her thoughts.

Leviathan traveled through time and through the world in the long dreams of her vanished kind. From time to time, she ventured out to forage among the canes and reeds of the riverbank. No one disturbed her. Had her dreams not held her attention, she might have been surprised.

At noon of the third day, Leviathan became aware that something was blocking her sunlight. She raised her head from its cradle on her massive forelegs, and looked up.

Noah stood before her, her former winged companions hovering about. They chirped delight at seeing her.

"I have come," said Noah, "to bid you join us in our escape."

"Behemoth is dead," Leviathan told Noah. "Our eggs are scattered. I am the last of our kind." She laid her head down again and wished for him to leave.

It was only when the sunlight fell upon her unimpaired that she knew she was alone once more.

Noah returned the next day, accompanied by his eldest son. The day was cloudy; their footfalls alerted her.

"I have come," said Noah, "to ask you to reconsider."

"I have no mate," Leviathan reminded him.

"You might find another," Noah suggested.

"I walk too slowly." Then, because she was an honest Leviathan, she added. "My scales are dulled with age."

"One of my sons might serve as go-between," Noah volunteered. "Or his son's son. They walk faster than you."

Leviathan whipped her head from side to side. "Your God says load two of every kind inside the ark. A mate and I could not board such a fragile thing without overturning it."

"I had planned . . ." Noah began.

"To leash me—and some mate?—to your ark? Your God holds by his rules, Noah. Look what he plans for the Anakim and do not test your luck." She raised her head and met the eyes of Noah's eldest son, endlessly patient, she saw, with how his father wasted time that might have been spent building this ark.

She feigned sleep. When she looked up, they had gone.

The day barely seemed to dawn, so heavy were the clouds. That God of Noah's must be herding them together before releasing their waters upon the Earth. Leviathan hoped that Noah could finish his ark and herd all his pairs of creatures safely on board. Perhaps she would rise later and see the ark, the last wonder, surely, she would ever see before the waters rose.

A figure blocked her way. To her surprise, it was a woman. Silver streaked her hair, but Leviathan remembered her from years ago, shepherding three unruly boys to the river to play with her last clutch. The woman walked as if she needed a birthstool more than she needed an ark. But that was the way of the daughters of men before the Anakim; the way daughters, mothers, and granddaughters brought forth their young for many years.

"I am Noah's wife," the woman said.

"And I, Leviathan. Do you have a name?"

The woman snorted. "I know perfectly well who you are, and who I am. What else do we need? And our time is short."

"Did Noah ask you to come to me?"

The woman shook her head. "My eldest grandchild brought me these."

She reached into the folds of her garments, draped not over the swell of a child to come but over . . .

Eggs. Two large, mottled eggs like those from Leviathan's lost clutch.

Leviathan's head darted forward so quickly that Noah's wife recoiled. The woman flushed with anger; she was not used to being put in fear.

"You recognize them?" asked Noah's wife.

"Where did you get them?" asked Leviathan.

"Does it matter?" the woman countered. "You, I know, will not come on board, lacking a mate. But surely, these deserve a chance at life. If I take them on the ark, how shall I keep them safe?"

"Let me see them," Leviathan begged. To feel a clutch against her scales once more. To sniff those leathery shells. To watch the sun beat down, urging her clutch toward ripeness. She wanted to live and see them grow.

Noah's wife glanced uneasily over her shoulder. Thunder rumbled.

"Do you hear that?" she asked. "I slipped away to ask you. How can I care for them on board? A box of sand, heated by fire?" A cloud crossed her brow. "How can I kindle fire on a wooden ark? How can I ensure no one will eat them?"

"Oh, give them to me!" Leviathan begged. "Just for a little." She would nuzzle them, hold them, and give them back. It would be a fine last thing to take with her into the deep waters.

Noah's wife held out the eggs, each the size of the woman's head. Leviathan edged forward, sniffing. "They are cold," she breathed.

Cold and wrong. Leviathan had raised too many clutches not to know these eggs would never hatch.

"Touch the shells," urged Noah's wife. "I have had them on heated sand since the boys brought them to me, not hours ago."

"How long did they have them?" asked Leviathan.

Noah's wife's head dropped, too. In that moment, Leviathan pitied her. She might have accepted her own fate, but hope for her, for Leviathan, shone so on this woman's face that it hurt to douse it.

"They will never hatch now," Leviathan said. "They have cooled too long."

Tears ran down the woman's face. She shook with sobs.

"Here," said Leviathan, "do not drop them, here. Give them to me. At least, they will not lack a mother's care here at the end of all things."

She set the eggs against her side. No motion within those leathery shells nor ever would there be. She curled her bulk around them as if they had hatched, producing live young.

"It is as well," Leviathan comforted the woman who would have saved her kindred from the flood. "You could not even know if the chicks were male or female—if you had violated Noah's God's commandments. Perhaps it is better so."

"When I was a little one, I remember clinging to a lizard's back in the water. I wanted my grandchildren's children to grow up knowing your race."

"Why, they will, child," said Leviathan. "Don't you know your own old songs?"

"Out of his mouth go burning lamps, and sparks of fire leap out.

Out of his nostrils goeth smoke, as of seething pot or caldron.

His breath kindleth coals, and a flame goeth out of his mouth.

In his neck remaineth strength, and sorrow is turned to joy before him."

"You will remember us always," Leviathan said. "We will be your dream of power, of sheer size, of ancient days before the flood. You will think of us in fear and in joy every time the songs are sung. And that will be a better future than being only two in a fearsome world."

Noah's wife wept into her skirts.

Leviathan nudged her with her nose.

"You will remember me, too. And you have my thanks, one mother to another. Now, go. Tend to your living children."

Thunder pealed overhead, echoing in the distance. Lightning danced across the sky, and the wind began to lash. The woman's head went up. "Do you hear them shouting?" she cried.

"For you?" asked Leviathan.

"Those are the children of the Anakim," said Noah's wife. "They are finally afraid. Oh, I must get back!"

"Will you be safe going alone?" Leviathan began to fret. She missed her winged companions; her shoulders itched—but not for much longer, she told herself.

"I must."

"You must not. Here, pick up the eggs, and I will come with you. Lay your arm across my neck. We will not be parted short of the loosing of the waters."

Together they walked toward the great ark Noah had built. He and his sons shouted, herding the living creatures, two by two, up into its bulk. Noah saw his wife, and ran toward her.

"Where have you been, woman?" he roared. "Get on board now! The storm is almost upon us."

Noah's wife knelt by Leviathan, settling the eggs against her flank. Quickly, she cut reeds and ferns and weeds, mounding them into a soft nest for the eggs that would never hatch.

Lightning flickered overhead, casting eerie shadows on the face of Noah's wife. It was drawn now with fear and sorrow. The clouds thickened, turning day to midnight. All of Leviathan's memories held no such clouds.

"Wife!" Noah cried. "Come, or we leave without you!"

"Go now," whispered Leviathan. "Or they will make songs about you, too."

"They may do so anyhow," said Noah's wife.

The woman tried to smile, flung her arms about Leviathan's neck, then ran for the ramp and the closing of the last door. Sealed in upon itself, the ark waited for the water that would lift it from its moorings. It was larger by far than Leviathan. It might withstand a flood.

Leviathan bent over her last two eggs, brooding over them as, it was said once, that God of Noah's brooded over the face of the waters. Now they would rise again, and when they receded, they would reveal a world lacking her presence, except in dreams.

The first fat raindrops spattered down. The skies opened, and the torrents followed.

The last thing Leviathan saw was the ark floating free, a Leviathan itself freighted with lives and souls . . . and the dreams of all their kinds.

Science Fiction Anthologies

Don't Miss These Exciting DAW Anthologies